T5-CQC-296

WAITING
FOR
RAIN

WAITING
FOR
RAIN

A NOVEL

INDIANA NELSON

RANDOM HOUSE
NEW YORK

Copyright © 1990 by Indiana Nelson

All rights reserved under International and
Pan-American Copyright Conventions.
Published in the United States by
Random House, Inc., New York, and
simultaneously in Canada by Random House
of Canada Limited, Toronto.

Library of Congress Cataloging-in-Publication Data
Nelson, Indiana.
Waiting for rain: a novel/by Indiana Nelson.
p. cm.
ISBN 0-394-57774-4
I. Title.
PS3564.E464W3   1990   813'.54—dc20   89-42774

Manufactured in the United States of America
24689753
First Edition

For Leo

all is clouded by desire;
as a fire by smoke,
a mirror by dust;
just as the embryo
rests deep within the womb,
so knowledge
is hidden by selfish desire.

—The *Bhagavad Gita*

WAITING
FOR
RAIN

PROLOGUE

AN OUT-of-town visitor from Dragoon, Arizona, dangled from a window ledge on the thirty-eighth floor of the Empire State Building one cold and dreary day in New York City. Help eventually came in the person of a janitor, who crawled along the ledge to reach the unhappy fellow. The visitor snatched hold of the janitor's pant leg, so that together they were hurled out into space, coming at last to a violent rest on the roof of the YWCA. On East Thirty-fourth Street, far below, the crawling procession of tiny cars had turned on their lights. It was Christmas Eve, 1955.

SEVERAL HOURS earlier a few blocks away on the West Side, a woman wearing a fur coat and high-heeled shoes opened the door to a room marked PRIVATE. Twelve businessmen were seated at a table that was empty but for a decanter of whiskey and some glasses.

The woman strolled up one side of the room and down the other, opening and closing the coat as she turned. Under it she wore a raw silk cocktail dress, also black, onto which there was pinned an ornament: a pavé diamond peacock with a luxurious fanning tail of emeralds, sapphires, and diamonds. She wore sapphire earclips and black kid gloves.

The woman did not speak or smile although several of the men touched the coat and spoke to her. A man smoking a cigar and wearing red cowboy boots slipped his card into her gloved hand: *Horace McAllister, Dragoon, Arizona.* On her way out she dropped the card into the ashtray next to the elevator.

She modeled three more coats, a leopard, a Russian sable, and a white mink, and returned to the ladies' room to undress. There she noticed someone slowly moving the handle on the door. Through the opaque glass she saw the heavy silhouette of a man she supposed to be Eddie, the guard from the fur store where she worked. She unlocked the door and the man with the cowboy boots pushed his way into the room.

"Get out," she said quietly, stepping into a wool skirt and reaching to zip it up the back.

"Why won't you have a little drink with me?" said Horace McAllister. "Or dinner?"

She removed the diamond peacock from the black dress and dropped it into her open handbag, which was balanced between two sinks. He watched her. Although she never glanced at him, she knew he was trembling. She drew a string of pearls from the handbag, clasped them about her neck, and leaned across the sink into the circle of light to powder her nose. The pearls cast dimpled violet shadows, fragile, like bruises, in the hollows of her throat. Horace had never seen anything so dainty. Alongside him she seemed so fine! He could crush her with one finger, Horace thought with a certain glum satisfaction. But he had no idea to hurt her. He just wanted her to look up once and see him.

He watched through half-closed eyes as she traced a fluff of pink swansdown along the delicate edge of her nose. His blood began to stir. Suddenly Horace did not see why he should be treated this way.

"Hey!" he said. "I'm not going to take no for an answer."

"Look," she said, snapping the compact shut, "why don't you go before you embarrass yourself?" Her voice was low, bored, odd. She slipped out of the satin high heels and bent to find her leather pumps. Horace lunged for her. Though taken aback, she laughed in his face.

They began to wrestle. Horace was surprised at how strong she was, and young, now that he saw her up close. She did not seem much more than a girl! A little wrassle, thought Horace, not to hurt her, just to show her a thing or two. But she began to fight him ferociously. Her eyes, unbearably close to his own, opened wide, dilated, a strange yellow color. It crossed his mind to be afraid of her. He had only thought to kiss her a little, there on the neck near the pearls, or maybe on the mouth, then let her go.

Now she threw her head back and came at him, mouth open wide, hissing like a snake, it sounded more horrible than anything he had ever heard. She spat in his face.

Horace was burning mad. He forced her down and the girl bent under him like a dry stick. Straddling her, he managed to twist her face with its terrible unblinking eyes off to one side, pressing her cheek down hard into the floor. Her pearls broke and rolled away. She saw the necks and bellies of toilets, like a row of soiled geese, mute witnesses to her disgrace.

Horace panted now, and bore down hard with his knee on her chest, pinned her arms with one hand, and reached the other up under her clothes. He had not planned to do this. He never hurt anyone. He was a big softie—everyone said so. She felt the tangle of his fingers in the delicate mesh of her stockings and then, a moment later, the rip, as the thin silk of her chemise gave way and his fingers raced like hairy spiders across her belly. And then there rose up in her a disgust so powerful she flung herself up onto him, and with the howling, uncanny strength of a beast began to rip at him, tearing at his eyes, throat, at his pants, ripping the buttons, and reaching in she grabbed and clawed at his tenderest parts. The man screamed and fell back but still she came after him, tearing with her teeth, gouging, digging at his flesh. He began to blubber and whine and from him came the smell of fear, rancid, disgusting. Somehow she felt strangely exhilarated. This moment seemed completely natural, as if all her life, until now, were a preparation for this moment, a long smothering silence suspended between brief terrible awakenings.

Someone rattled the door. A loud female voice called out, "Hey! Who the hell's got the door locked? What's going on in there anyway? We all gotta use this dump, you know!"

"You see!" she hissed into his ear, dropping him; Horace sagged onto the wall like a bag of soiled laundry, head lolling, face smeared, stunned. Crawling on his knees, jerking at his clothes, he slowly rose, staggered to the door, threw it open, and fled down the hallway.

"Hey! Wow! You're not supposed to—well, you sure got your nerve, honey!" Then catching sight of the deadly face on that other woman she fell silent. She eyed the twisted skirt, the tangle of dress, shoes, overturned bag, the scattering of pearls, and then pounced, first on one pearl, then another, crying, "Pearls! Lookit here! Hey—are they real?"

But the young woman had turned away to stare into

the mirror, astonished: she could not believe how changed she was.

A moment later there came a knock at the door and Eddie spoke through the glass. "Hiya, Princess, all set to go?" But she could not tear her eyes away from the mirror. For it really seemed as if now, at last, she were fully alive. Where there had been a pale mask only, lovely but frozen, coolly watching, an imposter, nothing more, there was now someone real, a face staring out, vivid and beautiful.

She followed Eddie, who pushed the rack of swaying coats like headless matrons down the deserted corridor. They passed the room marked PRIVATE. Glancing into the ashtray, she noticed the business card was gone.

"Want a lift over to the subway or are you going back to the shop?" said Eddie, as he loaded the furs into the back of the van with DORIAN WHOLESALE FURS etched in gilt across the side.

"I've got to go back to the shop," she replied, a strange lilt to her voice. "The jewelry is on loan from Van Cleef and Arpels and it has to be turned in tonight." She climbed up onto the passenger seat and carefully laid out the borrowed cocktail dress, the satin pumps, and her handbag.

Now what's with her? thought Eddie, who cast an expert eye over the girl's face. Tonight something was different. Remote as always, cool, something about her seemed lit up, disturbing.

"Any big spenders today?" he asked.

"No. But one man seemed interested in the Russian sable and another asked about the diamond peacock. Maybe after Christmas . . ." Her voice trailed off.

Something about this girl spooked him. She seemed to be gloating, she smiled to herself.

"This sure is going to be a mean Christmas," Eddie said.

The light changed. It began to drizzle. Through a mottled radiance of lights came the panic of honking. The girl seemed to be far away, as if between her and the world out there nothing more than a profound absence existed. Futile, whining sirens sounded in the rain somewhere to the east of them. The light turned red again and still they had not moved.

"God, I hate this city!" Eddie shouted, thumping the horn with both fists.

The girl stayed absolutely cool. Eddie couldn't wait to get her out of his van. They began to move again and Eddie shot through a red light at Fifty-fourth Street, but still she made no sound; she seemed wrapped in this exultant silence as if Eddie and all the millions like him did not exist. Along the avenues, in the dark plazas, they passed fragile trees whose leafless trembling branches were etched for Christmas in flimsy crowns of light. He gunned the motor and made a dive for the next light, taking the corner fast at Fifty-sixth Street.

She fumbled in her bag for a cigarette, then all at once she let out a little cry of terror.

"It's gone!" she cried. "My God, it's gone!" He could only stare.

"The diamond peacock! It's gone!" she shook her bag violently. "We must go back!" she demanded.

Eddie felt suddenly powerful. He coasted up to Dorian Furs on the next block and double-parked. "Please!" she cried. "Won't you help me? The peacock!"

He turned off the motor, turned to her, and smiled.

WHILE HORACE dangled from the thirty-eighth floor of the Empire State Building, his wife, Mary Lou, back at the

Waldorf-Astoria Hotel, listened to rhumba music on the radio and indulged in a little afternoon snack: one frozen daiquiri and a bowl of potato chips.

This was supposed to be her second honeymoon. One week in a fancy New York City hotel, ordering up room service and lying around in bed all day like the Queen of Sheba. Horace was on trial and he knew it.

Horace and Mary Lou came all the way from Dragoon by Pullman car. On their very first day in New York, Mary Lou had a thrill: one of the desk clerks—a small baggy man with a moustache—gave her the hot eye.

Horace didn't want to come in the first place. So he got back at her by spending as much time away from her as possible. Mary Lou didn't care. Horace's days were numbered. She was planning to leave him when this second honeymoon was over.

Horace had wanted to save the money and stay with his sister, Nanine McAllister Brown, who was married to a big shot. Mary Lou stood her ground: the honeymoon had to be in a hotel. Anyway, what did she care about these people the Browns who acted like royalty and knew all the right and wrong places. One thing Mary Lou hated was the "right places." What Mary Lou liked was shopping: charging up hats and shoes, then sending them back the next day. While Horace was out doing God knows what, prowling the streets, Mary Lou sat at her vanity table in the Waldorf wearing her brand-new Rose of Sharon negligee, her face done over to look like Joan Crawford in *Chained*, trying on hats. Wasn't it just like Horace to leave her alone?

When the New York Police detective came to her with the awful news about Horace, Mary Lou retired immediately into the reassuring solitude of the dove-gray dressing room and locked the door against the world. At first she could not believe Horace would die and leave her all

alone in New York City. Then she began to feel just
plain cheated. Maybe Horace hadn't been much but now
she wanted him back. He had been invisible almost all
those years, a face passing before hers without luster or
dazzle, creeping home after dark, night after night, sitting there like a silent lump, a stranger at the foot of her
table, gnawing on his dinner and wondering, always
wondering, what in hell she was thinking. What satisfaction is there in a man like that? Yet disappointing as
Horace was (especially now he had ruined their second
honeymoon), at least he had always been there. She
dreamed of fleeing, but now that she really was on her
own, Mary Lou felt petrified. What was she supposed to
do? For one thing, Mary Lou had no clear idea about
where money actually came from. Or how to go about
procuring such items as railroad tickets. Disagreeable as
it was being Mrs. Horace McAllister, at least it always
got her railroad tickets.

When Horace's sister arrived with her husband, Dinwiddie Brown, they were greeted at the door to Mary
Lou's suite by a Detective Tooney of the New York City
Police Department. He had disturbing news. It seemed
Horace might have been pushed, and there was evidence
that his assailant was a woman. Although it was impossible to make out anything conclusive, it appeared Horace
had engaged in a struggle: claw marks, teeth marks,
ripped flesh, and in the area of the genitals, confided the
detective, disgusting wounds. Was it possible, he inquired, lowering his voice and keeping an eye on the
boudoir door where Mary Lou had locked herself in, that
the deceased had been fooling around? They found
traces of female makeup, powder, rouge, of some lingering perfume on the body, and long, dark hairs tangled
around the buttons on his suit. In his breast pocket they
found a single pearl.

"Horace was no womanizer," said Nanine. "Mary Lou was the love of his life; they ran off together at age nineteen, twenty years ago. Of course the family never thought much of Mary Lou," she added, lowering her voice, "but then they never thought much of Horace either." But there had been no other woman, she felt sure of that.

"I heard that," said Mary Lou as she emerged from the boudoir. "You can go ahead and talk about me all you like," she said, "I don't care." Nanine gawked; this was a new Mary Lou. Her usual heavy-lidded languor replaced now by bright eyes, scarlet lips and cheeks, she wore a jaunty feathered hat tilted just so and a hibiscus-pink cocktail dress.

"Yes, that's right, go ahead and stare," said Mary Lou, as she pulled on black gloves, "but I don't see why I should have to give up *my* honeymoon, do you?" she demanded of the two men. "Not when Horace promised I could stay a whole week in a hotel. Anyway, we're paid up through Tuesday. Horace would be the *last* one who'd want to go and spoil everything for me." Mary Lou fixed huge eyes on the detective. "As far as I'm concerned, *I'm* here to have a good time," she continued. "There are his things." And with an airy toss of the hand Mary Lou pointed to an old Stetson parked on the hall table and a beat-up suitcase. "Do what you want with them but I'm going out, y' hear? Because I've had enough bad luck!"

"Now listen here, Mary Lou!" cried Nanine.

"No, *you* listen here, Miss High and Mighty!" screamed Mary Lou, who stamped her foot. "Horace was no prize. So the way I look at it, I deserve a medal or something for putting up with him all these years. Well, I'm tired of waiting around till something good comes

along. It isn't fair! Why did this happen to me?" She
squeezed out two tears.

"And your child?" asked Dinwiddie softly. But the
tone of reproach was unmistakable and Mary Lou
wheeled on him angrily.

"You're not going to make me feel bad about myself,
y' hear?" she shot back, pulling on her fur chubby. "If
you're so worried about Jewel, why don't *you* take care
of her? I've had it up to here with being a beast of burden. So the two of you can just—" But the words were
swallowed up by a loud slam. Mary Lou was out the
door.

As Mary Lou pranced through the lobby, the room
clerk hailed her. He held a small, neat package.

"Mr. McAllister left this for you just before—" he
said.

"Oh!" cried Mary Lou, who flushed to the roots. Horace! So he *had* thought of her after all! Not until she was
in the taxi speeding toward Radio City Music Hall did
she peek at Horace's last gift. Out of the box she pulled
a gorgeous pavé diamond peacock.

PART
ONE

1956

1

ONE MORNING in May a strange threesome stood before a
large house on East Ninetieth Street, discussing whether
or not to ring the bell.

"You can say what you like," said the child, a girl of
about fourteen, "but I'm not going in there."

"Now let's just get this straight," said the man, a
skinny cowboy in boots and brand-new Stetson hat. "My
orders from Miss Lou was to see to it Jewel here is
delivered to her aunt. No one said anything about me
goin' in there." He reached up under the hat to scratch.

"Well, hell, Alvin!" exclaimed Jewel. "If *you* won't
even go in there—"

"*Hell,* is it? Whoooee! Now we done gone off'n de
ranch dis chile be cussin' a blue streak. Huh!" said Twyla
Hoover with a snort. Twyla was Miss Lou McAllister's
maid. "You best be holdin' yo tongue, girl, cuz dat big
ole mansion over dere, it got eyes in its haid, an ears."

"Pooh!" said Jewel, but with none of her usual fire. A
shade snapped up just then in one of the upstairs windows. Just eight, the other shades were still drawn tight,
and the house wore a frozen, dejected air. The only sign

of life was high up above the somber brow where at the roof a wavy line of crimped lead-green hair fluttered with pigeons. Alvin was thinking, How could any person in his right mind live all cooped up with no cows or clean air or moonlight nights? Jewel always knew Alvin's thoughts.

"Well, I'm not lettin' no fancy New York mansion scare me off!" said Jewel at last, fighting back the lump of fear.

"That's right, darlin', no fancy New York mansion gonna skeer us off!" Twyla shot the cowboy a dirty look. "I done tole yo' granma Lou how's I'd fetch you here myself. You did, too, Alvin Gumm. And now we's here. We jes gonna wait for de right minute to come along," she added, but here Twyla's voice faltered, she squeezed Jewel's hand hard. "Den de three of us gonna ring dis here bell."

"Speak for yourself, Twyla. My place was to hand her in. That's all," said the cowboy. "No one said anything to me about sticking around. The way I figure it is I done what I came here to do. And now I might as well git on home. It's time for roundup. I got work to do."

"Alvin!" wailed Jewel. "Alvin, you swore you'd stick by me to the end!"

"I know what I said," the man answered quietly. "I said how if we got here and took a look around and the place felt bad I wasn't going to leave you. But the place don't look so bad, now does it, Jewel?"

But Jewel was no fool. She had eyes. The cabdriver made a joke of it, said it looked bad because there was a garbage strike going on. Everywhere along the curb stood sacks bursting with garbage. Here it was, almost June, but there was none of that bright hope in the air like there had been at home. The air seemed worn out, even at this hour, and it smelled of rat flesh. Twyla's face

had a look that said, Hmmmph! folks might be rich but
the richer they get, the sadder they get. And Alvin, well,
Jewel could see he had already gone away, the Alvin she
knew had stopped telling her the truth. In a way it felt
worse than death, this game of theirs: pretending it was
all right to leave her here—alone, far from all that mattered, pretend the place was fine so they could go off
quick, leaving Jewel behind. Just once, thought Jewel, I
wish some grown-up would admit he has done something wrong.

"Well," said Twyla brightly, "I guess we chickens better head on in! We isn't gonna know what we up agin till
we steps inside."

"Aw, hell," said Alvin, who slapped his hat once or
twice, "You gals don't need me for that. It's your job,
Twyla, to take her on in there and see she gits situated.
I'll wait for you over to the train station."

"De hell you is! Now lissen here, you big sissy—we
came here together, de three of us, an we is all three goin'
in dere together, you hear? Otherwise," muttered Twyla
ominously, and she fixed Alvin with the evil eye, "otherwise I'm gonna tell Miz Lou."

"Aw, crap," said Alvin, disgusted.

"If we go away now, they'd never know we was here,"
said Jewel.

"An who gonna be the one to tell you' granma Lou we
done changed our mind?" demanded Twyla. "Anyway,
chile, it's like yo' granma allu says: once destiny done put
its finger down you ain't got no choice." Twyla Hoover
was always going on about destiny.

On the train, coming east from Dragoon, Twyla made
them a little speech. "Either of you two ever hear of true
destiny? Well, true destiny is when from birth clean
through to death you got somewhere to go. I means
somewhere particular. A lotta people, you know, got

nowhere to go. And if you got true destiny you knows
it, too, 'cause dat what you born to do."

"I don't believe in stuff like that," said Alvin Gumm.

"You ain't got no choice in de matter." Twyla
scowled, and stared him down like he was a mental de-
fect. "I don't suppose you noticed lately you got true
destiny yourself?"

"What a lot of hogwash," said Alvin, slouching down
under his hat.

"Was you ever anything but a cowboy?" challenged
Twyla.

"What's that got to do with it?"

"Right from birth clear on through you was meant to
be a cowboy. I cain't see you doin' anything else, kin
you?"

"Aw hell, Twyla." She was right. Even if all the horses
and all the cows on earth were swallowed up in a big hole
suddenly, Alvin could never be anything else.

"It's like what old Miz Lou allus says: dey is four kinds
of destiny. Dey is lost destiny and found destiny and
borrowed destiny—dat's when you grabs what you kin,
honey, like yo' aunt Nanine—and last but not least dey
is true destiny."

"I ain't got any of those destinies," said Jewel. "I got
my own kind. I make it up as I go along."

"What kind of destiny is dat?" demanded Twyla suspi-
ciously.

"Waiting," said Jewel.

"Waiting?"

"Sure. Waiting," said Jewel. "You know—like when
you got no particular destiny at all, you haven't even
made up your mind and you're just waiting for something to come along. To rescue you maybe," she risked.
"You don't even know sometimes what you're waiting
for but you go on waiting."

"Sounds like lost destiny to me," piped up Alvin.

"Hush yo' mouth!" snapped Twyla. "Lost destiny be when dey is no hope. When you done blown it all away. Like yo' daddy jumpin' off'n de Empire State Buildin'. Now Jewel here, she got—" But to save her soul Twyla could not think what kind of destiny Jewel might have, so she said, "Well, Jewel here, she be in transit. But dey's hope for us all, chile. Take yo' granma Lou, now. She got herself found destiny, she done gone right out an foun' herself a rich fella an' a ranch and moved right in so's you'd hardly know dat ranch it wasn't hers from de beginnin'. But de trouble is, honey, most people, dey tries to bargain with destiny—but destiny, he cain't see, chile, and he cain't hear, and de sooner you realizes life ain't no more'n a big ole piece of flypaper de better off'n you'll be. Nosiree. Dere ain't no point resistin' what comes. You jes wants to be real particular where you lays down dat first foot, dat's all, chile, you hear?"

Jewel heard all right. Alvin could sit there winking and picking his nails with his pocketknife but Jewel knew the old woman was right.

JEWEL'S WORST fear, coming away from Dragoon, was that now she'd no longer be invisible. Like the lizard driven from his rock. Visible, her real self, that secret destiny fomenting there in the dark, must now be brought to light and accounted for. Jewel was different from other people: she did not know why this was so. It seemed to her one of those great awful mysteries that drove you wild in the dark, but clearly she had gotten into the wrong family. Maybe even into the wrong skin. Other people seemed perfectly satisfied to be here. Now her one great friend, the land with all its hiding places, was gone. She couldn't think how she would survive.

How does the lizard survive away from his rock? Like the others she must be a body now: walking around, visible, two legs, two arms, a head.

"Why is Granma sending me away?" she kept asking Twyla Hoover. "Doesn't she see I might die? People do die sometimes, you know. Anyway, it isn't fair. I hate it when things aren't fair," said Jewel.

"You ain't gonna die, Jewel honey," said Twyla.

"Maybe I will die. I wish I would," said the girl. "Fat lot you'd care." Then, when this got no response, "Maybe I'll go live with my mama. I could take care of her, see, and—"

"And where you gonna find her?" demanded Twyla. "You best forget her, you hear? Miz Lou says if'n she ever do come back she gonna shoot Miz Mary Lou clean between de eyes afore she let dat no good white trash step foot back on dis ranch. Anyways, chile, whoever tole you dat life was supposed to be fair?"

"It may not be fair," said Alvin Gumm, "but it's all we got till somethin' better comes along."

Jewel rocked herself to sleep in the deep fragrant hollows of Twyla's breasts, smelling so sweet, always, of powder biscuits and fresh folded wash. These days there was little enough to comfort her. Not that Jewel's mother had ever been much in the way of comfort. Or her father either; although sometimes Horace had picked the girl up and tossed her once, twice, barking out, "Whoops! Whoops!"

Sometimes, though, if Twyla was in a particularly good mood, she let Jewel suck on her arm to quiet down. Twyla Hoover's flesh tasted soft and oily like turkey meat.

"I guess dis here chile 'bout de unluckiest chile I ever seed," Twyla said over the girl's drowsy head. She aimed to make the best of it: five days cooped up with the

cowboy. She never did see why he had to come along,
too. But Old Lou remained adamant. The world out
there is a filthy rotten place. You need a man to get you
where you're going. None of them had ever been farther
east than Willcox. Anyway, Alvin Gumm might be the
man but it was Twyla who got them there.

"Yessiree," Twyla would sigh, "her pa done killed
heself, poor fool. And her ma run off. Her granma Slade
is dead—cose she was nothin' but a drunk anyway, no
wonder Miss Mary Lou turned out no good. And den dis
here Nanine!" Here Twyla cackled out loud.
"Whooooooee! Wait till dis chile seen her aunt Nanine!
Hah! Cose I ain't seed her myself in near on twenty
years, but honey—" This was addressed to Alvin Gumm,
who scrunched himself way down and pretended to
sleep. Jewel, eyes tightly shut, listened to every word.
Why, she thought, do they always talk about me as if I'm
deaf and dumb?

"Nosiree," continued Twyla philosophically, "people
don't change. You is what you is. From birth straight
through. All de rest is jes fancy clothes. Let's face it—dis
Aunt Nanine is downright peculiar. Dey say at de ranch
she rides elephants. An dat every two years she done
throws out everything: clothes, lamps, all de furniture,
an starts all over with a whole new set. But at least she
want de chile. An her husband I hears is one of dem
tycoons. One of de grandest gentlemuns left in dis here
world. So if I was in dis here chile's boots I wouldn't be
so all-fired quick to look a gift horse in de mouth."

At age fourteen Jewel McAllister had been off the
Dragoon Cattle Company, owned and operated by her
father's mother, Louise Beal McAllister, only to go to
school. This and the occasional trip to Tucson to visit
her granma Slade composed Jewel's entire experience in
the outside world. In the last five months this world had

heaved up violently and resettled itself without Jewel's having anything to say about it. Her own existence seemed mighty irrelevant.

"I'm sending you east, Miss, to see what you'll make of yourself," said Old Lou to her granddaughter on that fateful day a week ago. She had sent for Jewel to come to the "office"—always a bad sign—and Jewel, petrified of the old lady, as they all were, had kept her eyes glued on the gun rack behind Granma's head.

"Yessiree," said Granma slowly, savoring the words, "I'm sending you back east."

Jewel, scarcely breathing, said nothing.

"What you need, Miss, is a polishing-up. Oh, you've got your share of good blood, I suppose," continued Lou with a grimace of distaste, sizing up her granddaughter with an expert eye for flesh; Jewel was no beauty. "At least on the Beal-McAllister side. Although compared to the Beals the McAllisters got nothing special to write home about. I've seen better stock than McAllisters right here in my own backyard." The old woman snorted, jerking her head toward the corrals. "Lookit your pa! I always knew Horace for a pervert—bad enough he had to go kill himself, the little pipsqueak! What else was he doin' foolin' around on Christmas Eve with a whore in a fur coat? No, sir, I still can't believe a big sissy like that was a Beal *or* a McAllister." Through all this the old lady kept her eye fixed tight on Jewel, who turned redder and redder but stood her ground fiercely, eyes on the gun rack.

"Don't go getting hoity-toity with me, Miss, 'cause you've got your share of bad blood, too, so far as that goes! If I was you I sure as hell wouldn't go around blabbing you're part Slade! You've got a powerful lot to live down, you hear? We'll see how you like living high

off the hog in New York City with that fancy-pants
daughter of mine."

"Leave Dragoon?" Jewel began to understand.

"We'll see if that don't give you some polish—polish,
bah!" cackled Lou.

"Granma, are you really sending me away?"

"Yessiree! That damn fool daughter of mine, your
aunt Nanine, says she wants you. Beats me," the old lady
barked. "In forty-five years I never saw her do good for
anybody but herself. Now all of a sudden Miss Fancy
Pants has got a conscience! Says you can't have no
mother and father and grow up out here on a ranch. I
don't know why—she did! The Dragoon Cattle Company was good enough for her. But if she wants you—"

"I won't go!" Jewel screamed out, then fell back suddenly, terrified.

"What's that?" hollered the old woman, "*You* won't
go!" Lou was a little shrunken scrap of a woman not
much bigger than Jewel but she had a way of puffing up
with her eyes pushed out. She gawked at Jewel, rounded
those dry little lips into a terrible surprised *O*—the effect
was terrifying—and, though she remained in her chair,
somehow she crowded onto you, filling up the room, like
some horrifying rubberized figure blown up to bursting.
"You won't go?" spat out Old Lou with her dry laugh.

"Please, Granma," Jewel choked out. "I want to stay!"

"What you want don't interest me," snapped Granma.

"I could work real hard!" cried Jewel. "I could get up
early and—"

"It's no good," said Granma Lou. "I already decided."

"I could help in the kitchen, Granma! Twyla said—"
Old Lou began to slap her leather work gloves on the
desk once or twice to signal the meeting was over but
Jewel, her heart pounding, blurted out, "You hate me

because my dad killed hisself! You got no right to hate me but you do! You hate anyone who gets in the way of your idea. You just want to get me out of here so you won't have to see your disappointment. My dad, well, maybe he wasn't perfect, but I belong here, this is my place as much as it is anybody's. I don't care about any-place else, I never will!"

Old Lou looked pleased but she wasn't going to tell Jewel. "You'll do what I tell you, girl. The way I see it you've got no choice, none whatsoever," she said. But then in a quiet, almost gentle voice: "You've got no des-tiny, girl, so you'll have to borrow one. Like your aunt Nanine. She'll show you. If you look sharp you'll pick it up real fast, whatever it is they've got back there." It was a well-known fact what Lou McAllister thought of East-erners, but she went on in that quiet voice, "And then you'll come home. You're no good to me now. This land is in your bones, same as the rest of us, so I know you'll be coming home. You won't be happy anyplace else, none of us ever is. But it does no good to have a thing before you know its value. Look at my kids. There isn't one of them knows what this place is."

"My dad did!" cried Jewel. "I know he did, he taught me!"

"Four kids," muttered Lou, "and not one of them knows!"

Horace, Jewel's father, had been the youngest. The other three were girls. Aunt Louise, the oldest, was nearly fifty, then came Aunt Nanine, then Clara, who although past forty still acted like a big baby and lived with them on the ranch. Clara was funny in the head; even so, she had been Jewel's best friend—except for the cowboys and the land.

But it was Aunt Nanine people talked about. She had

not been seen in these parts since the day she ran off to
snag herself a sugar daddy. She got one, too—Dinwiddie
Brown. They talked about her in the kitchen, Twyla and
Eufemia and Rosie Gonzales. An "exotic," they called
her, who didn't want children because it would spoil her
figure. So, except for Jewel and Aunt Louise's little boy,
Johnnie Truesdale, there were no other children in the
family; the line was dying out. Jewel had never seen her
cousin Johnnie but he was famous on the ranch; he was
the little rich boy who lived in places like Greenwich,
Connecticut, and the south of France.

"Well, girl, maybe one of these days you'll see what
I'm doing is for your own good." Granma stood up; the
interview was over. "Maybe you'll be the one out of all
of them to understand. It won't be easy back there, I
admit—those Easterners, they got a lot of tricks and
you'd better watch out. They'll want to fool you."

"They won't fool me," Jewel said passionately as she
followed Granma out.

"Never trust anybody," the old woman grunted. "You
go and trust somebody, then they got their hooks in you.
Need people and the next thing you know, you've forgotten who you are. You come home to Arizona strong,
you hear? We don't need the weak; the land out here, it
chews up the weak ones and spits them out. And maybe
one day this powerful feeling will come over you," continued Granma, pulling on the gloves as she strode off
toward the corral. "A real powerful feeling. And then,
Jewel girl, there won't be a thing on earth that can keep
you away. That's when you'll come home."

"LET'S GO on in there and git this blasted thing over
with—it's past eight," said Alvin Gumm. "They ought

to be up by now." At the large second-story corner window another shade snapped up as the curtains were drawn back.

The front door was opened by a scowling person dressed all in black, the butler. They followed him through a strange egg-yellow room, an octagonal foyer with a dizzy black-and-white marble floor. At either side of the large entryway into an even larger front hall stood great tall palms in huge Chinese pots and near these immense brass cages, large enough each to house a full-grown ostrich. Jewel looked in and saw one parrot in each cage, bitter old antagonists whose entire purpose was to vituperate loudly against one another or anyone fool enough to pause and cluck admiringly.

The parrots reveled in their distress and began to hurl abuse at those three. Twyla, holding fast to her pocketbook, began to moan softly. The butler, without a word, left them.

On the balcony above them languid plaster nudes and leering gargoyles presided over a kingdom of staghorn ferns and thorny bromeliads; overhead, dim alcoves of leaded glass sent down faint bubbles of light onto a mélange of hothouse trees whose straining shadows left inky contortions along the paneled walls. The floor, lumpy beneath them with kilims piled one upon the other in crisscrossing pathways of lizard-colored stripes, darted the length of the long room, stopped at various doorways, and disappeared altogether up a twisting staircase.

"Well, I'm going to take a seat," declared Jewel, who took heart when she saw how abashed Twyla and the cowboy were.

"Now you hold tight, girl, you hear?" Alvin murmured. "This place looks to me like it's some kind of test—see?"

"What test, Alvin?" said Jewel as she settled herself on a tall claw-and-ball chair.

"Never you mind! Hush there, you!" Twyla hissed, crowding in close to Jewel. "Yo granma did wrong, chile, sendin' you to dis here place. But never you mind."

"You're going to be real brave, Jewel, I know you are," said Alvin. Then he said it again. But Jewel felt excited. Now that she'd seen the place she thought maybe her time in New York would not absolutely kill her. There were at least twelve good hiding places she could spot straight off and the house rose three full stories. She could lose herself in the bric-a-brac and they might not even notice her. Across the way she caught sight of herself in a long mirror. She sat up high, stretched out long and tall with the exotic trees behind. The face stared back a freckled blur, but as she gazed at her image it grew. The trees got smaller and Twyla, too, shrank back. Jewel's face became clear, stronger now—the eyes a little glassy, bold, the lips pursed—like Granma! Suddenly Jewel grinned and the face vanished from the mirror. "An I'll come, chile, an fetch you, hear?" Twyla said. "If'n dere be any way yo Twyla kin come, she be dere, you hear? Nosiree—dere isn't no way I gonna leave dis here chile all alone in New York City!" she moaned, rocking Jewel to her heart.

"I'll say one thing," Alvin volunteered as he inspected one of the naked statues. "They sure got some valuable stuff! You got any idea how much statues like this cost? You could git two yearlings at least—or maybe a bull for one of these! Might just be that Jewel here has hit the jackpot."

"Any more talk like dat, son, an Twyla is gonna kick yo ass! Don't you lissen, chile!"

"Remember what I was saying, Twyla—on the train? You know, about waiting? Like when you want something so bad it just grabs you here in your bones?" said Jewel, holding on to Twyla's hand. "And won't let go? But you can't say what it is, this thing you're waiting on, sometimes it don't even have a word. But you know it's in there, you go on waiting anyway because a voice inside, well, it tells you this thing will come to you if you wait."

"Yessiree, chile, dat be de voice all right, de voice of God."

"Plenty other voices in there, too," Alvin piped up. "How you going to know which of those voices to listen to? Why, I got a voice telling me right now to light up a cigarillo. Have a smoke. Got another voice sayin', Hey, Alvin! Let's clear on out! Now, which of those two voices is God?"

"You got another voice in dere, boy, but you jes ain' lissnin."

"This voice," said Jewel, "well, it's telling me I got to wait a long, long time. This is what I was trying to tell you on the train."

"Hush, chile!" Twyla moaned.

"And that I'm not afraid!" cried Jewel. "See, I'd a lot rather be surprised, Twyla, than know for sure how it'll all come out."

"Poor chile," Twyla muttered. "You done with missin' de ranch already, I kin see it in yo' eyes, girl! Well, Lord be! Les jes hope dat what you waitin' on so hard, Jewel honey, it don't turn out to be de wrong thing."

"Yup!" said Alvin.

"No such thing," said Jewel smartly, "as the wrong thing."

2

NANINE, A middle-aged redhead, lay suspended in a blissful twilight of lurid dreams. With a vicious yank the curtains shot apart and her maid, Lucy Cook, stomped toward the bed.

"Rise and shine!" she said and plopped a breakfast tray down on the covers.

"Ugh! What's that revolting smell?" cried Nanine, who raised a corner of the satin sleep mask to peer at the contents of the tray.

"Well, that's your breakfast, just the way you ordered it: soybean spread on Zwieback with no butter, Bran Buds, and a chaser of acidophilus. Gives me the goose bumps just to look at it. This here's the yeast. That's what stinks so." Nanine groaned.

"None of these fancy diets make you look a day younger if you ask me. You'll grind up your liver with that bran garbage. I heard of a woman who—"

"Haven't you got work to do downstairs?" demanded Nanine in icy tones.

"Suit yourself," said Lucy Cook spitefully. "You got visitors."

"Visitors! At this hour?" yawned Nanine.

Dinwiddie poked his head in at the door. "May I come in? I have just encountered the most peculiar group downstairs. A frightful-looking child, female, I think," said Dinwiddie, sinking his large bulk into a peach satin boudoir chair. "And a colored woman who glared at me and the damdest-looking—"

But Nanine did not listen. She tossed off her warm-ups, glancing meanwhile at the week's menu. "Poor darling," she murmured absentmindedly, as she pecked at the Bran Buds and executed a few listless scissor kicks. "You men will never understand"—she puffed, switching now to a rapid series of leg-overs, arm jerks, and head rolls—"just how gruesome it really is, what we have to go through for you—this unending quest for beauty! Here it is barely eight and I am simply exhausted!"

Behind Nanine's head the bed curved high up into a tufted shell of coral satin. With her two plump thighs swimming in air, she had the extraordinary appearance, he thought, of some huge underwater succulent. How could he have married such a creature! Not that he didn't adore her—Dinwiddie was mad about his wife—but he simply could not believe, even after twenty years, that he had married her. Archibaldo, the marmalade cat curled in a nest of silken Léron pillows at the end of the bed, glanced up, furious, as a pink foot shot through the air perilously close to his ear.

"Whoever they are," continued Dinwiddie, "I am afraid they mean to stay. The front hall is strewn with luggage. Whoever heard of uninvited guests at such an hour? And who, my dear, do you suppose they are?"

"Luggage? My God!" screamed Nanine, leaping out of bed with amazing agility. "They're here!"

"Who?" cried Dinwiddie as Nanine struggled into her negligee. "Who's here?"

"Don't you remember, darling?" his wife tossed over her shoulder as she rushed out the door. "That child we invited here to live with us! You know. Horace's little girl. We talked about it when he died."

"But that was months ago! And I don't remember saying anything about her *living* here!" he cried, trying to keep the rising panic out of his voice as he ran out into the hall after Nanine.

"You've just forgotten, that's all. Now darling, stop making these dreadful faces, you can't think how old and horrid it makes you look! After all, this is poor dead Horace's little girl! My only brother!"

"Whom you loathed!" he snapped. "Anyway, children make you nervous."

"Well, I might have said that once. But now I've changed my mind," said Nanine as she paused at the top of the stairs. "Anyway, we can't think only of ourselves, can we, darling?" She pecked his cheek.

"HOOHOO!" THE three waiting downstairs looked up. "What a delicious surprise!" cried Nanine, who floated down toward them in a cascade of maribou feathers and swirling silk that ballooned out all around and it seemed to Jewel for one startling moment that her aunt was a fearless, brilliant bird of prey with beak and feathers and beady eye. "Darling, how nice of you to come!"

Twyla Hoover, whom Nanine instantly divined as a foe, was swept off to the kitchen in the wake of Treacle, the butler.

"There's no need to look so glum; you haven't been sent to a labor camp," said Nanine flashing a taut smile. She engulfed her niece in voluminous sleeves and swept Jewel off to the Red Room. Dinwiddie followed and Alvin Gumm came slouching behind.

"Isn't this exciting?" asked Nanine. Dinwiddie sulked and the other two stayed mute. "My very own little girl! How old are you, darling—ten? Fourteen! Well, never mind—we're going to be the best of friends. We'll go shopping together and have lunch, it's going to be such fun, I can just tell!"

Jewel didn't seem very comforted by these words. She balked at the door to the Red Room, glancing around for Alvin.

"Do come in," said her aunt crisply. "I want you both to feel right at home."

Alvin, red-faced, stood rooted in the doorway. The room seemed larger and gaudier even than the lobby of the Fox theater back home, with painted skies overhead and gardens on the walls, babies swirling naked through the air, and endless trompe-l'oeil avenues wandering off into vanishing perspectives. Jewel could scarcely get her feet to move. Her aunt waved from the far end of the room and patted a place next to her on the love seat. A terrible panic rose up in Jewel. She thought: I'll die here. I'll never survive this. Alvin came from behind and prodded her shoulder. She stiffened and remembered Granma Lou. Slowly Jewel and Alvin walked toward her aunt. They picked their way through a sea of exotic doodads and upholstery. Halfway across the room Dinwiddie waited for them. He saw that the child gnawed at her lip and her eyes filled with tears. Jewel caught him looking. Surprised by a remarkable fierceness in her eyes, it had not occurred to Dinwiddie to feel sorry for the girl—it was his own plight he thought of—but this look of determination settled something for him. He admired her and as she came toward him, slow yet resolute, he felt they had reached a bargain, a solemn and secret arrangement not to interfere, each with the other, for now her glance softened a little. Was it with gratitude?

The moment she laid eyes on her aunt, Jewel hated her. She saw the disappointment in the woman's eyes. How long would this woman pretend to be her friend?

Jewel's heart was weighed down with ominous thoughts as she picked her way carefully through the tables filled with dainty gewgaws: snuffboxes, porcelain eggs, music boxes, ivory fans, photographs in silver frames, and everywhere bowls of sweet-smelling rose-buds. There were also pots of forced flowers; the air here felt sickly; Alvin looked drowsy. There were candies, too, bonbons and gumdrops and marzipan fruits in little birds'-nest baskets tucked in under vases of pussy willows and peacock feathers, and remnants of crumbling altars from foreign places, dingy icons studded with colored gems, an Aztec urn murky with the ashes of a long line of departed cats, decaying valentines, picture cards—and over there, forgotten in the lap of a paisley shawl, prayer beads lying fatly coiled like amber snakes. They made their way to the far corner where under a single tremendous window, the largest Jewel or Alvin had ever seen, Aunt Nanine was sitting beneath the dimpled deceitful light of a snooded lamp. Behind her, trembling in the morning light, were fringes and tassels that trailed across the ruby red swags of velvet in the window beyond. Nanine beckoned. Jewel was made to sit on the love seat beside her aunt. Nanine directed Alvin to a large pouf just there beside them on the floor. Uncle Dinwiddie positioned himself a little farther off on a straight chair. The pouf sank very low to the ground and quivered violently as Alvin sat down. Alvin held very still, afraid he would be thrown off, his knees poking up under his chin and lips tight together.

"Let's have a cozy chat. I want to hear everything!" Jewel stared. "One thing I'm not awfully good at is children. This is why most of it will have to be up to you,

Jewel darling." The child said nothing. Nanine found no
support from Dinwiddie, so she rang the bell for Treacle. Jewel stole a peek at her uncle, who seemed to find
the situation amusing. When she looked again he
winked.

With his moustache and beetling brow, his sleek hair
and blowzy jowl, his enormous lived-in bulk, Dinwiddie
looked to Jewel like a large amiable walrus in a pin-
striped suit. Not very old, a man of late middle age, he
appeared ancient to Jewel. His eyes seemed the most
hilarious, direct, and mischievous eyes she had ever seen,
but very old and sad, too. His eyebrows shot out every
which way, like antennae. As they talked, one of his feet,
encased in a long smooth shoe, rose up slowly, then
down, doing a little dance in space. Up came the irre-
pressible other, keeping time to the talk.

Treacle arrived carrying a silver tray with little sugared cakes and steaming chocolate in rattling, eggshell–
thin china cups. Alvin blew on his but then thought
maybe the cup would crack. He dared not drink from it
and held it straight out in front of him like a dead bird.
This made Jewel smile. She slurped hers down noisily
and ate several cakes while Nanine surveyed her behind
drooping hooded lids.

"Well now, what shall we talk about?" she said when
they had finished their treat and the silence was more
awful. "I know—plans! We can plan your future."

At this, Dinwiddie stood to excuse himself.

"Must you go?" Nanine glared.

Dinwiddie made his niece a pretty speech. "My dear,"
he said with a little bow, "welcome to Ninetieth Street.
We shall do our very best to make you comfortable and
you must tell us what you like. Whatever it is, I am sure
it can be found. If I can be of any use do not hesitate to
call on me. Mr. Gumm, I hope, sir, you enjoy your stay.

Now, good-bye, I must be off!" and with a wink to Jewel he took himself away.

"Oh, dear" said Nanine. "Where were we? Plans. Now, let's see. What do you want to be when you grow up? Not a rancher. I used to be a little ranch girl, too, you know. And I lived in Dragoon—it was awful. Let's face it, childhood is awful. Mine lasted and lasted. Never enough Christmas presents, never enough money." Nanine snatched up the last of the little cakes and popped it into her mouth. "Well, why not admit it?" continued her aunt as the cake went round and round in her mouth. "Luckily, though, I went from being twelve to forty. The one thing you've got to remember, dear, is that people will forgive anything if you are rich. Lots of money, we all need lots of money. Isn't that true, Mr. Gumm? Or if not money then at least background. It doesn't have to be *real*, you know—you can make it up as you go along. I did! In lieu of this it helps to be fascinating and of course if one has nothing else intelligence is a must. And it always helps to be beautiful." She looked Jewel over with a practiced eye, then looked away quickly. "Well, never mind. I wasn't beautiful either. But one works at it, my dear, works and works! And then if all else fails one simply has to make up one's mind to get on with all the right people. Don't you think, Alvin? Do you mind if I call you that?"

"Alvin," he said, clearing his throat. "Just plain Alvin."

Jewel noticed a pair of feet under a Chinese lacquer screen. Human feet. Bare with curving yellow toenails. She watched, transfixed, as one by one the toes lifted and began to wiggle.

"Don't you agree?" Nanine said. "Nothing nastier than childhood."

"Oh, well," said Alvin.

Jewel looked away and the feet were gone.

"Yes, and all those ungodly horrors in the country. Snakes! Spiders! Toads—ugh, toads in the summer after the rains." Nanine poured out the last of the chocolate and drank it down. "And nasty scorpions, eek, and centipedes crawling around, Gila monsters everywhere! But the worst, don't you think, are those disgusting June bugs darting in your hair! Thank God, dear Jewel, you will not have to encounter June bugs in New York. You can be thankful at least for that." She patted the child's thin shoulder but instantly snatched back her hand.

Why is this poor demented creature staring at me with her mouth wide open? wondered Nanine. Jewel's small shoulders poked out at the back of her dress like deformities. Not a stitch of grace, thought Nanine. With freckled flesh, taffy-colored and burnt by too much sun, Jewel had brazen eyes filled with—but Nanine could hardly even think the word—yes, with contempt! Contempt! And what was that unpleasant odor? The little dress smelled musty. The smell of an unloved child, thought Nanine. Well, really, this was a bit more than she bargained for. How was she supposed to cope with such an unlovely child?

Jewel gazed into Nanine's face and saw everything. Suddenly she leaped up and let loose a thin piercing scream. "Aiiiiiee!" screamed Jewel. "Alvin! I want to go home!" She threw herself onto the cowboy and sobbed into his chest. "June bugs!" she howled. "It's summer, Alvin, summer! I want to go home!"

Nanine jumped to her feet and began to ring for Treacle frantically.

"Green!" Jewel howled. "Green green!"

"What on earth is she talking about?" cried Nanine, but Alvin only shook his head.

Splinters of green glass: dazzling bottle-blue fluorescent green-glass June bugs: the smell—thick, sweetish, rotten sweet, a little disgusting, like stinkbugs when you crunch them underfoot: a powerful smell, intoxicating! And oh the splendor of those gold-shot whirring wings, the crash of brittle bodies up against the glass plunging down, curl and die—June bugs! "Aiiiieeee!" screamed Jewel.

"Well, my God! Have you ever seen anything so peculiar?" said Nanine.

"Aaaay there, Missy, aaay aaaay, Missy, whoa!" Alvin clucked tenderly and he patted the limp yellow hair once or twice. "Well, ma'am, she's mighty sensitive, you know, she's not like other girls—I guess you'll have to go slow at first."

"Go slow?" said Nanine. He couldn't have said anything more distasteful. Nanine made a face. "Go slow?"

"WHAT ON earth are we going to do with this terrifying child?" Nanine sighed as she handed Dinwiddie her glass for a refill. They were having a midnight nightcap in Nanine's boudoir.

"We?" exclaimed Dinwiddie with a chuckle. "We, my dear? I can't think what *you* are going to do about this mess, but personally, I find the child captivating."

"You do not!" she sulked. "You hate children."

"I don't hate anybody," he said as he added one brilliant drop of green crème de menthe to the concoction he handed her. "I thought it was you who loathed children."

"Well, of course I do!" cried his wife.

Dinwiddie, magnificent in a maroon silk dressing robe with black satin lapels and tassels on the tie, lowered himself into the flamingo pink chaise.

"I wish you wouldn't do that," she said. "You know

how cross it makes me. Why don't you sit over there? I
think you'd better have them make you a dressing gown
that looks good in my boudoir."

"I don't suppose you could have this chair done over,"
he said, moving. "I'm rather fond of this dressing gown."

"My dear, if you'll pay for it I'll have the whole boudoir done over!"

For a long moment neither of them said a word.

"Don't you think this is bound to have some effect on
our lives? I mean the child," he said.

"Well, I certainly hope not!" said his wife.

"We can hardly turn her over to the servants. I
thought we had plans to be in Marrakesh in the fall. And
Luxor for Christmas with the Slocums," he added petu-
lantly.

"Why on earth can't we go to Marrakesh? We'll take
the girl along," said Nanine. She patted a spot next to
herself on the bed for Archibaldo. Then she selected a
petit fours from a silver dish and dangled the morsel
before the cat.

"And what about school?"

"School?" said Nanine. "I don't think school is nice at
all. It didn't do me any good. Why should everyone have
to go to school? Have you ever known anyone who was
made fascinating by going to school?" Dinwiddie
watched as the tom cat dragged his hairy swaying belly
across the satin coverlet to examine the bait. Neck out,
eyes sluggish, he sniffed: slowly and with the weary disdain of a very grand potentate Archibaldo turned his
back in her face, tail stiff and straight up, the tip of his
tail quivering with disgust, and he stalked off, resettling
himself far away on her shins.

"What arrogance!" cried Nanine. She flicked on the
light in the aquarium in the wall beside her bed. A horny

creature, spiked, mottled black and orange, wriggled at the window.

"Oh, well." Nanine sighed. "I suppose she will have to go to school." Suctioned to the glass inches from her head: a black fish, dense as mud, swayed from his gums. "We could send her to Miss Hall's or Miss Porter's or one of those. Then we'd only have to cope at Thanksgiving and Christmas. We could send the girl somewhere for spring break. Summer, of course, will be awful. And what about that name? We can hardly introduce her as Jewel! Have you ever heard of anything so tacky? So like Mary Lou. The name will simply have to go," declared Nanine. Then: "ARCHI-*bal*-Do! Yoohoo, here Archie!" sang Nanine as she prodded the cat with a toe. "Lookee here, Archie—dindins!" and she scratched at the aquarium window. The cat rotated his great fat neck, and regarded her contemptuously.

"I expect Jewel might have something to say about that."

"Well, I hope she knows enough to be grateful!" Nanine said.

"Grateful? No, darling, I think not!"

"You think I'm awful," she said. "Yes, you do! Oh, you *are* polite, I see that, and always *so* tremendously correct. Well, I hate it, I hate all that correctness. You're always criticizing me, looking down your nose, I see it in your eyes."

"My dear, I wouldn't *dream* of judging you," he said pleasantly. "Now that we've got her here, though, shouldn't we think of something for her to do? The cowboy, you know, and Twyla are leaving tomorrow and Jewel might feel—"

"*Jewel* might feel? What about *me*? How can I help it if the poor thing's had a rotten life and looks simply

ghastly, can't talk, grunts only, rubs her nose with the
back of her hand, and has no conversation skills whatsoever? Was it my fault we had to dine out her very first
evening? It was you who insisted we accept the Wiley
Andersons. We never go there. I *hate* the Andersons. I
would never go back if it was left to me. How was I to
know it would be her first evening? I didn't even remember she was coming! Anyway, she looked relieved to see
us go, cocktail hour was a disaster, she'd much rather be
with the servants. She hates me already!" Nanine burst
into loud sobs.

"Now darling, you are very brave," Dinwiddie said as
he perched at the edge of the slippery coverlet. "I think
it's wonderful that you've taken her on."

"You do?" asked Nanine.

"Yes, I do. It was a grand thing to do, and I admire you
for it. All I want is that everything goes on as, well, as
pleasantly as always, my dear. I don't see why we can't
stretch ourselves a little, and make the child feel perfectly at home, that's all."

"Oh, Dinsie!" Nanine buried her wet face in the satin
lapels of his large maroon bosom. "You can't imagine
how hard all this is on me! I was so sure she would love
me! I've made such an effort to please the girl, really I
have, you should have seen me this morning! But she's
got the saddest eyes, a little bit gruesome in fact—like a
hare caught in the headlights. How am I supposed to
have a conversation with anybody who stares like that
and eats peas off her knife—"

"Hush, darling," he crooned, patting her stiff curls.
"And when you're feeling better we'll think what to do."

"You don't hate me for bringing her here?" Nanine
peeked up at him.

"No, of course I don't! It'll all turn out, I know it will,"
he said. "Would you like me to?" he asked softly.

"Please, darling, not tonight, though you really are the best man alive."

"And you—" he murmured, creaking slightly as he bent to kiss her cheek, "—are adorable!" He turned out the bedside light and tiptoed out of the room.

Nanine waited a full three minutes in the dark before she switched on the light. She reached into the drawer of her bedside table and brought out a copy of Rex Stout's *Black Orchids*. She found her place and began to read: ". . . so I reached a hand to feel of it, and the end of my finger went right into a hole in his skull, away in, and it was like sticking your finger into a warm apple pie."

IN HIS room, Dinwiddie poured himself a tumbler of brandy and soda and crossed over to his favorite chair, a deep leather with balding arms. For nearly one hour he sat lost in thought, his eyes fixed on the single ornament in his entire room: a tapestry hanging opposite his bed on which some ten or twelve monkeys cavorted on a leafy ground. The monkeys turned, as if to an audience, pale epicene faces stitched into half-raucous, half-entreating grimaces, their malevolent little eyes open wide as if in defiance of his pathetic human need for sleep.

One monkey, the leader, turned toward Dinwiddie. He hung from a vine by one wrinkled paw while the other paw hung down limply and concealed that disappointing place down below where his private parts, had the weaver endowed him with any, should have been. Twenty years ago Nanine had presented her husband with this tapestry as a wedding present.

Dinwiddie heard the hall clock chime twice. He rose and went to his desk, unlocked the top right drawer, and withdrew a black jeweler's box. He carried it over to the lamp, swallowed the last of the brandy, and opened the box. His fingers began to tremble. There, carefully laid out on creamy satin, was the pavé diamond peacock, its tiny facets shooting off a million glittering stars and its gleaming ruby eye mocking him.

3

"ARE YOU really an orphan? I never saw an orphan before!"

Jewel opened an eye. Still she could not think where she was. A canopy mushroomed overhead into a fussy bonnet tied back with twisted cord, the tassels dropping down near her cheek. Useless, like dry pods, thought Jewel. She felt bruised, changed by the night. Then she remembered that Twyla and Alvin were gone. Yesterday evening they had left for Dragoon.

"And I brought oatmeal," said the voice, more insistent now, "but I wouldn't eat mine so you don't have to eat yours. And blueberry muffins. Boy, were they good. And fried ham. I might have another piece if you'll let me."

Jewel peeked out from under the mountain of covers. A small boy with a wonderful mop of golden hair stood there. She thought him the most beautiful human being she had ever seen. "You're Johnnie Truesdale," she said.

He beamed at her. "I brought you breakfast in bed. You being an orphan, I figured you never had breakfast in bed. My mama does. Every day. Here, move over."

A smothering of coverlets tucked in all around held
Jewel tightly pinned: a place to hide, she thought, feeling
small and warmly buried. Twyla had tucked her in for
the last time.

"Dis sho ain't no fit place for a chile," Twyla grumbled
as she snatched away Jewel's pillows. "Lord, I never seed
sech queer goin's on—look at dis place! H'ain't right,
nosiree, an somfin' mighty bad gonna come of it, hear?
You best be watchin' yo' step, Jewel honey, 'cause dis
here place done puts out a powerful spell."

"Please, Twyla, can't I keep just one pillow?"

"An git a crick up yo' spine? Now don't go gittin' no
fancy ideas now yo' Twyla done gone. You be livin' high
off'n de hawg, girl, thas true, but if'n it be no pillows in
Dragoon dere gonna be no pillows in New Yawk City,
you hear?" Twyla growled, smacking, viciously whop-
ping the pillows as she carried them away. She jerked at
the coverlets, smoothed them, kneaded Jewel down in
her rough businesslike way till nothing but the nose
poked out for air. "Lord, I sure do hates to think what
yo granma Lou'd say if'n she could see her little Jewel
right now wallowin' in all dis here luxury," muttered
Twyla, and placed the worn saddle shoes and rolled-up
socks beneath the bed.

Immensely tall and square, Jewel's new room was
swathed from floor to chandelier in a chartreuse moiré,
and this spiraled out in gathered pleats like the lining in
a hatbox; the windows, too, long and very narrow, were
cosseted in this same tart stuff, trailing out over dense
undercurtains so the room seemed permanently sealed
shut. It had an awful silence.

She had a vague recollection of Alvin Gumm carrying
her up to bed, then Twyla said good night. Did she
dream or had Twyla wept a little, tucking her in? Yes,
and Jewel remembered saying, "Anyway—who cares

what Granma thinks? She's gone, Twyla, she can't get me now."

"Gone! Hah! We'll see who be gone!" Twyla cackled. "Don't you be foolin' yoself, Miss, imaginin' you be safe fum Miz Lou. Cuz dat ole woman, she got a long arm, hear? Yessiree, a *looooong* arm! None of us'n be safe fum Miz Lou. She de boss. You wait an see! Dere ain't *no one* mo' powerful dan Miz Lou. Dis other one, yo' aunt Nanine, why, she be a misruble runt, a chitlin', longside Miz Lou! Gone! Whooooee!" And then, for the last time, Twyla turned out the light.

Sleep had come thick and mysterious. How good it felt to tumble over the edge into that purple abyss, hidden in the huge soft bed, buried in satin, with crisp sheets smelling of lavender and dust. Now she remembered: slipping past that last color-shot edge, a gleam of last consciousness, down and down, the rush of airless sleep, the black of velvet wings enfolding, carrying her away. If the morning ever came she would be new, brand new and changed—and for the first time unafraid.

"Aunt Nanine says nobody wanted you," persisted the voice, and Johnnie climbed up beside her and helped himself to ham and syrup. "So she got you. And that she's going to do a makeover. New everything. You'll be all new, she says."

"The hell I will!" cried Jewel.

"You're not supposed to say 'hell,'" he said.

"Listen, where I come from we say 'hell' whenever we want."

"You do?" exclaimed Johnnie.

"Sure! Anyway," continued Jewel, disgusted, "I am not an orphan. I got a perfectly good mother, only no one knows where she is exactly. But as soon as she hears where they took me she'll come and get me, you can count on that!"

"Oh!" said Johnnie, and he put down the ham. "I sort
of hoped you were an orphan."

"Well, you can forget that right now," she said
roughly, pushing away the breakfast tray. "Anyway, one
of these days I'll be clearing out of here. I'm planning on
running away."

"You are? Why?" asked Johnnie, who settled himself
next to her, propped up on one elbow, and regarded
Jewel with huge, admiring eyes.

"Why, you don't think I could live in a place like *this*,
do you!" she exclaimed.

"But Aunt Nanine says how she's adopting you.
They're even giving you a new name—Deedee, I think,
or something like that."

"What a lie!" Jewel snorted. He had never seen anyone
so outraged or magnificent. "Why, anyone can see the
place I belong is the ranch! Did you think I'd let them
hold me here? You sure don't know me."

"I guess not," he murmured sadly.

"Shoot, no! Why, as soon as I get me some money
together I'll be on my way. I got it all figured out. I'm
just pretending to fit in around here, but it's an act, see?
The real me is out there."

"Out there!" he cried, electrified. "The *real* you!"

"Sure!"

"If it was me and I had a ranch," Johnnie blurted out,
"hell! I'd'a done it by now, run away!"

"Oh, you would! Well, it isn't you, hear? You don't
know anything about it. How you going to run away
with no money, huh? How old are you anyway? Nine?
Hah! Nine years old!" The way she said it it went
through him like a knife. He was mortified to his soul.
"Well, lahdeedah!, Mister Nine!" she sang. He held his
tongue, afraid he was going to cry. Then Jewel reached
out and touched his hair.

"Hey! Quit that!" he said.

"It's like real gold," she examined his hair. This was true. Something about the boy's hair was extraordinary. It shimmered and rose up all around his head like a fluffy crown of gold, wonderful to touch, silky fine, curly. His skin, too, glowed silky white, almost opaline, not at all like the boys at home, coarse, bitten by the sun. And he smelled fine, too, like expensive soap, he smelled clean and sweet, especially around the neck; and now Jewel sniffed him there, poked her nose in; he held his breath, it felt good—strange but awful good—only she had hurt his feelings and he didn't like her to see him cry. His eyes, she saw, were luminous and brown; they looked old in a curious sort of way, like the eyes in certain animals that look straight down into you, deeply, and with a message; eyes that do not look away but stay there and wait.

"How old are you?" he asked her.

"Fourteen," she said.

"I'm not a baby," he said. Then, "Do you think I'll ever catch up with you?"

"No," said Jewel philosophically. "You see, I guess I'm going to be special. Now that Twyla's gone, and Alvin Gumm, I guess I don't belong to no one. I'm on my own. I got no particular destiny, see. It's different when you don't belong. In my case somebody made a mistake. It's like I got into the wrong family."

"You did?" said Johnnie enviously.

"Take a look," she said. "Do I look like these people?"

"No," said Johnnie slowly, and he scrutinized Jewel, "you don't." Jewel's hair, cropped like a boy's, poked out every which way in strange yellow spikes, this being the unhappy result of an arduous session yesterday at Elizabeth Arden's, where she had undergone a complete makeover, toes, fingers, everything. But the hair, which had been cut by a maestro and slicked down into a svelte cap, had gone berserk ten minutes after Jewel hit the street. And then everything else about his cousin seemed slightly askew; but charmingly so, thought John, who admired her with all his heart. Maybe she was a little wild-looking and what adults called uncouth but she had about her the thrilling taint of the west: hers were the unsavory manners, the dialect, and rough gestures of those people who lived out there, he knew, beyond the world. Out beyond the edge.

"I guess I'm special, too," said John. "I was a love child."

Jewel did not want to admit she had no idea what a love child is.

"Yes. Even before I'd been born they loved me. Mama says she and Papa knew I would be special. See, they wanted me awful bad. My mama was an old mother when I came—she's *very* old," confided John. "They said she could never have a baby. But then she had me. My papa died, too, you know," he continued, gazing at Jewel with a sweetness she had never encountered before in anyone. "Before I was born. I never saw him. I guess that leaves me at the head of the family. I'm the only male, you know. Mama says Granma McAllister is leaving the ranch to me. In her will. I'm the heir." Johnnie pronounced it hair. "You can come live there, too—with me! It'll be the two of us. Then you'll belong somewhere, won't you, Jewel?"

Jewel thought about this for a minute. She was tempted to resent him. But then she said to herself, I like to be near him. Anyway, maybe some of his luck would rub onto her. She said, "You can count on me."

"I knew you'd understand!" he cried. "And Mama says I'm going to be loved. No matter what. And the ones who are loved," continued Johnnie, his eyes shining, "well, they get all the luck. They shine like gold, the lucky ones—that's what Mama says, and the shinier they get, the luckier they get. Do you think that sounds silly?" he asked her.

"No, Johnnie, I don't," said Jewel slowly, and she reached to put her arm around him.

"I didn't think you would," said Johnnie, allowing her to squeeze him tight.

"WHERE IS Johnnie's *real* father?" Jewel asked Nanine, who was doing her nails. Jewel watched the buff fly back and forth across the nails.

"Jack Truesdale! Now *there* was a divine man!" cried Nanine. "And a great catch. Lord knows how Louise got him. His death was simply ghastly, they were skiing at Gstaad, Jack and Louise, they had been told by everybody not to go—Louise was pregnant at the time and let's face it, she was no spring chicken! Then an avalanche hit. So unfair. He died on the advanced slope. What a heavenly skier, and so good-looking! A great success with the ladies and of course his son will be, too, Johnnie is just like him, a magical little being. Lord knows how poor crazy Louise could be married to this god and turn right around one year later and latch on to an old bore like Marshall Trimble! But he's rich," sighed Nanine, wiping and patting. She began to work on her face. This ritual both fascinated Jewel and revolted her. After a great deal of massaging and creaming, off it all came; and now Nanine began to dust those oily cheeks with a huge swansdown puff, chatting all the while. "And if there is one person on this earth who craves money, it's your aunt Louise! Have you met her? No! Well, they'll be here tomorrow, I'm afraid."

"Who?" cried Jewel.

"Aunt Louise, my boring old warthog of a sister, and Uncle Marshall. I shall put them in the Tourmaline Room. And Johnnie in Moonstone, next to you. Won't that be fun! A little friend!"

"But he's just a baby," scoffed Jewel. "I won't like him at all."

"Then Dinwiddie's sister is arriving, too, alas, with a smelly old husband. They take up two rooms; they hate each other. We'll put them in Jade and Topaz, far apart . . . Tootie, Dinwiddie's sister, hates everybody, she's a dreadful snob, hates me so I'm sure she'll hate you, too . . . and what a prude! It's always the ones who sneak around *doing it,* who say the most awful things about the rest of us . . . and it's all so boring, sex, not worth all the hullabaloo! So messy, so icky poo! I can't imagine why anyone bothers with it. You'll see," continued her aunt, and on went two dabs of rouge—smear, smear—with little violent pinches Nanine worked these into the powder, then began on the eyes, and selected a pot of turquoise, dabbing with her pinky finger so as not to stretch the eyelids. Nanine's dressing table was entirely filled with little pots of color and cream and with jewels everywhere, ropes of pearls and diamond rings, rubies and emeralds thrown in with the jars of cream. She threw off her wrapper (Jewel had been told to call it a peignoir) and sat there on the little fluffy stool in a large black girdle with stockings and a large black bra and satin mules and now she wound on ropes of pearls and what she called her sapphire clips. Not that Jewel thought her aunt Nanine ugly; she couldn't even put a word to it. The woman was stupefying: as Old Lou put it, Nanine was a freak in nature. But then suddenly Jewel wondered, what if I am some kind of freak in nature also? Only no one's seen it yet—no one but Granma! If only I could stay invisible . . .

"So why are all these people coming if you hate them so much?" asked Jewel.

"Hate? Heavens, I don't *hate* anybody!" exclaimed Nanine, as she disappeared into her closet. "They're coming to look you over," said the voice, floating out. "I suppose they'll make a great fuss over you, now you are one of us."

"I don't want a fuss!" declared Jewel. "No one made a fuss before."

"Yes, well, now you're somebody," said her aunt Nanine, who emerged from the closet in a sapphire-blue shantung with a waltz skirt, dyed shoes, and a little bag, a hat even, all this same blue, what she called her Mamie Eisenhower blue, and she twirled around once for Jewel to admire.

"I was somebody before!" muttered Jewel.

"You know what I mean." Nanine clasped on her bracelets. "*Somebody.* Now we're not going through all that again. It isn't your fault you had a tacky mother and poor foolish Horace for a father, but now—"

"He was not a fool!" cried Jewel. "No one's going to say bad things about my pa!"

"What a fierce little thing you are!" her aunt exclaimed, staring at the child. Too bad, thought Nanine, she isn't a beauty, I might have made something magnificent out of her! The child stood her ground. Really she was uncanny. Nanine looked away first, she had the feeling sometimes that this creature had strange powers, could see into her mind. For this reason she decided to tell the truth. Otherwise the truth bored Nanine. As a rule she found it a great irksome encumbrance.

"Look, Jewel—I still can't get used to that awful name—do you want me to be straight with you? Or shall we lie? Very well: the truth is none of us liked your father at all. Mother simply loathed him, I guess you've

figured that out, and Father—well, Father was a
dreamer. I don't suppose he ever really noticed Horace
much."

"But why?" insisted Jewel, "What did my pa ever do?"

"He was a disappointment, that's all. Some people just
are. His ears stuck out as I remember. And I guess he
wasn't very amusing. And also, you know, he was the
youngest. Mother used to say that by the time they got
to Horace the genes were watered down. But you
mustn't let this interfere with you," her aunt went on.
"Once we get you fixed up, Jewel, you can overcome
anything. We're going to send you to all the right
schools. Your friends will be the girls who count. How
do you suppose I got all this?" cried Nanine, waving an
airy hand over Jewel's head toward all the rooms
beyond. "My dear, I *worked* for it! *Worked!*" She breathed
the word "worked" a third time. "And you can have this,
too!"

". . . AND *you, yew,*" whooped Jewel, and she collapsed in
peals of laughter, "can have all this, too! Lord, I sure do
wish Twyla and Alvin had stuck around to hear this!"

"Tell about Alvin and Lucy Cook!" Johnnie pleaded.
Jewel had been telling him stories all day. "Tell about
the soufflé!"

"Well, it's that first day at lunch," began Jewel, "and
the three of us are sitting in that big ole dining room at
the table. Nanine, Alvin, and me. In comes Lucy Cook,
she's heading straight for Alvin, see, and she's carrying
this bowl of wobbling cheese—"

"Soufflé!" cried Johnnie. "It was a cheese soufflé!"

"Well, if you know so much," Jewel growled, "you go
on and tell the story." Johnnie clapped a hand over his

mouth. " 'Maybe she'd better go first,' says Alvin, point-
ing to Aunt Nanine, but Lucy Cook, she says, 'Naw,
she's on a diet. Grapefruit is all she eats on Tuesdays for
lunch, and celery soup. Hey!' she says to Alvin, winking,
'Hurry up! My arm's about to fall off—go ahead, take a
poke at it!' and she shoots Alvin this look of pure lust.
'You've made a great conquest, Alvin!' says Aunt Nanine. 'Hey,' I say, 'he's married!' 'Well, I don't really
think Mrs. Gumm will mind,' says Aunt Nanine, 'if
Alvin Gumm has a teensy flirt with my maid!' You
should've seen Alvin! He's backed way up against the
table as far from that woman as he can get and she's
pushin' that soufflé at him. So then Alvin says, 'Hold
tight now!' and he takes a whack at it. There's this pitiful
little sigh and down it sinks. Alvin, he says 'Aw, hell! I
guess I ruined it!' Lucy Cook whispers, 'What a hunk!'
in his ear—only I heard! Can you believe it! And there's
Alvin, married and with four kids!"

"I guess I ruined it! Heehee!" cried Johnnie, kicking
his feet with excitement.

"That Lucy Cook," said Jewel, "is a mess! They all are,
I never saw so many freaks in one house!"

"Well, how about the time," said Johnnie, "when
Uncle Dinwiddie and Aunt Nanine had all these people
to dinner, I think it was the president of the United
States or something"—actually it was Estes Kefauver—
"and Lucy Cook was passing around the lamb chops and
someone said something funny and Lucy Cook's mouth
flew open—like this!—and out flew her false teeth! And
stuck on top of the lamb chops!"

"Hee!" screamed Jewel, and the two of them rolled
with laughter.

Suddenly with a loud thump the door flew open and
there stood Lucy Cook. "So!" she barked at them. "*So!*"

Johnnie was so scared he dove down under the covers. "I see you, you little vermin!" hollered Lucy Cook and she switched on the light.

Lucy Cook, a pinch-faced acerbic virgin of about fifty, with a long drawn-out horse face and a pointed nose, beady eyes, pale red hair poking out from under the confines of a hairnet, was tougher even than Alvin Gumm and talked out of the side of her mouth like a man. She slapped her thigh a lot and wore men's shoes. At the dinner table Jewel heard her placing whispered bets into the pantry telephone between courses. Fond of racing, particularly greyhound, Lucy Cook kept a detailed track record posted on the pantry wall that she consulted whenever conversation lagged in the dining room.

"Alrightie!" bellowed Lucy Cook, "I heard what you two said! Think you're real smart, I suppose, ripping people apart. Well, it's lucky I don't get hurt feelings real quick. I guess I know who my friends are, though. You there," and she pointed a finger at Jewel, "I thought we was friends! I took you to the zoo yesterday! Spent my money on you! But I guess you got so many friends," she sniffed, "you can afford to treat people bad. Me—I got to be real choosy, see? But I guess stuck-up folk like you don't care." Although this was said in the flattest possible voice each word sat on them with a terrible force. Suddenly Johnnie began to blubber. Jewel felt pretty rotten herself.

"I feel so sad!" sobbed Johnnie. "If only you'd give us another chance, Lucy!" He slid down from the bed and ran fast out of the room.

"We didn't mean anything by it—he's just a little kid," began Jewel, and she hoped Lucy Cook might relent a little and tuck her in but the woman stood there, stone-faced. "Don't be too hard on him, he's awful sensitive," she went on. "Anyway—you're wrong, I got no friends, only Aunt Clara and Alvin, Twyla—but they're gone. So I'm available."

Still the woman said nothing, only stood waiting, but her eyes, hard as agate pebbles, got a little film of something moist and almost tender, not wet exactly, but friendly, and her voice, when she finally answered Jewel, was scratchy. "Well, I'll think about it. Maybe I'll give this thing a second chance. But you didn't even say you're sorry!" she added as she stomped toward the door. "And if you aim to be my friend you'll have to show some respect. The way I look at it, you're going to need a friend. These people"— she jerked her head toward the endless hallway beyond—"they stick with their own kind. And you aren't like them. No, you're not, I spotted it straight off. They'd as soon feed you to the alligators, girl, as do it your way. So think it over." And with that, Lucy Cook put out the light.

4

DINWIDDIE BROWN adored the ladies. In his day he had
been thought quite a rascal. All the great beauties of the
twenties and thirties were seen at one time or another
hanging on his arm. More than a few of them hatched
desperate plots to snare the man but Dinwiddie had not
been the marrying kind.

In 1935, when Dinwiddie met Nanine McAllister, he
was thirty-nine and she was twenty-eight. Even then he
had seemed much older. He liked to say, "The trouble
with old age is that by the time any of us gets there he
is too damn old to enjoy it!" Dinwiddie's idea was to
spare himself any of the usual degradations of youth: the
shenanigans and the disgraceful downward slide into
that twilight of foolish last dreams and befuddlement—
not for him! He meant to be prepared. And so, although
the prevailing fashion was to remain aggressively young,
whatever the cost and for as long as humanly possible,
Dinwiddie rushed headlong, the moment he married,
into a soothing old age. Before long the raffish beau of
yesterday became everybody's naughty, harmless old
darling; and if the gay, new young people exchanged

glances when Dinwiddie's admirers recalled his conquests, referring to him as a tremendous old buffalo,
what did it matter? He maintained a stalwart elegance
they might never hope to imitate. What did they know,
these new young boys, of gallantry and manliness, of the
beau ideal, phantom of a better age, swept aside, all but
gobbled up by the brusque forties? His sort were nearly
extinct and perhaps even a little absurd now in the howling, yapping wake of these new fellows. Let them have
the field. He watched them go to war, these giddy boys,
and come limping home; still, they had no idea. A new
and horrifying playfulness, frantic happiness, and a terrible bright insincerity characterized these years; as if all
the world were tricked out with palm trees and dames
in slinky dresses; boys and girls together dancing in the
rain; no more ladies and no more men; only a stunning
hodgepodge of dressed-up children.

Until he met Nanine McAllister, nothing, it seems,
ever really happened to Dinwiddie Brown. Oh, he had
gone off to war and ridden out the Depression, then set
out in the thirties quietly to amass another respectable
fortune to add to the one he already had. His friends (the
same friends he had always had, those from Groton and
Yale) all called Brown the best man alive. Ladies vied for
the place next to his at the dinner table; no one knew
why exactly; he would not flirt, only gazed fondly with
that little twinkle of perfect recognition as his admirers
carried on. His great fault, if he had one, seemed to be
a slight superiority he permitted himself on the subject
of emotional entrapments. He stood back and watched in
horror as the best fellows ran amok; sank down in the
murky waters of bad marriages, or, God forbid, even
worse, of love affairs. One by one they vanished, Groton
and Yale's finest, in the mud of love that he somehow
avoided. Who could blame him for gloating a little as his

own life proceeded along a safely charted course through tepid peaceful waters? And yet Dinwiddie adored the ladies. He would have been the first to tell you so.

Twenty when his father died, Dinwiddie chose to continue on in the family mansion at East Ninetieth Street, sharing the house with his mother, Charmagne, Mrs. Mortimer Brown. Although they had coexisted in perfect harmony, Mrs. Brown did the correct thing when her son turned thirty; she left the house to Dinwiddie and moved out; there, across the street in the corner building, where she had the penthouse apartment, Mrs. Brown peered down on her son in fond approbation. His personal well-being she entrusted to Cook and her maid of many years, Thatcher, who between them remained as devoted to her son as a dog to its bone.

Dinwiddie's daily routine was a triumph of orderliness: up at seven, oatmeal in the dining room at seven-twenty (kippers on Sundays); then, brief exercise in the form of a ten-minute walk down Fifth Avenue followed at a respectful distance by his chauffeur; picked up near the Metropolitan Museum and driven some thirty blocks to Brown, Brown and Cadwalader, he invariably began work at his desk by nine o'clock.

On Mondays, Wednesdays, and Fridays he met with his roommate from Groton, Talbot Rutherford, for a game of squash at the Union Club after which they each had a rubdown and one drink. On Tuesdays and Thursdays he met Morley Barrett at the Knickerbocker Club, where they had an hour of backgammon. It was a rare day when he found himself unable to enter his own house at six-thirty in the afternoon, bathe, and be seated downstairs in his library at seven-fifteen for a glass of whiskey before dinner.

The advent of Nanine changed all that.

Nobody knew how she got him. Nanine was no

beauty. She could boast of none of the fascinations of the
women in his set. True, she did have a dazzling thatch
of red hair, mountains of hair, and long silky legs. But
everything in between seemed wonderfully awry: big
teeth, big nose, slightly vulturine eyes, hooded even then
and sly; white skin, too white, and red elbows; huge
bosoms, which, depending on the prevailing fashion, got
strapped down for a decade and concealed or were thrust
up and out, suddenly, so that they must be, everyone
thought, amazingly false. She was so real, in fact, she
seemed false; certainly none of them could believe their
darling Dinwiddie Brown had run off and married such
a person.

It began incongruously one day at sea. They met in the
first-class saloon on the *Queen Mary,* as it sailed from
New York to Southampton. At the last moment Dinwiddie threw in with the Talbot Rutherford party, who
were off to Scotland for the August shoot. Binkie Rutherford found her, they needed someone to fill up a rubber
at bridge, and Binkie, feeling pleased with herself, produced the amusing little redhead from some absurd place
in Arizona. Actually, Nanine was traveling second class
on the *Queen Mary* but such was her skill that no one ever
found out, not even Dinwiddie after twenty years of
marriage.

"But who *is* she?" everyone asked.

"My dears, she's *nobody.* But for one afternoon I don't
think it matters much, do you?" said poor Binkie Rutherford. Of course they all blamed her afterward.

How Nanine managed it no one ever found out. Five
days later when they docked in Southampton, Dinwiddie was besotted. A month later in Scotland he married
her. He never knew what hit him; if he had awakened
from a perfectly innocuous sleep in his very own bed in
Ninetieth Street and found himself miraculously and all

unaccountably entwined with Betty Brattle, his cook, he could not have been more amazed than he was to find himself back in New York presenting his new wife to his mother, Charmagne Brown.

Nanine took them on, all of them: the old dragon of a mother, the gloomy family mansion, Cook and Thatcher, the Rockingham dessert sets, the creaking Hepplewhite; before a year was out she managed the impossible: to throw out everything, expunge the moldering old house of its awesome grandeur, drive Charmagne mad, or nearly so, utterly destroy all domestic order, ruining her husband's perfect digestion forever. And yet she made him laugh.

If there were moments in Dinwiddie's life with Nanine when he felt bound, gagged, shot from a cannon, heart in throat, and head awhirl, even so, he always landed back on earth. He could think of nothing about her of which he approved: pitiless, petulant, tyrannical, stingy, provocative, horrifyingly indiscreet, irrational, sly; definitely no lady, she caused his mother nearly unendurable suffering and embarrassment. Yet she proved generous to the point of madness, forthright, humane, whimsical, childlike, brave, amusing, adorable—the pulse and vivid thrum of life itself; with Nanine gone he could only imagine a dim resettling of all the life forces back into a dark and stymied coagulation.

Even so, Dinwiddie had begun to feel increasingly less satisfied of late. He could not say why. It was not his marriage, certainly. And no one had a more amusing, orderly, and useful life, did he? And yet, despite the best-laid plans, he began to detect to his infinite regret a certain deep furtive rumbling down there in his innards. It would not go away. He told no one, of course. The horror was that now at fifty-nine, just as he had thought he might be quite safe at last, the snake (years and years too late!) suddenly reared its ugly head.

THEY HAD told him at the police station the woman called herself Madeleine. The name on her passport, however, read: Boldiszar, Magda. She was very young, seventeen, but Dinwiddie noticed a triumphant savvy about her that belied her years. She agreed to see him. In her cell that first night she refused, though, to speak, would only stare him down contemptuously despite Dinwiddie's gentlest, most temperate appeals. The fact is, he loved her from that first moment.

When Jewel McAllister's father, Horace, leaped from the Empire State Building and her mother, Mary Lou, disappeared, it had been decided Dinwiddie should go see the foreign woman. Clearly she was mixed up with Horace's death. Her name, it seems, was scrawled on a slip of paper next to "Dorian Furs" and a West Side address. She had been brought in for questioning and detained for nearly a week. They found damaging evidence on the dead man's body of intimate contact with this woman. Then, too, a valuable piece of jewelry was missing: a pavé diamond peacock of unusual beauty, and this turned up only much later in the possession of Mary Lou McAllister. No one believed this foreign woman to be innocent—except Dinwiddie, who loved her on sight, loved for the first time in his life, and who then prevailed upon his close friend, the famous trial lawyer Morley Barrett, to get her off. Barrett would do anything he could for Dinwiddie Brown, but all the same he thought the woman a bad lot. He got the thing hushed up and she went free. If he had only known! Later, he almost regretted setting the woman free.

Nothing came of it, of course; Dinwiddie gave the girl money to return to wherever it was in Europe she said she lived. And then one night several months later he spotted her at the Stork Club. At first he wasn't sure. She wore a skirt and blouse, very simple, almost playful, and had pulled her hair back into a pony tail: how helpless she looked, and young! She danced with a fat, much older man and appeared so out of place Dinwiddie brought himself to do something previously unthinkable: he asked the majordomo about her.

Dinwiddie was alone that evening. Without, that is, Nanine. She had gone to Long Island for the weekend with her sister Louise. Nanine's idea had been that he treat Miss Plank, his secretary of some years, and her fiancé, to whom she had just become engaged, to an evening at the Stork Club. It was the sort of thing he never did.

Smart women in cocktail dresses, sleek predators, moved about from table to table, ordered fresh cocktails, eyeing one another indolently; the waiters hovered; Miss Plank gasped out one more time about some famous face whirling about on the dance floor and the soufflé arrived; Dinwiddie could not remember if they had eaten the rack of lamb or if it was still to come; he was signaling for the check when he saw her spinning in the arms of the beefy baron, a young girl down from college for a gay, grown-up evening. She wore flat-heeled shoes. Her mass of dusky, heavy hair had been caught up in a gleaming tail at the back of her head, and alongside such unadorned simplicity the other women, coarse, almost garish, seemed indecent. His heart stopped as she flew by.

The majordomo did not prove very helpful. Yes, she did seem very charming, the little lady, and must be, he thought, a Polish countess. Her friends were Poles and

Hungarians—the baron, he knew, was German, one of the newer titles. Dinwiddie, his heart in his throat, actually managed to brave the table of noisy foreigners and ask her to dance; her friends let her go with a great deal of noisy joking at his expense but he did not care, she was in his arms.

"And so, you did not leave," he said at last when they had spun about the floor once or twice and still she said nothing. He even had the idea she did not recognize him but this he knew must be impossible.

"No," she said in that slow, curious voice that sounded so strange to him, ugly almost, guttural, yet somehow thrilling. "As you see, I did not leave." She smiled at him for the first time. "Are you sorry?" she added. He said nothing, only looked down into her eyes with unbearable sweetness until at last she looked away. She knew.

"Have you eaten anything?" he said finally, feeling, for the first time in his life, at a loss for conversation. "Will you join me for dessert?"

"Yes," she said.

Introductions were made and then Miss Plank, just struggling into her coat, sat back down uncertainly. Dinwiddie murmured something about what a shame it was Miss Plank and her beau must leave so early and Miss Plank sprang back up, blushing furiously, and fled. Dinwiddie ordered Champagne.

They said little; she did not expect him to be a conversationalist. In the jail, certainly, theirs had not been a very vivacious intercourse. He saw though with a great tug of happiness how hungrily her eyes devoured everything on the dessert cart and at last she settled on a mound of fragrant strawberries, glancing at him for approval when the waiter offered to surround these with zabaglione and a dollop of bitter black chocolate mousse. He felt moved nearly to tears as he watched her devour the whole rich mess and he felt sure she was the only woman alive who could lick a tiny morsel of chocolate from the outer edge of one small pink finger without appearing instantly wrong. Dinwiddie was enchanted.

She toyed with her Champagne as she answered his questions. The foreigners at the other table were not really her friends at all; she hardly knew them; the fat baron was a boor. The awful thing about being alone in a foreign city was that one had to be grateful for whatever came along. To model fur coats, for instance, she thought a stupid job—well, if not for that she might have starved.

"Have you no family?" he inquired in his courtly fashion, but this she chose not to hear. He knew nothing of her. In the jailhouse he had discovered nothing. That woman, the hard-faced glaring little person of those days, had nothing to do with this creature. And it was part of Dinwiddie's amazing delicacy that he would never refer to those days or betray even the slightest curiosity as to why she had not used the money he gave her to return, as she said she would, to Europe. In this he differed from the men she knew and instantly won her gratitude. If she wondered what he must think of her she said nothing, behaving that night as if everything between them had always been perfectly easy.

(Much later, in the following months, he felt sorely tempted to speak of the past to Madeleine in the week he managed to track down his sister-in-law, Mary Lou, and wrest from her the diamond peacock. This had been accomplished only with several detectives and a fat bribe worth far more than the bird itself. He did it for Madeleine. Mary Lou expressed great reluctance in parting with the pretty bird. It was the only thing decent, she said, Horace had ever given her—what did she care if he stole it? But she was down on her luck, living in a trailer park with some sleaze, a two-bit used-car salesman.)

Dinwiddie wanted so to share the amusing little story with Madeleine. He could hardly tell Nanine! She would have snatched the jewel away from him on the spot! And worn it, brazen creature, triumphantly! But something stopped him, some sense that Madeleine might feel he needed proof of her innocence after all. No, better to let it lie. The evil bird he locked up. No one would know. Van Cleef and Arpels he had paid off long ago. Madeleine was free, he had gotten the charges dropped, and this was all that mattered.

She appeared not to notice the purring Bentley at the curb before the Stork Club, and Gustavo Mendez, Dinwiddie's chauffeur, behind the wheel. Dinwiddie coaxed her into the car, that first evening, although he hardly knew what to do with her. She slid in as effortlessly as she had mounted Eddie's Dorian van a bare five months before, her head held high, oblivious to the rowdy jests of her companions who came gushing out just then and hailed her loudly. For Dinwiddie the moment was very terrible.

"Please," she said in her low voice, "will you take me to the subway at Lexington Avenue and Fifty-ninth Street?"

"My dear, we'll take you home!" cried Dinwiddie, acutely aware that Mendez eyed them lasciviously in the rearview mirror.

At the Fifty-ninth Street subway station, where she insisted he drop her, Dinwiddie protested but she leaped out, a little cat. She would have run off except that, almost desperately, he called her back.

"Let me take you home," he entreated. Then: "When will I see you?"

"And is it so important?" she cried playfully as he reached out a hand to detain her. He was so taken aback by this he said, miserably (hang Gustavo Mendez, who gawked, the impudent cur! He would settle with him later), "Can you ask? Don't you see?"

For answer she leaned in and placed a kiss on either cheek, saying, with a sweet laugh, "Well, then—perhaps I will call you tomorrow!" She disappeared down the subway stairs while he burned, still, from the two little kisses. He tapped on the glass and signaled to be taken home.

Dim and snug, he gazed out from the back seat. There was the Plaza as they rounded the corner and slid up Fifth, her banners drawn in against the night. There, too, on the next corner, the Pierre. From deep within the soft hushed gray vacuum of the Bentley the world out there seemed a wonderful place. His world, his city. And what did it matter to him, her disappointed face, her terrible late-night face full of awful yearnings; and her scavengers, her hungry late-night crawlers? Let the city howl. What did this mean to him?

Ah, here was the Knickerbocker standing guard over the good life. Yes, and here, too, that haughty dame immured against the chilly night, his old friend the Frick. All was as it should be . . . but then, alone in the dark, his thoughts rushed in, beat down with whirring wings. I love! cried his heart. Ah! So it isn't too late! I love! So this is life!

Then, a moment later, hopeless: Sodden old fool! Fifty-nine, you are fifty-nine, a revolting old heap, a smelly, ancient old human wreck—and she is seventeen! Please, dear God! he groaned, covering his face in agony. Please don't let this be! Then, astonished, he felt his face was hot with tears. All gone, slid away, the delightful world. All gone! He looked out again. Where was his city now? He saw only the wavering, sadly tarnished ribbon of ghostly lights going nowhere, attached to nothing. So then it really is all for nothing, this long life! No matter how one tries! He almost howled out loud, thinking with disgust on the foolishness, the long banal satisfaction of his life. So then, said a mocking voice, you, too, are nothing but a fool!

But then, a moment later, dizzy with wonder and joy, he fell back, crying out softly, I love! Oh, my God, at last I love!

5

THE NIGHT of the much-dreaded Brown family gathering in her honor, which Jewel remembered all her life, her uncle Dinwiddie was nowhere to be found. Though this seemed remarkable at the time, when he did show up, the next day, he refused to account for his whereabouts.

Jewel and her cousin Johnnie were fetched downstairs to the Red Room by their new ally, Lucy Cook. "Something mighty terrible is going on in there," Lucy hissed, pushing them in at the door. With cocktail hour nearly over, Nanine had forgotten to send for the children, and now it was too late, dinner would be spoiled, they must say their hellos quickly and run along to the kitchen for their supper. Nanine did not believe in children in the dining room after six o'clock at night.

Jewel, twitching with embarrassment in her new Lanz of Salzburg dress, tucked all over and way too babyish for a girl of fourteen, loped around the room after Johnnie, who seemed amazingly at ease, kissing all the aunts and saying Howdydo? to the aged uncles. It was an august crowd. No one took any notice of Jewel, and she was on the point of sneaking away when Johnnie came run-

ning up, very excited, and said, "Uncle Dinwiddie has
run away!"

"How do you know?" exclaimed Jewel.

"They can't find him anywhere! They've called all the
clubs and anyway, it's Saturday, he doesn't go to his club
on Saturday, and they've called his friends."

"Pooh!" said Jewel. "He's probably taking a walk."

"Or maybe he died," said Johnnie, "In the park. On a
bench somewhere."

"Uncle Dinwiddie doesn't sit on park benches. He
doesn't go to the park," said Jewel. "Gee, I'm sorry about
this," she mused. "He was my favorite person around
here."

"I thought I was!" Johnnie scowled.

At nine o'clock the children were sent to the servants'
hall and Nanine said the rest of them might as well go
in to dinner. Dinwiddie Brown had never been late but
as he had not been found it seemed silly to spoil a perfectly good dinner. Jewel and Johnnie heard them in
there every time the pantry door swung open: screaming, all jabbering at once like deranged birds.

"I don't ever want to grow up," said Johnnie.

"I'd kill myself first, acting like that," said Jewel
glumly.

When dinner was over at eleven o'clock they sent to
the basement for Gustavo Mendez. Although the basement was not very nice Gustavo had balked at living in
the attic with the other servants and so they let him have
the little room off the storeroom downstairs, which
meant he had his own entrance. Alarming noises sometimes emanated from that quarter and then Treacle
would be sent to investigate. Treacle, suave and judi-
cious, would report back that it must have been the
radio. The Puerto Rican station, perhaps.

Gustavo Mendez emerged from the basement fingering his fly, as always, when he knew he was going to be grilled. Although he swore most violently as to his innocence in knowing anything of his master's whereabouts, his face was full of innuendos. He had an annoying way of hesitating before answering mistress's questions, as if to spare her the worst. At last, after many sly squints and shrugs, he intimated he knew why the master did not come home. But not even when she threatened him with prison would Gustavo tell. Nanine summoned Treacle and the other servants, Lucy Cook, and Thatcher the upstairs maid, Chee, and Betty Brattle, known as Cook, but they all stood, abashed and hang-faced, silent as to the master's whereabouts. Actually, some weeks ago, the Mexican, Mendez, whispered the details of the master's affair into the butler's ear and Treacle told Cook. . . . There were disappointingly few facts; they had been together several times, Gustavo swore to this, but as to what they did—

This was all very confusing for the dinner guests: one by one they began to creep home, and those who were staying in the house crept off to their rooms. Nanine could be heard, at midnight, shrieking in the hallways. The servants, lined up in their bathrobes, were all brought down and grilled again.

"Why doesn't she call the police?" asked Johnnie, spying on the lineup from his cousin's room.

"Because she doesn't really want to find him," murmured Jewel.

DINWIDDIE DID not call his wife because he could not bear to tell a lie. Once long ago he had told a lie: they sent him home from Trinity School in the fourth grade for telling the boys his grandfather Brown kept a quadroon locked up as his mistress in the Ambassador Hotel. Dinwiddie suffered greatly for this crime. Mrs. Edgar Slocum Brown, his grandmother, a tower of awesome female outrage, gloomy and infallible, unimaginably ancient, sent for him. She peered down from what seemed an awful distance and made him recite his treacherous tale once again. He could have borne it if she banished him from the family forever: instead, beckoning him to come close, she leaned down, his grandmother Brown, swaying and creaking most dangerously, and grabbed ahold of his ear. *"The Browns don't tell lies!"* she boomed.

Not that truth was sacrosanct. In the present instance, what good could come of blurting out the truth? His feelings for Madeleine were an embarrassment, to the girl most of all! What should he tell his wife? For the first time in twenty years he had not come home to dinner. Dinwiddie completely forgot what night it was and that Jewel was being feted with the whole family gathering. But if the truth was unthinkable, still he would not concoct some lie. It did not matter that his wife lied continually, that she did it, he knew, as a sport. To keep her wits agile! Ugh, how sordid it had begun to seem, his precious love!

"TELL ME," Madeleine had said, "why do you look so furious? What can you be thinking?"

They sat together on a chaise longue in the little sitting room of a suite Dinwiddie had taken at the Plaza Hotel. Madeleine lay stretched out, her long legs in their high heels crossed prettily at the ankle. Dinwiddie perched along the arm, his great uncomfortable bulk balanced uneasily. He yearned to stroke her hair. Opposite, with the door left partway open to reveal the other room, was the bed.

"I was remembering my grandmother," he said at last.

"Was she nice?"

"No, not at all."

"Am I like her?" she smiled, and leaned her head back against his leg.

"You're not like anybody, Madeleine," he brought out slowly.

Madeleine pulled away, and crossed the room to take a cigarette from her bag. "Tonight you don't like me." She struck a match, then drew in deeply. "You want something—but I haven't got it. Still you don't believe me."

"I haven't said—"

"No, you wouldn't . . . but all the same, you think if we fuck . . ."

"I told you not to use that word. It has nothing to do with us."

"Ah," she said wearily. "Well, it's all the same to me. Call it what you like. If it isn't *that* you want, what *do* you want from me?"

"I don't know."

Sometimes he almost hated her. He watched as she paced and smoked. He could not think of a time when he had been so untrue to himself. Not even in the war. Oh, he had done things before now he did not like to do. But somehow his great impulse remained an abiding fastidiousness by which he knew himself. Now all that seemed betrayed. He still could not think why this was happening to him. Monstrous, unspeakable desires had overwhelmed him. Besotted with this woman whom he knew nothing about, not even where she lived or where she came from, he thought only of dissolving into her, of the dizzy, slow-devouring rapture of her nearness. And even though each new encounter left him weak and frightened, his one thought remained to see Madeleine and be near her again.

What she thought of him he could not imagine and he felt grateful she tolerated his attentions. He supposed she put up with him because he let her alone. Men, she said, were in the habit of pawing her. This he would not do. He supposed she must be grateful for that at least.

They had been meeting these last three months, innocently at first (or so he persisted in thinking of it), and then he had the idea of finding some place they could meet in private. He hardly knew what he hoped for. She had not as yet made him a happy man. He seemed amazingly inept at seduction and felt repelled, in any event, by the idea of seducing a seventeen-year-old girl; he knew only that he must see her as often as she might allow. They could not go on meeting in the street. True, Madeleine liked the excitement of lunching in fashionable places; they arrived at "21" one day and were told by the maître d' Nanine had gone in just ahead of them with a party of friends. Next Madeleine goaded him into taking her to Giovanni's, where they met his sister Tootie and Irene Driscoll coming down the stairs!

Usually Madeleine asked if they could drive around in his car. What must Gustavo Mendez think! First she had him stop at Nat Sherman's for Russian cigarettes. Then drive around the corner to the St. Regis for magazines, then way over to the east twenties to pick up her dry cleaning; or perhaps they crawled through traffic at a murderously slow pace to some obscure address in the Bronx and he would wait in the car while she ran in to pick up a dress from her seamstress. At the subway she leaped out, sometimes without even a little peck goodbye, and he returned to the office limp and exhausted, resolved never to see her again. He knew he was making an ass of himself but what could he do? Not to see her again was out of the question. He had to see her. In the hours and sometimes days when they were apart he drove himself nearly mad with sensations conjured up by her silky beauty: a gleam of skin remembered, the fall of thick healthy hair tucked back behind the little ear, the slender fingers curled about a cigarette, the pink of her nails, unvarnished, plain as a baby's.

"Why won't you tell me where you are from?" he asked her one day. Madeleine stiffened, and he never asked again. He suspected she might be Polish or Hungarian; her accent struck him as curious—French perhaps, but with some odd guttural undercurrent not quite pleasant to the ear. It was inconceivable to him, not being connected to a place or having people know who you were. Yet somehow he loved her for this childish game, for what else could it be? Only criminals and low types hid their origins and he could see she was not that. He saw perfectly how fine she was; next to Madeleine his wife appeared coarse and as rough as an old shoe.

"Tell me, Madeleine," he said at last, sinking down into her place in the chaise longue, "have you ever desired a man? Because if you—because if you could— well, don't you see how it is, Madeleine?" Then, a moment later, he said very quietly so that she must lean to hear, "I am trying to tell you I am suffering—not that this is your fault, my darling."

She came to him quickly, shhhshing him, putting her fingers on his lips. "Don't say these words! Don't say anything more!" she cried. It amazed him to see how bright her eyes suddenly became. Were there tears? Gently she leaned to kiss his cheek, then vanished into the other room. He sat waiting for her to return. At last he got up and opened the door, pushing it wide, and saw her. She kept very still, watching him. She had taken away the bedspread and placed herself, stretched full out, completely naked upon the white coverlet.

"Not like this," he brought out awkwardly. He felt

deeply shocked but could not take his eyes from the vision of that strangely immature body sprawled naked upon the bed.

One arm curled up behind her neck, the other lay loosely across her belly; not, he thought, to shield her flesh but to suggest a languor that he found terrifying. He felt old: a tremendous fat old sorrowful sod, a beast spying on a very young child. But in fact she was not a child. How I must revolt her! came the sickening thought.

"You want too much," she said at last, yawning at him indolently, and Madeleine rolled over onto her side, curling one long leg, then the other, up tightly against the tiny breasts so that he had a full view of the slender neck and the long curve of her spine relaxing down into the foolish, rounded little buttocks, two pink globes absurdly exposed, tenderly offered up, and suddenly he forgot to think, forgot Nanine and his dinner, forgot all he had ever been or hoped to be; dropping to his knees beside her on the bed, moaning, sobbing almost with the agony of his love for her, he reached to touch the soft shoulder, the slender spine, felt her shudder, and buried his face deep down in the fragrant tangle of wonderful dusky hair.

AS DINWIDDIE let himself into the house late that night, Isidor, one of the parrots, shrieked, *"Thief! Thief!"* It did seem he had taken away something settled and inviolable; he had been gone only a few hours, yet the place appeared changed.

The lights, both upstairs and down, were all left on and the effect of so much unwonted brilliance shocked him. For a moment he did not move. He felt a disastrous silence and knew at once something terrible had happened and he was to blame. It came to him: a sense of the old order suddenly disappearing. Even so, Dinwiddie felt armored by happiness. More than anything he wanted to slip away to his room and hide with his secret, mull over his good fortune in the dark. How light he felt tonight, and buoyant! Dinwiddie gave way to an irresistible urge to kick up his heels and dance: slowly, once around the room, swaying with delight.

But the violence of so much light actually seemed menacing. It held him pinned. Old presences lingered here. He looked around, astonished by the old house: how disfigured it appeared! By some odd trick the dear belongings of his father and grandfather, hidden in long-forgotten corners of the great hall, appeared to have been pushed forward in this light. Ah, how absurdly out of place they were next to the mocking prominence of these newer things. The worn Turkey carpets upon which, as a baby, he had tried his first steps—in this very room!— shown up as ragged, pathetic almost, and absurdly out of place near these bold new carpets, the new chairs with their flaming colors, and the shocking furbelow Nanine had insinuated into the house. How was it he had not noticed? As he gazed at this appalling transformation of his mother's house, whose tone of soothing refinement he depended upon always to smooth away the jarrings of the outside world he thought, I have lost everything.

But then in the next moment he remembered and said to his heart, Never mind! A wonderful seed of new life is hidden here! A curious thing happened as Dinwiddie crossed the hall. He thought: I am an actor posturing on some absurd stage. He took the steps two at a time—and at the bend in the staircase stopped short, for there sat the child, his niece Jewel. She watched him with an eagerness that made him laugh out loud.

"Hullo!" she said in a friendly way.

"Why, hello there!" he cried. "And what, may I ask, are you doing up so late? Waiting for the moon?"

"You're going to catch it," said the child solemnly, gazing at him with big eyes. "They're awful mad."

"They?" he inquired delicately, with a slight bow, his hands clasped behind his back. How droll she was!

"They're all here, you know. All the aunts." Jewel wrinkled her nose at him humorously.

Suddenly his expression changed. He had forgotten! A look of such horror crossed his face she was frightened. Then he understood: she had waited, she wanted to warn him. He tucked his arm through hers, tenderly, and said, "Shall we retire, my dear?" and at the top of the stairs he watched as she disappeared, a wiry, skittish, oddly angled, and slightly unsure figure wafting down the hall.

Nanine, stiff as a cadaver, lay with her face to the wall. He knew she waited for him. Still holding to his new seed of joy, he stood beside her bed. In her room, also lit with what seemed a mad, incisive clarity, he saw what he had not noticed before: a plethora of disgusting jars and bottles, creams and sinister unguents on his wife's dressing table—some with the caps left off, he had to look away; and oozing out from the closet and across the floor, a spill of lingerie, discarded shoes, a girdle dragged off, the stockings still attached, and other nasty souvenirs no decent man should ever have to confront. And all this had the effect of enlisting him in some conspiracy, he knew, a conspiracy to trample down dignity. Even as he had these sensations he felt how dated they were. How Nanine would have teased him! He was *musty,* reeking of sanctity, she always said, when the whole point was to have fun! She was right, he felt as much, nothing seemed very amusing about virtue. And hadn't he married Nanine for just that—to be amused?

"Don't," he said at last, "please, Nanine, don't do this."

For a long moment she stayed silent. Finally, without glancing around, she said, "You came home."

"Of course I came home." He groaned. "Please, Nanine!"

He saw something in that fat, slightly creased, reddish neck that repulsed yet moved him nearly to tears. At that moment he even felt close to loving her, he envisioned himself giving up Madeleine. Nothing could be as dastardly as wounding this pathetic creature. Also—and this was very powerful—he had never seen Nanine like this before.

"What time is it, Dinsie?" she asked weakly. He said nothing, he knew it to be past three in the morning. Coming home he had decided: the worst disgrace is a concocted lie. If there is nothing to say, I will be silent. Nothing she might suspect him of seemed as bad as the truth itself.

Suddenly: *"Fucking sonofabitch!"* She rose up screaming. He fell back from her, horrified. *"Bastard!"* she screamed out wildly, flailing at him with her fists. *"Do you have any idea what I've suffered?"*

Her face, a disgusting livid red, so appalled him after that other face he almost couldn't look. He fell back from her, shuddering, but she came after him, throwing herself up off the bed. *"Bastard!"* He saw way down her throat to the angry little dancing tonsils as she shrieked at him and pounded. He determined to meet her eye. This was the least he could do.

"What makes you think I give a rat's ass about where you've been? I don't even want to hear! Who cares if you've been out screwing some pathetic whore somewhere? Just keep away, you hear? Don't think you can climb on top of me, I don't want you anywhere near me,

Hear?" But when Dinwiddie turned and began slowly walking toward the door she screamed so violently he really felt afraid for her. She came rushing after him, pummeling his back with her weak little fists, loudly choking, weeping. "Twenty years, twenty goddamn years I've wasted! I'm old! I coulda had anybody I goddamn wanted but I stuck it out with you you faggot and what for? I actually believed you loved me! I actually believed we had something! Now what'm I supposed to do? Go stand in the corner? Is this what I get for loving you? I've loved you more than my own life, yes, almost to distraction, no one can say I haven't! Who else would love you as I did? Oh, Dinsie!" she sobbed, and Nanine collapsed, dragging at his lapels. "For chrissakes think of your family, think of this child—and your mother, think of Charmagne! What would Charmagne say if she could see—" Through all this Dinwiddie stood straight as a ramrod. Her abuse flowed over him, and he kept holding to the new seed; but something chilling began to steal over him: the unbearable sweetness of those hours with Madeleine took on an ominous hue. Wasn't there something almost insidious about happiness that cost so dear? It began to taunt him, this newfound joy, the new buoyancy, and twist him around. He turned on himself with loathing suddenly, hating the new little seed.

"And even if none of it was true, if you never did care for me like you pretended to all those years—"

Pretended! He had never pretended anything in his life. If only he *could* pretend! And all those years came crushing in on him, the moments added up, the hours and weeks, and it struck him as a monstrous lie, the whole of it, futile, self-satisfied, and something in his face must have finally caved in for she sprang at him.

"You do care, don't you! Ah, you care! Some chippy has got her clutches in you, that's all. Or maybe it's that

vile Miss Plank." Nanine scowled viciously. "Well, I'll
see about Miss Plank—" she hissed, then twined herself
around him. She cried, "Do you care?" searching his
face, and it seemed to her she frightened him. His usual
pink turned to ash. She clung to him, savored this one
small triumph.

"Tell her I'll never let you go! Send her to me, Dinsie,
if she bothers you again. Nannie will take care of her, yes
and by God I will!" cried his wife, and she ground her
teeth, "Yes, and your Nannie loves you, darling, she
really really loves you, don't you believe her?" she demanded, pulling away to look into his face.

"Yes! Yes!" he gasped. As he dragged himself off to his
room, an old and beaten man, Dinwiddie thought, This
is the first time in fifty years I have told a lie. Yes! yes!
he nearly screamed. Yes, I believe you!

6

"HEY, KID!" said Lucy Cook, who stood in the doorway watching Jewel. "I've been looking for you everywhere."

Jewel, a small intrusion at the edge of a polished lake, sat at the dining-room table, all alone. Silvery undulations of morning light stirred the waxy pools: a long-necked silver pot followed by a tea service swam in the shadows of watery cathedrals, silver candelabra sinking slowly down. How many days, wondered Jewel, have I been here?

They had been working on her to change. To be someone else, not Jewel. Sometimes it scared her, feeling so alone. What if she lost the way to that little voice inside? The voice had kept her going. That and Lucy Cook. She and Jewel were best friends. Because of Jewel, Lucy Cook got three afternoons a week. They went everywhere together. Chee acted jealous. He followed them sometimes.

But the hardest part was that Johnnie had gone away. He was only nine but Jewel liked him better than anyone. For a little kid he had amazing powers. She did not even have to finish the sentence sometimes: he knew what she meant and felt her feelings with a quick glance. She had told him about the ranch, he knew the Mexicans by name, the cowboys, he knew all about Aunt Clara and Granma, too, he even knew how to say *chingón* and *hijuela* like a vaquero.

"I don't see why he had to leave," said Jewel to her aunt Nanine.

"They're always on the go," said Nanine as she wrapped her head in a turban, then layered slices of cucumber on the bags under her eyes. "Poor Louise gets depressed if she stays in one place too long. So they winter in Palm Beach and Nassau, then spend a week here with us in May, then Greenwich in June and maybe a quick dash up to Bar Harbor; then down again for a week or two in Southampton in July. Salzburg in August, or Capri. Then Scotland for the shoot. A week sometimes in London, or Paris, then New York in the fall . . ."

"But where does Johnnie go to school?" exclaimed Jewel, who stood by, riveted, as Nanine, head thrown back, laid on more cucumbers. The lips, surrounded by cucumbers, worked up and down like guppy lips.

"School, my dear," said the lips, "is for those who have nothing better to do."

NOT THAT Lucy Cook hadn't tried. She took Jewel everywhere: to Ripley's Believe It Or Not, to the Automat, to hang out at the back entrance of the Copacabana to see the gangsters and cigarette girls. But nothing had worked. That very first day when Jewel and Alvin were sent to Central Park with Lucy, Jewel made a pact with her soul not ever to let go of that place where she belonged. Twyla was right: this place had an awful power.

"Hell!" said Lucy Cook. "This place is where the action is! Where else in the world are you going to see a Rockefeller and a movie star or a gangster, maybe? Or someone like Adlai Stevenson walking down the street? Same as us, in the same block?"

"If it's a gangster," Alvin replied, "how'll we know?"

"Don't it give you goose bumps?" said Lucy Cook. They had to run a little to catch up with her. "To think that right now, right this minute, someone famous might be looking down on us from one of them big windows?"

Alvin, though, did not seem very impressed. Jewel remembered this later. "If it's a gangster," Alvin persisted, but Lucy Cook rode him down with the last word.

"Oh, pooh! You can tell one of them anywhere," she declared. "All you gotta do is get a good look at their socks. Gangsters always wear silk socks. Real silk." Lucy sniffed. "Now, are you two coming on an adventure or not?"

She had taken them, that first day, on an odyssey Jewel would not forget. They sat together, the three of them, on a park bench, and Lucy produced a rumpled packet of birdseed. She pushed it at Jewel and said, "Go on, kid, it's your turn to feed the birds!" Then in the next moment she hollered, "Not like that, dummy! Don't they teach you ranch kids how to feed a pigeon?" Then Lucy Cook began an easy sleepwalking bird dance, cooing, swaying, scattering seed. At the end of the bench a woman in a red coat sat watching the pigeons waddle. She wore pancake-flat shoes and at the back of these Jewel saw large bleached white heels, bare as soup bones. She hadn't liked to say it but the sight of those heels made her want to cry. Then the woman opened up a large black pocketbook on her lap and looked inside.

"We got raven," said Alvin, "and fruit bats. And red-tailed hawk. We got all kinds of owl." Oh, it was hard to remember that sweet singsong voice of Alvin Gumm without a terrible pang! "We got vultures and turkey buzzard. And once—once in Dragoon," said Alvin, "I even saw a bald eagle."

Next to them the woman with the soup bone heels leaned down and put her head in the black pocketbook and began screaming dirty words. The birds scattered.

"Why is she doing that?" asked Jewel.

"A person can scream if he wants to. C'mon, let's beat it," said Lucy Cook briskly. "What'll we do now?"

"We don't care," said Alvin, who tried not to look at the woman in the red coat.

"I got plenty of money," said Lucy Cook. "My own, too—not Miz Brown's. We could check out the zoo, then head on over to Times Square. There's always something going on over there."

They walked through the park: music came pumping, floating through the trees, carousel music. They started to run, Alvin in his boots bringing up the rear.

Around and around it flew, a riderless carousel. Galloping horses, unicorns in scarlet plumes, zebra, coolly unconcerned, flying round and round; tigers crouching, implacable geese: spinning, spinning!

"See what I mean? Have you ever seen anything so wonderful as Central Park?" shouted Lucy Cook excitedly. It seemed strange to think a week ago Jewel and her aunt Clara McAllister had been crouching out in the back meadow watching for the stallion to mount the mare.

"Yup!" said Lucy Cook. "I guess life just don't get any more exciting than this."

"There's no one here," said Alvin. "It's like a runaway circus." And the animals flew past desolate, dismayed: mouths open, grimacing.

Jewel said, "It's the saddest thing I ever saw." But no one heard.

Lucy Cook began to tramp around the machine, calling for the operator. Maybe he died or was murdered or something, she called over her shoulder to Alvin and Jewel.

"Yoohoo! Where are you, you big dumdum? Yoohoo!"

It seemed to Jewel as she followed them she had already forgotten what was real. She tried to remember the cottonwood tree at the ranch but her mind drew a blank. The kitchen at home: beans on the back burner, the smell of tortillas scorching on a round of cut iron—yes, she remembered! And the fights, the gossiping: Twyla and Eufemia and Rosie Gonzales, the cowboys filing in late for the noonday meal: somebody passed around a plate piled with slices of white bread and hot folded tortillas in a towel; and gravy, they brought in a roast and ate till it was gone. Granma sat at the top of the table and talked to the men about late calves. Or about some cow's cancered eye. Or about rain. Sure wish it'd rain, someone would say. Summer. And someone else would say, It rained over to the Guevavi last week, they got grass this high! Then Rosie would dish up a lemon meringue pie. No—she could still remember.

They wound through the park toward the zoo and passed a bald meadow beginning to sprout grass. A nipping breeze stirred gum wrappers in the path, and across the paved footpath came the rustle of cardboard lids and an occasional rolling cup. Lucy Cook was in seventh heaven.

"Yessiree bub," she said, "this city's got everything! Summer's coming, don't it just thrill you? Once a place like New York gets into your blood it makes every place else seem plain and stupid. You'll see." She grinned at Jewel. They had to push to keep up with her gangling stride. Summer! Jewel could almost smell the June bugs! Buzz buzz, down they swoop! And the horseflies, the

ants, the rubb-rubbing of crickets so loud, on hot nights!
And vibrant—all the earth thrummed with their small
fevered music so you got caught up in it heart and soul;
no longer separate but part of it all, the busy, rubbing,
vibrant earth!

Once they passed an old stew bum wrapped in rags
and laid out on a park bench. Groaning in his sleep. But
only Jewel noticed.

"Yessiree bub," said Lucy Cook, "when the time
comes I'd be willing to bet nine to one you won't even
want to go back to that lonesome ranch." She pulled out
her wallet to pay for three tickets to the zoo and gave
Jewel a friendly poke.

"Fat lot you know about it," scoffed Alvin, who rose
to the bait like a trout to a fly.

"Well, all I know is when Miz Brown gets a plan in
her head no one on this earth can stop her—she's got
what she calls her projects. And it looks like you are the
big new project," Lucy Cook said to Jewel.

They passed through a room with a giraffe, a yak, then
a lion all cooped up in bare little stinking cages. Jewel
scurried past. A gorilla, over in the corner, cowered with
shame.

"Projects!" cried Alvin. "Well, I guess you just haven't
met the big honcho, ole lady McAllister! Now there's a
big shot!"

"What kind of project?" Jewel asked as Lucy Cook
paused to take in the bear.

"Well, I guess she means to turn you into a lady—
hawhaw!" Lucy Cook chuckled.

"A lady!" echoed Jewel. She wasn't sure what being a
lady meant exactly. "Are you a lady?" she asked.

"Me! A lady! Hell no, I ain't no lady!" Lucy Cook
guffawed.

A man stuck his tongue out at the bear. A big sign said,

PLEASE DO NOT FEED THE BEAR. The man tossed the bear a
bologna sandwich.

"Will you look at that!" exclaimed Lucy Cook.

"Well, is Aunt Nanine one? Or Granma?" asked Jewel.

"Your aunt is many things," said Lucy Cook who
glowered at the man as he wadded up an empty brown
sack and shot it at the bear. "But she is definitely no
lady."

"The only genuine lady I ever met in person," mused
Alvin, "was my mother. Oh, she's not rich or anything
like your granma but she's a lady all the same, and real
gentle with sick folks," continued Alvin, "and she always puts on her bonnet to go down to the chicken
house."

"We got plenty of ladies right here in New York
City," said Lucy Cook. "The thing you got to get into
your head is that if you're a big shot somewhere else it
don't count for anything in New York City."

"Do you have any idea how big the Dragoon Cattle
Company is?" demanded Alvin. "I bet you don't even
know how much land Miz Lou McAllister's got! Why,
it's a lot bigger than anything you got here—it's bigger
than New York City!" he spat out.

"Big deal," said Lucy Cook. As she said this the man
threw a rock at the bear. Lucy Cook whirled on him,
stamped her foot, and shouted, "*You rat!* Go on home,
bum—beat it! Damn you anyway—who the hell lets people like you in the zoo in the first place? Can't you read?
It says DO NOT FEED THE BEAR! He's not even an American,
I bet," she said to Alvin and Jewel as the man slunk off.
"If there's one thing I hate it's foreigners. Now what do
you want to see next?"

"I want to go home," said Jewel.

"Home! What's the matter, doesn't she like zoos?"
Lucy Cook asked Alvin, flabbergasted.

"I guess she's never seen one before," said Alvin. They stood a moment in the thin light and discussed Jewel. As if she were deaf and couldn't hear them. She began to feel smaller and smaller, she was shrinking. It seemed a relief almost.

"What do you mean—she's sensitive?" said Lucy Cook.

"Well, she's a strange kid," said Alvin. "She talks to herself most of the time. No one paid much attention to her at the ranch, she ran wild, mostly, foolin' around with her aunt Clara. Two of them were quite a pair. Oh, she's a good kid, only they let her run to seed—can't say how it'll turn out. But she's mighty sensitive. Smart, too! You tell her something once and she's got it down for life. She just watches it all with those big eyes, like she's waiting all the time for a signal or something."

"A signal!" said Lucy Cook, who stared hard at Jewel. "Don't it get lonesome out there on a ranch?" said Lucy, and she turned her back to the monkeys. One of the monkeys began to do something dirty; Alvin looked away.

"Nothing lonesome about land or clean air or sky," he said.

"It's people that make you lonesome," Jewel piped up.

"Lonesome! This city! Why, I come here to this zoo every Thursday on my day off!" said Lucy Cook, astounded. "I just don't get it—I never met a kid don't like zoos!"

"C'mon," said Alvin, who saw Jewel's face starting to crumple, "let's get the kid out of here."

"There's plenty more to see," said Lucy Cook. "Hey! If she doesn't go for the zoo we could head on over to Times Square and take in the sights—"

"I guess we've seen enough sights," said Alvin.

"You haven't seen Ripley's Believe It Or Not or the

Empire State Building!" cried Lucy Cook, who chased after them.

"*Alvin!*" Suddenly Jewel let loose with a high thin howl, like a snared rabbit. People stared, Alvin bent down, scooped Jewel up effortlessly, and slung her over his shoulder like a sack of meal.

"Well, who can figure kids out?" said Lucy Cook, as she brought up the rear.

"LOOK, KID, what's the use of remembering?" said Lucy Cook, who sat down next to Jewel at the dining-room table. "Why, if I let myself remember things—"

"Is that what life is, Lucy?" asked Jewel. "Forgetting? What is it grown-ups try so hard to forget?"

"No use looking back," said Lucy Cook. "What was it the Bible said, about Ruth and that pillar of salt? Well, you keep lookin' back, girl, and you going to be frozen to stone! See, the secret is to always keep moving. You stand still and well, hell, nothing lives if it stands still. Now, sure you love that ranch out there in the boondocks, I can see that—but lovin' a thing too hard, squeezin' the life outta something, well, there ain't no better way to kill a thing."

"But I'm afraid if I let go I—"

"Afraid! See! There's the word you gotta look out for! Why, if you knew the things old Lucy here has had to fear! But I won't do it, nosiree, I won't! You put that fear in a box, kid, and put the lid on it—throw it to the hogs, that's what Lucy'd do . . . now c'mon," she added in her gruff voice, "I got something real exciting for us to do today."

Jewel knew this meant the health club. Not that Lucy Cook went there to get health. No, she went there every week to check up on her friend Mrs. Feeny. Jewel had to admit if there was one place exciting in New York City it was the health club.

Mrs. Feeny lived in the basement of the Ansonia Hotel. It was over on the West Side; all Lucy Cook's secret places were over on the West Side; Nanine would have been shocked if she knew Jewel had been to the West Side—and liked it better than the East Side. The East Side was just a lot of ladies in fancy clothes and lizard bags but the West Side was full of friends. Mrs. Feeny didn't really live in the basement of the Ansonia but she worked down there where the blubbery fat ladies came to swim. Mrs. Feeny was the chatelaine, as she called it, of the Al Roon Swim Club.

It felt like going down into hell in a slow bucket, the descent down to Al Roon's. As the elevator went down the steam and smoke of slow baking human flesh rose up; the elevator even smelled of wet flesh.

The elevator doors opened onto a small room. On the walls were a hundred pictures of movie stars in swim-suits, the kind with a flap over the crotch and the crotch pulled way down over the thighs. The messages on the photos said, on a slant in black ink, "To Roberta Feeny with gratitude!" or "With Best Regards! Keep up the Great Work!" Then there would be a name like Maureen O'Hara or Dorothy Lamour or Gloria De Haven. Esther Williams was there, too, Jewel's great hero.

"She autographs them herself," said Lucy Cook proudly, the second time they went.

The floor of this first little room was wall-to-wall carpeted in a bristly shimmering black nylon, sticky on the bare toes and entirely covered with huge red and orange roses. This rug felt so stiff with the grease of the fat ladies' massage lotions that it was like standing on a used Brillo pad. There was only one chair to sit down on; this had gone from leather to plastic to bald foam and had the

imprint of a moist fat back, always, and two greasy run-
nels where the fanny went and the thighs; shiny, always,
with a slick of sweat.

"Tell her to take a seat" was always the first thing Mrs.
Feeny, Roberta, said to Lucy Cook, and so Jewel would
have to sit in the terrible chair. She only sat on the edge
though.

"Tell her to make herself comfortable," said Mrs.
Feeny, not looking up. She was always doing something
important. Then when she finished she would come
around and perch herself on the edge of her desk, one
hock up, arms akimbo: like the boss man of the dock
strikers or something. She was enormous, the biggest
human Jewel had ever seen up close. Roberta only wore
muumuus. These were black usually, like the rug, and
with hot tomato-red roses all over. The muumuus were
scoop-necked to show peeps of Roberta's best features.
These were two tremendous pendulous bosoms that
swayed back and forth from side to side under the muu-
muu.

"If you got a best feature for God's sakes put 'em in a
showcase," said Roberta to Jewel, and leaned way over
good and low so that the best features dangled and tickled across the ball-point pens in their holder and the
ashtrays which were always full so that butts were scattered, usually, onto the floor.

"Give the customers their money's worth," said
Roberta.

The second-best feature, Jewel discovered, was the
black beehive that stood on Roberta's head.

"If the whole world caught on fire," said Lucy Cook
happily, "Roberta Feeny's beehive would be the last
thing to go!" This beehive seemed indestructible. She
took it down once a week to air it. Once, said Roberta,
proud as punch, she had let it go two weeks. When she

took it down she found (loud guffaws) a spider had laid its nest in there and had babies. Once Jewel got to see the hair being aired. It stood way off Roberta's head in wiry black spindles; stiff, like she'd been electrocuted; her scalp was gray and almost bald—like a dead man's.

The first day they went to Al Roon's Roberta let Jewel swim free. There was a long smelly warren filled with tiny pink cubicles where the ladies changed. Each cubicle was so tight you could hardly turn around or get your elbows up. In the next cubicle Jewel saw four feet instead of two. She heard whispering and giggling, then the feet moved around a lot as the ladies got their clothes off. Now suddenly a tremendous loud clunk and one of the ladies gasped, screamed: a large black gun fell between the four feet. Roberta came scooting sideways down the hall, fast.

"What the hell!" she shouted. "Hey! You two slimes had better clear on out—*pronto*!" she roared.

The pool was slippery and all covered with steam. Like a swamp. Blue-gray vapors rose up mysteriously and over on the far side you could see huge fat ladies, gray, too, naked or holding towels, wandering around in the fog. Or sitting on recliners like they were sunbathing or relaxing. Only there was no sun. Jewel crept into the water. The steps were greasy, you couldn't even see them the water was so thick and gray. Women swam by, keeping their heads out.

"Tell her not to swallow any of that water," said Roberta. Then, in an aside to Lucy Cook: "Every other night the men use this place. If you knew what was in that water!" She sniggered.

At the edge of the pool near where Jewel inched along she came eye to eye with an enormous cockroach. He was alive all right, Jewel saw his antennae quiver sluggishly, but he didn't move, he acted drugged.

"Here. Let's get the kid fixed up," said Roberta afterward. "What do you say to some color—poor kid, does
she like color?" The orange lipstick looked like a grease
crayon that melted in the sun and was grafted back together again with some wiry black hairs. They put a dab
of blue on her eyes.

"Who does she look like?" said Roberta, standing back,
legs wide apart, to look.

"Someone famous?" said Jewel.

"Naw—c'mon, let's beat it," said Lucy Cook. "You
look more like one of them little old midgets. Sad. Here,
git it off quick—I sure hope your aunt don't see you."

"Bring the kid back real soon, you hear?" shouted
Roberta as the door slid closed and the elevator jerked up
and up. But that night Jewel broke out in red welts all
over and she never got to go back to the health club.

Every morning Jewel was invited to visit with her
aunt Nanine in the boudoir—"boo-dwar," Lucy called
it. Nanine polished off the last of a vigorous series of
scissor kicks when Jewel entered the boudoir. Dinwiddie
was there in his maroon dressing gown and when he saw
Jewel his eyes lit up. Behind Nanine as she kicked the
bed hangings trembled mightily: speckled veils all shimmering and dappled with the fickle, translucent colors of
the sea; and watered silks, one floating over the other like
watery grasses. A pink foam of buoyant cushions floated
around her aunt's head as she counted out loud, puffing:
one two *three* four *six* seven *nine* eleven—Dinwiddie's
eyes met Jewel's. Behind her in the wall one or two
yellow-and-black zigzagged fish were scooting about
frantically—but even this hadn't the power to lift Jewel's
spirits today.

"My dear, if you are going to hang around looking like
a frightened goat you will drive me mad!" gasped Nanine. "There! Over there!" she said to Jewel and pointed

in the general direction of her desk. "Get my list. Be quick about it, please—we can be going over our agenda for the day, we have tons to do, so hurry along!" Jewel found a place beside the bed and waited with the pencil. "Yes, now hair first and nails; feet, facial, lunch at '21'— be sure to wear the mouse-gray georgette, dear, so becoming!" And then Nanine glanced up. "EEeek!" she screamed, *"Spots!* My God, child, what *have* you been doing to yourself? Well, that settles it." She groaned. "We'll simply have to cancel '21' and settle for Schrafft's. What a bore. Now pay attention—only one week left and we are off for the country. We'll be gone a long long time, three months, and I've got tons to do. So try, please, to be a little useful, darling, won't you?" Then Nanine picked up the housephone and shouted into it: "Tell that lazy Chinaman I want to see him immediately!"

"DID I ever tell you, Miss Jewel McAllister, that I'm awfully glad you are here?" said Dinwiddie into her ear as they slipped out of the room.

"You are?" she cried, scrutinizing his face for some sign. They stood in the hallway just beyond Nanine's room, whispering.

It was on her tongue to ask him why. He must have known something of this for he added, "I was old, you know, before you were even born. I never had a child. I see now that I have missed out on all the fun!" and he gave her arm a friendly little squeeze. "Besides—" and he shot her a wicked grin, "—I might have gotten away with it if you hadn't come along."

"Gotten away with what, sir?"

"Thinking I am a good person!" And with a belly laugh he was off.

7

SUMMER IN the Brown family was a serious affair. In some respects the other nine months seemed little more than a preparatory adjunct to those three lighthearted airy months by the sea.

A great deal of labor was devoted to all that airiness. Jewel thought Long Island must be some wild and woolly outpost very far away. Great lists were in the offing and Chee was sent scurrying day and night, that last week, to procure the little delicacies that make life— as Nanine put it—worth living: Schaller & Weber liverwursts and the most heavenly slabs of sweet country butter; brownies and sand tarts from Greenberg Desserts; artichoke pâté and barbecue sauce from Zabar's; ravioli from Canal Street. Hampers lined the hallways; the maids flew upstairs and down all day long and looked as if they wanted to cry. Cook yelled in the kitchen and bit your head off if you asked for a glass of milk.

But the great preoccupation of those last days seemed to be with the contents of the basement. There was much discussing and maneuvering; arguments erupted all over the house and the servants swore they would quit; Na-

nine shrieked and cajoled. The situation was this: whatever could not be made to fit in the city had been saved
up, all through the year, for the country: lamps and
clocks and Hoovers that would not work, toasters, gad-
gets of every sort, Christmas presents, carpets, curtains,
clothes, unloved paintings, lame chairs, chipped teapots,
unread magazines—friends even, and the people who
were all wrong for the city, these, too, were saved up and
given a second chance in Ox Pasture Lane, where they
were carted off and miraculously revived. Even the most
recalcitrant beings were thought to be calmed by the
balmy influence of sea breezes.

The *modus operandi* was always the same. They left
town the day before Memorial Day and returned the day
after Labor Day in a cavalcade headed by Dinwiddie,
whose idea was to disassociate himself as best he could
from the flotilla of debris behind. Like a very great pasha
he traveled alone in the back seat of the Bentley with
Mendez behind the wheel. The Bentley was followed at
a discreet distance by an assortment of hired vehicles:
first came Nanine in a station wagon with Jewel in the
front seat and Archibaldo, who snarled and urinated in
the back seat. The two parrots followed in a rented bread
van chauffeured by Chee, their cages hooded in mono-
grammed snoods. Treacle followed in another station
wagon with Cook and a large picnic hamper stuffed with
cucumber sandwiches and other delicacies. Lucy Cook,
silent as the tomb, occupied the back seat. At the very
rear of the cavalcade came an enormous orange U-Haul
truck loaded to the roof with the contents of the basement.

The journey was arduous with many stops along the
way to soothe any ruffled nerves and water the animals.
One hundred miles from Manhattan, Southampton was
a three-hour drive at the very most but for the Browns

the drive took an entire day. Dinwiddie sped on ahead, arriving in time for a leisurely round of golf at the National, after which Mendez drove him to Ox Pasture Lane. Here Dinwiddie disappeared into his own quarters and was not seen again until the house had been made to successfully ingest each and every broken-down toaster. At which point, in a wonderful mood, Dinwiddie reemerged, ready to begin the summer.

The month of June was devoted to the delicate business of pacifying the servants and animals, all of whom must be convinced they liked the country. Cook had evil things to say on nearly every subject: sand in the picnic baskets, houseguests who wanted breakfast sent up at unusual hours, and, of course, the formidable preoccupation with summer bugs. Cook, whose real name was Betty Brattle, had one purpose in life and this was to protect the master from the mistress. In her heart she remained convinced mistress was a dangerous woman. This seemed more apparent here in the country, where there were all sorts of unsavory goings-on.

It was Treacle's duty to meet the innumerable trains and cart houseguests and their luggage up and down the three flights of stairs all summer. And, burning with indignation, to promenade the visiting Shih Tzus and Yorkshire terriers in Ox Pasture Lane until coaxed to do their business. Treacle, whose real name was Eddie Ginch, fancied himself something of an Errol Flynn. His hero was the master: it seemed plain indecent that such a fine gentleman as Mr. Brown who never raised his voice should be stuck with that shrew. He knew: old Eddie Ginch saw it all, he knew how the master suffered.

Within the Brown household there existed two factions. The older, more august faction consisted of Cook (not to be confused with Lucy Cook), Treacle, and Thatcher the upstairs maid, who consolidated behind

the master. Thatcher remained in the city for the summer months to look after master. The above three were
Catholic, Irish, and as respectable as master himself.

The other faction, which consisted of Lucy Cook,
Chee, and Gustavo Mendez, grouped themselves in Nanine's camp. As these three had been "found" by the
mistress and not, as was proper, "hired," they had no
references, no history or known background, at least
none anyone knew of, they were not from New York
City, and they were viewed by the Dinwiddie faction as
nasty suspicious foreigners.

This rankled Lucy Cook for if nothing else she consid-
ered herself American to the teeth. Nonetheless, like
Mendez and Chee, she maintained a perverse silence as
to her origins. The fact is that in Lucy Cook's younger
days she had a little run-in with the law and Nanine,
who found her in Colorado, encouraged the woman to
jump parole. This detail, however, was kept a secret,
even from Dinwiddie. But when Lucy Cook arrived in
Southampton she made it her own particular crusade to
let all the Domkowskis and Skrebnevskis, the butcher,
plumber, laundress, and day char, know exactly what
sort of an American she was; they found her an intrepid
adversary.

But there could be no more vehement crusade than
that of Lucy Cook against Chee. Each viewed the other
as having repulsive and unforgivable habits. The minute
they arrived in the country Nanine must speak to the
Chinaman about nude sunbathing, swinging in the trees,
Buddhist saber leaps out on the lawn, T'ai Chi, chanting:
he had never managed to integrate himself into the family with a proper spirit and no one felt this more than
Lucy Cook.

Their rooms in the servants' attic were side by side
and neither was above stooping to the wall, ear pressed

to glass. Many a late-night vigil sustained those two as they strained in the dark to catch each appalling and suggestive noise emanating through the wall. Chee's nightly ritual featured Oriental leaps punctuated by growls, hisses, provocative grunts: a disgusting heathen sex act, no doubt, said Lucy Cook to Jewel, whom she invited to the attic to listen.

Chee, momentarily expecting ambush from the other side, remained convinced Lucy Cook lusted after him. Night after night he must endure the terrible misleading sounds of slapping, squeezing, and violent rubbings as Lucy Cook washed out girdle and stockings, and now, in the country, her bathing costume. Nor could he fathom, deep in the night, groans and certain raucous female sniggerings as Lucy Cook rolled on the mattress and abandoned herself to the funny papers, to Dick Tracy, her great hero, and Fearless Fosdick. Most appalling were the summer afternoons when Chee, shivering with disgust, smelled singeing hair or other worse tokens of female perversity as Lucy Cook and Jewel crimped their hair with steaming tongs or gave one another finger waves.

No one proved a greater problem in the country than Gustavo Mendez. Although Gustavo would have nothing more to do with the other two than they with him, the three did have something in common. Mendez, a native of the Mexican state of Chihuahua, had made his way to New York circuitously, as Nanine put it, and only after many discouraging and unfair encounters with the law. Mendez found his mistress in the street one day as she emerged from Bergdorf Goodman. His intention was to hold her up for the lizard bag; something stopped him—Nanine had that effect on people—and he attached himself instead, passionately, like a stray cat who instantly recognizes his one best chance and latches himself to a passing pant leg, refusing to be shaken off. It so happened the Browns needed a chauffeur. This was Mendez's official role but he viewed himself as Nanine's bodyguard as well and hoped that somehow before too long the killing monotony of life among the upper classes might be relieved by a shoot-out or a stabbing.

Mendez turned into a sex maniac in the hot months. He was a nuisance in Southampton, cruising Main Street with the radio turned up loud, hissing, staring at the ladies with the insolent torpor of the Mexican as he licked his chops over what he called the merchandise, and made rude suggestions to every female, even the old ones, and Nanine was forced to return him to the city only to be called back for special occasions.

The animals proved to be the most mutinous. Directly upon his arrival in the country, Archibaldo was buckled into a reeking flea collar. This put him in the worst possible mood. Then, set free for the first time in nine months, he was expected to behave like a gentleman. But the delicious freedom proved too much for Archibaldo. His smallest gesture was inevitably misconstrued as a piece of fiendish perversity. They all applied themselves to protecting Archibaldo from his baser instincts. If spied slinking through the thrilling greenery, hot on the scent of some delicious rodent, he was snatched up and left to cool his heels in the laundry room. If, on the other hand, he proved lucky in the laundry and snagged a mouse, and dragged it off to the linen closet, to lurk among the crisp stacks of immaculate Porthault sheets and munch in private, his feat encountered shrieks. Often they clubbed him with brooms and mops till he relinquished the wonderful morsel and then drove him rudely from the house. Not only that, he was expected to look good and smell nice at all times: they even carted him off once a month to a beauty establishment (shud-

der!) to be dipped and pomaded: hurrying home, he
slunk off to the dung heap in the potting shed and wallowed and rolled and kicked; but they always found him.
There were more shrieks; again he was quarantined in
the laundry room. But for Archibaldo the very worst
trial was that of the insufferable canine houseguests to
which he was expected to be civil.

"Now, the Mellons are coming and I do not want to
hear you've been unkind to Fifi. Last time, as I recall,"
said Nanine, "Cook found you urinating in Fifi's dog
dish. Now if there is anything disagreeable this year,
anything at all— Are you listening, Archibaldo?"

As for the two parrots, the day spent in the bread van
had been so mortifying that for weeks after they drooped
and hung upside down in their cages, just to frighten
Nanine. At last, when they could be coaxed right side up
again, Nanine felt the summer really could begin. This
day was almost always celebrated in the same way: Isidor
and Maria Guadalupe, the two parrots (but actually
Maria Guadalupe was a boy—only Nanine would not
admit to gay parrots), were carried outside by Chee and
as a great treat allowed to play in the lower branches of
the apple tree. Tea was brought and they all had tea
under the apple tree. Isidor and Maria Guadalupe, their
moods quite restored, would perch, one on either shoulder, and nibble on Nanine's pearls. There followed a
tremendous excited flirting between the three of them,
and Dinwiddie and Jewel and the various houseguests
could scarcely get a word in edgewise.

Then always there would be this little drama: one of
the parrots and then both disappeared into the chestnut
tree. Now the chestnut tree, being much taller than the
apple tree, a statuesque, tremendously noble old tree,
was off limits to the parrots and they knew it. Nonetheless, feeling their oats, they always felt they must try the

tree. High up in the pungent fleshy leaves, Isidor and Maria Guadalupe became delirious and forgot how to come down. Chee shrieked at them from below. Nanine coaxed, then threatened. Soon it will be dark! Owls, vultures, hawks! cried Nanine. Predatory turkeys! But still the birds did not come down. Ladders were brought and Chee scaled the tree. But the parrots did not like Chee and they inched up higher and higher until at last, marooned way out on the highest, most frightening branch, they began to squawk their hearts out piteously. Then Jewel tried but the parrots despised Jewel.

At last Nanine had Chee bring the ladder around to the laundry room roof and she hoisted herself up, satin pantaloons and all, and cooed across seductively at Isidor and Maria Guadalupe. She was nearly eye level with them on the laundry room roof but they did not budge. Then Chee sent up the Georgian silver teapot and the cream and the wonderful Fortnum & Mason brown sugar crystals, and Nanine, perched on the shingles, drank her tea. At last, when they saw Nanine take her tea, pour out cream, and rattle the little sugar crystals, Maria Guadalupe and Isidor made up their minds: down they came hurtling out from the tree with desperate squeaks, bat squeaks of terror, and glided from chestnut to laundry roof, and fell on Nanine's neck with passionate relief, clinging for dear life: and Archibaldo, his lip curled in disgust, sneered at them from the laundry and plotted his revenge, biding his time.

JEWEL DID not feel lulled by all that heavenly green, by the days of ordered ease, the blissful quiet. She didn't trust the polite chatter, the awesome politeness, the likes of which she had never seen, or the dreamy complaisance of the snug seaside village: no, some fatiferous twinge of disaster lurked there in all that repose, and she was the first to sense that this summer all would be violently upheaved.

All was green, a rolling, effortless green. It seemed to Jewel she had never noticed the color before. In Arizona the browns and lilacs and dusty blues have a way of seeming green but in fact there is not much of that true viridian color in the desert. It should have been perfect, to lie cradled in that acre of oblivious green, stupid with tranquillity, gazing out by the hour over the indefatigable lawn stretching to the sea. She asked little, asked no questions. But somehow the question was always there.

To come out of that thudding other world into this! The world of long desolate valleys, and of dust, of jagged mountains, of heat! To be always aware as they were at home of the nearness of large beasts whose needs ruled the order of that other world. Why, Jewel wondered, wasn't this green world a relief? But all was hidden here and self-satisfied. She felt a vague menace in these meandering lawns, in the easiness of life that belied what she knew: that life was hard and not meant to be easy. You noticed life, felt the hardness of it there on your skin where it pinched. How else were you to know what was real?

She did love to bury her nose deep within the sweet-smelling grass and breathe the pungent bristle, go far down; and she ate the grass like a cat, feeling clean; little by little Jewel found herself being changed; maybe this wouldn't be all bad—but she aimed to stay alert: the earth here smelled of death.

Jewel hid in the apple tree and watched. She saw how fraudulent it was, this guise of harmony; she wished just once they would scream out some truth, clear the air. It disgusted her, this calling everybody darling. Nanine, she knew, had no idea who Jewel was; Jewel the impostor parading around in new clothes. Jewel wanted to be invisible yet she yearned to be seen; in her heart was this boiling soreness: no one had ever seen her! And Dinwiddie—it almost broke your heart to see his face. Sometimes Jewel thought he might crack right open, he seemed so tender and the ache in him so transparent. They had spurned the deep intention of life, these people, this much Jewel knew: and one of these days the earth would open up her jaw and yawn, swallowing the whole lot of them down.

Except for the house itself, a sprawling three-story weathered shingle "cottage" of the Stanford White vintage, with wide porches and a flying roof, gaily curved, nothing disturbed the implacable lawn. A kitchen garden grew out of sight at the back, Chee's pride and joy, and a cutting garden of roses, dahlia, zinnias, and marigolds; also luscious bearded iris with velvety tongues and tremendous translucent heads all atremble in the morning light; and tiger lilies in the field, large speckled bouquets. But this was Chee's domain; Jewel stayed at the front of the house unless the Chinaman went to the movies.

The lawn stretched on and on, arriving at last at the tall hedges: prim, impenetrable, neatly clipped, the front guard of privet facing the house grew perhaps four feet deep and twelve feet high and this was flanked by an even taller rear guard of privet whose spiny ribs umbrellaed out into wild and thorny crowns with strange blossoms and these stretched down to the sea. Beyond the privet, the narrow lane was further bordered against invasion by long avenues of chestnut and elm, old and tall, their long wavy satiny gray arms arched and interlocked, as if forsworn against the light. The aspect was one of pleasing largesse. Jewel had explored the dark

little lanes, peeking in at other large old houses, some
with names like Pheasant's Crossing or The Forge or
Pride's Folly. To Jewel they all seemed frozen and self-
centered, these manor houses posing as cottages by the
sea; staid and a little bit silly, like pretty postcard houses.
None of it felt real enough to seem menacing to Jewel.
That is, until Johnnie came to stay. With him came the
self-consciousness; he was the witness to her absolute
insignificance; and although he did not care, she did.

There were other children here, she supposed; behind
the hedges one sometimes heard the high glad shout, but
just as quick the sound was gone. One didn't feel quite
certain humans lived here. Nothing ever seemed to jar
that sedate and dreamy world of lawns whose lush monotony was broken only by the flattering intrusion of
white-frocked nannies reading novels in the shade and
calling to the children; this and the querulous drone of
the old people sipping bull shots in the heat, discussing,
on the wide porches, taxes and servants and the new
people who inveigled their way in. Not for this neighborhood the squalid clues to life: swing sets and garbage
cans, barbecues; or, out back in a field, the telltale anoma-
lies: the jalopy, the abandoned icebox or stained bathtub
left to die, as they do in Dragoon and everywhere else,
a slow, matter-of-fact death. This remained the cleaned-
up world. You didn't see people in hair curlers either.

But all that was changing! Only yesterday Dinwiddie
had staggered home from the market (as a summer sport
Dinwiddie enjoyed an occasional foray into Herbert's
market in Southampton to pick up something: canapés
in packages or Danish butter cookies), where he had seen
a person in pedal pushers. Dinwiddie only used the word
person when nothing else could be said. She was a white
woman in ghastly shoes and Dinwiddie had gazed on in

horror as this poor creature shelled out forty dollars for a roast pork. Forty dollars! What sort of people had that kind of money—for pork?

This incident precipitated Dinwiddie's last excursion to Herbert's. Actually a blessing because a few years later—say, in 1979—he might have seen that same woman wearing short shorts, her buttocks hanging out and her bare thighs and belly stuck to the butcher's glass, order up a roast pork and pay more than sixty dollars! People like the Browns were better off at home. What was the point of seeing too much? Jewel, poor child, had seen nearly everything, one way or another, by the time she was twelve; and although he was beginning to adore this child (and he could never tell you why) Dinwiddie found her candid Sturm und Drang approach to life a little frightening. The whole point he felt was to remain innocent for as long as possible.

But if Southampton had begun to change there were still, thank God, people one knew. Nice people. And in this snug world it did not matter if you slept with the gardener, or cheated at cards, or got drunk and molested your best friend's wife on Saturday nights, as long as you were one of the nice people. The boundaries of this world ran from that corner of the Atlantic Ocean enclosed by the Southampton Bathing Corporation (known as the beach club) and St. Andrew's Church on the dunes, which nobody went into except for weddings but at least it was there, and the Meadow Club for tennis, and of course Herbert's grocery store and the two golf clubs, Shinnecock and the National. Occasionally the Browns would wander as far astray as the Maidstone Club in East Hampton for a cocktail party but this they felt to be a dreadful bore. Nanine in all those years had never been to Westhampton or Quogue or Sag Harbor or Amagansett, a few miles away; she didn't even know they were there.

They had their world: Thursday-night lobsters on the porch of the Irving Hotel; Friday evening at the train station: all the wives came and the children in pajamas to meet the seven o'clock from Penn Station with its extravagant load of husbands and houseguests; then Friday steaks at Ridgely's Grill, everyone was there; and planter's punches Saturday at the beach club: Emilio Puccis in the sand. Striped tents Saturday night if some debutante was coming out in Gin Lane or there was a fund-raiser at the Parrish Museum. And golf golf golf, always golf. Sunday lunch at the National and Sunday supper at Shippy's for those who didn't take the train. This was life in the country.

Jewel could not see what all the ruckus was about. She had seen a million ladies in pedal pushers. And these people were busy always but they never seemed to be doing anything. On the ranch you had to be doing something every minute. It seemed to Jewel she lived in a private world all alone. Oh, she could hear people all right, they mouthed the words, the same words she used, but nonetheless theirs seemed a foreign language.

Take the word "God," for instance. She asked Nanine what she thought of God. Not now, said her aunt the first time.

"My dear," said Nanine haughtily, the second time, "if you persist in using that word at the dinner table I shall scream!"

"God!" said Dinwiddie with a snort. "God! Oho!" he guffawed, disappearing into his study, where she could hear him chortling behind the door.

"If there is a God," said Johnnie, "why did my father die?"

"God!" exclaimed Cook, rolling her eyes ferociously. "You'd better be mighty careful how you use that name, child, because *He hears,* He hears *everything!*"

"God? Where this famous man God? I no see him, do you?" demanded Chee.

And Lucy Cook made a fist, curled in all fingers but the two at either end, and those she jabbed at the air. "Horns!" she cackled. "If *He* exists, then so do the other one, heehee! The devil!"

But here's what Gustavo Mendez said when he took Jewel for a ride in the car one day. Now, of the people Jewel had met since she came east, the only ones she respected were those who did not try to convince you they were good: Dinwiddie, Lucy Cook, and Mendez. They were like the people at home, real.

"What about God?" she said to Mendez.

"What about Him?" said the Mexican.

"How do you know there is a God?"

"How do you know there isn't?" he said.

Jewel thought about this. "Well, what proof is there?" she demanded.

"Proof! Hey! How many things you can prove? Anyway, I got all the proof I want. I got a voice, man, he lives inside me. Don't you got a little voice? She always whispering, Hey, man, don't *do* that! Course you got to go and do it anyway but still you got the voice. And God, He understand."

"So there isn't any proof?" said Jewel.

"People, they say, Hey, man, what did God ever do for you? Hey! What did people ever do for God? It goes both ways, man. He's in there but you gotta *look.* You gotta be real quiet to hear that little voice. You gotta *believe* first, see, then it comes true. But hey, man, if you lookin' for proof you never gonna find him. He isn't gonna make it too easy, see? The ones who don't find him, well, hell, maybe they jes' don't look in the right places, man. You ain't gotta be no genius to figure that one out."

"Well, how do you know if it's really Him you're seeing and not someone else? Not the devil? Not some trick?" said Jewel.

"Hey! Who's ever seen the wind? But the wind you feel her, she is there, no? There's a lotta things no one ever sees but you go on believing, no matter what."

"I just don't get it." Jewel sighed.

"Hey! There ain't nothing to get! You ain't never going to understand God, see? Then he wouldn't be God if you could understand Him."

"But why is there so much sadness then, if there is a God?"

"There gotta be sadness. How you gonna know you happy if there ain't no sadness?" said Gustavo. Jewel said nothing as he laid a hand on her thigh. "Here. It's like this. There are all these people, see, and they're waiting for rain. The rain don't come. The crops don't grow. Nothing grows without rain, see? Okay, so here comes the rain. Now it rains over here, see, and the corn grows tall, the corn she feels herself good. But when the rains come over *here* it washes out the seed. No corn. It's the same rain, see? The same earth, same corn. But over here the corn don't grow. They can wait and they can wait but the corn, she don't grow."

"Well, why's that?" asked Jewel.

"Who can say?" Gustavo shrugged, rolling a weed.

"Well, what's it got to do with God?" demanded Jewel. "I still don't understand."

"Understand—hah! You gotta forget about that word, see? No one understands anything," said Gustavo with a grin as he sucked in a long slow draw. "The earth, she don't know. The corn don't know. The rain, he don't know what makes the things to grow. But the ones who

wait, they know. Some of them do. It all got to do with
how you wait. That's the test, see? That's how you know.
Like when you wait for rain. Some people they give up,
they lie down, and they die. But the others—they *know*
He's there! He's in there, He's in your heart, He waits
for you to see. The wait, she isn't so bad. But the others,
they wait alone. And the seed, he don't grow."

"Oh," said Jewel, "I see."

But the days were so long! It seemed they were all in
on some secret, the rest of them, and she stayed on the
outside. Even Johnnie knew their language.

"Don't you wonder sometime if maybe you aren't
real?" Jewel asked him one afternoon. "Or maybe you
are the real one and all of them are pretend."

"Seems like everybody's real to me," said Johnnie after
he thought about it. "Only, there's just lots of different
reals."

"Phoo!" said Jewel. "Dummy. There's only one real!
Everyone knows that!"

"Well, what is it then?" he challenged. "What is the
one real?"

"You wouldn't have to ask that," cried Jewel fiercely,
"if you'd been to the ranch. It's the ranch! I guess that's
the one real."

IN THOSE weeks before her cousin arrived, Jewel occupied herself by watching over Dinwiddie. It was a
strange thing, the way in which she came to be his secret
guardian. Jewel had always been the insignificant one in
whatever setting she found herself, but here was someone large; that is, powerful, the master in his own house,
rich, established, above all comfortable—comfort, she
saw, was at the center of everything they did—and yet
he seemed absolutely irrelevant to that carefully con-

structed edifice in which they all lived. He was the one essential glue to all their lives, you might even say he was the meaning beyond the commotion, this much at least is what he had become for Jewel, of late; but she saw that if he evaporated suddenly the commotion would continue of its own momentum. This seemed terrible to Jewel. For although he was nothing like her heroes, those rugged individuals who *claimed* life, she recognized that thing in him of which heroes are made. Call it a dilemma. He remained poised, she knew, on some terrible precipice and could not jump or turn back. She knew in her bones he was a good man. The only other good man she had ever known was Dwight Eisenhower. Not that she had ever met President Eisenhower. But in 1952 when Jewel was ten years old she sat up all night waiting to hear that he had been elected, she actually said a prayer that he might be; then when everyone else, Granma Lou and all the cowboys, screamed and hollered and ran around celebrating, Jewel went to her room and cried her eyes out. That's what it felt like, knowing someone was deep-down good.

Of course Dinwiddie was nothing like General Eisenhower. No one ever talked about the good things he did; if they did he would have shushed them on the spot. He didn't like to talk about who he was the way others did, but when you were near him you felt good, he made you feel like laughing. She asked him about this once in those first weeks in Southampton.

"What I want to know," she said as she plunked down near him on a wicker chaise on the porch, "is why these people here don't ever look happy. People at home look happy—at least sometimes they do," she added.

He chuckled, patting her knee in that brusque, friendly way he had. "The thing about New Yorkers," he said, "is that if one of them actually admits to being happy he is made to feel he has let the rest of them down. Like links in a chain fence, they depend upon one another, my dear, to keep the perfect enclosure."

"But you're not that way!" she cried.

"I'm not?" he said, screwing up his eyes. "Well, then, I must be a great deal worse!" he cried. "If anything, dear Jewel, I have given myself over to the conspiracy wholeheartedly!"

"Conspiracy?" she inquired, delicately.

"Well, yes, there is a conspiracy, I think, not to be too happy. Or, if you like, a conspiracy to believe in one another's pain."

"You mean the pain isn't real?" she persisted.

"Oh, it's real all right!" he chortled, almost to himself.

"Then I don't understand."

"Sometimes the kindest thing, my dear, is not to take away someone's pain."

"I thought people were supposed to be good to each other," she ventured.

"Oh, they are! But there are so many ways to be good, don't you see, and some of them, Jewel, are quite evil."

She thought about this a long time. "How does a person know, then, what really is good?"

"He doesn't know, sometimes, until it's too late." Her uncle sighed.

"Well, a person knows he shouldn't steal. He knows that," declared Jewel.

"There are even moments when one feels he must steal. There are moments," he said slowly, "when one finds he has become that very thing he always despised. When a circumstance—well, when life becomes absolutely real and to deny it—" he paused, "—to deny it is perhaps to die."

"Then there are good reasons," said Jewel, "even for the bad things people do?"

"I suppose you could say that."

"Then every person has to make up his own law?" she replied. "What about killers, what about bad people?"

"Sometimes I wonder"—and he sighed again, deeply—"if there really are very many bad people out there. Perhaps there are only bad moments. Circumstances . . ."

Jewel thought fleetingly of her father: of Horace dangling, dangling . . . then letting go. Had he been bad?

"The thing about pain," he continued, almost with a groan, "is to understand why we need it. Most of us learn very little through happiness. Sad but true. Contrary to what a lot of us think, we earn our pain. But happiness, my darling, is given to us. Take away a fellow's pain and you take away, perhaps, his only means of expressing how he really feels. The trick, don't you see, is for a fellow to *behave* as if his actions matter. But if they don't? Ah! Good Lord!" he exclaimed. "How you let me blither on! Look what a fool I've made of myself, what? Why don't you say something for a change, my dear? What a wise little monkey face you have! Heavens! They're making them smarter and smarter these days, it makes me feel like an absolute cretin. Now tell me about your fabulous Dragoon. Are they smarter out there, your cowboys? I wouldn't be surprised! Oh, city boys are smart all right, but I'm never quite sure we *know* anything. But my Lord, it gets tiresome, doesn't it, Jewel, being around people who know things! I'm waiting for a person to come along and say, 'I don't know *anything*! Hoo!' " he cried, delighted, and his belly wobbled in the most wonderful way; he wore the palest of pink linen pants, a huge size, very loose and breezy, and a soft old frayed polo shirt, pistachio green, very pale, so if you squinted your eyes in the heat he looked like a mirage, like a wonderful boysenberry cone melting down slowly: and his skin, too, felt cool to touch, smooth and very white like a big baby, no hair, no sweat anywhere. Only his eyes were old, very very old.

Suddenly she cried: "Have you ever said I love you to anybody? Well, I never have!" she declared, going very red in the face, and strange. He remained silent, a little frightened by her intensity. She jumped up suddenly and threw at him, roughly, "Well, I do love you, you know!" Then Jewel ran quickly away and burst into loud sobs.

8

DINWIDDIE WAS suffering. These halcyon days were anything but soothing. Beneath everything there wriggled the creeping vermicular truth: *betrayer!* Not simply of wife and creed, and now this young girl placed in his care—see how she trusted him!—but of order and all reason, of sanctity itself. He remembered a line from Santayana: *Sonent voces omnium liliorum florem*, Let everything bloom that has within it the seed of a flower. So this was the flowering of his precious new seed!

The old customs had fallen away. Instead of taking the train into the city on Tuesdays and returning Thursdays, as of old, he now went up to town on Sunday night with the younger men and did not return to the country until Friday. Nanine knew, the whole of their little world knew, Dinwiddie had fallen in love. Rotten as this was, to throw off their whole summer agenda, what should he do? Nanine must make his excuses: Monday-night bridge with the Vanderpoels, Thursday evenings with the Talbot Rutherfords—Nanine would know what to say. It seemed a shame to lay this on her but he was too far gone to be of any use in the matter.

Madeleine remained exacting but in a subtle way. They met, always, on a whim. Madeleine would not be tied to an arrangement of any sort. She said it made her feel like chattel and so they had not arrived at any "understanding." And if she had fancied herself his "mistress" he would have been horrified. The only means he had of seeing Madeleine was simply to be available: as a "friend." She had a conviction of how a friend ought to behave: expect nothing and always be sensitive to her needs without having to be told. Having to tell men things destroyed the mood. For example, when she didn't feel "in the mood" he ought to know; she should never be made to reject him. They made love rarely, Dinwiddie refused to impose himself or wheedle. His understanding of the situation and her great conviction remained thus: he had no claim on her. Also, he must never offer her money. Which indiscretion would only cause her to refuse—and she sorely needed his gifts. Far better to tuck some lovely jewel or a nice wad of bank notes in a secret place; she could think what she liked about how it got there and perhaps she would mention it later. Perhaps! But it really did not matter. It was awful to offend her. Once he gave her the wrong flowers, an arranged bouquet in a basket, terribly expensive, but she refused to look at it, she was indignant. Later he inquired as to her favorite flowers but she only smiled, as if to say, No, I will not force you to please me, you must find the way yourself. He liked her for this, liked her more than he had ever liked anyone. She did not reduce herself to scale. Then one day he came across a miraculous bouquet of lilies: unimaginably slender and graceful, tiny, only seven or eight inches long and of the strangest faint yellow color: each flower curved around itself in a single translucent tongue and died away at the edges in a crimson flame. They had no scent. Madeleine hadn't either, a fact that always surprised him. This, as much as anything, caused him to feel she was not entirely real, that he had not been with Madeleine, did not know her. He could not get her scent—and this caused him sorrow.

The strange lilies delighted her. She knew exactly that she was like this flower: rare and incandescent, oh, infinitely more incandescent than other beings! This pleased him, that she knew how rare she was. It would never occur to Madeleine to ask, Am I too fat? Too thin? Her identity did not depend on his view of her. She knew who she was even if he did not. Madeleine seemed calm, unbelievably incandescent and calm. But she had no scent.

He did not feel calm. Now that he had her, so to speak, he began to agonize over how to keep her. All this must be done in secret since the slightest hint of a plan would frighten her off. A nature so sensitive as hers, so high-strung and fine, must not be jostled with coarse intrusions. He would never have asked her if she loved him. Or, What do you expect of me? Or, What is it you see in me? He knew there could be no plausible answers, at least not answers he might like to hear. His restraint, his incredible degree of civilized restraint, drew her to him, coaxed her near: for that first tentative sniff, like some wild creature, coming at last to the salt lick.

Hard as it was not to smother her with attentions he concocted ways to let her know he adored her and she smiled over this. What did that smile mean? The miracle was she accepted him! There were even moments when Madeleine looked deep into Dinwiddie's eyes, down into his very soul, and saw him with perfect intelligence. A comprehension—more, a compassion such as he had never experienced from any other being, except perhaps his mother, Charmagne, long ago. This seemed no small thing, to be recognized! Now that he knew the sensation he supposed it was the very thing he had yearned for all his life. Yet he had never thought of it before now; it was only the recognition that had been missing. She knew him, she looked deep in and understood! Yet it made him feel bottomlessly alone. Not so much with Madeleine; but knowing her made him see what a sham it all was, the others, all the rest of it—ah, his whole life! Suddenly he must see that not a single moment of the last fifty-nine years felt *true*. A nearly invisible webbing of claustro-phobic deceit wrapped itself round the whole of his life and held him in place. Yet he wanted to be true. No one had devoted himself more disinterestedly to the truth, had he? And now that he knew what the truth was—of all those years!—he must lie! Caught between Scylla and Charybdis! Should he throw over the whole mess—or remain in the lie? Whatever else, he could not bring himself to leave Madeleine. She *was* the truth! But nei-ther would he dispose of his wife. Nothing appalled Dinwiddie as much as the way people turned one an-other in, these days, for something better. No, he had taken her on, offered her his name and protection, there could be no question of abandoning her now, regret it as he may. Might as well regret Yale or the war! If he knew anything it was this: you are what you are. No use wishing.

But there was still this question, How could he enlist Madeleine into his life, join with her—and, more impor-tantly, be of some use to the girl? The fact remained—he knew it perfectly—he did not have her. He did not even know where she lived! She seemed ashamed of the place. Lived in some hideous surrounding, no doubt. He could only adore her more for sparing him the sadness of the place, wherever it was. Only once had he made the error of asking, Won't you let me help? She turned and gazed at him with such chilling hauteur as had frozen his blood. It left him with the sense of being entirely expendable. If only he could think of something to give her she would never have from anyone else! How then could she bring herself to leave him? For beneath everything here was the agony: he knew she would leave. She might let him be useful to her in little ways, endure his attentions, admire him even—but one day she would leave. He knew her life was hard, perhaps even degrading to such a soul as Madeleine's, but she had not been contaminated, she was not so desperate to wriggle free as he might have thought, at least not yet . . . but when she left him he knew it would absolutely kill him! The thought frightened and sickened him so that he almost imagined it must rise out of his flesh as a repulsive smell—terror! What could smell worse?

But perhaps she had not noticed. Not yet. At least he could spare her that—his torment. He understood he must leave her alone: not ever ask or hint that one day she might leave him. Go home—if there was a home! She was seventeen! At the jail they had showed him her passport, a French passport, yet she was not French. He still had no clue as to what she was! Yet Madeleine did not seem deceitful. His own conjecture was that Madeleine had been born in some concentration camp in Poland perhaps, or Germany. She might be Hungarian or Russian. If it meant so much to the girl not to say, why should he persecute her with his curiosity? And if indeed she had been the victim of such a destiny as that, he would gratefully honor her reticence.

At the office he could scarcely think. He saw Miss Plank staring, glistening at him with pity when a call from the girl came through. He had no way of contacting Madeleine except to leave a message at Macy's, where she currently worked, and this was loathsome to him after the first attempt. So he spent his days waiting for her call. Once or twice a week he and Madeleine met for lunch and sometimes, when the gods were smiling, she would retire with him to their little love nest at the Plaza. But this was not always wonderful! Sometimes she paced the little sitting room angrily, refused to take away the high heels and the hat, rubbed against things rudely, like a cat, touched the flowers, the mirrors and curtains with loathing, then suddenly, hissing a good-bye, ran out the door. He suffered this rebuff without a word for he absolutely understood. And although he himself had nothing of the quick irascibility of the cat, the scathing quick-fire disdain—for in his nobility he was more doglike—he respected her unwillingness to linger in a wrong spot. She always came back. And then sometimes she was so gay and mischievous! She might hide herself in the closet and spring out at him; or he pretended to hunt for her—and together they hid in that dark place to devour one another with greedy kisses, laugh wildly, sink down—and she gave herself to him as never before. He who had always been fastidious and shy! And then for a little while, a week perhaps or a day, Dinwiddie would forget. Only Madeleine, only this grand happiness, nothing else mattered; not Nanine or his life or any tortured ruminations on the truth. Here now, for the first time, was happiness.

TODAY HE decided to take her to "21" Club for lunch. She liked the way they treated him in these places. She liked a long sumptuous luncheon: chilled Senegalese, hamburger "21," and some sensational dessert with Champagne, one glass. The end of July was approaching; just that morning Madeleine had been fired at Macy's. She was too careless, they said, in keeping their hours. Madeleine laughed about it, tossing off the experience as a lark, although now she had no job, had, in fact, nothing, not even enough to make it through the week—but she did not tell him this.

"Won't you come with me today, my darling, to our little place at the Plaza?" he asked, just as she finished her dessert.

"No," she said at last, slowly, and bit off the last delicious rim of bitter chocolate from her fork, then relinquished it with a sigh. "Not today. I think not." His heart sank.

Why, he wondered, did she glower at him? She had been so pleasant an hour ago! He never knew. Ah—she was dangerous! When she became this way he tried to still himself to the point of nearly vanishing, and wait for the mood to pass. Not that Dinwiddie was subservient—never that. But he believed in giving women room when they felt dangerous; and she seemed to expand while he, shrinking, became unobtrusive. This he did with wonderful restraint. Normally it worked because there was nothing of the martyr in his bearing, however bruised he might feel about being treated as an irritant. She would flare up passionately, lash out; and when he effaced himself it sometimes made her cruel. But the very thing that appeased her mood one day proved incendiary the next.

"I am so completely tired of everything," she said in her odd, guttural tones, staring at the table, the wineglasses and silver forks, almost with loathing, as if this table, this place were an impossible eyesore, an insult she must endure. As she must endure him. "I am so tired," she went on, listlessly, "of feeling like meat."

Of all her moods, he dreaded this one most. Meat! And what was he? The gnawing, slavering butcher slobbering for meat! He said nothing, only straightened himself slightly, and in this small gesture managed to convey his sorrow.

"God! How I hate this American thing you have—all of you!" she spat the words in a twisting, low voice, unbelievably ugly to his ear—yet how he loved her! "This grotesque determination to own everything, possess what cannot be possessed! To degrade—" She let it hang, waited to see if he would respond, but he kept his silence. "Degrade what should never be ordinary. Smother it, contaminate it! Do you listen?" she demanded. He saw she had tears in her eyes but still he said nothing, his glance showed no reproach, only a small clue to his sorrow. "Oh, what's the point!" she exclaimed, turning her face so he would not see.

He reached into his pocket and drew forth a small package, placing it before her. Madeleine stared at it almost with dread.

"I had wanted to give it to you there," he said softly. "In our little place, but this will do." He smiled but still she did not reach for the box. "It is not so much a material object as something—well, as something prophetic. A good omen—call it, if you like, a hint of something yet to come—although as you will see it has already served us well, in a sense, this little trinket. At least I think so, for it has brought us together . . . In fact, my dear, it belongs to you." She reached for the thing and opened it. "You see, I couldn't think what to do with it!" he said, as Madeleine stared with blank horror at the pavé diamond peacock.

"But why?" she exclaimed, disdaining to touch it. Dinwiddie gazed into her eyes with such full, adoring love, eyes spilling over—that Madeleine felt afraid. The absence of all love for him suddenly shamed her. There must be something vile, she thought, in my refusal to

worship such a man! But no—she could not bring herself
to love him, not even a little. Ah, she was a monster! This
is what Madeleine thought. What torture to be loved so.
It would choke her. She could not find it in her heart to
love him in return. Now she understood: he had given
her the peacock so she could go free! He trusted her!
How simple the man! Until now she had been absolutely
trustworthy! But was there not a deadly obligation in
such a trust? A trust that seemed to her now the ultimate
act of possession.

"And so!" she cried in that taut, low voice. "You be-
stow on me my freedom! Freedom even from you—if
necessary!" And she laughed harshly. "And so you trust
Madeleine not to go," she challenged, taking up the glittering bird, holding it between two fingers delicately, as
her own tears spilled out, but she brushed them away,
almost angrily. How dazzling the peacock! Hundreds of
winking, glittering little pavé diamonds twinkled up at
her outrageously as, mesmerized, she twisted the pretty
creature this way and that.

"Oh, as to trusting you," he chuckled, "to take the bird
and not go— Shall we just say you must do as you please.
There are no strings attached. At least I hope not," he
exclaimed gently and still with that pouring love. Then:
"In fact, my darling, I do trust you!"

Ah! This was unbearable. Madeleine placed the bird in
the box.

"Well, you needn't," she said abruptly. How grand
this man, how pleased he seemed by his own stunning
magnanimity! Ugh—it choked her! So much love, really
it was obscene! And how should she repay him? But
no—she refused to step into that terrible trap. Very well,
if he insisted she have the horrid bird, then she would go
free!

It came to him suddenly that he ought not to have

given her the bird. Perhaps after all, he thought, she cannot be trusted. He heard the false note. I am nothing more than an old fool, he sighed, sagging a little. She will crush me. A small shriek of fear caught at his heart but he beat it down. What does it matter? said another voice within. What difference can it possibly make if she dashes you down, grinds you, spits on you, smears you underfoot—as long as you might be near her one more time? Truly he did not think Madeleine would use the bird to leave him—not yet! But oh! why had he given it to her?

He took the bird from its box and pinned it to her jacket.

"There!" he exclaimed, almost exultant. He would not be cowed. "See how the peacock becomes you! Now, my darling girl, you are free!"

9

"BOY, IT sure is lucky you showed up!" Jewel said to Johnnie that last week in July. "I was beginning to get real weird! One more day on my own and I might've bit someone on the ankle. Things are getting peculiar around here if you ask me."

"They are?" exclaimed Johnnie, and his eyes lit up.

"Well, for a place where nothing is ever supposed to happen things sure are leaping. They had to send Mendez away—you know, the chauffeur." This was pronounced *show*-furrr, which tickled Johnnie. "I guess he did some pretty disgusting things to some lady in the village but he was the only one in this place who seemed normal to me. This Chinaman—he's a real lowlife! He gives me the creeps. Do you know what that little snake whispered into my ear? That I ought to run away! Can you believe it? He's dying to get rid of me!"

"I thought you wanted to run away—you said you did!" protested Johnnie.

"Not unless it's *my* idea, see? Gad—if I want to do it, I'll do it! But I'm not having some two-bit Chinaman put ideas in my head. The next thing you know, you're brainwashed. Yessiree," continued Jewel, "there are some mighty funny things going on around here!"

"Like what?" said Johnnie.

"Well, Aunt Nanine, she sure is picking some funny ways to get back at Uncle Dinwiddie for having a girl friend," said Jewel.

"How do you know it's a girl friend?" he cried. "Who's seen her?"

"Phoo! Everyone knows! Chee, he's seen her! Says she lookee like a slick blown foxy, do missy!"

"So, what has Aunt Nanine done about it?"

"You know how Uncle Dinwiddie hates the China-man. Well, she's got him cooking! Yup! She sent Cook off to New Jersey on vacation! You should've seen Cook go! My God, you never saw so much crying and squealing and goings-on! It nearly broke her spirit—but Cook, she shook her fist and said she'd be back soon as master got some brains in his head about what's going on! Boy, was it exciting! You should see what Chee stuck in the kitchen cupboards! Nasty bottles, ugh, and potions called names like Lotus Pod Elephant Ears—ooh, and do they stink! And the first morning at breakfast he brought out this weird little heap of something that looks like jelly beans in hair for Dinwiddie, and Dinwiddie—"

"In hair!" shrieked John. "How gross!"

"Well, some kind of hairy little nest. He's always con-cocting these things, see? And Dinwiddie, he looked so cross, he says, 'What the devil's this?' And Nanine says, 'Those, my darling, are wild Blue Jay eggs! Chee hand-painted them just for you! Do you have *any* idea, dar-ling,' she says, like this—looking at him with those razor-blade eyeballs but always 'darling' this and 'dar-ling' that—'how hard it is to find a Blue Jay egg on Ox Pasture Lane? Why, he's spent hours and hours squat-ting in the—' 'But all I want is oatmeal. I always have

oatmeal on Saturdays,' Uncle Dinwiddie says in this pitiful voice. 'Not while Cook is away,' smirks Aunt Nanine—you know, like, Well, you big doodoo, what can
you expect?"

"Poor Uncle Dinwiddie!" cried Johnnie. "Do you
think it will work? Can she starve him out?"

"Who knows?" Jewel sighed. "But I sure am getting
hungry for some plain old lamb stew and a plate of
mashed potatoes. You should see what he cooks us. He
spends hours and hours, see, sharpening that collection
of long knives he keeps hidden in his room. Then out
come all the smelly little bottles which by the way I
would not be surprised to hear were poison—"

"Poison!"

"And then he hacks up all these vegetables, he makes
teeny little flowers out of everything, radishes, cucumbers. It's pretty awful. Then he stands in there on a stool
spying on everybody through the pantry window to see
what they think. On Thursdays when Aunt Nanine has
her ladies over he shakes his fists at them and makes faces
through the glass if they don't coo over the carrots."

"God almighty!" And Johnnie whistled through his
teeth appreciatively.

"Yes, and you can see how it makes Uncle Dinwiddie
feel. It's like this isn't even his house anymore, like he's
just some stupid old houseguest and he can eat toads for
all she cares. And the worst thing," continued Jewel,
who scowled at the thought, "is that she's sicked the
Chinaman on him wherever he goes. When he isn't
whipping up his poison pellets in the kitchen, he's spying on Dinwiddie in the city."

"What for?" exclaimed Johnnie.

"What for? Why, Uncle Dinwiddie's got some terrible
secret, he's got this girl friend, see? And he's in trouble—
that's what for!" cried Jewel passionately.

"How do you know?" said Johnnie.

"What a dumb question!"

"It is not! I don't think it's so dumb!" he muttered.

"Can't you even see we're sitting on top of a big fat bomb around here? God, why can't anybody *see*! Listen, Johnnie, maybe we can help him!"

"Gee!"

"See, that's the problem—no one ever goes out of their way to help anybody. This woman in the park—"

"The one with the soup bone heels!" he said eagerly.

"Well, she was crazy, I tell you, and no one even looked! Like, what does a person have to do to be seen?"

"You always said you *wanted* to be invisible," he reminded her.

"Look," she said impatiently. He did not like this bossy new voice at all. "We all *are* invisible! Don't you get it? No one has to try—we already *are* invisible!"

"Nope!" he said. "Not me! Not my mama, either! And what about Lucy Cook and Aunt Nanine—and Chee? What about them? Are they invisible?"

Jewel found this exceedingly frustrating. "Listen, nit-wit—" she exclaimed.

And he went rigid, his cheeks blanched, and he drew himself up and said, "Listen—you! I am not going to be called bad names!" Slowly he turned his back on her and left the room. Jewel was awfully impressed. She waited a moment and then ran after him.

"I'm sorry," she said. "Please, Johnnie—I really am!"

She thought he would say, It doesn't matter. Instead, he looked her straight in the eye, flushing a little, and said, "I want to be important, too."

"Well, sure!" said Jewel, quickly.

"No—what I want is for people to understand who I *am*," he added solemnly.

"You mean *be* somebody," she assented. Jewel felt suddenly, although he had only just turned ten, he was years older than she was.

"Yes. I want people to know I'm not just some kid."

"That's it!" she cried. "What I was trying to tell you! You see, it isn't *you* they see, it's who they think you are! Like when your mama looks at you, what she sees is not what I see! It isn't Lucy Cook we see, it's who we think she is. So no one ever really sees anyone." She struggled to hold back the tears. "What is the point of trying to be invisible if you already are invisible? And that woman in the park, well, she was trying to say something, only no one wanted to hear!"

"Well, what could anybody say to a crazy person?" asked Johnnie softly.

Jewel thought about this for some time. Then she said, "Hello! They could just say hello!"

"DO YOU think he's gotten himself a real mistress, my dear," said Louise Trimble, settling herself across the foot of her sister's bed. Archibaldo beat a hasty retreat. "Or perhaps he's only tumbled into the sack with Maude Fish or Lally Slocum once or twice—you know, just for a quickie. And really, darling, if that's all there is to this, I don't think it's so very awful, do you?"

Nanine stared out morosely from under an avocado face pack. Around her head she had wound a length of Scalamandre silk into an acid Nile-green turban and fastened this together with a large ruby starfish. Louise thought how used up and positively yellow her sister looked in the morning light, and she could not repress a little shiver of satisfaction. Although one year older than Nanine, she felt at a disadvantage with her sister. Nanine always seemed so amused by everything. Louise did not find life amusing. She saw no smiles on Nanine

today, however. What could be more aging to a woman,
thought Louise, bending to remove an invisible speck
from the lap of her Lilly Pulitzer, than plain old-fash-
ioned meanness? Nanine had been ranting and raving
about Dinwiddie for two months now!

"You know, Louise dear, I can't figure you out," said
her sister, who roused herself at last to swish away a few
flies from the avocado goop. "The other day when you
found the children in there indulging in a harmless little
diddle you screeched and and carried on like Caryl
Chessman had gotten into the house! But now that I'm
losing my husband to some whore—"

"I told you not to bring up that nasty other business,
you know I can't bear to think about it." Louise shuddered. "Anyway—what other woman? You don't even
know who she is! Frankly, your position isn't so bad.
Marshall says you'll get everything. Why, in a case like
this you can absolutely clean him out, Dinwiddie hasn't
a leg to stand on! In fact, if I were you—"

"For chrissakes, Weezie, will you stop! I haven't made
up my mind to get rid of him yet! As you say, I don't even
know who or what this other creature is. . . . I just hope
nothing like this ever happens to your precious Marshall, my dear!" she said spitefully. "The trouble is,
Louise—you've never had anything really awful happen!"

"Why Nanine! I can't believe I heard you say that!"
cried Louise. "After everything I've been through! What
a ghastly year this has been. Do you know how much I
had to shell out coming through customs last week?
They socked us for the new Vuitton trunk, you know.
And of course they discovered every new dress. I had cut
out all the labels, too, but they found them . . ."

"Found the labels?"

"You don't think I threw them away, do you? I'm

planning to sew them back in. What's the point of a Givenchy with no label? And they caught me with this little sapphire guard ring. Poor Marshall, he had to shell out a bundle. We're simply impoverished, it's too mean!"

"Poor you," said Nanine. "And off to Italy in a few weeks. We can't go anywhere this year. The roof has to be reshingled in Southampton and of course now with the child there'll be hideous expenses. Boarding school and all those clothes, it's really quite depressing."

"Well, maybe now you can understand," said Louise, who had tried for years to tell Nanine how expensive children are.

"A boy—pooh! Try having a girl. Can you imagine what her first bill was at Elizabeth Arden? Not to mention DePinna and Best and Co.?"

"Yes, well, you and Dinsie can be thankful you aren't stuck in the ninety percent bracket. We won't have a nickel left after taxes." Louise sighed.

This brought the conversation to a close. Nothing irritated Nanine more than this reminder that Louise was in a slightly higher tax bracket. And the maddening thing was that although Nanine had *less* than her sister, Louise always came to her for a loan. How can I possibly buy a new fur if it means selling off Daddy Henry's Continental Oil stock? You *do* see my problem? Why, the cost basis on that stock is about three cents!

"Well, for chrissakes, Weezie, my Continental stock cost exactly the same! Why should I have to pay the capital gains?"

"My dear, you're *not* in the ninety percent bracket— thank God! Think what it would cost Marshall and me!"

No one who saw them would guess they were sisters. Louise appeared as respectable as Nanine was dubious. A blonde, Louise had the bewildered face of a baby. In fact, she had practiced up a look and always seemed to be blinking in amazement at anything nasty and untoward. Nanine proved a great embarrassment to her idea of niceness. Not just the appalling clothes, the dyed hair, but the way she walked and talked like some border babe. And Nanine went out of her way to use the F word when Louise was around. Louise still could not say the word "bosom." She was famous for asking the butcher for chicken chests, that's how genteel Louise was.

"I just can't imagine why Nanine carries on like she's some sort of white trash or something," Louise would say with her endearing giggle at dinner parties. Nanine, in her element, would regale the company with off-color bad-girl yarns about life on the ranch.

"Why, all a person has to do is look at you, darling Louise, and they can see all the breeding they want. What nonsense all this is about Louise's family," Marshall Trimble would say in an aside to his dinner partner. And then: "Tremendously attractive people, the McAllisters of Dragoon. I went out there once . . . they own half the state, you know. Tremendously attractive."

Nanine told everybody her mother was a cattle rustler. Or sometimes she would describe Lou as the illegitimate daughter of an itinerant preacher and the onetime mistress of Pancho Villa. The one that really got their attention and made Louise the maddest was Lou as a *Mormon.* She said these things to annoy Louise and, when she was still alive, her mother-in-law, Charmagne Brown. Not that the plain truth wouldn't have annoyed Charmagne just as much: nothing about Old Lou would have been palatable to Charmagne Brown. The curious thing was that although Nanine and her mother were nothing alike, agreed over no single thing, they would have shared a good laugh over this.

"There's only one thing you can do with a snob—give 'em a ride on your fastest horse," Old Lou would say.

"Beat 'em at their own game: if you can't pull a duke out of the family hat, give 'em a scoundrel. One does just as much good as the other."

In this case, there were no dukes or scoundrels either, which did not seem fair. Nanine felt herself to be a woman who should have come from a long line of scoundrels; and Louise, who was more refined than anybody, deserved at least one real duke.

"Well, anyway, I know what I'm going to do about this bimbo or whatever the hell she is," said Nanine when their tempers cooled, "R-E-V-E-N-G-E! That's what keeps old Nanine warm at night."

"Revenge! Really, Nanine, I never heard anything so silly. Or unattractive. You ought to see it's beneath you. I do hope you're not going to become a bore about all this. I mean, we're all tremendously sorry Dinwiddie's gone off with a mistress or whatever she is and spoiled your summer, but—"

"We! *We all?* And who exactly is we all?" cried Nanine who rose up out of the bedclothes. "Louise dear, I certainly hope you haven't been blabbing about this behind my back! Because if you have—" She let the words hang ominously.

"What twaddle! Nobody knows anything," lied Louise surveying her sister through slits. Let's face it, thought Louise, is *anything* more unattractive than a woman who's been dumped? "But seriously, Nanine, you are a fool if you think people haven't been talking. . . ."

"Oh, Louise!" her sister cried suddenly. "What am I going to do? I feel so alone!" And Nanine began to sob noisily.

"No one cares—no one!" sobbed Nanine bitterly. True, there was not one real friend. Unless you counted Lucy Cook, who was only a servant. Certainly no one in Nanine's family gave a damn. And look at

Louise over there with that prissed-up swizzle stick of a body! No love! Oh, it isn't fair! For the first time Nanine came right up close to the edge and looked in: there really is no one! No one cares! I am absolutely unloved. Why? Even that creature I took in out of the goodness of my heart—Dinwiddie hadn't wanted the girl!—Jewel, even she turns away! Scuttles off when she sees me coming through the hall! And my friends! That impossible Betty Peabody had actually crossed the street yesterday in Job's Lane to avoid saying hello. Betty Peabody! I wouldn't hire that Peabody woman as a housemaid! "Louise!" shrieked Nanine in a shrill mouse voice. "Louise! What will happen to me? My best friends won't look me in the eye—and Dinwiddie, I can't bring myself to say another word about this to him! He won't discuss it, Louise, not a single word, and I'm afraid to push . . ."

"No," said Louise quickly, "don't push."

"Do you realize I have only seen him seven weekends—fourteen days!—and it is almost August? And people have stopped asking. Everyone knows," Nanine moaned. "And they don't say a word, which is worse. And the awful thing, Louise, is that I almost feel it's *me* they don't like! That it's me they've turned against instead of him! Can you imagine? It's too unfair!" she wailed, giving way to loud sobs.

"Of course the more you need people the less you can expect from them," said Louise at last.

"Well then, for God's sakes, Louise, tell me what to do!"

Louise might well have tasted some small, albeit bitter, triumph. This had never happened before. How Nanine had lorded it over them all!

"I suppose it's just that people feel awkward. They're

embarrassed. You can understand that, surely," said Louise when Nanine stopped crying.

"Embarrassed!" cried Nanine, stung. "But I haven't done anything embarrassing!"

"Well, you know—it's all so *real*. If this didn't matter to you it wouldn't mean anything to them. Do you remember what Lou used to say about the chicken with the speck of blood on its head? That the other chickens would peck it to death? I mean, it's awful but suddenly now you are the vulnerable one they can't stand to look at. It isn't Dinwiddie—it's you. Because you represent this *realness* none of us are accustomed to; the realness of—well, of suffering. It's just too real," said Louise flatly but not unkindly.

"So I'm to be shunned!" cried Nanine bitterly. "All because my husband has gone off with a tart!"

"Well—yes. Perhaps for a little while. You have to be reasonable, Nanine, and see it their way—no one wants to be inconvenienced," drawled Louise.

"Inconvenienced!" said Nanine. "When I think of those bores who have been sucking around me for invitations to this house for years—my God! This will drive me mad! Do you mean to tell me a pack of morons and oafs I wouldn't use to clean my boots really mean to snub me?" Nanine turned a hideous red.

"Oh, Nanine, do grow up. You know how it is! People just don't want to get involved in anything messy. And why should they? When it's all settled, they'll be back . . ."

"And what makes you think I would have them back?" screamed Nanine. "And you wonder why I'm being driven to revenge? What else can I do? Do you know I wasn't even asked to Viola Simms's coming-out party— she's my goddaughter, for chrissakes! And the party's in two weeks! Oh, Louise—think of something! You've got to help! You could speak to Angela Simms—she likes you."

"Nanine, I feel just as wretched about this as you do. Honestly I do. But you are going to have to pull yourself together, you hear? Revenge just isn't the point. Believe me, it will only make everyone turn against you. And what good is there in driving him away? Look at how wonderfully Anne Bratlett handled the whole thing when Monty went off on a toot with that awful Powers woman. Remember? And he was gone a year! When people asked Anne where Monty was, she said he was resting. As if he had just stepped into the next room! I must say I admire that. And no one felt inconvenienced. No one had to take sides. And then Monty came home and there she was: mixing his Martini just the way she always had; and they sat down to a divine dinner and not a word was said about it, then or ever. Because really, Nanine, *what is there* to be said?"

But Nanine felt as if she were suffocating. "This is going to kill me dead, Louise, I know it is," Nanine cried pitifully.

"Nonsense! Think of it as character building," said Louise briskly as she stood to go.

"Louise! Don't go, Louise! My God—there's no one!" Nanine wept. "And I need your help. If you'll stay by me."

Louise gave one or two efficient pats to the mound that was Nanine under the coverlet. "You know perfectly well why we have to go," said Louise. "It was not my idea to leave so soon but you know how things are." She sighed.

"You mean the children—you mean Jewel? I'll get rid of her, Louise! Say you'll stay! Pooh, Louise, you don't have to be such a virgin!" cried Nanine. Louise froze.

"Oh, Louise—is it really so terrible? Don't you think it's all rather healthy, that sort of thing?" said Nanine with a giggle. "I mean, after all, if children do have to do those things, it's better, don't you agree, to keep it in the family—no?"

"Nanine! I shall leave this instant and never come back if you mention it one more time!" snapped Louise.

At that moment Johnnie came in to bid his aunt goodbye. They had said he might be allowed to stay on the whole summer but now he was being dragged away to Biarritz or some other stupid place. His face looked surprisingly sullen as he leaned over to peck at Nanine's cheek.

"This has been the best summer I ever had, Auntie!" he whispered, fighting back the tears.

"Dear Louise," said Nanine firmly, "would you mind awfully if I had a word with the boy? Just for a moment? Don't be offended."

"Yes, but not if—"

"Heavens, no! We won't speak of that nasty other business, will we, John?"

"Oh, no!" cried John, but he went fiery red.

"Now, John darling," said his aunt, who patted a place beside her on the bed as soon as Louise had gone, "I suppose you had better tell me everything." John, though, only hung his head. "Did you do something *very* dreadful?" continued his aunt softly. She waited a moment, then: "Or was it your cousin Jewel, did she get you to do something?" whispered Nanine. At this Johnnie grew even redder but he drew himself up like a little man and answered her stoutly.

"Jewel's been nicer to me than anyone!" he declared.

"Yes, well, of course she has!" sniffed his aunt, not at all pleased by this declaration. It seemed too provoking: they all saw something marvelous in that unfortunate

child. "But the two of you must have been doing something?" prodded Nanine.

"It was something nice!" he cried.

"Nice! Well, I don't think your mother thought it very
nice!" said Nanine with a taut smile.

"My mother!" he began, then stopped, unsure. But
then he gathered himself and glared at his aunt quite
ferociously, almost as his cousin Jewel might have done.
Nanine was taken aback. He said firmly, "My mother,
you see, doesn't know." He had been tempted to add
"anything" but caught himself.

The events of these last days had changed around
Johnnie's world. He remembered the incredible uproar
two summers ago when his luscious blond cousin
Samantha had been taking a bath and discovered the
gardener boy was peeping. My God, the screams and
shrieks! And they had flushed that boy out of the neighbor's shed and pummeled him into admitting he had
done something wrong—something unspeakably wicked
and dirty. But Johnnie had seen the fellow's face, would
never forget the absolute befuddlement mixed in with
the shame. What had he done wrong? The incident remained with Johnnie because he had said to his mama,
Well, what *is* wrong with spying on a lady in her bath?
And then he had mentioned King David, whom they
were just studying in Sunday school, and his mother
slapped his face for talking smut. It had been the first and
only time Louise ever struck him so he knew it must be
bad. But he also knew, for the first time, there was a
dividing line: on one side was everybody old and on the
other everybody young and they did not think at all
alike.

The thing that seemed especially hard to Johnnie was
that he inspired confidence in grown-ups. He could not
say why but this was so. Until lately it had pleased him.

With the advent of Jewel he saw he must take a side. That it is like being in a secret society: you are privy to mysteries, the rites of your sect, young or old; mysteries that make no sense unless you are joined to your society. And without access to these mysteries you are stranded away from your kind. Grown-ups had taught him their odd, self-conscious behaviors, behaviors that chased away the fascinating questions, the delicious blank spaces of the young. But then along came Jewel to save him.

Of course he had had adventures; that is, he had been everywhere: he knew the names of all the doormen at the George V in Paris and the Ritz in Barcelona. Jewel, on the other hand, had been nowhere. But she seemed to him the source of all life, the oracle! She might not know how to eat an artichoke but what was that compared to her thrilling yarns about Aunt Clara loping off into the night to have sex with a Yaqui Indian? Or the sheriff of Tombstone who shot off his toe at Rodeo Days? Or about Alvin and Marge Gumm and all the little Gumms? And Twyla Hoover and Rosie Gonzales and Granma Lou and the horse called Spider and the cowboys and the Mexicans! The vaqueros! The ranch! Johnnie could think of nothing these days but the ranch. True, he had been down the Nile, but what were Abu Simbel and Karnak compared to Dead Man's Gulch and the Silver Dollar Saloon? Why, the idea of a shopping spree in Paris or another interminable summer at Como seemed flat and silly compared to the tantalizing image of Old Lou, who stampeded the cows in a lightning storm to get them home!

Then, too, although only ten, Johnnie had a terrible carnal craving for his cousin Jewel. In this new society of theirs, the society of the young, it didn't seem wrong to creep in close, burrow near someone nice. But of course that other society—the old—they called every-

thing wrong. It seemed strange to Johnnie that something so pleasant could be wrong. Maybe this happened
to old people because they were all used up and for them
it really wasn't so nice: his mother looked like a frozen
stick of a woman, no flesh anywhere, no bum at all, only
two lifeless globes that hung down mortified; no breasts
at all, only two hard unwilling little boobs, nothing
comfy to bump against; dry arms, thin and dry with
loose, unjuicy chicken skin: tan, and with many jangling
bracelets, chunks of gold—horrible arms! Who could get
near an arm with all those bracelets! And she had had a
face-lift. Kissing his mother, Louise, felt like kissing the
lampshade. She turned her face always and he had to kiss
the taut cheek. Sometimes Johnnie wished he could lie
down in a field of huge jiggling titties and just roll and
roll and suck and roll some more. He felt starved for
flesh.

And of course he had lost his father. Jack Truesdale
died before his son was born. No father! He did not feel
sorry for himself but sometimes he felt like a person who
had everything in the world but a left hand.

Marshall, his stepfather, was amazingly decent. A
more civilized fellow there never had been. He never
touched Johnnie, though, and would shake hands only.
They shook hands every night before Johnnie went to
bed.

"Good night, John, pleasant dreams," said Marshall,
hand extended.

"Good night, sir," said John. Then his mother, who
did not really look up, leaned the waxen face out toward
him sideways so he could peck at that cheek. Also, she
smelled like department store. Her hair, lacquered and
sprayed, and the formaldehyde cheek, and the earlobes
and neck: they all smelled like Bergdorf Goodman. Johnnie wanted a mother who smelled real.

He had had a governess until a year ago. Then one day, he was almost nine, his mother discovered he did not know how to tie his shoes. What an outrage! She set up a frightful row and fired Miss Lovering on the spot. But anyway, the governess had smelled of Vicks cough drops and Hu-Kwa tea and she had no flesh or it always looked so packed in in its girdle and he'd never been allowed to kiss or look or feel her body.

By now Jewel let him come in bed with her most of the time. Sometimes she let him lift the nightie and take a look. He felt absolutely amazed by what he saw. It was so completely right! So natural! The way he had always known it should be! Johnnie could describe the sensation, it felt like at last he had that left hand back. Those small, tenderly sloping mounds were all that had ever been missing on this earth. Although he had never before seen an actual bosom, or felt one, in his soul he had known: warm, oh, achingly, maddeningly warm, soft beyond imagining! And small though they were, these thrusting mounds, they had a wondrous springing life all their own! That and the other place down below, that other mound, filled the terrible ache and gave him back what was missing. Jewel understood nothing of this and everything—she had almost no curiosity about his body—but she let him creep near.

Louise walked in and found them there. They had become very careless. Their probings, by now, were so comfortable. There they were—but Louise almost could not look! That vile child lay there with her legs open, sprawled back lazily, bored, it seemed, by the experiment. Oh, the sumptuous look on her own child's face! The horror of it! And Jewel—the shameless inertia! Like one of those depraved filthpots lying around—and John fully clothed (it was the middle of the afternoon—they had abandoned themselves on the window seat, and not

even pulled down the shade!) and he lay half across her
ankles idly looking in. What is he doing? had been
Louise's first thought. Then she saw! Oh, the horror!
Then, to the amazement of the children, Louise opened
her mouth wide and began to scream. What a scream! It
rattled her whole body: a wild, deranged shriek! A piercing incoherent shrieking scream that tore your heart
right out of your throat—and the two of them leaped up
terrified, hardly able to comprehend; completely dazed,
stupefied, yet disgracefully flushed and rosy—ah, the
sweet bliss of it! To lie together in the sunshine, drowsy
and content. But all this was now torn apart! She flew at
them like a madwoman, mouth open wide, tongue gurgling, a demented shriek ripping them in two, and she
would not stop, her body shuddered with horror, my
God the horror and the loathing, and she rattled, Johnnie
would never forget her loud rattling as she threw herself
down onto them with little knotted fists: *Get off oh get off!*
Dirty filthy slut dogs filthy beasts! Get off! and then dragged
him, with great howls, out of the room.

And now they were taking him away. It might be
years before they let him see Jewel again. Jewel had
warned him: people like his mother and Aunt Nanine,
old people, are dangerous because they believe they are
right.

Jewel devised a plan. The idea was to get Granma Lou
to send for him. Jewel suffered over this solution but she
felt the situation called for some major sacrifice—that
Johnnie should go to Dragoon and come to know the
ranch without her. A sacrifice indeed. But if John could
be saved— And Jewel knew her grandmother: the old
woman would love to get her hands on this boy-heir
before it became too late. But would Louise ever give
him up?

They met in secret late that last night long after the others had gone to bed. Jewel helped Johnnie phrase a letter to his grandmother.

"Please Granma, I want to come see you," the letter said. "I feel if I'm going to be a rancher man someday I ought to know what to do. Besides, this life here is stupid and I am sick of Europe and always being around grown-ups. I want to ride a horse and see some cows, also I want to know you better and learn things. Please Granma rescue me. They got me here against my will. Jewel says I should tell you, she says you will help. Love, your grandson John Truesdale."

Jewel made him stick in that line about "they got me here against my will" on account of Granma being some-thing of an old-time hero and she would see right away he had to be rescued. John was against anything crafty. Jewel said, "Look, you want to win this thing, don't you?" Jewel mailed the letter herself the day they took Johnnie away.

"Well," said Jewel in those last moments together, "so you're going off to my land and I get to stay here in your place—in captivity. It's like I'm a hostage or some-thing—you probably won't even remember me pretty soon." She sighed.

"I'm only going for a visit," he said.

"Haw! Visit, my foot! You don't know Granma. Once she gets her hooks in you she'll never send you back! Not if she's got some use for you. No, Johnnie—if you go through with this you'd better be ready to stick to it, hear? Are you feeling scared?"

Johnnie mulled this over. "I suppose I ought to be scared," he brought out slowly. "But I'm not. See, the funny thing is I feel like I'm doing what I ought to do. Have you ever felt that way?" he asked. "Like something

is right even when it might look wrong? Well, that's how
I feel—like something right is happening and now I'm
going to be different all of a sudden."

"You probably won't even miss me—" she mourned.

"Like now, see," continued Johnnie dreamily, "I'll get
to be the *real* me."

10

ONE WEEK later the summons came. Granma did not communicate by letter; she sent telegrams. Johnnie was to report to the ranch immediately.

Louise was beside herself. What about their summer plans? They had booked passage aboard the *Queen Elizabeth* and were to sail that very moment! Lou would hear no excuses: she wanted the heir in Dragoon—pronto!

Marshall fumed: let the old harridan wait. But John was the heir to thousands of acres of prime Arizona ranchland—and now the old lady muttered to them about finding another heir! So Louise gave way. She could not fathom the boy's passion to go west; she still had not heard of the letter and surely this was an outrage, to have John snatched away from her—but still, it was only for a month and he was the heir. This is what Louise said to herself as she and Marshall sailed for Europe and that very day, all alone, Johnnie set off by airplane to be with his grandmother in Dragoon.

Now although Johnnie had never before been afraid, suddenly he felt anxious. The plane journey was arduous: they transferred him from one blimplike constella-

tion to another, first in St. Louis, then in Oklahoma City
(an airport filled with Indians), then in a place called
Albuquerque, where he got wretchedly sick, disgracing
himself in the airport; then finally they put him on a
noisy, rickety twin-engine Beechcraft and sent him to
Tucson out in the middle of the desert. With each stop
Johnnie felt himself carried farther and farther from the
center of his safe world, sailing into some vast unknown:
and at the pulse of all this vastness dwelled the gorgon—
his grandmother! That muttering, unsafe creature of
whom they all felt petrified! She could eat him alive,
swallow him down in one gulp, of this he did not doubt;
the stories Jewel had filled him with made his hair stand
on end—yet he yearned to know this dragon woman! He
had needed only to send that one obscure appeal and
whoooom! She sent for him! Not even his mother or
Marshall Trimble stood up to the old lady's summons!
And Jewel had said, Do not be afraid of her! What, then,
had the rest of them so terrified?

There were those in Dragoon who nurtured suspicions about Lou McAllister. Some thought she murdered her husband. Then, too, where had all the money
come from, and the mystique? No one knew. As to
Henry McAllister, he never worked a day in his life.

Henry McAllister, Johnnie's grandfather, had been a
soft-spoken fine old gentleman with delicate hands and
soft eyes. A scholar, said some, and a traveler: he had
ventured to far places on the swaying backs of elephants
and camels, bringing home emeralds from India and
blowguns and shrunken heads from New Guinea. This
grandfather, a favorite topic with Jewel and Johnnie,
seemed a mystery; all his effects had disappeared or been
hidden by Lou. When she murdered him! cried Jewel.

Henry met Louise Beal, the ferocious, last-surviving
member of a family of Colorado miners, the only daugh-

ter among eleven sons (and all the sons had died of fever!), on one of his travels into Colorado. They met in 1905 and married that spring. Henry, who had saved himself, remained a virgin until age forty-six. Louise, just twenty, had grown up wild but she knew everything a woman ought to know. Everything, that is, except how to be gentle.

Henry always said that when he saw the right woman he would know. He asked for her hand in marriage the first day he set eyes on Louise. Her dashing bravado and the head of vigorous red curls captured his imagination. Henry, left to his own devices, was something of a dreamer, a gentle, almost reticent fellow, who counted on his young bride to breathe some adventure into his musty life. Of course Louise Beal, strictly speaking, did not prove to be the right woman. A fierce little thing no more than five foot two, Louise sized up slow-moving, leisurely Henry and came down hard, chomping, stamping her feet when necessary or until she got her way. Henry was dazzled at first by so much unbridled female energy. Given rein, Lou roared up and down the land, rode and shot as well as any man, scandalized the neighbors, hobnobbed with the Mexicans, and made life miserable one way or another for poor Henry. All this Jewel managed to impart to Johnnie in lurid detail.

After they were married Henry McAllister retired into his cool dark study and shut the door. He spent long hours with his eyes shut. Dreaming of other times. Although no one heard Henry complain, people swore Lou drove him to death—as she did her son thirty years later. Lou gave Henry three daughters; the youngest, Clara, proved a great disappointment. Then came Horace, their only son, Jewel's father, and he turned out to be nothing his mother wanted in a son. She harassed the boy and bullied him till it almost drove a person mad to see.

There wasn't a thing in the world Henry could do to protect his son without making it worse. It broke his heart to see young Horace ground down, whipped, abased; but there wasn't a thing Henry could do.

Before many years passed, Louise had the men coming to her for their orders. Henry never fancied himself a cowboy but he had ideas about how things ought to be run. It was his custom several times a year to ride out to the water tanks and the branding pens to check fences and look around. His foreman, Robert Castillo, was the best vaquero in the county and had been running the Dragoon Cattle Company for years. That left nothing much for Henry to do—he couldn't hang around the corrals, could he? But this is exactly what Lou did and the men grew afraid of her. Soon Lou knew everything there was to know about a horse. The men respected her; her feats in the saddle were nothing short of spectacular. And Lou made it it her business to learn about cows. Lou loved branding and dehorning; loading the bulls; the stink and fear of castration she found positively intoxicating. Henry, disgusted to the core, shut himself in on those days.

Then one day Henry did not come out of the study: he swallowed poison. This at least is what Lou told everybody. But there were those who felt she wanted him out of the way. Nanine, her own daughter, had suspicions. Henry and Louise had been married twenty years. The same day as the funeral Lou got rid of everything: the blowguns, the emeralds, the withered skulls, everything, and now the ranch became hers. Nothing at the Big Earth, the Dragoon Cattle Company, had been the same ever since.

Louise McAllister—or, as she was known through Cochise County, Old Lou, a term of respect and begrudging affection—did not seem what you would call a natural mother. Loveta Hoover, mammy for the first ten years to the four McAllister children, had no recall of Miz Lou ever touching those kids. Clara she had a positive aversion to and the little boy as well. Defects (Lou always said *de*-fects) ought to be strangled at birth. When they brought in Clara as a newborn Lou took one look at this wrinkled swarthy abomination and bellowed, "Get her out!" Besides the unfortunate complexion, which never did improve, and a head of kinky black hair—all other Beal-McAllisters were golden—Clara was downright peculiar.

There was no end to the embarrassment Clara caused her family down through the years. A year or so ago, when Clara turned forty, she eloped. That is, she climbed out the second-story window and loped off with Eddie Pesquiera, a Yaqui Indian with vile intentions. They fetched Clara home the next day. Manny Castillo found her abandoned and weeping in the vicinity of the village dump. Her gray silk stockings, a Christmas present from Twyla, hung shredded off her legs like dead skin. Matted in Clara's hair were bits of debris: eggshells and what looked like shrimp skins. Her best dress, the black silk, gaped open to reveal red underwear. This last proved the worst aspect of the seamy affair so far as Lou was concerned. A horny daughter seemed bad enough but the idea of a Beal-McAllister running around the country in red nylon undies was flat-out depraved.

This was Clara's only dalliance with the other sex. The fact is, right from the beginning, from the moment of that first scream on her mother's lips, Clara knew she was different. She knew it was hopeless pretending to be like the rest of them, and in a funny sort of way—at least this is how Jewel explained it to Johnnie—that scream liberated Clara from the awfulness of being like everyone else. Maybe she looked swarthy and ugly and fat but

Clara seemed to get a big kick out of it, especially if she could shock people. She always talked to different parts of her body like they were people: like they had a mind of their own.

"Whoa there, Charley—where're you goin'?" she would say to her feet if they started to run fast. "Where's the fire?" Or sometimes Clara would jiggle the fat rolls on her belly and ask what they wanted for supper. "You girls want seconds?" she'd cackle. "Or is we on a diet?" For Clara, everything in life had a feeling. If you stepped on a flower it squeaked, Hey! You hurt me, fatso! Clara could hear the prairie grass sing, and she got messages, too, from lizards, snakes, everything. And usually she was right! Clara knew things, oh, she knew a million things, but why say much? Who would believe her? Jewel: Jewel loved Clara—but Jewel had gone away and they might never let Jewel come back. The interesting fact is that when Clara was little the one person she loved most was Nanine. And Nanine, strangely enough, had been good to Clara.

Clara, at least, had some life to her. If not for Clara, Nanine would almost have gone mad on the ranch. It had been one long-drawn-out series of disgraceful defeats. As soon as she got her toe up to the next rung it seemed to Nanine she'd go back to the bottom. Like the winter they were sent up to town to dancing school. Town being nearby Tucson. She and Louise each had a party dress. Nanine's was seafoam-green taffeta; it crackled when she danced, and all the way up to town she had to sit forward so as not to muss her bow. Manny drove them in the pickup truck and they freshened up in the ladies' room of the El Conquistador Hotel.

Louise in rosebud sateen turned out to be the belle of the ball. How Nanine hated her! Week after week Nanine sat marooned on the sidelines, waiting in mute appeal as the boys rushed the floor to grab the pretty girls; then afterward the nasty reluctant pimpled boys, the leftovers, crows in black feathers, came slouching over to take a look and carry away the last of her mewing rivals. Louise, flushed, victorious, sent sympathetic smirks as she whirled past in the arms of some squeaky Lothario, and Nanine sat out the first dance all alone in an agony of defeat, multiplied, many times over, on her gilt party chair along the wall of long mirrors. Then Miss Witherspoon spied her there and swooped down, clucking sympathetically, to mate her up for the next dance with some damp, frightened boy. Louise saw: Nanine would never forgive her for seeing.

Then Louise had been sent away to school. It seemed like that year, 1920, Nanine did nothing but lie, steal, and cry. She was bused to junior high school in Willcox, where she got some small satisfaction from tormenting the sons of the local pig farmers. Then at last they sent Nanine away to boarding school. Clara, left all alone with poor abject Horace, became so desolate when Nanine went away she did nothing but lie around in the dark; or sometimes she stepped into the closet for a good loud scream. Boarding school did little for Nanine: the fact is, she got tired of swallowing her sister Louise's dust. At eighteen Louise had so many beaux she hardly knew what to do with them. But if it was Louise they came to see, they hung around to visit with Nanine. No one knew for sure but the word was that Nanine had done it with just about everybody. Actually this proved untrue. She had tried it once or twice and felt appalled. She just couldn't believe the people one knew had any fun doing something so unattractive. It amused Nanine, though, to let them think of her as a vamp. And although not pretty (Louise was one of those petite blondes), neither did Nanine appear hampered by prissy clichés and boring virtues. So although everyone wanted to marry Louise—five years down the line—Nanine had all the fun.

The hardest thing of all, for both Nanine and Louise, had been to come home to the ranch after a round of debutante parties in the east. Lou waited for them: and no comedown on earth seemed so mean as the sight of their mother parked there at the airport, one foot up high on the running board of a Chevy truck, wearing 501's like a man and a J. C. Penney's workshirt, beat-up boots, and an old hat, talking cows with Spike Miller or some ranch hand.

"Well! Get a load of the day-*bu*-tonts!" sniggered Lou. Then: "Awright, girls, you kin toss your duds in the back and squeeze on in with me here up front." One hundred miles to the ranch and neither Louise nor Nanine said one word.

Sooner or later they had to go home. Lou kept them on a five-dollar allowance; she watched every penny. And although Lou understood their dilemma perfectly she refused to lift a finger to help. Girls like the McAllisters did not go out and get jobs. For one thing, what could they do? They were absolutely useless.

"You two still hanging around?" said Old Lou. "You mean to tell me one of you couldn't snag some moneybag to finance the high life? Well, godalmighty, what's the point of me bankrolling you two to all those fancy schools?"

No one helped *me*, she liked to say.

Nanine's liberation came about like this: in 1932 she bet her mother a thousand dollars she could mount Gold Rush and stay on him one hundred yards. Without falling off. Now, if there is one thing Lou McAllister had a weakness for it was a good horse, and there had never been a finer piece of Thoroughbred horseflesh than her

stallion Gold Rush. The thing is, Gold Rush was mean.
Beautiful but mean. A real killer. There wasn't a man on
the ranch could get near his stall to groom him, let alone
mount the beast, but when he saw Lou coming he
swished and stomped and backed and forthed, making
a fearful ruckus: breathing, snorting, carrying on in a
most terrible way so that anyone in their right mind
would run clear out of the barn, quick. Then Miss Lou
stepped right up and slapped open the stall door like
nothing was going on in there; this skinny little flea of
a woman, and she only had to touch his flesh and Gold
Rush went rigid all over, legs out, the back in a spasm
of ripples; it was incredible to see, the horse and the
woman.

The day of the famous bet began like any other. Lou
held forth in the dining room, where Louise, Clara, and
Horace sat imprisoned at the breakfast table. Nanine
took her breakfast in bed. This proved a great bone of
contention between Nanine and her mother. "The hell
you will!" shouted Lou when Nanine defended her right
at age twenty-five to breakfast in bed. "What the hell do
you think I'm running around here—a boardinghouse
for floozies?" Nonetheless, Nanine prevailed. Each
morning good and early she ran down the back stairs to
the kitchen and fixed a tray, then crawled back in bed
and lay there awhile. At this time of day Nanine allowed
certain half-lit fantasies to have their way with her: a
slow, dreamy, soft-around-the-edges time of day. But on
this particular morning Nanine conceived a plan. She
knew her mother would never give her the money to get
away and more than anything in the world Nanine
wanted to go to Europe. Nanine knew perfectly well,
however, that her mother was not averse to an occasional
bet. Lou would bet anything on a horse.

Now Nanine was no horsewoman. She could ride,

same as any other ranch kid, she had grown up on a
horse, but Nanine never had shown any great passion for
horses, probably because this would have pleased Old
Lou too well. But Nanine, at least, felt no fear of horses
the way Louise did. Every fiber of her being balked at the
idea of being cowed by anything, let alone a beast.

At a quarter to eight Nanine showed up in the dining
room all done up for riding. The conversation stopped
dead.

"And to what do we owe this great honor, Your Royal
Highness?" demanded Lou as Nanine flung herself into
a chair and poured out a cup of black coffee, swallowing
it straight down. Lou, regarding the flaccid eye of her
egg without mercy, jabbed at it. Yellow drops splurted
onto the plate. Louise, on the other side, held her handkerchief to her nose.

"Nosiree!" continued Lou, twirling a rind of ham into
the yellow mess. "I never could abide crumbs in the bed.
Nothing more ridiculous than a female who gives herself
airs—isn't that so, boy?" she hollered down the table to
where Horace, seventeen, stuffed himself on hot cakes.
Horace giggled.

"Lookit that! For chrissakes, boy, if you're going to
whinny like a mule, do it in the barn! My God, all I asked
for was an opinion!" she fumed. "You there! Is that all
you're going to eat?" she roared over at Louise, her
mouth full of egg. "There'll be nothing till lunchtime,
you hear? Not one thing. God knows where you two
girls get your highfalutin ideas, peckin' away at a little
scrap of toast like you was Mrs. Astor—and you!" she
continued, addressing Nanine with an egg-sodden belch.
"Well, I never thought I'd see the day when one of my
kin thinks she's too good to eat with the family! The only
one outta the whole lot of you is half normal is Clara!"
From her side of the table Clara snorted.

Every morning had been exactly the same.

Old Lou glanced around the table and she said, "Well! Who is going to ride Gold Rush today? Hah! You mean to tell me you're going to let the finest stud in the county kick his stall to bits just 'cause none of you here got the balls to mount him?" Then, after an awful pause: "Well, Louise, what about you?" Louise, fighting back tears, shook her head, always the same. "Well, what'm I going to have to do to get my oldest child up on a horse?" demanded the old lady, inexorable. "Well?"

"I'll ride him," said Nanine quietly.

"You'll what! What's that you said?" demanded her mother.

"Oh no, Nanine—you can't!" cried Louise, aghast. "You know how he is!"

"But only under one condition," Nanine continued, staring her mother down. "And that is: if I ride him a hundred yards and stay on, I want one thousand dollars, payable immediately."

"One thousand dollars—my Lord, girl, are you sure you asked for enough?" grunted Lou. "A thousand dollars for *what*? To ride an animal I kin ride myself every day of my life for free? Hah, you sure got your nerve, girl! And if you lose, what'll you give me?"

"Nothing," said Nanine. Two feverish spots stood out on her cheeks.

"Nothing! Nothing! Did you hear that?" cackled Lou. Horace, Clara, and Louise all stared with their mouths open.

"That's right—nothing. I figure if I lose, my having to stay on here like this at the ranch, against my will, as a prisoner, is payment enough. Anyway," she added, evenly, watching her mother's fury mount, "I'm not going to lose."

"Oh, you're not!" shouted Lou. "Well, guess what,

girl! Just for that I'll take your bet! Bet's on! But if I win you'll do things my way from now on, hear? No more lounging around in bed. Is that a deal?"

"Deal!" said Nanine, sick with fright. But to see her there so cool and arrogant you would never know. Old Lou looked her daughter over. Here was a girl she could respect—not that she'd ever let on. There wasn't a chance in hell Nanine could stay on that horse but Lou liked her for trying.

The whole family walked down to the stables. Ozzie, Inez Hoover's son, Twyla's brother, the stable hand, cowered outside Gold Rush's stall. "Nosiree! I sho' woun' go in dere, Miss, if'n ise you!" cried Ozzie, rolling his eyes at the stud. "He done bit one fella already today an he done kicked Sapphire Blue in de withers. He's mean as fire, dat one is!"

"All right, everybody, out of the barn!" cried Nanine, who shooed them away with her riding crop. Horace, Louise, and Clara turned tail and ran to the fence as fast as they could, clambering up, and Ozzie, too, disappeared suddenly into the tack room. Only Lou stood her ground.

"I don't want you touchin' my horse with a stick," she said. "I've never laid a finger on him. Hear? So don't go gettin' any fancy ideas. And I don't want you tearin' at his mouth any, either. That horse is so sensitive he could—"

"Are you going to let me ride him or not?" said Nanine.

Gold Dust, meanwhile, stood there so quiet and easy you might think he was drowsing. Every once in a while, though, he'd roll his eye sideways, all the way around, and glare at Nanine out of one fiery red eyeball. He thrust his head down low, nostrils tense, distended, and

every minute he'd blow a little and snort. He was all
saddled up, ready to go.

"Well then, what the hell's keepin' you?" snapped
Lou, but she hung to the reins. Suddenly it seemed to her
she could just as easily say, Stop! Hey, girl—don't go!
Way down inside her gut something unfamiliar stirred,
a terrible doubt. It circled around, a knot of fury tightly
held, a furiously guarded lump that did not go away;
around this came the teasing thought: What if she is
killed? After all, this is my child! But the knot would not
loosen. By God, she had mothered three monsters,
hadn't she—no, four! She was always forgetting Horace.
For what else were they? To have dragged about those
four all those months in her womb—and for what! To
think that Lou McAllister of all people could produce
four creatures so unfit! The first two, those females—
why, they were nothing like *real* women! Imagine
Louise homesteading! Or giving birth out in a wild little
hut somewhere! Imagine Nanine boiling up soup for her
family in an iron kettle over a fire; or beating the wash
on a rock; or loading a shotgun! And look at Clara! Good
God, poor Clara—sly as a raccoon, sooty, devious, without purpose or destiny! Then worst of all—Lou gnashed
her teeth—Horace! Puling, flimsy, a sissy-boy who
hadn't the balls God gave a jackrabbit. So why shouldn't
she be bitter? What the hell had she ever done to deserve
the disgrace of four such abject specimens?

Something remarkably like compassion flickered a
brief second in her mother's eye—Nanine saw it, or
thought she did; but whatever hovered there died back
almost immediately. Lou, her eyes tight and mean,
hissed at Nanine, "Well—get on with it!"

Nanine turned her back on her mother and fooled
with something in her hand. A powerful smell suddenly

broke loose in the stall. Gold Rush stayed dreamy and almost apathetic as Nanine crawled up onto his back and rode him out the barn door.

"Hey!" shouted Lou. "What's that smell? It smells like perfume—why, it smells like my Shalimar—hey!"

It was exactly one hundred yards from the barn door to the first cattle guard. Gold Dust, sighing, stumbling along, sauntered like a being lost in fog. Then, just as he neared the cattle guard, his ears perked up. He seemed to remember; gnashing his teeth, he took off. Lou came streaking down the road after them. The others would not get down from the fence but watched in horror as Gold Dust hurled himself at the cattle guard: high up he arched with a tremendous gallant thrust: and they hung there in the sky for a thrilling moment: to Nanine it seemed they were one, the girl and the horse, so deep was she dug down into his flesh, laid along his neck, nose, eyes, lips choking in the stinging tendrils of mane, the foaming smell of beast: high they flew, high up! Then suddenly down they came: crashing down, down they plunged, a terrible falling down: and she knew, even before the fall, how terrible it was and sad, coming back to earth. But down they came, he dashed her down: bones and hooves, the slashing, now the blood: loud, loud, eyes filled with blood! Then darkness! All was black and broken.

"AND THEN what happened?" cried Johnnie, who had begged Jewel to tell him the story of Gold Rush and Aunt Nanine over and over that summer.

"Well, Aunt Nanine, she won her bet! Imagine! She lay there all smashed up, see, they strapped her down for nearly a year. She broke her back. That's what a horse can do to you if you don't get on its right side."

"But at least she rode it!" he cried admiringly. "I never thought that old lady had the guts, did you?"

"Oh, she's plenty tough!" said Jewel. "You gotta be tough if you're going to get on with Granma Lou. When she sends for you, Johnnie, you remember that. Never let her see you're scared. She'll ride all over you! But if she likes you—"

"Gee—I wonder if she'll like me?" he sighed.

"A person can never tell what Old Lou will like. But you, Johnnie." This was the last thing he remembered her saying to him, they had taken him away the next morning. "I got a real strong feeling that old lady is going to take one look at you and something in her heart, something that's always been stuck, will pop loose, see, and I got a feeling she'll love you."

"You do?" he cried.

"She never loved anyone, I expect—but I got this feeling it'll be you."

The Beechcraft put down in the desert near Tucson, and Johnnie had a vision, suddenly, of home. It must be dark outside back east, they'd be calling for me to come to bed. Probably I'd hide awhile in the garden there behind the lilacs; not too long, just long enough to stir things up a little. How far away it was, that other place! Like a tiny speck on the horizon—gone! See how bright it is here! Yes, and here is the sun, balanced, just as Jewel said it would be, like a flaming eyeball in the sky. And nothing else for miles around except for jagged mountains—and over there, one or two pickup trucks. The door to one of the trucks, a Chevy, stood open and leaning against the running board, one foot up, he saw an old cowboy. No—it was an old lady! Dressed like a man but it was her all right, hat pulled low, talking to a cowboy who stood angled against the next truck. The plane pulled in close, stopped before the trucks. Now she

looked up, squinted his way. It was Old Lou! His grandmother—he'd know her anywhere! And she looked wonderful! No one had told him how wonderful she'd be!
What a face! And here she was!

"I knew it!" he cried. Tired as he felt, Johnnie mus-
tered a happy laugh. "I knew it was you soon as we set
down—and you're just like I thought you'd be!" He
could hardly repress his happiness as he stood there
beaming at her.

"Well, can you beat that?" exclaimed Lou, standing
back to look as he shot past her and scrambled up into
the truck. "I never saw such a kid! Hey, you!" she called
to him. "Think you're man enough to handle that
Chevy? Haw! Can you drive? Well, dad gum it wouldn't
surprise me if he could!" She cackled happily and
climbed in next to him. "Kid!" she said. "Guess what? I
got a hunch you and me are going to be friends!"

11

ONE MORNING in August Nanine emerged from the house in Ox Pasture Lane and climbed into the back seat of a rented station wagon with Gustavo Mendez behind the wheel. Over her own red curls she wore a blond wig.

"What in hell is she up to now?" exclaimed Lucy Cook.

"Chee is at the bottom of this, I bet you anything," said Jewel as Nanine zoomed off. The two of them were spying on her from an upstairs window.

Chee had been sent to the city on numerous occasions to spy on the master and his fancy lady. He had followed Madeleine on the subway and saw where she lived in the Bronx; in one week he saw a lot. Then Nanine hired a private detective and now she knew almost everything about Madeleine except where the girl actually came from; no one knew this. Nanine went into a state of shock when she realized who Dinwiddie's floozie was: none other than the creature embroiled with Horace in that horrid mess. And she had been in prison! Seventeen years old! This was far more disgraceful than anything she had imagined. And to think—they had lunched at

"21" Club and Giovanni's—repeatedly! Where anyone
might see them!

Beside Mendez on the front seat were a bottle of dry
sherry for sustenance and a wicker basket filled with
sliver-thin ham sandwiches from Fraser Morris. Nanine
had no very exact idea where the Bronx was but she
thought it must be very far away.

At last they pulled up before a house on Meyer Avenue, Madeleine's address in the Bronx.

"Maybe I'd better go in there first," said Mendez, hoping for some action at last. But Nanine said no. She had
no definite plan of attack but she was resolved to end this
thing today. Munching ham sandwiches, they contem-
plated the house, a gray, squat row house with a stingy
porch hanging off the front, set slightly apart from the
sidewalk by a torn fence and a strip of dirty grass. A
boardinghouse with rooms to let. Over the windows
they noted venetian blinds pulled tightly shut. Depressing as it appeared, and unrelentingly gray, the street
boasted a row of trees: with trunks of bloodless gray,
anemic and with soiled leaves, an inert green. Still, the
trees did exist, lending the row of little houses a dejected
bravado.

"Oh, dear," said Nanine at last. "I suppose I'd better
go in there and get this thing over with."

"I still think it's better if I go with you," said the
Mexican.

"No, I'll go alone," she said firmly as Mendez leaped
out to open the door.

She was a woman after his own heart. Hah, thought
Mendez, admiring the plump rump of his mistress as it
teetered up the rickety steps, she has the courage, the
fire! Maybe she isn't so beautiful, although personally he
liked redheads, the fatter the better, and so what if they
were a little old? So what! Actually mistress was not

sexy. But she had the fire! He would stick his hand in the flame for her all right. Yes, this little lady was a real *tigre*—eeejola! And Mendez chuckled to himself.

Nanine examined the names on the mail slots at the door. Madeleine Boldiszar, 5B. But what was this? Ernst Stupfelfinger—also 5B. So! And under Stupfelfinger, this card:

> *Piano Tunings*
> *By Appointment AT3-9984*
> *Evenings*

Was he her lover? How many did she have? All the names, Nanine noticed, were either Polish or German except for Madeleine's. Nanine rang the bell.

The door opened a crack. The landlady, Mrs. Stubbs, had been watching her the last five minutes through a chink in the blinds. She had seen Gustavo Mendez in his hunter-green custom-made serge uniform and matching hat; she took in every detail of Nanine's costume from the snub-toed narrow lizard shoes and matching bag to the blond wig; and Mrs. Stubbs was not fooled.

She opened the door another inch, releasing a smelly plethora of sauerbraten. Undaunted, Nanine inquired if Miss Boldiszar was at home.

"There's no Miss Boldiszar here."

"I believe her name is written here on the mailbox," said Nanine firmly.

"Where?" demanded the woman in great surprise. And she poked her head out and around, craning slightly, like a long-necked pinheaded bird, her red dewlap throat flapping, and peered at the mailboxes, at the spot where Nanine put one gloved finger. She reached a bony hand across to the boxes and tore off the name Boldiszar, stuffed it into her pocket.

"I don't see nothin'," she cackled. The other hand, yellow and bony, plucked at the waist of her cotton housedress. Although it was insufferably hot, Mrs. Stubbs wore woolen hose and fur bedroom slippers. Nanine felt faint, she was so revolted by the woman.

"When will Miss Boldiszar return?" she inquired delicately.

"What do you want her for?" said the woman.

"I have good news!" said Nanine, in a moment of sheer inspiration.

"What news?" said the woman shrewdly, and she squinted at Nanine sideways.

"Are you a relative of Miss Boldiszar's?" demanded Nanine.

"There's nobody by that name lives here," and the woman shut the door.

Nanine jotted down Mr. Ernst Stupfelfinger's phone number and retreated to a drugstore to telephone the piano tuner. He seemed very dubious, but when Nanine insisted she had good news and wanted to speak to him about an urgent matter, Stupfelfinger allowed himself to be persuaded.

"How do you do? Mr. Stupfelfinger?" said Nanine, moments later, pushing past a small baggy man at the front door. She brushed past Mrs. Stubbs as though the woman were some unsavory smell lingering in the hallway, puffed up five flights of stairs until they arrived at the piano tuner's meager quarters on the top floor.

"But *hello*! This must be *her* room!" exclaimed Nanine, who noted the 5B on the door. "Are you lovers?" she demanded.

But Mr. Stupfelfinger was so overcome by the spectacle of his visitor struggling out of her suit jacket, the blond wig askew and the straggling red hairs peeping out, that for a moment he could not trust himself to speak. In these surroundings Nanine looked positively menacing. She actually seemed to soak up all the oxygen. He felt afraid of her.

"Oh, hang it!" said Nanine, who snatched off the wig and shoved it into her handbag. "I don't suppose I really need this, do I?"

"Won't you sit down, Mrs.—?" he asked shyly.

She gave him the name: Mrs. Arthur Pringle. She removed a pile of sheet music from the only comfortable chair, a faded lump of eglantine horsehair, placed the music on the floor, and lowered herself into the chair.

"Do you have anything to drink?" she asked. "I'm dying of thirst. Oh, I don't mean whiskey. Although if you have any I wouldn't mind a shot." Vanishing into a tiny Pullman closet, he rinsed out a glass. "Anything but water," she called out. "I'd adore iced tea. And something to nibble on, please. I could hardly concentrate on lunch. I'm ravenous."

Mr. Stupfelfinger decided to revolt; he appeared in the doorway, his pale face suddenly animated by two angry red spots. "This is very unusual!" he protested.

"My dear Stupfelfinger, *life* is unusual. Now hurry along and get my tea. I am mean as a snake when I haven't been fed." Mr. Stupfelfinger ducked back into the kitchen.

Nanine occupied herself with a quick snoop through the room and bath, this last being filled with unappetizing black socks and dingy Jockey shorts dripping from the shower rod. A quick peek into the medicine cabinet and closet revealed no feminine apparatus. The little room gave off a weary impression of soot and poverty: a sofa bed with straying sheet, a few books, Schopenhauer and Hegel in paperback, a pedestal table draped in soiled lace, and on this, in a saucer, the remains of a half-eaten bagel and an open volume of Goethe's *Italian Journey*, the place marked by a pair of eye spectacles.

One lamp, a gaudy lilac vase with a tattered rose-silk shade, lent a voluptuous intimacy to what might otherwise be a despondent room. Miss Boldiszar's lamp, thought Nanine. All this she took in with a swiftness that would have rattled Mr. Stupfelfinger's teeth had he seen. Nanine began to think her journey a dismal waste when her eye lit upon a piece of furniture standing in the corner. Shabby and yet still somehow elegant, the little piece, an étagère, appeared, in this surrounding, a surprise: not unlike a grand duchess stranded among poor relations, thought Nanine. She pounced on it. She could hear Mr. Stupfelfinger scratching around in the closet kitchen. Peering in, Nanine decided the little cupboard must belong to a woman: among the bric-a-brac she spied a corsage of withered tea roses tied with a curling scrap of silver ribbon, stuck through with a pearl hatpin. She fiddled with the little glass door and had just pried it open when Stupfelfinger came up behind with biscuits and glasses of tea.

"Yes! It is beautiful, is it not? Do you like it?" he asked softly. Nanine jumped back. She had spotted something in the étagère she yearned to investigate.

"Tell me, Mr. Stupfelfinger," said Nanine, her mouth full of biscuits, "does it belong to *her*?" He seemed flattered by the question and watched with the large gullible eyes of an unwholesome baby as she settled herself in the eglantine chair, thinking at first to tell her nothing, this gross, noisy, impertinent woman. But she had noticed his one treasure and so he relented. Perhaps she would listen and be sympathetic.

"Yes! The piece you admire is hers—that is, it *was* hers until today. She gave it to me," he brought out timidly.

"Don't you think it casts a spell upon this room?" he ventured.

"Oh, I do!" exclaimed Nanine. "Why yes, it does absolutely cast a wonderful spell! Why, the piece is enchanted, I really believe it is!" she burbled.

"You do?" he cried, brightening. "Yes! I think you must be right."

"I hope you are not offended by my suggesting—well, you know—" continued Nanine, slyly, "that you two are lovers. I didn't mean to—oh, dear! Will you forgive me, Mr. Stupfelfinger, but you *are* in love with her, no? Or perhaps," she risked, but in a gentle voice, "the lady is in love with you?"

"Oh, dear me, no!" he exclaimed quickly, horrified by the suggestion. "It is true this was her room. She lived here." He let it hang a moment. "You see, I lived there— across the hall." He pointed. "We were neighbors these last months."

"Ah!"

"Ah, then," he cried, taking her up on it, "why am I in her room?" But for a moment he only shook his head sadly, gazing across at the étagère. Then he made up his mind. He felt so lonely! Madeleine had gone, why should he not talk of her a little? "She came to me yesterday, she came flying in over there, across the hall to my room. I was eating my supper—and she said I mustn't ask why but that she would be leaving here momentarily, today perhaps, or tomorrow! When she could make the arrangement. That she would need to leave behind a few things for a day or two. Ah! Such a rush! And she begged me to take her room. Immediately! The landlady, you see!—that Stubbs woman!" And he lowered his voice. "The thought of that vulture picking through *her* things! She stayed here last night, Madeleine did, and I was to come over in the morning. She even helped bring my things," he added, blushing. "The books—even my wash! Yes, she took it down and hung it there herself, to dry . . . she has almost nothing of her own. Just that," he indicated the sofa bed and the wonderful étagère. "Those are her things over there," and Stupfelfinger nodded toward a homely brown valise parked against the door.

"I see," said Nanine ominously. "And do you think she will come to collect them soon?" She felt quite weak: what if they were planning to fly away tonight, this woman and her husband?

"Ah, you see, I cannot be sure!"

"But her things? Surely if they are all she has?" Unless of course, she thought bitterly, he buys her all new things! Stupfelfinger, watching her, felt horrified by her sinister expression.

"Perhaps she will have me bring them to her," he said enigmatically. "She has left one or two valuable things in my care," he could not resist adding as his eye strayed involuntarily toward the étagère.

"So," said Nanine, "she asked you to move in here to guard her things?"

"Yes," he said sullenly, "her things."

"Perhaps she is going home. Let me see—where did you say she is from? Boldiszar. Hungarian, is it not?"

"I have never inquired!" he said loftily.

"Why did she have to leave so suddenly?"

"You make a great mistake, madame, if you judge Madeleine by this surrounding! Miss Boldiszar is a lady, believe me! So refined, so quiet! Such a person as that never lived in this neighborhood before, I tell you! She was poor, yes, like so many of us today—exiles, but—"

"*Was?*" demanded Nanine, leaping on it. "Has she gotten some money?"

"She has—well, let us say she has come into a small good fortune." He smiled secretly, his eye straying again toward the little cupboard. "Of course she did not discuss this with me. She only said, 'Ernst! Now I am free!'"

"Hmmmm!" said Nanine, dangerously. "I see."

"You have not said why you are here," he brought out suddenly.

"I have a wonderful surprise for Miss Boldiszar if she ever turns up. Do you think she will?"

Stupfelfinger agonized over this. He certainly did not want to be the reason for Madeleine's losing out on a wonderful surprise. Yet her instructions to him were to tell no one, absolutely *no one* anything. She might return for the suitcase and her few valuables at any moment. She had asked him not to leave the room and he had been good to his word. But what should he do?

"If you would leave your telephone number," he said reluctantly.

"Fine," said Nanine, who by now was bored to death with the little man. "Do you have paper and pen?" Stupfelfinger glanced about the room wildly but saw no pen. If he left the door open and dashed across the hall, quickly—

What luck! Quick as a snake Nanine ran to the corner, the minute he had gone, and opened the étagère. Without even pausing to think she reached in and snatched the tantalizing object, a box she had spied tucked in among the souvenirs, stuffing it into her handbag. When Stupfelfinger returned a second or two later—and the door had stood open all the time!—Nanine sat as he had left her in the eglantine chair. The curious thing was, Stupfelfinger looked immediately in the direction of the étagère. He suspected nothing—and yet he looked! And the door of the pretty little piece stood wide open! Stupfelfinger gazed, transfixed. Two vivid spots began slowly to burn on his cheeks as he stared at the étagère. Then glancing around, he encountered Nanine. Steady and bright, she faced him straight on without a blink. She saw him deliberate. Then crossing over, he looked inside; carefully he latched shut the little door. A terrible moment for Nanine, lasting, she felt, an hour! A dreadful heat climbed her scalp but she felt ready for anything. But no, he hadn't seen!

He turned to her at last and Nanine, struggling into her jacket, put out her hand in a most winning fashion, girlish almost, and said, "The time! Heavens, do look! Well, I can't *believe* how wonderful you've been, Mr. Stupfelfinger, but really I must go! Do give Miss Boldiszar this note, please, and tell her she has a marvelous treat in store. Got to go!" And suddenly Nanine was gone.

Two flights down, hovering, cackling to herself like an evil chicken, Mrs. Stubbs waited. "She left without any notice—that type always does! Royalty-heehee!" shrieked Mrs. Stubbs. "She acted like she was royalty! The slut! She never had *me* fooled!" But Nanine flew on past and out the door.

They reached the Long Island Expressway, yet still Nanine did not peek at the contents of the box. If she opened it now Mendez would see, he was dying to know some tidbit! She began to be afraid of what she might find. What if she had stolen some rare thing? Thank God she gave him a false name! Why had she taken it? But hadn't this woman stolen everything from her? Everything! No, surely she had a right to it. And how curious that she was so drawn to that little cupboard, placing her hand on that one thing as being of any consequence. The little box: tantalizing, rich-looking. She burned to know what lay inside but in a way she did not want to know. It burned in her pocket like a great molten lump; she itched to open it yet would not. Probably there was

something quite worthless and disappointing inside. If
nothing else it might furnish a clue to her adversary, she
felt sure it would. More than ever she needed some
means of quashing this thing absolutely before it con-
sumed her husband. Free! So now Madeleine was free.
This could mean only one thing: that he meant to set her
up in style in the Plaza Hotel. Where all their friends
might goggle at them in the Oyster Bar. How obscene!
Free! So then she had him—he belonged to her! Nanine
moaned out loud in the back seat, thinking about it.

Home at last. Alone, Nanine opened the box. At first
she could not fathom what she saw. How bright the
jewel, falsely bright and dazzling! But surely it could not
be real, this pavé diamond peacock! Nanine examined it
carefully. Yes—it appeared to be real. But this must be
worth thousands of dollars! And then she thought, And
he gave it to her! Dazzled by the bird, Nanine almost
could not think. But something about a peacock came
back to her. Yes, here it was in the detective's report.
And there had been some messy business about Mary
Lou running off after Horace died with a valuable pavé
diamond peacock. But this did not explain the Boldiszar
woman's having the bird—unless it had been given her
by Dinwiddie. Thousands of dollars! Yes, that must be
it—this sly seducer of little girls showered his child-
mistress with jewels! The fiend! Why, it must be costing
him thousands and more thousands to keep her! And
what had he ever given *her*? Nanine ground her teeth
thinking on it. Twenty years of devotion and he treated
her like dirt! With money snatched from her very mouth!
Ah, but if she had one real regret it was that she had
given Stupfelfinger an assumed name. How delicious her
revenge, how perfect, if only the girl might know who
had taken the jewel!

12

THERE CAME a faint tap at the door. Before Ernst could open it Madeleine rushed into the room. Ernst had never seen her so splendid. Her cheeks flushed pink with happiness and her eyes, always so guarded, were wide, excited. She came into the stale little room like some wonderful gush of vibrant wind, teasing, laughing at him.

"The room looks good! We should have done this sooner—yes?" she cried playfully. Rushing at him suddenly, she planted a kiss on his cheek. How beautiful she was! Stupfelfinger went fiery red. Madeleine was so delighted with his confusion she thought to kiss him again, on the lips perhaps, but then changed her mind, whirling off instead to the étagère.

"Ernst," she cried, opening the door, "I cannot tell you how it has come about, my dear fellow, but this time I really will be free!" And she smiled on him like an angel.

"Free!" he breathed. "But how? Does this mean you are going away?"

"Ernst," said Madeleine gently, and she came to him, "these years in America have been for me very terrible." And to his great amazement, her eyes filled. Ernst looked away. They had lived across the hall from each other, yes, but she had taken no more notice of him than you would the neighbor's cat. Oh, she had been pleasant always, civil; but distant. Until one week not so long ago when Madeleine had waylaid him in the hallway and begged him in whispers to look out for her room, saying she would be gone sometimes and did not want that wretched Stubbs woman prying through her things. Ernst had been thrilled with the request—she chose him! Every so often, after that, she would pass him in the hallway and thank him with what he could only describe as a heavenly glance. He would never call her a snob although the others did—no, not a snob, only that she seemed so far above the rest of them. She was rare, they were not.

"But don't worry, Ernst," she continued, "I am not going to tell you how miserable I have been. You are from over there too." She stood very close and gazed into his eyes solemnly.

Ernst thought he would faint. He knew that by "over there" she meant not just Europe or any particular place, her country or his own, but that other world: that difference, bottomless and inconsolable; and he understood.

"So you know. It has to be forgotten immediately, doesn't it—all the horror, else how can one bear to go on? I came here two years ago, my God, I was only a child! This place, you see, has nearly crushed me. I'm not meant to live like that. Oh, I don't mean just this room. But here in America. They want too much! They want everything from you—everything! It costs everything,

and you are defiled, absolutely defiled, Ernst! And they
do not notice—" she dragged out with a low moan,
standing so close, and Ernst felt scorched!

"But if one of us," she continued, "gets the chance to
go free— You do not begrudge me that? No?"

"Oh, no!" he cried passionately. He would have
thrown himself down like a rug if it would be of any use.

"But where will you go?"

"Oh, I don't know—Paris maybe, or even Italy. Yes,
Rome would be wonderful!" she cried liltingly, her eyes
radiant. She seemed completely transformed from the
guarded creature who whispered at him sometimes in
the hallway. "Yes, in fact I shall probably have enough
money when I sell the horrid thing to go to both! And
Ernst"—she lowered her voice and looked at him almost
shyly—"when I sell the bird I shall be very rich. But
probably only for a short time. This is my nature, you
know—I should tell you, Ernst, I am rather extravagant!
But if you . . . I mean, do you . . . do you need money?"
she asked gently. "Because if you do I would gladly—"

"No, no!" cried Ernst. "Nothing! Go—take it and go.
But where will you sell it?" Ernst still had no clear idea
what she meant by "the bird." "But do you know how
to do this?"

"Yes, yes! I know now where to go, I have just found
out everything in these last days. Look, Ernst, I will
show you!"

Madeleine turned again to the étagère. She reached in
and groped for the little box, but did not find it. At first,
in her terror, she laughed. Then she began to scratch
through the heap of trinkets frantically. No—it was not
there! She turned to look at Ernst. There was such naked
terror in his face, such duplicity! Ernst nearly died of
fright! He knew! He knew! Desperate, snarling like an
animal, Madeleine hurled herself onto him, she fell onto

him with a shriek of hate, cunning as a wolf, panting, she searched his pockets, again that scream—ach! what an ungodly scream, it would ring forever in his ear! And in a snarling voice, not human, horrible beyond anything, she howled, *"Give it to me!"* But what could Ernst do? Nothing, absolutely nothing. And she saw this, mad creature, frenzied, deranged, and threw herself once again at the étagère, pawed, tore at the trinkets, up-turned everything, wild, feverish, then threw the whole thing over, heaved it onto the floor and crawled on her hands and knees through the mess and searched, turning on him, at last, a ghastly face and cried, *"The peacock! It's gone! Ernst—you have killed me!"*

13

SUMMER WAS over. Somehow Jewel had survived the last three months. In two weeks she was going to boarding school. They were sending her with a whole trunkful of new clothes and although she would rather go home to the ranch, she did think school in the east might be something of an adventure. At least it would be something to write Johnnie about. His last letter from the ranch sounded pretty cocky. In the first he said Granma let him ride Spider. In the next, and Johnnie did not sound like a baby anymore, he said Granma had gotten him a horse. And Johnnie planned to call the horse Gold Rush II. He was not a stallion though, only a mustang, but he and Granma were pretty much best friends now, she let him shoot snakes with her Luger. It sounded pretty obvious to Jewel he had won the old lady over. But then Jewel had known he would. The big news was this: Granma had sent about nine cables to Europe and at last his mama said Granma could keep Johnnie until Christmas but no more—but Granma gave a big snort and said, "We'll see," and Johnnie was going to fifth grade in Dragoon. But in neither letter had he said any-

thing to Jewel about all her news: that Cook had returned and Uncle Dinwiddie was victorious, while Aunt
Nanine crept around the place like a whipped dog.
There was general rejoicing all over the place—except
for Lucy Cook, mean as a rattler these days, no one could
get near her, and Chee, too, skulking around in a gloom.
But Jewel felt awful proud of her uncle. In a way she was
almost sorry to have fixed things so Johnnie could go off
to Dragoon, especially if he couldn't even remember
who his real friends were.

It was Labor Day weekend, the night of Viola Simms's
coming-out ball. Not that Jewel cared two hoots about a
ball but everyone else did, all Southampton was going;
that is, all Southampton that mattered, including the
Dinwiddie Browns. Dinwiddie had mentioned the thing
in passing to Archie Simms out on the tenth green and
the thing was settled.

Dinwiddie stood waiting for his wife that evening in
the downstairs hall thinking how altered he was. What
a change from the Dinwiddie Brown of old! It was hard
not to preen a little. If any one of his acquaintances had
dared to suggest six months ago that he would keep a
child-mistress (a foreigner!) closeted in the Plaza Hotel
he would have called them a damned liar. Pacing slowly,
luxuriously, back and forth in the downstairs hall, Dinwiddie pondered these things, tracing a path on that
gleaming, familiar old floor that had been his mother's,
his grandmother's. But he did not think of them now.
Ah! cried Dinwiddie, breathing in the heavenly salt
breeze so refreshing to the soul, wafting in through the
wide oak door left open, just now, to the thickish Southampton air; and he preened a little in his custom-made
tuxedo that had needed to be taken in a hefty two inches
all around, only recently; and he could not help but
ruminate on the delightful changes in his life. How

pleasant it feels when one stiffens a little and takes charge! Why hadn't he done it years ago? To think that a bare six months ago he would have been frightened out of his wits at the idea of keeping a mistress—and to have anyone know! What a thought! And to think, back then, of having to beard Nanine in her den—for Nanine could be very fierce, very unpleasant indeed, if crossed. Why, only a few weeks ago she had yapped and carried on like a big baby over their not having been invited to this silly ball, all because, she said, he had a mistress! Imagine! But how effortlessly he had smoothed down this whole thing—without giving an inch. No, he wouldn't be run by women.

And what about the amazing turnaround in Madeleine of late? She seemed so amenable it almost frightened him. Why, the day he gave her the peacock, now nearly three weeks ago, he had had to grovel, as he remembered, to have lunch with her! And he had actually managed to convince himself, that day when they departed "21," he might never see her again! How he had wept and bitterly cursed his idiocy in giving her the jewel—for surely she would dispose of him! Fool! Foolish honor—how it had bogged him down! And of course she was right: it had been a test: he thought he could not go on without knowing if she did really care. If he meant nothing to Madeleine, wouldn't she have taken the bird and flown with it? Sold it, disappeared? This is exactly what she would have done. She had seemed so glittering and sly, so ungrateful that day after lunch—but he was the ungrateful one, stupid male! She had not gone away!

Then the most surprising thing happened: she asked him one day a few weeks ago if she might come live in their little nest in the Plaza—where he could see her whenever he liked! Oh, it was too good to be true! And after all, hadn't his grandfather kept a quadroon in a hotel?

Of late there might be some deeper shade to the girl. Certainly some of her fire was gone. But he felt glad. She had been nearly too much for him. Too fierce—or was it proud? Yes, perhaps her pride had left her. He certainly hoped not! But something was changed: she appeared almost listless sometimes, dispirited; and under her lovely eyes he noticed bruises; yes, she reminded him of some dark-eyed, soiled—but no, he didn't want to think of that. After all, he treated the girl decently, gave her money, whatever she asked for, which really wasn't a lot, not like Nanine. And he did love her. How many girls in that position could say they were loved?

Ah, but imagine it! Dinwiddie Brown having a mistress! He caught, just then, a long oblique angle of himself flatteringly framed in his tuxedo in the hall mirror and paused, arrested. You know, he said to himself with a chuckle, for an old blowhard of fifty-nine I don't look half bad! Oh, I'm no Cary Grant, let's face it, but in fact I'm quite presentable. And the face gazing back from his grandmother Brown's Queen Anne mirror did appear distinguished, if a little paunchy around the jowls. He had grown a neat bristle moustache. Madeleine liked that! And his was a fine manly nose, nothing remarkable but decent enough, not without breeding at least; thank God he didn't look common or deformed! And his eyes gazed straight out, the woolly brows might not be fashionable but the girls didn't seem to mind. The girls! My word, they had multiplied! Jewel was one of them. He called her his "best girl." He couldn't resist a fatuous little smirk—which luckily he knew was fatuous. So now he had a harem! Back and forth he paced in the hall, pausing sometimes to light his cigar, which he only pretended to smoke. Actually, none of the girls could stand the cigar. But my, how it pleased him after all these years to light up in the house! Instead of skulking out to the porch to have his smoke. No, let's face it: he wouldn't let her pull any more of her tricks, her horrendous bullying. If a female doesn't finally get the point, figure out who pays the bills, who is boss, then she ought to have her head examined. Well, for chrissakes, what did Nanine think would happen if she had actually stormed out? She could kiss the good life good-bye! And imagine—she had threatened to pick him clean like a buzzard! What rot! Well, he supposed he might have given her something, he didn't plan on behaving like a scoundrel; of course there is no way he would have parted with either of the Brown family establishments. She could have settled in New Jersey or somewhere. No point sticking around here; they hadn't even wanted to ask her to the Simmses' ball! Everyone planned to go. The fact remained: if she wanted all the jewels and dinner invitations she'd better take him as he was. Toe the line. After all, it wasn't as if he had cheated her out of a wonderful sex life—heavens! She had gone cold on that years ago! Hell, he had even needed to beg for it! To beg from both of them! Well, no more begging, nosiree! I'm master now! I'll do what I like around here, yes, and by God I will!

Out of the corner of his eye Dinwiddie caught a glimpse of a malevolent face staring, spying on him there enjoying his cigar: that hideous Lucy Cook! Gad—he would certainly get rid of her now that he was in charge, and rid them of that sly Chinaman as well. What had his darling Jewel tried to tell him? That the Chinaman was following him? But no, the child had too much imagination. But imagine the nerve of anyone spying on him in his own house! How dare she grin at me in that insinuating fashion—why, she is gloating, the old cat!

He heard Nanine approaching in the upstairs hall. Slowly and with a strange sort of deliberation, she began to descend the stairs. She looks quite good, he thought. In fact, he had not really looked at her in days; even so, through his fog of blissful well-being he did just notice, in this moment, that she looked rather good. She came closer, then stopped.

"What's that?" she said, sniffing.

"My cigar." The words rang out pleasantly in clear, manly tones. Might as well let her know. Nanine stood there a moment on the staircase, poised, but still he did not flinch. She waited; he supposed he ought to take notice of her costume, which sparkled and looked fluttery and pink, but then he thought, Let her wait.

"Put it out," she said suddenly.

He was taken aback by the tone. She had not dared to speak to him in that voice for weeks now.

"What do you mean, put it out?" He snorted. But it was a little snort for Dinwiddie was master now, he did not feel any particular need to roar. He caught another satisfying view of himself in the mirror and thought, My, how well that fellow is behaving in what must be a trying situation! Ah, but life was pleasant. It made him chuckle happily.

But now Nanine was there, just before his nose, he must notice her now. Truthfully, he did not at all like how she looked. And he had married her! Gad, how vivid she seemed, how blatant! All lit up like— But wait! And then he saw! My God, what was that she wore on her breast? But no—it couldn't be! The peacock! Pinned there triumphantly! Ah, could it be possible?

Madeleine would never have given it to her, would she? No! Why, they had never seen each other! He reeled, thinking on it. And how would Nanine even know the bird existed? For surely she had never seen it!

She could not have known it belonged to Madeleine, that I gave it to her . . . or did she? But then how did she get it from Madeleine? Madeleine would never betray me! And if it was possible, if she has found some way to sell my wife the bird, wouldn't she have flown with all the money? Is she scheming to flee from me even now? All this raced through his mind evilly, poisoning him, and Dinwiddie nearly swooned with the horror of it—of what he imagined. He looked again—yes! There it was! The exact same pavé diamond peacock, ah, he knew it well! But how? Dinwiddie fell back from his wife, gasping.

"Put it out," said Nanine again in that ringing, insistent tone. He was conscious of that same malevolent face, near the pantry door, leering at him; he thought he heard a lewd giggle. He did not stop to think but quietly turned; and Dinwiddie went out onto the porch and threw away his cigar.

PART
TWO

1981

14

AS THEY bring down the banners on a summer night, slowly, slowly, there is a moment in the sky, a pause, when the world is without light. There is sky, air, lagoon: in place of light there is only atmosphere itself, suspended, gentle, undisturbed. Here, just before dark, the mists blow in from the sea—languorous, indolent, blown by idle clouds.

One July evening, a Venetian count, Alvise Priolio Dal Bezo, known to the world as Lalo, made his way through the piazzetta, stopping for a moment to sniff the desultory Venetian air. Lalo sighed deeply; he spotted a beautiful woman.

Jewel noticed the count. His tragic air and intent surveillance of the basilica interested her. He was sleek and handsome with a touch of poetic gloom—exactly the sort of rare being one hoped to see in foreign places. Just then a beggar passed and the count drew from his purse a crisp five-thousand-lira note. The man's gratitude seemed to sadden him. Jewel felt sure it pained him to part with the money. The count gazed freely at Jewel; Lalo never tired of admiring a beautiful woman. His

frank admiration seemed harmless enough—but if he
thought to engage her in a flirtation he was mistaken.
Jewel gazed past him into the basilica with its cupolas
nestling down like camels crouched against the night,
dim in this absent light, glinting dully here and there
with crushed glass, and she thought how glad she was to
be free. Still, the count stared; he seemed to be waiting.
Suddenly the mists vanished, quickly drawn into the sea.
Lalo seemed pleased by her astonishment and smiled his
sorrowful smile as if to say, You see! After all, these little
moments of harmless ecstasy will pass away. Then he,
too, turned away from her. She stared after him as he
vanished into Piazza San Marco, waited, then wandered
toward Riva Degli Schiavoni to lose herself in the throng
of holiday people strolling along the quay.

It amused the count to stop a moment and bend his
knee in that corner of the basilica lit for vespers with the
sour little red-eyed, mean-eyed glass lamps swaying in
the gloom. Not to pray, he didn't believe in that, but it
would not hurt to breathe in the pious hush; then, triumphant over the sepulcher, issue forth to greet the night.
He positioned himself at the front of the basilica where
a thrilling azure light came leaping out from sullen
greens and silent inward-folding grays, while higher up
the angels and a languid lion lifted arduous marble
wings from the azure bed of stars. Higher still, a thousand leaping lights came falling down from rich sapphire
blues, from golden stones and emeralds, from carnelians
and rubies and the soft old rubbed marbles of Byzan-
tium.

Now in the descending night the sky is deepened to a
pool of blue. In the piazza, in the hundreds of stone
colonnades above and below, and in the arches so solemnly redundant, the lamps are lit. Above each arch two
tapers reach slender arms to light the night while below,

within the arches, the globes are lit, one echoing the other like descending moons. Within the arches, sails: billowing cloth filled with shadows. As a child Lalo came here with his grandfather Dal Bezo, a terrible and ancient buzzard, a cackling predator who stalked Venice with his ebony cane looking for some worthy adversary. The old man called the sails "Il drago di San Giorgio!"— the Dragon!—and poked at them so that the wings flew out, filled with shadowy wriggling light, then came swooping down onto Lalo, who clung to that withered ancestral palm. Again the wings puffed out and out slowly, then collapsed to earth. A ghostly hiss, the weak fluttering as, not quite slain, the dragon breathed his last. Who could pass by the curtains of San Marco and remain unmoved? thought Lalo. Was there any more satisfying consolation for the horror of life than the vision of San Marco for even the beggars to see? The count suddenly felt desolate as he remembered. Beggars! How was it possible that such as he, scion of a grand race, cultured, flawless in appearance and breeding, should be reduced through absolutely no fault of his own to poverty and degradation? Why, only this afternoon he had been forced to haggle—*haggle*—in a haberdashery for the first time in his life with the lowest of merchants over the price of a dozen lisle socks. The impertinent man snatched back the socks and demanded his money on the spot. Since his father had died several months ago Lalo had tasted bitter insults from his creditors, rude remarks from his lady friends, and even rancor from his mistress, who despised him for his poverty and demanded he return her latchkey.

This was only the beginning. Earlier in the day he met with his attorney, DiCicci, who had the impudence to suggest his client find employment. At fifty-nine! He had never worked in his life—the outrage! No one had

treated his father this way. DiCicci persisted: what other
means had Lalo to sustain himself? As he crossed the
piazza and turned in under the columned arches of the
Procuratie Nuove he kicked at a pigeon in his path and
searched out some distraction in the shuttered shops.
What riches: icy aquamarines waiting in the dark, tour-
malines, topaz, pink sapphires, smoldering garnets
awaiting the fat finger, black pearls, ropes of coral and
lapis lazuli for the well-fed neck. Here, too, the lamps
were lit, dusty amethyst teardrops of old Venetian glass.
It was his own recently departed father who had cast
him out. His father and that foul hussy, the contessa, had
ruined him. Lalo gave himself up to the full horror of it,
and thinking of all he had lost, he wept a few tears in the
arcade and groaned out loud.

Lalo's father, Aloysious Alvise, the old Count Priolio
Dal Bezo, had been killed in an extraordinary fashion.
He sat one day in the last pew of the apse in that hunch-
backed dowager of Venetian churches, Santa Maria della
Salute, lost in angry dreams. The old count went to
church on occasion, but did not sit closer to God than
absolutely necessary. He was in the most voluptuous
part of his dream (the mass, which he slept through,
being long over) when an iron pineapple hanging some
forty feet above in the dim recesses of the apse and filled
with watery, evilly twinkling lights burst its threadbare
iron chain and plunged straight down with vicious ve-
locity, irresistibly drawn to the nodding, stertorous skull
of the count, who was instantly and ignominiously
crushed as though his life were absolutely irrelevant. It
was not exactly a shameful end to die in church at age
seventy-nine, yet for a Priolio Dal Bezo such an exit
seemed disgraceful. Far better, said those who knew him,
a death by pistol or sword!

The cause of Lalo's present embarrassments was the

old count's widow, the Contessa Priolia Dal Bezo, a
woman much younger than her husband. It was well
known that she had loathed the old count and stayed
away from him, maintaining a villa nearby in Asolo. The
moment her husband died, however, she descended on
Venice and took possession of the family palazzo on the
Grand Canal.

Her presence there was intolerable—not just because
Lalo refused to leave his apartment on the top floors of
Palazzo Prioli but because once, shortly after her arrival
in Venice as his father's bride ten years ago, Lalo had
attempted a seduction. With any other woman it might
have worked, but this woman was a monster. She was
ravishing, the contessa, and clearly the old man had revolted her. It broke Lalo's heart to see the young bride
languishing. What could be more natural than to comfort her? He had been so sure she desired him that he
crept into her room late one night. A fiend waited there
for him! Lalo shuddered to remember it. The woman had
hurled herself at his head, bit and clawed him. And of
course she betrayed him to his father. The old man was
beside himself. This had been ten years ago. Aloysious
Alvise swore he would strike his son from the will but
in fact no one believed him. An only son! The two lived
together in the same house for a decade, father and son
on separate floors, and never spoke a word. Occasionally
the old count visited his wife in Asolo, but the contessa
was rarely seen in Venice. Aloysious Alvise blamed his
son for the failure of his marriage. It had been his ardent
wish to sire a new son and although the contessa did her
duty and swallowed any disgust she might feel, no child
was forthcoming. The contessa had every reason to do
her duty, for without an heir she was at risk of losing
everything upon the old count's death.

The contessa became a figure of great interest in Ven-

ice. No one knew where she came from, though there
were many rumors: perhaps she was a Hungarian of low
birth or the illegitimate daughter of Tartars, or Cossacks,
or even gypsies. Or maybe she was a Polish Jewess, sent
into the concentration camps as a young girl, where she
had been used, people said, as a whore. The old count
found her in Bavaria, where he went to take the cure—
nothing short of dropsy could remove the count from
Venice. He knew nothing of her, except that she was
beautiful, more beautiful than any woman he had ever
seen before. The count had a great weakness for beauty.
The only thing known about the contessa was that she
was penniless when Aloysious Alvise found her.

Neither Lalo nor his father had left Venice more than
twice. These voyages into the outside world had not
proved successful. The first, in both cases, had been to
England, where each was sent at the proper time to
acquire an education, but this did not take. Both fled
almost immediately. More recently the younger Priolio
traveled to Bologna in pursuit of a lady and the father
had gone to Bavaria but this so upset the two Priolios
they determined never to venture abroad again. There-
after, they might be seen in Venice, father and son, always separate but occupying themselves similarly:
taking a coffee, walking about, pausing for an *aperitivo*,
reading a newspaper, smoking a cigarette. They each
enjoyed a good risotto, a *fegato con polenta*, a Carpaccio
(both the meat and the artist, though the meat was better), and a perfect peach. The old count enjoyed stopping
a moment to exchange some pleasant nonsense with Baronne Ruspoli or young Sforza; the younger Priolio
flirted with the baronne as well, old as she was, and with
her daughter, too. On the appropriate occasions father
and son could be seen emerging from Fenice or Teatro
Malibran pleasantly dazed by Wagner or an imported

ballet. Occasionally the contessa joined her husband and before all Venice they seemed amiable, nodding, pausing to say some word to an acquaintance.

The sexual feats of the younger Priolio were a great source of continuing animosity between the old count and his son. It almost seemed God created the son to spite the father and shame him, so numerous were the conquests of the dashing Lalo. The father had been known to indulge in an occasional peccadillo but finally he thought sex a squalid middle-class preoccupation, not at all nice, an embarrassment in fact, perpetrated on the Italian male by a misbegotten code of Italian honor. Why couldn't something like stamp collecting, for instance, be just as sustaining to the Italian honor?

Until the son came along to disprove everything, nobody bothered about whether Aloysious Alvise's exploits were real or fictitious. In Venice it is the discussion of these *faits*, more than the deed itself, that pleases one's friends so much. The old count kept up an amiable façade of intrigue; terrible things were said about him, hints of bacchanalias and delightful perversions, which pleased the count. Of late, however, the son eclipsed the father.

There was no one in Venice who had not heard by now the story of Lalo's seduction of his stepmother. (Venice generally agreed he must have succeeded.) For this, and his other numerous amorous exploits, Lalo was petted and much adored; all Venice seemed enchanted by the intrigues of this dashing lover. The old man, a fool for disinheriting his son in favor of a foreigner, had no doubt deserved his ignominious death.

Now the question remained, Who would gain control of Palazzo Prioli and the small inheritance? The old count left his affairs in a muddle and no one knew exactly what remained. The villa in Asolo had been put up for sale. The entire Prioli property, however, was heavily entailed by debts. Lalo could not imagine what the contessa lived on. Perhaps she sold off a few dingy tiaras. In the meantime, he himself had parted with everything not absolutely hammered down—that is, everything his father had not already sold. It had become a familiar sight over the years to see either Priolio hurrying to the antiques dealer with ormolu clocks poking out from under his overcoat. What would Lalo and his stepmother live on once the clocks ran out? It was said the young count, who, after all, at fifty-nine was not so young, would rather swab out bathrooms at Florian Caffé than part with this last specter of Prioli honor, the sinking, rotting palazzo.

Without money, neither of them could keep the place afloat. The count feared that his stepmother would find some way to sell the place before he could somehow claim it as his own. The contessa had taken possession of the two lower floors and seemed to view the entire palazzo as hers. Though it had been in the family keep for five hundred years, she had recently put it up for sale. All Venice waited to see what would happen next. The contessa, it was said, was on the lookout for an American, but they proved scarce of late.

15

THE MUSICIANS arrived in Piazza San Marco, stubbed out their cigarettes, found their places. It was just nine. After the sluggish day, the cafés came alive with pumping, beckoning music. A flux of damp bodies pressed in at the sidewalk tables, squeezing into the florid little rooms at Florian's to devour whipped cream concoctions in the awful heat. The count could not pass Florian's without peeking in; however tiresome his existence, it would not do to be seen skulking in the passageways. He felt a wonderful allure in the little burnished coffee rooms tucked in under the Procuratie Nuove. Their slim glass doors opened out invitingly to the flow of excited people streaming past in the arcade. As a child Lalo had stolen in to peek at the fat ladies painted on the ceilings, languishing on clouds, pressed beneath glass like swooning hothouse flowers. The air seemed enticing here, he had always felt it so—the lingering sighs, the murmurings in foreign tongues, the assignations and love affairs—and he sucked it in gratefully as he surveyed the crowd. And in that dingy twilight of old Venetian glass it seemed to Lalo nothing bad could happen, that these

people were figurines in marzipan tucked within a sugared egg. For a brief hilarious moment his hopes returned.

The count scanned the crowd with a practiced eye. A
black girl eating ice cream rolled her pink tongue around
the spoon. Was she looking at him? At a nearby table an
old man with frightened eyes watched his life slip away
in tiny gasps between sips of coffee. Two adversaries, a
man and a woman, fought desperately, bitterly, in whispers. In the arcade a moron made ecstatic faces. Middle-
aged ladies glanced about, smiling bravely. Lumpy,
blank-faced virgins, and young men with murderous
glances—what had these creatures to do with him? He
could not imagine what it meant to be ordinary and exist
in this pool of communal fates. He was separate, rare!
Could anything be more ridiculous than hoping for some
sign of appreciation from this crowd? Disgusted, he had
turned to leave when suddenly he spotted the face of the
American woman he had seen earlier. He knew her for
an American; she had that rapt, transparent joy peculiar
to a certain type of American female. She seemed nothing like the others, he saw it immediately. He hoped she
might notice him, but she was absorbed by the crowd.
He looked on with amusement as she sought a place
among the tables spilling out onto San Marco. When she
found a table she appeared delighted. Surely there was
something imbecilic in so much pleasure so easily found.
What did it mean? But she was adorable, so unlike the
shellacked and armored ladies he knew; he thought her
absurdly unguarded and unsophisticated. An innocent?
No, he did not believe in innocence.

Small squeaks: the violins were warming up, now the
cello, the clarinet. The American glanced his way. She
seemed startled, he saw it, then she looked away quickly.
Lalo felt a small rush of pleasure and decided to stay.

Perhaps she would signal him to join her. For some
moments she refused to look but at last he found her
scrutinizing him—her eyes sped from the glossy wing-
tip shoes straight up to the wavy hair. Did she smirk? She
looked away. Indifferent? The outrage! To be passed
over like a stone column—by an American!

In fact, Lalo was a wonderful specimen of the aging
Italian male. In this crowd he felt certain he must be
noticed for he had placed himself beneath the caressing
light of a moon-globe lamp under an archway where
contorting nudes and drowsy scowling lions framed his
slight figure beguilingly. Although slender and not very
tall, he was perfectly proportioned, not unlike a small
but exquisite warrior, a Praxiteles or a Donatello. He
had thick wavy gray hair, which he wore slightly rumpled and long in the manner of a famous symphony
conductor. Women liked to dangle their fingers in this
marvelous mound of hair. The eyes had a candid tristesse
that spoke to women as well. Of course he had the Venetian nose, remarkable for its historic length, size, and
passionate, always flared nostrils. Lalo's best features,
however, were the aristocratic hands and feet: the taper-
ing square-cut toes, each one perfectly carved, the graceful ankles and marmoreal arches, slim but muscular
calves, and the wonderful long fingers of David. The
count was not a little vain about his anatomy. His con-
temporaries, so beefy and grizzled, had all succumbed to
the elements while Lalo's skin had softened to the tex-
ture of fine parchment, faintly creased, as in rare manuscripts.

He wore his new suit, a dashing mole-gray linen collected from the tailor's that very afternoon, and a pale
lilac shirt, lilac socks. Surely she must see him. Other
ladies passed by, he knew, more than once, to shoot him
excited glances. He could not think why he stayed. She

was luscious, sweet-faced, but not at all his type. There was even something slightly askew, a bruised quality in the angle of her features, and yet something determined, too. He had seen that in the once-over she gave him; a fierceness, sudden and unpredictable, just as babies and animals are unpredictable—snoozing, scratching their bellies in one moment, and howling out wildly the next. The image excited him. He noted a willful set to the jaw, but also something unsure. A young man stopped at her table and introduced himself to her with a bow. She drew back as if bitten by a snake.

Lalo guessed her to be thirty-five, although she could have been younger and in fact was older. Slim, girlish, taller than he, she wore jeans, a soft white shirt, and a wide belt of fine old Indian conchos. Her bare feet were strapped in sandals. Her hair, a soft, loose baby blond, fell away from her face in curls. He was not fooled by the little smile; and felt sure she must be exciting, perhaps even wild. He had been told again and again that he was a great judge of women.

Lalo watched as she leaned to say something to the waiter.

"Alfredo," said Jewel, "do you think it will rain?"

"Ah, signorina—I hope not."

"In Arizona we *pray* for rain!"

Alfredo shook his head as he walked away.

I'll miss the summer rains in Dragoon this year, Jewel thought. How odd—alone in Venice in a rented room. In a few months I will be forty. How shall I fill up the rest of my life?

The music began, a waltz, and at the first scritching of violins Jewel was swept away. Now the gasp, the wheeze of an accordion, now the startled clarinet; falling away, farther out, good-bye the old stopping places, endlessly out and out, falling away from that tight circle of a solitary existence, joined, safe now. How leaping this music, how it whirls me away!

One day Jewel followed a man without knowing why. An American. She had been in Venice for a few weeks. She met no one, spoke only to the waiters and the concierge. The man must have been about forty, he had a dreaming face, he made his way smoothly through the crowds in a white summer suit surrounded by a silence. Up and down bridges and through the narrow streets, she followed him in the noonday heat. Was it that she hoped he would turn at last and recognize her? Say, there you are! I have been looking for you everywhere!

Why had she chosen Venice? It was as far away from her world as she could go.

Everything he looked at she looked at, too. People passed, nudged by gusts of wind. Here is the curious thing: his every gesture seemed familiar. He had the habit of touching walls, of trailing his fingers along the glass of shop fronts as she did, then stopping before a blank wall for a moment to stare at nothing. The idea of a stranger being exactly like her thrilled Jewel. She recognized him! She even imagined that no one else ever had—because no one had ever recognized her. How was it he did not notice her?

Sometimes, alone in her room, Jewel thought she might go mad without those things that had anchored her to reality: dog, horse, cow, Johnnie and Dinwiddie, even Granma Lou and Aunt Nanine. Mountain, sky, earth, the desert—and now what? What if reality is nothing more than feeding the cat—and there is no cat?

It was lovely at first to escape the crushing realness of that other world, to exist out of a suitcase. She outfitted her room at the Palazzo del Giglio with two Bolivian ponchos slung over an armoire, and with photographs of the three men in her life, Dinwiddie, Johnnie, and her

father. She could not bring herself even to look at her
paints. A pile of books. A vase of outrageously beautiful
flowers seeping a heady perfume bewitched her belongings, soaked the walls and the sheets with their fra-
grance, so that she awakened in the mornings dazed,
almost stupid with unreconcilable yearnings. Her solitude was torture. She had never been so alone. Yet each
day that she survived, a deeper and more excruciating
awareness filled her with joy, and with fear, as though
something long buried inside would fly out now that she
was far from home.

More and more, Jewel felt her solitude growing into
something marvelous. Yesterday in the crushing heat she
crossed the lagoon to the island of Torcello and sat in a
gravel garden bordered by delphinium, and tall swaying
cosmos filled with bees, and gladiolus dazed with heat.
She lunched on crusty golden gnocchi and cold beans,
narrow as shoelaces, wriggling in a pool of olive oil and
lemon seeds. White butterflies darted up from the
smooth white pebbles in the noonday heat. All around
her families lunched in the sunshine. How settled and
complete they seemed, these thin brown women wearing violet glasses, with their necks wound in gold, their
long arms, long brown hands with quick fingers, ruby
nails, ruby rings, flashing in the heat like dangerous butterflies. The men, the children, families—the stunning
order, all in balance, all complete.

Suddenly it grew late. The women began to drip and
scowl. Their faces drooped, the dazzling fingers fell back
into laps like listless fish. In the kitchen the hired help
knocked kettles about in resignation. Jewel heard the
drone of dissent, a whirring of disgruntled servants beating the air with grievances. Plates of fish soured in the
heat. The children laid their heads to weep in puddles of
spilled cream and melting meringue swans, while the

men, purple with wine, called out loudly for the check.
Alone at her table Jewel felt absurdly happy.

JEWEL LOOKED up at Lalo. How could she miss him in his
new summer suit? She was the kind of person who always noticed things. Her uncle Dinwiddie used to say,
if there was a pervert in the supermarket four aisles
away, crouching down behind the canned pineapples,
Jewel would know he was there. The count offered up
his profile and Jewel chuckled out loud. Who does he
think he is, Cesar Romero?

"The signorina is happy?" said Alfredo the waiter.
"This is good. There is no other reason, I think, to come
to Venice, no?"

"Do you know, Alfredo, I really began to think I came
here to be sad. In private, you know."

"In private?" He was horrified. "But why would the
signorina choose to be sad?"

Jewel smiled at him almost tenderly. "You're right.
Why *would* anyone choose to be sad? Well, then, perhaps
I have come here to be transformed."

"Ah! *Transformata! Naturalmente!*" cried the waiter.
"Venice is good for this! But, signorina, you must take
good care never to look down into *la laguna.* Do you
remember how it was when the *imperatore,* he came to
conquer us?"

"What emperor?" asked Jewel.

"The Imperator Napoleone! You see, signorina, all the
ships who came before was lost, the sailors, you see, they
was—how you say it?—*ipnotizzato*—"

"Hypnotized!" said Jewel.

"*Sì, ipnotizzato.* They look down and what you think
they see? They see a *miracolo!* Sailors, *sì,* but not like
before. Transform-ed, beautiful sailors, *sì,* signorina!

And then they lose their way! So the Imperator Napole-one, he hear all about these famous lost sailors and *la laguna* and he say he come here to see. But Napoleone, he's very smart, see." Alfredo tapped the side of his nose and winked. "He is the *imperator*! He never look down; he look always to the sky. *Allora,* we was conquer-ed, signorina. The sky is the same sky here as everywhere. If you look up you can find your way. But the others, they forget to look, they look-ed down, so they was lost!"

"Lost?" said Jewel.

"*Sì!* You must remember, signorina, always look to the sky!"

Lalo began to lose hope. It grew late and he wanted his dinner. As he walked away he glanced back one last time. She had given her whole attention to the evening sky across which now in the deepening night a single star was seen to stray. He had forgotten about her by the time he reached the far side of the piazza. His only regret, if he had one, was that she had not noticed his new summer suit.

16

JEWEL STOOD alone in the entryway to the arbor called
Locanda Montin and endured the wary gaze of the pro-
prietress for some moments before she was seated. The
waiter beckoned and Jewel followed him through a lat-
ticed tunnel of soft green branches whose blue flowers
dripped down over the diners' heads. The arbor was
surrounded by high red walls banded in green—the
chalky, disappearing reds and alkaline greens of old clay
pots. The evening air felt moist with the sticky perfume
of ripe figs.

Two broad aisles ran the distance of the arbor. Here
beneath flowering oleanders the tables had been placed
near one another in congenial groupings, like conver-
sants in a country play. Jewel was seated at a table directly opposite that of the count, who slowly,
meticulously dissected a peach. He saw her immediately:
the slim figure in narrow jeans, her easy walk which
rustled the arbor like a hot wind. He watched as she
came straight toward him, looked him dead in the eye,
flushed, then looked away.

It felt too awkward to ask for another table but Jewel

could barely endure his gaze. He was horrid, she decided. Far too handsome, smug, bristling with a nasty
monkeylike curiosity. She had never seen a man polished
to such a shine.

Jewel had a warlike response to admiration, if indeed
this was admiration. She did not feel receptive to lingering glances from strange men. When some watery old
man hissed at the sight of her, Jewel shot him a look so
ferocious he froze in his tracks. She did not imagine that
she was beautiful. Determined not to look across the way
again, she occupied herself with a family of baby cats
rolling in the aisle, snatching at their shadows or at any
little offering of a fish head or some juicy gristle.

For dessert, Jewel ordered figs. The waiter led her by
the hand through a small gate in the red wall and into
a wild little garden. Jewel held the ladder while Gino,
tender-eyed, with a beautiful oval head, shimmied up
and disappeared over the wall. The fig tree smelled of
ants and summer. Jewel remembered Dragoon, the air so
sweet with the thick sickish smell of ants, beetles, June
bugs, and grasshoppers that it sometimes turned yellow
in the heat. But this was nothing like that wild place at
the edge of the world with yellow air and flat hot skies.
Her eyes filled. Gino reappeared with three pale-green
figs.

He gently peeled them for her and served them in a
saucer of thick cream. They left her feeling soothed and
dreamy, until the count at last approached her table, sat
down, and signaled to Gino to bring a carafe of wine. He
took no notice of her protest, seemed amused by her
furious looks, and continued to speak in a gliding, lazy
monologue.

Why was she here? Did she plan to stay? She must be
rich. Was there a husband in the picture? An *ex*-hus-
band? How many? A lover? *No* lover! Did she dislike

men? He had heard that in America it was currently fashionable to dislike men.

Jewel was amused in spite of herself, and every moment or two his eyes would droop at her in the funniest way so that, against her will, she felt pulled into his spell. She felt too shy to say much and he did not seem very interested in her answers. If she muttered some dissent he flowed over her, his words coming out like oiled pebbles, scattering her thoughts. Her most sincere responses amused him most of all. These he tossed aside with loud happy snorts. Her less than truthful replies he snatched at eagerly, for he laid traps and challenged her in low, insinuating tones. Jewel felt the earth around her was laid with mines; she must leap and keep moving or suddenly be blown to pieces.

"But you say almost nothing!" he said, seeming to notice her reticence for the first time. "Is it that you do not like me? Or perhaps it is all Venetians you despise. Are you shy? No, I think not. I think you are not at all shy but that it suits some false idea of virtue to pretend some dislike."

"You don't understand anything about it," she said, and signaled for the check.

"How old do you think I am?" he asked.

"Oh, quite old!" she tossed back. As she gave the money to Gino she noticed she was charged for his carafe of wine. But it gave her a sense of power to pay for it. "Look here, I'm not at all interested in how old you are, so if you please—" Again that terrible low chuckle and the eyes drooped.

"Closer—" he leaned across the table toward her, almost whispering, "closer to fifty? Or to sixty? What do you think—eh? Tell the truth. I am not so terrible-looking, you think? No? Very well—I am fifty-two! Not so bad—eh?" he declared, paring off the last seven years.

"Look, I'm really not interested—"

"There is nothing more interesting than age. Ah! You make a face! I will tell you something—you are afraid!" he said.

Jewel stood to go. "I'm not afraid," said Jewel. She moved away from him quickly and headed out the door. He followed behind.

"Afraid!" he said again. "See how you walk! And see, you refuse to look at the men. They like you, you know. Yes, yes, you *look* strong, you pretend this very well, but Lalo is not fooled." He slipped his hand under her arm, but she snatched it away.

"No one asked you to be fooled! Why don't you leave me alone? I never heard anything so ridiculous! You don't even know me, I tell you I *like* to be alone, I came here to be alone, do you understand?" But he steered her to the vaporetto stop. People passed by and stared at them. Women, Jewel noticed, glanced at them with soft, sly eyes. It was an outrage, preposterous the way he clung to her arm and insisted on attention. She had to admit he was not unattractive. Nanine would have swooned over him. He seemed very different from the sort of man she was used to. And he was an impostor, she felt sure of it, that little scene with the beggar the other night had been for her benefit, she knew it, not a single thing he had done or said seemed natural or easy or disinterested. He was full of contrivances and she was not impressed. He stood beside her and waited for the vaporetto. She felt a certain charm to the conversation, a Venetian splendor in his facade, a mirageous gleam, however fraudulent, in his glances. He pressed her to take a drink with him; she hesitated. Her anger had gone. The boat came thudding in at the dock. Keep your eye on the sky—was that what the waiter had said? She began to laugh out loud, she had nearly weakened. She leaped aboard the vaporetto and when she looked around he waited there, still with that impudent little smile.

WITHIN THE week the count discovered her name, her brief history in Venice, her hotel, and her habits. He did not have to move very strenuously; in Venice it is not difficult to find out what one's friends are doing—all life floats past in the Grand Canal.

She was a solitary creature, he learned, and this mystified him. It was her custom to position herself morning and evening at either end of the terrace at the Gritti Palace, near the gondolier station, where she was apparently lulled by the insistent half-amused, half-disgusted growlings of the gondoliers. He had spied her breakfasting in the fog; later, in that glittering blue hour when the hard light gives way to a leaping, fizzy twilight on the Grand Canal, he saw her dreaming eyes partway closed. Suddenly she produced a little notebook and jotted something down. He decided she must be very rich. After all, one didn't live in the Palazzo del Giglio for less than two hundred thousand lire a day. The Palazzo del Giglio, a *residenza*, was next door to the Gritti and owned by the hotel.

Lalo found himself rushing once or twice to catch the vaporetto that would carry him past the place where she sat. She never looked at him. He saw, even from a distance, that she seemed absorbed in the view of that dropping-off place at the edge of the world, the enchanted abyss between sea and sky—the Basin of San Marco, where for those who wait there might be seen a soft dancing in the basin, a rosy simulacrum of wavering towers, of drowsy lions and amethyst lamps, a listless swaying in the morbid heat of boats and palaces. And then, sliding out silently from behind the Salute and the golden Dogana, there comes a vast ship emerging from Giudecca like some horrendous mirage, a sluggish beast dragging herself into the basin to be swallowed down by the lagoon beyond. The lagoon! Placid and blue, flat in the heat and with marooned tankers moaning in the fog—the lagoon! And beyond the lagoon, invisible from here, yet waiting, dropping away at the edge of the world, the sea. He would have liked her to glance up and see him once, yet he admired her more for giving herself to the view.

One morning he appeared on the Gritti terrace. Jewel finished her breakfast at the far table and looked up as if sensing a disturbance in the air. It was early still, one of those clammy Venetian mornings when the fog clung in straying vapors to the awnings, and the air, filled with hot needles, gathered itself for an immense heat. The waiters lounging about with sly eyes, leaped to one side as the count sauntered past. Nothing about Lalo appeared very jocular in the early morning. He came straight at her as if he brought bad news.

"Well!" he exclaimed. "Are you finished with that?" As if they were old friends! He squinted down at the contents on her breakfast plate, then, not bothering about a response, said, "I am taking you to an island— you will like it, come! My boat, as you see, is here at the dock."

An elegant, highly polished, slope-back motorboat was bobbing, Jewel noticed, and gurgling at the Gritti dock. Beyond it, at the Traghetto, two gondoliers haggled over the fare with a flock of nuns, blackbirds all in a row, standing in a gondola. Jewel watched until they reached the far shore. She felt afraid of him.

"Come, come," the count said irritably. "None of these boring pruderies. We haven't time for all that, so come along, my dear." She managed a tight little laugh

but he saw her shrink back. "How stupid you are," he
said quietly, and sat down.

This had been her hiding place, beneath the lazy snap
of awnings holding back the fog. No one knew her here.

"I don't know what to say to you," said Jewel at last.
"You see, I came here to—"

"It doesn't matter why you came here," he said. Her
cheeks were flushed and hot. She looked angry but he
went on. "I know why you came—to hide. But the day
is so wonderful. Why don't you hide tomorrow?"

"What is it you want from me?" she blurted out.

"Aren't you behaving like a child?" he said to her. "Is
it so insulting to be asked out to be happy, to amuse
yourself for a few hours? Have you something better to
do? What is it you are afraid of?"

"I told you, I'm not afraid. I just want to be up front
about everything. I don't see what's wrong with that—"

"Up front? What is this?" he demanded.

"No fooling around. You know perfectly well what I
mean," said Jewel.

"My dear absurd American!" he cried happily.

Jewel was mortified. She saw it suddenly: he had not
thought of her in that way. A slow flush rose up her neck
and cheeks.

"I assure you," he continued in his most reasonable
tone, "I am not the least bit interested in *that*. We shall
leave your body undisturbed." He smiled. She looked,
just then, like a large child about to cry. "You are not at
all my type, you know—although it is true you have
splendid eyes," he continued. "A bit warlike perhaps,
but splendid, nonetheless. I have plenty of women—
more than I know what to do with."

Jewel said nothing. She wondered how it was she
ended up in these situations. He stood to go.

"Are you coming?" he said.

"But where are you going?" asked Jewel. The count turned and walked across the Gritti terrace, moving with a wonderful, slow grace. Sleek and gray—like a whippet. He stepped down into his boat. Suddenly, the thought of not seeing him again sent two slow tears rolling from her eyes. How flat the day, how long now! Her solitude, so sweet the day before, bore down on her as something unnatural.

Jewel leaped up and ran toward the boat. The count removed his linen jacket, folded it carefully inside out, lit a cigarette, and leaned to speak some word to the driver. He said nothing as Jewel stepped into the boat, did not glance at her, yet Jewel knew he was pleased. A moment later, still in silence, they churned away from the dock and headed out into the lagoon.

17

"I MUST warn you," said Lalo, "I do not live here alone."
He led Jewel up the damp staircase to Palazzo Prioli
from the sad inner courtyard, a mausoleum reeking of
cats. The sole ornament was a padlocked cistern, which
Jewel did not think very remarkable, but Lalo paused
here to wait for her opinion.

"She lives here, too, you know, my stepmother," he
continued. "But of course you know all about it, everyone does. She has made it the scandal of Venice."

"I don't know anything about your stepmother,"
Jewel said. They passed a large mahogany door bearing
a brass plate with the name PRIOLIO. Lalo jabbed two
fingers in the *cornuti* and said *"Putana!"* quite loudly as
they continued on to the top.

"You never heard anything?" he asked, turning to
scrutinize Jewel's face. "You must have heard something."

"I don't know anyone here!" she said. Lalo seemed
disappointed. "What's so terrible about her, anyway?"

He thought how pleasant it might be to enlist her
sympathy. He had nearly won her over, he could feel it.

She would not be so difficult after all, this one. In fact, he liked them a little more difficult.

"You see, I really am in terrible trouble," he began. They stood at the top of the staircase in the dark little landing. She couldn't see his face. "I don't like to mention these things," he said softly.

"No, please do," said Jewel.

"Well, then. You see, I have been robbed."

"Robbed!"

"Yes, by my stepmother. She has robbed me of my birthright, of this palazzo, of everything."

"Are you sure?" said Jewel.

He stamped his foot and shouted, "*Sure?* Of course I'm sure. Do you think Lalo doesn't know when he's being robbed? Sure!"

"Lalo, I am so sorry!"

"To be dispossessed!" said Lalo. Jewel felt unsure what to do. This was an altogether different man from the one she had seen so far. He had been delightful this morning, playful, mischievous, teasing her; she had no idea he could be this sensitive, and vulnerable.

The morning had been so fine. He took her to Isola dei Armeni, where a young Armenian friar rushed down to the dock to greet their boat and escort them through the monastery. Jewel was enchanted. This was the Venice she yearned to see. In the library they lingered over the rare manuscripts and Lalo entertained her with wonderful stories, referring now and then to his own books, the Prioli collection. A friar brought them glasses of sugared tea and saucers of a delicious marmalade, a nectar of crushed white roses dripping in honey and made only once a year by the friars.

Lalo fumbled over the keys at his door and Jewel's apprehension returned. She felt like saying she couldn't

go in, that she was ill. He opened the door and smiled at
her strangely.

"Will you come in?" An icy gasp of air ushered her
into the entry hall, a large unhappy chamber in which
their footsteps reverberated.

The count did not put on the light so Jewel followed
close behind until they reached a larger salon, where
Lalo drew back soiled and very old pea velvet curtains
gathered here and there with tattered epaulets of gold
braid. The heavy gold fringe scampered along the bottom when pulled open, like mice on frozen marble. Bubbled glass and half-parted shutters admitted a weak pink
light. Far below in the Grand Canal, Jewel heard the
churning of boats.

"Shall I show it to you?" he asked softly. Jewel stared.
"My house—shall I show you?" He switched on the huge
chandelier, indecently bright, sagging toward the
ground under a pink and white burden of glass flowers.
The display over, Lalo switched off the light.

The room was bare except for a sofa near the windows,
a faded old thing of mouse-colored velvet, and a couple
of gilt end tables placed at various far outposts next to
the occasional stranded chair. Also, a marble coffee table,
bereft of ornament, and a bookcase with several old and
very beautiful books which Jewel examined. On the
walls hung two fine old engravings of Venice and the
lagoon. Lalo waited for her to say something. Now she
felt she understood—and how much nicer he seemed to
her in his poverty.

"I think your house is wonderful," she said. "And I
think you are wonderful, too."

"Come," said Lalo. He looked pleased. She followed
him down a long hallway. Jewel glimpsed a bed and had
a quick hilarious image of herself rolling here with the

count. Again she felt repelled by some unsaid feeling
toward the man. It seemed extraordinary to find herself
here, closed in—with a stranger, with someone of an
altogether different species. She was a creature of the
earth, of open places. And he was human. He turned and
looked at her.

"Are you afraid?" he said, and held out his hand.

"Afraid?"

He heard the indignation and smiled. Jewel followed
him into the bathroom and Lalo said, "Here it is! The
room of which I am most proud—see, very modern, no?"
He pointed to the pink marble sink. She saw his tooth-
brush.

"Would you like a *douche*?" he asked. "*Un bagno?*"

"No," said Jewel firmly, "I would not."

"But it is so *hot*!" Lalo smiled.

"Well, I'm not hot," said Jewel. The bathroom felt
humid, close, with a slit of light high up in the smooth
slippery pink marble wall. Everything was that same
intense cloying pink. It made her think of sickening secrets. Lalo stared at her. Suddenly he seemed to press
close. This pink reminded her of hopeless hot afternoons
in Granma Slade's terrible pink stucco house in Tucson,
interminable summer days swatting flies; a drunken fizz
of summer flies hissing around Granma—that and
Granma's thick rubber girdle, pink, too, and scary.

"Are you feeling ill?" he asked her. These Americans—did they want you to seduce them or not?

"I don't know," she said, "maybe I ate something
funny." Her voice squeaked oddly inside her head. They
had left her alone with Granma and the old woman died
suddenly. Out she passed from the bright afternoon like
the sudden cessation of a small irksome squeak.

"How do you say it? I won't bite!" He laughed,
touched her arm, she sprang back. He said something,

she saw his teeth, the lips. Granma's mouth wetly sliding across her face. Pressed to the glass like a fish in a tank, drowning in lousy memories. A last gassy sigh: how pathetic it is, dying.

"Tell me then what you want," he said, wondering at her queasy face. "You won't let me tempt you?"

"I don't want a bath," said Jewel, who pushed past him and out the door.

"You are tired," he said, "and cross. Like a child. Go, wait for me there. I will bring you a sweet. Do you take coffee?" Jewel found her way to the salon and collapsed on the sofa.

How smooth here and dim, she thought, this marble room! Cool and gray: an oyster shell. A stray slant of jittery light stole between the shutters. Far below in the Grand Canal, boats and high young voices. A day at the sea, mused Jewel, rocking into sleep. Young girls and boys screaming in the heat. Somewhere a clock ticks. Nearby, the rush of water. Slowly it came, pieces of the past floating downstream, in and out of fitful sleep, the debris catching here and there. Jewel dreamed: this time I shall be found—the note is sent. The bottle is sent to sea, it waits only to be found.

"YOU HAVE been weeping!" said Lalo. How long had he been standing there with that rattling tiny cup of coffee?

He was quite naked except for a pair of white boxer shorts. He had showered, his hair was slicked down and still damp. Jewel said nothing.

"You don't have to look away," he teased as he handed her the coffee. He looked pleased with himself. "For myself I am never bothered by these things. And you see, it is too hot! Don't you agree it is hot?"

Still Jewel said nothing. She thought of walking to the door but this seemed foolish.

"In any event, I am not planning to devour you," said Lalo, who swallowed his coffee in one gulp, then sank down next to her. "But perhaps you are disappointed? What a face you make! Who can understand you Americans? What a pity. You see, unfortunately I am quite swept away by you!"

"No you're not," said Jewel.

He was fascinated. She would *not* be wooed. He lit a cigarette. Perhaps this one liked to do it on the ground. Should he grab her neck by the teeth and attempt to carry her off? Yes, this she would like. He watched her closely. There was nothing civilized about these New World women with their checkbooks, their charge-card tickets around the world with stops everywhere. He began to understand. Here was a woman who would be mortified by the peeling away of socks and shoes but a gallop across the plain with some sweaty beef of a cowboy, lewd noises, the stink of horseflesh, scorpions under the rocks, this is what she liked. He curled his lip thinking about it.

"Well, are you going to sit there in your underwear?" said Jewel at last.

Lalo stubbed out his cigarette and crossed his knees; as he did so one long elegant thigh touched her leg.

"Would it seem too strange," he said, "if we were to lie here together for a little while? Oh, just to sleep a moment, nothing more."

"Go ahead," said Jewel. "Suit yourself."

The count stretched himself out as if this were the most natural posture in the world. The top of his head, gray, wavy, pushed against Jewel's leg. She detected a whiff of pomade. Lalo, stretched out like a cadaver, slept. Jewel sat with her hands in the skirt of her damp linen

dress and sweated quietly, deeply, like a housemaid waiting to be interviewed for a position.

DID ANYONE *ever tell you you look like a hibiscus? said Johnnie
in the garden one day. He smiled and reached to take a leaf or
an ant, something from her hair. And the light is coming
through your ear, said Johnnie, there at the back. Your ear is
filled with red and gold fire.*

*They had lain down in the grass there where the blue plum-
bago and the mound of sweet peas trailed along the earth in a
fragrant tangle and the delphinium and the fresh, stiff young
hollyhocks were just poking through. The banana trees, the hibiscus, and shallow young limes fluttering tender new leaves. Have
you ever loved anyone, I mean really loved? he asked, but she
hadn't let him take away her clothes. I have only loved you, he
said, but she had not believed him.*

AT LAST, nearly suffocating, Jewel slid away. Lalo was
flung out stiffly, he really appeared to sleep. She looked
down at him a moment and decided she pitied him. She
felt something heartbreaking in that neat little body all
stretched out. Jewel stood a moment, undecided. His
breath came in slow static whispers. His feet, sticking
out over the tense arms of the sofa like the Mantegna feet
of Christ, were perfect.

Jewel wandered through the salon examining the tables, the few objects too ugly to sell, a portrait of an
ancestor—a minor canon in the church too insignificant
to be sold; if he had been a doge he would be gone by
now. Lalo watched. Her pacing gratified him deeply. If
she had come to him, soothed him, stroked his spine with
gentle caresses, how he would have hated her. She was
struggling, she still might slip away. In one sense the

outcome did not even matter. This struggle is what he liked. She would have secrets; slowly she would part with them, weepy confessions, they all did. Little indiscretions—he would listen.

In the hall mirror Jewel examined herself. Is this really how I look? Am I this person? Like a field, I feel overplanted with too many seasons of corn and cotton. Now I want to lie fallow, then begin again. Perhaps as a field of almond trees.

She saw he watched her. Now he stole from behind and lifted the mass of damp curling apricot hair and placed his lips on her neck to savor the shudder. She was shocked by how sad she felt. She had forgotten the terrible sadness that precedes desire. He looked into her eyes with something she knew to be hatred. Lalo pulled open the front of her dress. In the mirror, Jewel watched.

18

August 15, 1981
Venice

"Darlings—

"Today I am happy! Last night it rained. The world is clean again. Big sobbing clouds, lightning, thunder roaring up the passageways! It seemed the world was dying and I hid beneath my sheets."

Dinwiddie paused to unfold a handkerchief and began vigorously polishing the silver box on his desk. Miss Antwerp tiptoed out. Those faint scratches on the box were the names of his ushers fifty years before.

"To that nice man at the Gritti I said this morning: In Arizona, you know, people sometimes die in such a storm.

"'Ah! But not in Venice,' he said in that way they have, smiling, 'or perhaps only a mouse. Yes, a mouse may have died in the night.'

"Who could be sad in Venice?"

Dinwiddie smiled to himself. He would go slow, not rush Jewel's letter. He instructed Miss Antwerp to hold all calls. There might be a particular coded message for him in these pages, although he had not found it yet. He might even send Jewel a little check.

Nanine appropriated the letter the minute it arrived. "Lambie, look! A letter from Venice!" She wagged a thick envelope at him from the bedclothes. Archibaldo III, a cranky ill-favored marmalade cat, glanced up in disgust as Nanine snatched the letter from Dinwiddie, who bent to examine the familiar handwriting.

"Here!" she said. "First part quite boring, a lot of silly nonsense about Venice, but listen to this!

> " '. . . *older man, a count, he has no money at all, nothing, he's flat broke and no, Dinsie, he is not a golddigger—*'

Here it is!

> " '*—madly in love, he's nothing like the people we know, thank God!, and he doesn't believe in God or any of those boring truisms about right and wrong or good or bad, all of which he finds too middle class for words—I must say this is refreshing, what a relief to be with someone who is candidly bad. He also says in my case it isn't sex he's after—*'

Nanine shrieked.

> " '*And that I have the rump of a well-fed horse. Can you believe it?*' "

Dinwiddie was so appalled he sank into a boudoir chair and did not hear another word but Nanine, relentless, read on:

" '*I can't possibly explain what it is I see in him, he's sort of
an engaging fop, I feel a little bit like one of those eastern
ninnies who go west and fall for some cowboy but trust me,
he's better than that, after all, he's coaxed me back to life, I
don't think any of you knew how sad I was and lost, I had
come unglued from life. Being loved, well, it restores me to
some purpose, I feel useful again although I can't say how. Oh,
and Dinwiddie—will you be awfully disappointed if I stay
over here awhile? I'm so happy! Trust me. And thank you,
Dinsie, for giving me this trip to Europe—all my gloom
about turning forty is gone. I love you—Jewel.*' "

"Well!" declared Nanine.

Sometimes he still hated Nanine. How had his mother
put it? People like us, said Charmagne, are meant to be
dull. Dull and dependable as a pair of fine old Chippen-
dale chairs. Leave it to the parvenus to be quick. He was
awfully glad she could not see her daughter-in-law at this
moment: flopping about in the bedclothes at age seventy-
four like a large decadent fish.

"I just hope you haven't done something very
naughty, Dinsie," said his wife. "Giving that child Venice for her birthday—wouldn't it be awful if she married
some bogus count? Oh, dear—well, I suppose you knew
what you were doing." Dinwiddie said nothing. What
did this mean? Rump of a well-fed horse—did fellows
really say these things to the girls nowdays?

He sometimes wondered if the years in New York
added up to anything worth a damn. Jewel had a way of
seeing clear down to the bone when it suited her, yet the
next moment she turned around and did some fool thing.
She was so grateful for anything you did for her but then
she would flail out suddenly, howl against the "system,"
flout it, then tear off to her beloved Arizona. She said a
curious thing: that you either had to be absolutely pure

in heart to live in the desert or absolutely evil; and that whatever it was she had dreamed all those years about home, it had gone. If only he knew how to help.

"Sunday is family day in Venice,"

Jewel wrote.

"All the world streams past in snug two-by-twos harnessed together like oxen, bumping, touching shoulders. There is a lovely old fellow whom I sometimes see on the Gritti terrace and he reminds me of you, Dinwiddie. He wears a white linen suit, like yours, and a navy polka-dot hankie tucked in at his breast, white shoes, smooth, very clean like yours, white lisle socks, and a heavenly Panama hat exactly the right shape. His hands are like yours; they flutter in and out of his lap like speckled birds dipping beautifully, swooping down onto the almonds and little dishes of olives.

"I didn't think he noticed me. But one afternoon, without turning his head, he said, 'Have you been to the Lido? To the Excelsior? Don't go!' he cried. Just then a flotilla of gondolas rounded the corner at the Gritti carrying a parcel of Americans, all female, and turned into the Grand Canal. At that same moment the CIGA motor launch pulled up at the dock to disgorge the bathers from Lido, the hot red-faced people, oiled and full of sunlight, red fingernails in the sunlight.

" 'They wear no tops, you know,' the old man sighed. Who? I asked him. 'Why, these brand-new people!' he exclaimed. 'They lie in the sand breast up, like creatures washed in from the sea.' He shuddered.

"The CIGA boat driver, one of those snappy young fellows with mirrored sunglasses, white ducks, slick hair, and a grin, was backing and forthing up to the dock. A snaggled blonde stood up in one of the gondolas and screamed, HEY, GOR-GEOUS! I'M AVAILABLE!

" 'Of course you don't remember the world as I do,' sighed my friend as he stood to go. 'The Excelsior. The Hotel des

*Bains. Those heavenly creatures in their summer hats. Beauty
meant something—ah, well, perhaps I am wrong, perhaps in
the end it means nothing.'"*

Dinwiddie carefully replaced the silver box on his
desk. He remembered Mortimer Carruthers, who had
resigned from the Athletic Club after sixty years. The
attendant, one of those new young fellows in tight trousers and a T-shirt, stopped old Carruthers at the door:
Sir! No one is to use the pool without showering first! Of
course Carruthers had no choice but to send in his resignation.

*"Imagine a day devoted to the pursuit of a perfect mozza-
rella. Or a sour green apple, a pear. I sniff my way along the
fruit stalls. Colors: green, the Venetian black—no black on
earth is so satisfying as that of the gondola slicing through
the lacquered silver of a small canal. Vacant grays leached
from the sea: the fog lifts, I dream the day, change my mind;
boats slide by in the sunlight. Tugboats called Carlotta and
Esmeralda and Dionysio; now a ship, vast and white. I stop
at the Traghetto to place a flower for the Little Madonna, say
a prayer, pass on. 'GONDOLA? GONDOLA, LADY, GON-
DOLA? AIIEE MI GONDOLA?' Just after Campo San
Maurizio he sits and waits, the gondolier with yellow hair,
wearing a straw hat with ribbons.*

" 'GONDOLA? GONDOLA, LADY?'

" 'Not today,' I say, 'maybe tomorrow.'

*" 'Ah!' says the voice. 'Tomorrow? There are a million
tomorrows!'*

*"Down the bridge and through the narrow passageway
smelling of chocolates and freshly ironed lingerie, custom-
made shoes, new umbrellas. The apotheke with bottles of corn-
flower-blue eyewash on a bed of yellow leaves. Gold bracelets
in the window and pearls: see, a slim young man buys his girl
her first pearls!"*

"Sir? Sir! I beg your pardon, Mr. Brown, sir!" How long had Miss Antwerp been standing in the door leering at him? What's that she was saying? The car? Ah, yes, Little was here with the car.

Little tucked the lap robe around his knees and shut the door. They had not far to go: around the block only and six blocks up Park. He always had one whiskey and a game of backgammon with his friend Talbot at the Knickerbocker before going home. Dinwiddie waited to hear the discreet cough of his old friend the Bentley as it shuddered to life, then he sank back weakly into its lush, plump gray arms. Today, as they eased away from the curb, two black boys looked in, thumped the roof loudly, and stuck tongues on the glass just near his face. Inside his head Dinwiddie felt his brain squeak like a trapped mouse.

All he wanted tonight was a hot soup and a bath but his wife, he knew, would have plans. At seventy-four she really was remarkable, she was unstoppable. Not that she had aged gracefully. Lucy Cook, who stuck around, as she put it, to see what would happen next, had the opinion that forty years of booze, fats, and cigarettes could not do anywhere near the damage those birdseed diets had done. All that deprivation worked its havoc on the mistress's brain. Oh, she stayed thin all right, but mean, just plain *mean*. And for all that she sacrificed Nanine still didn't feel thin enough! The styles had changed: just as she squeezed down to a size ten, tens were out. You couldn't even buy a ten anymore in New York City. You had to go to Tall Gals or the Forgotten Woman or one of those places over on the West Side if you were a ten or over. So she worked down to a size eight but then eights were passé. Now she was aiming at size six. Her biggest fear was she would get to size six only to find out six was out—finished! She told Lucy

Cook if this happened she was going down to Bergdorf's
and kill herself in the fur department.

Nanine was waiting for him when he arrived home.
Quick! He must dress and be ready to leave in fifteen
minutes, a wonderful last-minute invitation had come
through: first, cocktails somewhere over on the West
Side with people they scarcely knew, then the opening
of one of the Off-Off Broadway plays, just the sort he
hated, everyone running around in his underwear shouting. No dinner. We don't *need* food, Nanine screamed at
him from the top stair. The whole goddamn world is
choking to death on all this food! He murmured something about taking a chill at the office and wanting to stay
in this evening and she whirled on him, stamped her
foot, and screamed at the top of her lungs how for fifty
years he was never there for her when she'd done nothing but entertain colossal old farts like Mortimer Carruthers and now all he could think of was a bowl of
consommé, well, either he came with her or she would—
but Dinwiddie crept up the stairs nodding assent and
carried himself off to his dressing room to change for the
evening.

Hours later Dinwiddie awoke from a fitful sleep and
turned on the light. There it was, Jewel's letter.

*"And in the long evenings whose silences are punctuated by
Vivaldi or a Bach concerto floating out from the Church of
the Pietà, or by bells calling, I wonder over the ache that is
life. How is it the good times make us so sad? I always thought
there would be resting places. There is only the ongoing disturbance, the yearning not to see; the sheer bulk of all the
deceits piled on top, the absurd triumphs that hide the truth.
Lalo says we need only that perfect mozzarella and a glass
of wine, that this is the truth. And Johnnie says whatever we
do, the outcome is always the same."*

What did she mean, the outcome is always the same? This didn't sound like a woman in love! Deceits—did she suspect something? She may not have known it as she wrote the letter but this seemed a cry for help, he felt it with his whole being—only what must he do? He had sent her there, given her the money. She had some sort of a breakdown last year and no one knew what to do—so he sent her away. Alone in a foreign country! She isn't a bit strong, not really, not since her collapse; doesn't this prove it? It almost seemed she had determined to give herself away! A suffocating darkness crushed in all around him. What if I die tonight?

Dinwiddie struggled up out of his bed and stood a moment, bewildered, in his pajamas, and tried to think. He began the arduous business of trying to cross the room. His teeth chattered loudly. Amazed, he stopped to listen, then looked around wildly to make sure he was alone. Dinwiddie swayed, then struggled to stand erect; he proceeded toward the secretary, slowly, carefully, as if he were an enormous bowl full of soup that might spill over if tilted. He said Jewel's name out loud. Hold on, Old Boy. He began to cry. He had to tell her. She wasn't so fierce after all; they had been wrong about her.

At last Dinwiddie arrived at the secretary. He reached inside and found the box where long ago he had hidden the pavé diamond peacock that had been Madeleine's and then was mysteriously confiscated by his wife. The bird had come to signify his one great treasure. Madeleine. He said the name out loud once again: Madeleine! The peacock belonged to her, he must find some way to get it to her! Miss Plank—no, now it was Miss Antwerp, he could trust her to find Madeleine and send it to her. Yes, that was it! Dinwiddie found a pencil and began to scratch out a message. "This diamond peacock belongs to—" but then suddenly he could not think of the name.

A pain worked in his skull; his brain felt awash with loose wriggling words. Dinwiddie clung to the peacock. What had he wanted to say? Jewel would know. She always understood those things you could not say, thoughts that could not bear the light. Now he remembered and wrote the word: Jewel. "This diamond peacock belongs to Jewel."

19

NOW THAT fall branding was over, Old Lou decided
something had better be done about Jewel. They had all
read the letter. Nanine sent it out to the ranch after
Dinwiddie fell ill. As to the Italian's opinions on good
and evil, or God, they didn't mind that so much. God
meant nothing to Old Lou. She had done fine without
him all these years. And that bit about the horse's rump:
the McAllisters were ranching people, they had heard
worse. But what in hell did that foreign sissy mean,
saying it wasn't sex he was after? What the hell was he
after then?

"No commie pinko fruitcake is going to get away with
insulting a McAllister!" roared Old Lou. It was decided,
therefore, that her cousin Johnnie had better go fetch
Jewel home. It wouldn't be the first time. It seemed to
Johnnie he was always the one to go after her.

SHE HAD come home in a fur coat, got off the plane in it. Like
a movie star, said Bucky, who went with John to fetch her.
Bucky had waited for her all those years. She came swinging and

*sashaying toward them in flashing red cowboy boots, 501 jeans,
and dangle earrings.*

*"Where'd you get the fur?" Johnnie asked. Bucky drove, Jewel
sat in the middle.*

"I got it from George Chatfield," said Jewel.

*"Who the hell's George Chatfield?" said John. He was fifteen
but now suddenly he looked ten years younger than his cousin.
Jewel was nineteen, she had scarlet lips and mascara and blue
eyelids. Only the nails were the same—bitten down to the quick.*

*Finally Jewel said, "George Chatfield is the man I married."
The man! She said* man! *Bucky's face stared straight ahead at
the road and the knuckles on his fist went white to the bone.*

*"Married! Is that why you did it—to get the fur?" Johnnie
cried. Jewel's cheeks flamed up red. Her eyes, Johnnie saw, were
full of tears but he said it again, hating her. "Is that why? Shit,
Jewel, at least you could've held out for a sable, I'd say she's
worth at least a sable, Bucky, don't you think?" Bucky glared
at the road, he never looked her way once. "Nosiree, I'd've held
out for a sable or a chinchilla," said Johnnie bitterly. "If a
person's going to sell themself he might as well go for the jackpot.
What else has this guy given you? What'd you say his name was?
Chatfield? God, Chatfield!" The tears started down Jewel's face
and she began to stroke the fur, which was laid out across her
lap like a sleeping animal. "I sure never figured you for a person
who'd sell out for a fur coat and some guy from the east," cried
Johnnie, but still Jewel said nothing, she kept on patting the coat
as the tears came down. She was changed, he didn't know her.
"You said you were coming home as soon as you could get out
of there, you always swore you'd come back to the ranch, Jewel!
You remind me of your mother!"*

*"You shut up, John, goddamn you, shut your mouth! What
do you know about it? What was I supposed to do here? Wrassle
cows?"*

*"Well, what in hell are you going to do back there?" de-
manded Johnnie. "What's got into you, Jewel?"*

"You don't know me," she said. "None of you knows me."

"Bucky and me—we know you," cried Johnnie. "Why do you think Bucky waited?"

"Look, I'm sorry, Bucky!" she cried. Bucky jerked the pickup truck off onto the side of the road and slammed his fist on the wheel, fell over onto it facedown, never cried or made a sound. Johnnie would never forget: Bucky Lamott, all-around cowboy and best man he ever saw, a strapping tenderhearted fellow, one of those great and pure hunks, handsome, devoted, sincere, not stupid by any means but so good he might as well be stupid, there he was facedown.

"Please, Bucky, oh God, please don't do this!" cried Jewel, and she reached to touch his arm but he jerked away, he threw her off violently and smashed out the door, and ran off. They saw him run like a crazy man down the highway. Johnnie, who didn't even have a driver's license, drove them home because Jewel wouldn't stop crying. She cried her guts out and blew her nose, wiping it on the sleeve of her mink coat.

She was wearing that mink the time she came blasting up to Andover on the back of a big old Harley behind a black poet friend and there was never any girl so exciting, his friends all said so. They came gawking out from chapel to take a look, then hung back when she passed around a silver case full of black Sobranie cigarettes. Once he forgave her for George Chatfield he gave himself up to adoring her.

She dragged that fur coat around the big Park Avenue apartment like a dustcloth, slept under it, lent it to the Puerto Rican maid, wrapped the litter of beagle dogs in it, and finally lost it in Hamburger Heaven.

Johnnie spent Christmas with his mother and summers in Arizona but every Thanksgiving and spring break he spent with Jewel. She took him to nightclubs. George was always busy with important clients so Johnnie and Jewel went to the Hippopotamus and El Morocco. Jewel told the maître d' he was eighteen. She ordered Dom Pérignon and left him alone at the table,

*sometimes for a very long time, while she whirled off with some
guy in a pinstripe suit. The agony he knew in watching her smile
up into their eyes, dip and sway, felt worse at seventeen, more
excruciating than anything he was to experience in the next
twenty years of his life. Just to be in the same room with Jewel
was to forget everything. She pulled you along; out they came,
those trapped and embarrassing sensations, sharp, sweetly uncomfortable; she laughed or cried over them; but she listened. He
hated dancing yet she taught him the rumba secretly at home. It
was wonderful to have her so close and swirl around and around.*

*He stayed outside her bathroom with his back against the door
listening to her splash around in there. He loved to hear her slap
on the hand lotion. She sang ranchero; she had a terrible voice,
on anyone else it would be embarrassing. And while Jewel sang
in the tub he played his guitar. "Margarita" was their favorite.*

*She and George went to parties in a rented limousine, George
in a three-piece suit and a Turnbull and Asser shirt and Jewel
in a leather mini from Carnaby Street and the red cowboy boots.
And at the door George would turn, look, then say, "Are you
sure you want to wear that? We're going out to Locust Valley,
you know." And Jewel gave him her sideways lynx-eyed look
and off they went. Alone, Johnnie looked through her closets. Her
nightgowns hung all in a row on hangers. Sometimes he sniffed
them. He went into her studio and switched on the lights. Jewel
painted; someday she might be famous. The paintings were
SOS's, she told him; flying parts wriggling through the air,
messages stranded in a fantastic sea of color. He wanted to like
them. She said they were pieces of her soul, that nothing else
about her was so real. After a few years, though, she put a
padlock on the studio door. She said the paintings were too
naked, she couldn't look at them anymore.*

*Around this time she would lie on the sofa all day and stare
at the ceiling. She had seen a body slumped over the curb out there
on Park Avenue. George had stepped over it like it was a dead
rat. Jewel stared at the walls and the big rooms with all the new*

furniture; she hated George, hated the James Robinson sugar tongs and the Stark carpet and the Brunschwig leopard toile— but most of all she hated George.

"I don't see why you had to get married," said Johnnie.

"Well, what else was I supposed to do? Join the Peace Corps? Go to college? I had to do something, you know."

"You could have waited! If it's the money you wanted I could have given you some of mine."

"It isn't the money," she said.

"You could have asked Uncle Dinwiddie, he would give it to you."

"That would be the worst of all. He's so good to me—how can I take money from someone who is so good to me? No, it's better like this. At least I don't feel I owe George anything. He keeps a tally, you know. Makes me beg for it, write it all down, every penny I take. If I felt like it I could walk right out that door and never come back."

"Bucky would take you back, I know he would," said Johnnie. "You could be free with Bucky, he really loves you, Jewel."

"And spend every Saturday night for the next fifty years doing the cowboy polka at the Buckskin? No, thank you."

She left George Chatfield for an air-conditioner man. Paulie Manatucci was his name. He looked like Brando, she told him so immediately. He had never heard of Marlon Brando; he was young, twenty-five at the most. He said someday he was going to write.

"Mind if I take this off?" he asked her, and laid his shirt over a chair. In his undershirt he looked so real. George didn't even own an undershirt.

"What are you staring at?" said Paulie. "You East Side ladies are all the same." Lady? She wasn't even thirty-five!

One day Jewel showed up in Tucson with Paulie. They settled into the little studio house Dinwiddie had given her long ago. Paulie could write here. Jewel showed Johnnie the first poem, an ode to her in uninhibited gibberish—and this was the man she

*was wild about! And yet Johnnie could not stay away. He came
to see them often. It really did amaze him to see her in this new
guise: here was his glamorous cousin Jewel scrubbing and baking
in the kitchen while Paulie Manatucci sat under the lemon tree
napping, scratching his belly, waiting for his lunch.*

*"Look at him," said Jewel, gazing from the kitchen window,
"he's so damn pure he doesn't even know it. He's undiluted—it's
just plain intoxicating, Johnnie."*

*"Does he ever do anything?" said Johnnie. "At least George
did things."*

*"Like what? Make money? Serve on boards? Is that what you
call doing something? What about me—do I do anything? For
the first time in my life I don't have to prove I'm smart or
interesting or bake gourmet dinners to show how clever I am or
dress right or know the right people. Paulie, he's happy with
lasagne. Is there anything wrong with that?" "Not if you're
happy," he said to her. She did not answer.*

*Johnnie wanted no part of the system any more than his cousin
did. In those first years after Andover and Yale he went back
to the Big Earth not, as his mother and stepfather thought, to
settle down and run the place, but to run free. He hung out with
the Mexican cowboys from Agua Prieta, drank, talked cows,
danced in the bars along the border, brought home flashy girls.
He got together a wildcat polo team of cowboys and rough little
ponies and sometimes they disappeared into Mexico for weeks at
a time. Lou was pleased. If he had brought home one of those nice
blondes from Connecticut it would have sickened her. True, she
could have used a good man around the place, she wasn't getting
any younger, but it was better this way. A man had to be half
wild or he never would know who he was. Lou waited, she knew
at bottom he was good value. Maybe too good. Johnnie kicked
up a lot of dust in those years but he didn't fool Lou. Under the
swagger, the hard guise of manliness which he wore with a
beautiful nonchalance, he was strangely quiet, absent. As if none
of it meant anything; he knew the outcome, knew what you*

*would say, and heard it all again with an almost tender forbear-
ance. This unnerved her. Johnnie was the only person alive she
had any respect for because he didn't want anything from her
or from anybody for that matter. Even women, they did not hold
any power over the man, Lou felt sure of it. He had married a
local beauty, a little spitfire cowgirl from Douglas, and divorced
her before the year ran out because when he brought her home to
the Big Earth she suddenly began referring to herself as Mrs.
Johnnie Truesdale and dropping hints that maybe he ought to
wear a suit when they went up to town. What's the point of
being so rich, she said, if we can't go places: St. Louis, Oklahoma
City, Denver. That had been six years ago and Johnnie still
hadn't found the right one although there wasn't a finer-looking
man in Cochise County and plenty of women were after him.
Lou boasted of it, told people her grandson was a maverick. But
lately, in secret, she nursed a certain fear. Now he'd passed
thirty-six, how long could a man last without a partner? He
stayed alone always, said he'd rather sleep out under the starlight on some far butte than come home. Even the wild mustang
had a mate. When would he start building a family? She hadn't
knocked herself out all these years just to see her breed die out.*

*It nauseated Johnnie to see Jewel hanging all over Paulie
Manatucci. He couldn't figure it out. She would be forty soon;
her friends all had children, their husbands owned Ford dealer-
ships and played golf. Or taught botany and hiked the Catalinas
on weekends and kept a boat at Kino Bay. Paulie spent Saturday
and Sunday under the hood of his Pontiac GTO; his idea of
excitement was to peel out from the curb and hit sixty before the
guy in the next lane shifted into second. Paulie didn't even like
Tucson; he sat around the house in his undershirt with a six-pack
of beer and watched TV, making rude remarks about the locals,
life in the wild west. Johnnie knew he was scared of the desert;
he once admitted that the saguaros made him feel insignificant.*

*"Name me one thing you respect about the guy," said Johnnie
one day.*

"He doesn't play golf," said Jewel.

"You know what turns you on—that he's so unsuitable. You never did go for the suitable ones."

"Don't forget George."

"He was the most unsuitable of all."

"You should talk. What about Chiquita whatsername? Or the one you married—Glenda Gumm? Are you so sure either one of us would know who the right person was?" He was stung. He would know the right person if he saw her.

"You want some guy to change you," he said. *"You'd never settle for someone like Bucky who'd just accept you. Bucky could have made you happy."*

"Well, maybe I'm afraid to be happy," she said.

Jewel called Johnnie to come get her one day. She and Paulie had broken down in the desert near Locheil in the San Rafael Valley. It wasn't so much desert as a strip of wild pastureland out at the edge of nowhere with streaming yellow grasses and gullies filled with cradles of soft light where the cows hide and there is nobody for miles around. He heard something new in her voice.

"I've had it with being the reliable one," she said into the telephone, *"with being strong. I'm sick to death of giving."*

"Hell, honey, you've just been giving the wrong thing."

They had a blowout on the abandoned San Rafael road: first one tire, then a second, and Paulie said, *"We're not stopping here, I mean this place is a dump, I haven't seen a horse, a goddamn human, not even a cow for forty goddamn miles."* *"You can't drive on the rims,"* she said, *"just pull over, someone will come."* *"I'm not stopping."* On and on he drove, past the one deserted house, past the squatters' shack with its yard of snarling dogs, and farther out until at last, with the rubber blown off the rims, they had to stop. They were in the middle of a bull pasture. Far off to the east they could see black shapes. *"Well, what the fuck do you expect me to do?"* Paulie shouted. *"You're the mechanic,"* she said. *"Fucking goddamn Arizona!"*

*he screamed, pounding the horn. "Goddamn nowhere dump!"
Jewel climbed into the back seat. "You brought me here!"
screamed Paulie. Jewel lay down. She said, "You're a big boy
now—I'm taking a nap."*

*Far off down the road Paulie saw a speck. It came straight
at them in a swirling haze of yellow dust, larger now, coming
fast. It thundered down onto them, a ramshackle two-ton ranch
truck with homemade wooden slats tacked on behind and two
horses hitched to the flatbed with rifles at their saddles. "Hey,
you'd better get up here, Jewel," he cried, but she stayed in the
back. The truck squeezed in alongside the GTO in the narrow
path. Two Mexicans in huge hats eyed Paulie, grinned. What
were they waiting for? One of them said something, grunted, the
other one laughed. They were two feet away at most. "You'd
better get up here!" said Paulie. In the back seat Jewel began to
giggle. "Bitch! You bitch!" he hissed. Jewel leaned out the window and said something to the men in Spanish, laughing, grinning at them, she wasn't afraid. Then suddenly Jewel got out
of the car. "Are you going with them?" he cried. "Paulie, it's
okay," she said quietly, "they'll give us a ride." "You think I'd
leave my GTO?" he said. "Christ, I'm not leaving my car—you
go with them. Why can't they go get help, go to a gas station
or something? Are you really going with them?" He hated her
guts, hated the Mexicans, pulsing, grinning at him. He couldn't
believe she actually went with them, happy, excited. He hadn't
seen her so excited in a long time.*

*One night he disappeared. They had been together four years.
He left her a note tacked to the refrigerator door. "You take up
all the space," it said. "I'm not Marlon Brando."*

*She took it hard. No one understood why she fell apart. What
had she seen in Paulie Manatucci? There were other men with
beautiful bodies, big beautiful babies who grinned at you softly.
If it was just sex they could have understood, but Jewel found
the guy fascinating. Especially in the beginning when he was
an air-conditioner man. Yet she worked like a dog to change*

him. Later, when he became a writer, when he understood about her world and wanted to change, wanted things—he hungered after a Porsche—she was appalled. He wanted her to say it over and over again: how good he was, and smart—but he hated her for saying it. She was the wise one, she knew things. She knew what to wear, how to say hello—and she didn't care. The smarter he got the harder it was to say hello. If only he had stayed an air-conditioner man! Now he looked like everybody else, and he couldn't even remember how to fix the air-conditioner anymore, she should have been glad he was gone. But she loved him anyway, loved him bitterly, she had watched him grow, he was hers.

Jewel came disconnected from life. She grew afraid, set herself adrift. Freedom, once so intoxicating, seemed a burden. The things she delighted in now seemed pointless. She no longer had the courage to work; her paintings weren't good enough to make a difference. What else could she do? The only experience she had was being a rich man's wife. She had torn loose from everything she had once believed in and saw there was nowhere to go. Her friends stayed away; anyway, she was sick of faking an interest in their little worlds. There had to be a larger world. If only she could have been a Hopi Indian, for example: simple, complete, pressed in all around by the earth, the tribe, pinned to something large: ancient mysteries couched in an ear of corn. Without a tribe who were you supposed to live for? Even if you did manage to find the right man, someone permanent, would it solve anything?

She got a gun; it lay beside her in bed at night. A gun at least you could count on. If one olive dropped in the tree outside her window she was ready, aimed, click: ready to blow its head off. She lay in the dark waiting for rapists to crawl through the window so she could splat the sonsofbitches up against the wall. All those years and she still had nothing to show for her life but this fear.

Not long after Paulie left, Jewel went on a spree. She drove

*her car through the plate-glass window at Baker's Shoes in
downtown Tucson with all the Indians standing around rooting
for her. Doc Pusey drove out to the ranch and told them she was
having a breakdown.*

*"Breakdown!" hollered Old Lou. "No one in this family ever
broke down before!"*

*"Well, now, Lou, don't you remember, her father went and
killed hisself," said Doc Pusey. "I sure hope this little gal isn't
going to do some fool crazy—"*

*"Crazy! She's a McAllister, ain't she? Godalmighty, I never
heard such talk! Nothing the matter with her a good man won't
fix. She's no different than any other female. She's scared, that's
all, she ain't gettin' any younger and she's just begun to notice.
She'll be fine. Johnnie here can fix her up with one of his friends."*

*"It isn't a man she wants," said Johnnie ominously. "She
wants someone to tell her why she's here. She wants a reason."*

*"A reason? Well, for God's sakes! No one ever gave me a
reason!" snapped Old Lou.*

*"You've got the land, so do I," he said. "But it won't work
for Jewel until she comes up with a reason for being here."*

*"I don't know if she will," said Doc Pusey. "I went to see her
over to the hospital the other day and you know what she said?
'Doc,' she said, 'I'm never going to grow up. I always thought
I'd change. You know, grow, get better—get smart. But I'm still
that child. With all my disguises, Doc, that child doesn't go
away, she's still here.'"*

NOT LONG before Jewel was due to leave for Venice she
called Johnnie at the ranch and asked him to come see
her in Tucson. He heard the uncertainty in her voice, a
tentative quality so unlike her, and said he would come.
Everything had changed for him, too, since Paulie left.
Jewel didn't seem so irresistible anymore. As he left the
ranch that evening and pulled out onto I-10 in his pickup

truck, driving into the western sky, it came to him how glad he felt to be free of her. He couldn't remember exactly when it passed away, that old yearning. Maybe watching her pour her soul into that lover boy Manatucci all those years finally wore him down. A person could wait only so long—and what had he been waiting for? He still wasn't sure. His own life felt pretty satisfying these days.

He ran a sixty-thousand-acre cattle ranch, had as many as thirty vaqueros under him during roundup, and he still managed a polo team; his days were packed with the fever of ranching, of doing it better than Lou, of working the land. He had all he ever wanted. He knew enough to be grateful clear through to his bones so the excitement grew, the challenge. And the nights were filled with solitude: he prowled the land, it belonged to him, he gloried in the vast spaces.

She stayed in his thoughts though, especially on nights like this when all the world seemed eaten up with some bone-dry glow of last light. It was June, the hardest month in the desert. The hot months had settled on Dragoon like a long lament. A small promise of rain teased the air but Johnnie knew it would not come and he ached over it: the land shorn of all finery, desiccated, the cows desolate, listless in the heat, and the humans, too, gone sour. And yet there was a terrible beauty to it as all the earth lay dying; he almost gloried in it, the hard wait.

The day died out flat, a lifeless bleached green draining softly down from out the desert sky: now yellow, inert, an exhausted sky, too hot for clouds or some wonderful gay streamer of last light. The sun vanished, the day passed away unremarked. Johnnie switched on the radio. It was Country Roland, "Kicker Daddy," singing "Margarita," and he threw back his head and yodeled the words into the wind. These times he liked best: the silence, nothingness, he was a speck of life, nothing more, vanishing on the wind. Silence! It made him laugh, this roar of desert air, the roaring down into the heart of night, joining, fused with all the dark presences; the whoosh of hot tires on asphalt, the blur of headlights that drew him down into the dark nothingness, the speed, roar; a bright gleam high up as now a livid ray singed the sky with crimson flocking, a fervid last light. Then came night, moon and stars; high over the desert a few straying flinders of starlight. Johnnie pulled over to the side of the road to listen: the hiss of night, a dry crackle of feverish creatures working, filling up the dark. Now the night air coming up cool, that moment in the desert when the night, hot as fire, is invaded by a sudden cool sluit of liquid air, mysterious currents eking out from some deep place, a cave or some moist rock.

It was late when Johnnie arrived at the little house in Tucson.

"You stopped at the market," she said, "for beer. You feed me—" and she smiled in that odd new way, the smile bringing tears, and took the sack of groceries from his arms. He followed her. The house smelled musty. The windows and shutters were drawn shut; the air in her studio and in the little kitchen felt dead.

"We'll go into the garden," she said, feeling his thoughts. "Although I seldom come out here anymore." They stood a moment in the small dry garden; he seemed reluctant to sit down. It was dark but he saw she had let things die, wizened yucca, fig, and olive, the flowerless ocotillo. The air felt absolutely without life. Beyond the wall they heard the hiss of tires on hot asphalt.

"What is it, honey?" he said gently. "What's going on?" She stood before him, she wanted him to say things he couldn't say.

"You are a baby," he said at last. "You always were the baby."

"You were the witness," she said. "You waited outside the bathroom door—remember?"

"Yes," he said quietly, "I was the witness."

"The spectator," said Jewel. "I was the sport, you were the spectator."

"The way I see it, Jewel, you were damn lucky to have me."

"It's you who has changed," she said at last, softly. He stood in front of her a moment, glaring. He wouldn't sit near her, he still wore his hat, and now he began to pace the little garden—she almost thought he would leave. "Sit here beside me," she said. He had nothing of the old need to please, the confiding, easy manners of that engaging boy who had always adored her. He was hard with her now. She remembered once telling him what a man Paulie was but Paulie had only been a boy, she saw it now. Johnnie was the man—it scared her to see him so. She felt the fierceness, a sudden raw energy in his stride, his very posture; she had not seen this before, it made him seem too large for her garden, for any walled-in place. Yes, he had become a man suddenly, his legs had thickened, his arms, his neck so broad and hard, burnt by too much sun; he wore a moustache to lend a certain swaggering air; she didn't like it. But he was golden still, with golden eyes and hair, and although he was tall, much taller than Paulie, he had an almost feline grace. She saw it now as he swung around and came near her, dropping into a chair soundlessly in a languid long curve, legs out, arms hung down beside his chair, the fingers curled, the feet in black boots, near her own but not touching.

"You make me afraid of you," she said, "of your silence." On the other side of the wall a cop car cruised by,

its radio blasting ugliness. Every once in a while a crazy
filament of sizzling light wriggled nervously across the
sky. The air grew torpid with the promise of rain but he
knew the rains would not come.

"Do you ever think of Southampton on a night like
this?" he said at last. Between them the image of something sumptuous and green and indiscribably moist
floated in the night air. "They're sitting on the porch,"
he continued softly, "at this moment, Dinwiddie in his
pistachio shirt and seersucker jacket and the pink linen
pants." Visions of green velvet lawns rolling to the sea
and clipped privet, endless avenues of elm and plane; and
in the garden, tree peonies, lilac; and on the porches,
wicker painted dark green and snug fat people; a world
as narrow, thought Johnnie, as this is wide. A dose of
chloroform to her soul—Jewel nearly said it out loud.

"No," said Jewel, almost to herself, "I never think of
Southampton."

It grew late. Dry hacking thunder crashed down
around them but still the rains did not come and the
earth sizzled up, it hissed all around them with an unfor-
giving heat.

"You could still go back," he said. "You have a world
back there, you have Dinwiddie, friends. You might
meet someone."

"You used to think I belonged here. It was my land
before it was yours," she said. He reached in the dark to
take her hand.

"It isn't the land you want," he said.

"What do I want?" She said it so softly.

"You want to die. To go away." The words were flat,
uneventful; they took her breath away. "To be changed."

"I've spoiled it, haven't I?" she cried. He gave her hand
a squeeze. "My life was so beautiful and I've spoiled it.
Is this why you're angry?" He did not answer, only held

her hand in his own. She felt his heat and the calluses. "Do you remember? It was one night long ago here in this little garden."

"Yes," he said, "I remember. I couldn't sleep."

"That's right—and I couldn't either. You stood over there, remember? And you kept looking in at me through the screen door. Many times, all through the night." He pulled his hand away. "I saw you leap onto the garden wall. Over there in the moonlight. There was a moon, and crickets. I remember the slow rubbing, monotonous and slow. You in those cowboy boots, very quiet, a cat in boots, and you paced along the garden wall. My God, I never saw anything so exciting." It was dark but she saw his eyes were closed. "It was lovely to feel you watch over me. Is it spoiled, Johnnie?"

"How old are you? Forty? Christ, Jewel—what do you think? Do you have any idea how long I waited? Don't you get it? It isn't me you want, it never was! I'm not going to sit here now and pretend—" but he let it hang, she sat so quiet he could scarcely hear her breathe. Shocked by what he'd said he then began to feel a savage exhilaration and the old tightness came loose around his heart, the pain of loving her, and he didn't care. The silence was so unlike her, she had always been quick; what did this lassitude mean? Was she dozing? It gave him an eerie sensation. She dipped forward slightly, her head tilted toward her breast. He saw her picked out in a trickle of light coming out of the house; she had always been in motion—at least he thought of her so—and now she was still.

"Jewel? Goddamn it, Jewel," he said softly.

After a long time she said, "You were my best friend." He had to bend to hear her.

"Were you ever going to love me, Jewel?"

"You never even knew," she said.

"By God, I'm not going to listen to this," said Johnnie suddenly, and he stood to go.

"It made me feel like an impostor, to know that none of you could see me. Or that I could just cease to exist when you were through with me. I mean what the hell point is there to anything if we're all disposable?"

"Things end, Jewel, they have to, there's no point hanging on. If it's Paulie you mean, you're better off without the little runt, he was a kid, a dumb beautiful kid. Hell, Jewel, next time try a man for chrissakes, you might like it." She stood up suddenly to block his way, grabbed at him.

"You shut up about Paulie!" she cried. "You were jealous!"

"I'm getting out of here—"

"Damn you—it's not too late!" She came after him but he sprang back. Again she lunged for him. "Johnnie! Say it! It's not too late!" She ran after him into the house. "You loved me! You said you loved me—you wanted me once. Johnnie!"

He felt her crashing down. He was young, he was the golden one and he had never felt it so much as now; he had loved her but now she came falling past, bruised, rearranged, down and down. She looked into his face and saw. "Bastard!" she cried softly. "Oh, you bastard! You never did love me." He crossed the studio and let himself out. She waited, sure he would come back, he had always been there; all those years—he had said it was love. But then she remembered the look in his eyes, the triumph, his eagerness to get away. She heard his truck pull away and now there was no one, for the first time she was truly alone.

20

JOHNNIE ARRIVED in Venice during that dusky blue hour when the sky melts down suddenly and is lost in the silver sea and all that wavers in between. He came by vaporetto from the railroad station, feeling led astray as they made their way through a drifting fog—*la nebbia,* as the Italians call it. The little lights of evening sprang to life in the Grand Canal, squares of mellow gold light tucked in softly among the old rose and ochre of wavering palazzi sinking slowly down on either side, a soft blur punctuated here and there by a gliding black fin. But for the whine of vaporetti bumping now and then against some dock in the mist and the plash of an oar close by, the world seemed strangely absent.

He arrived at the Gritti Palace, a fifteenth-century palazzo, its terrace floating over the Grand Canal, and to Johnnie it seemed like some buoyant steamer ship bound for irresistible places. There were tipsy swaying mooring poles, striped awnings, pink hibiscus waving at the railings, and deck chairs, their arms opened out in endless anticipation of the dazzling ladies in their summer dresses—a world as far from his own as any on earth.

Now the fog lifted and they rolled back the awnings to let in the coming starlight.

He meant to stay only a day or two, a week at the most. He could not be sure what kind of a reception Jewel would give him. Whatever chagrin he had felt toward her was forgotten. He booked himself a room with a balcony at the Gritti.

Night came, slippery and black, as he stood on his balcony and waited for Jewel. He felt it at once, something dangerous and softly glittering in this vitreous sea that had nothing of the desert candor, the clean and spacious black of nights at home, the solemn hush of desert evenings gathering last wisps of fiery light high up, floating to the heavens. He had forgotten how seductive the sea could be, with her dreamy mists and lush watering places. How enchanted, this world, floating beneath him, with candles guttering in crystal shades and tables in starched pink skirts, a buffet laden with summer flowers trailing down over an antipasto of pungent fishes, how rich it was and deadly. It filled him with sudden yearnings.

A woman dined alone on the terrace below. She sat against the railing with her head in profile, white as a cameo and perfectly etched against the oily black waters of the Grand Canal. It seemed to John that the light sought her out, threading loosely, languorously through the silver forks and spoons, the polished chafing dishes with their tiny licking flame, to find her, to wind a long ribbon of light around her loveliness.

She sat perfectly still while all around her was in motion: the continual slapping of canal waters, the excited buzz of waiters, the colors floating in sanguine circles of light. Trolleys laden with delicious cakes, mounds of raspberries and *fraises des bois,* waxy pears nesting in

baskets, summer melons wheeled to and fro. She looks
frozen and alert, he thought, like a creature in the wild,
poised to escape. She doesn't belong here either; she is as
removed from the hairdos and the chatter as the moon
is aloof from some watery far-off reflection of itself somewhere down on earth.

Did she glance up? She held her head at a high angle,
like a horse. He suspected that if startled or caressed she
might jerk back suddenly, rear up. The upper part of her
face with its decisive modeling and smooth, square brow
was made even more vivid by wings of black hair sweep-
ing back from the moon-pale face. Her eyes were deep,
unlit smudges staring out over full cheekbones that gave
her a wild and foreign aspect. The nose, too, was splendid—long, finely chiseled, downward curving like the
nose of a Turk in a fiercely rounded line, an unlikely
companion to the full lips and round chin. Her throat,
strong and muscular, rose up very white from out of a
dark, almost monastic dress. Her head dipped slightly as
the waiter brought her plate. She began to eat, almost
cautiously, as if she knew she were being watched.

Jewel appeared on the balcony behind him and any
strange feeling he had about seeing his cousin again after
their unhappy meeting some months ago in her garden
quickly vanished. She wound her arms around him with
all the old affection, the same naughty teasing laugh, the
quick happy tears. He had not seen her so radiant for
many years.

"My God, I'm glad to see you!" she cried, and placed
a resounding smack on his neck.

"I'm glad to see you, too."

"So you've come to rescue me." Again that laugh.

"I *thought* that was why I came," said Johnnie, grinning at her.

"I knew this place would change your mind."

"I've brought you something," he said, handing her a small box.

"From you?" He never gave her presents. "But what is it? A joke? It's not real, is it? No—it couldn't be—you never give women jewels. You didn't buy this, did you—I hope not—" and she laughed. "It's incredibly ugly, don't you think?"

"The ugliest thing I ever saw," said Johnnie, who watched her lift the pavé diamond peacock from the box and twist it in the light. "By the way—it isn't from me."

"Do you know," she said, "I almost think this thing is evil. That's silly, isn't it? And I've seen it before, years ago. Is it Nanine's? Did she send it to me? No wonder it feels so evil. Don't you remember—a long time ago? She used to wear it sometimes."

"Aren't you curious how I got it? I came through New York and went to see Dinwiddie. As I left the house your old pal Lucy Cook grabbed me and took me into the pantry and she gave me this. She made me swear not to tell Nanine. Anyway, it seems that when Dinwiddie had his stroke Lucy found him and he was clutching this." Johnnie took the bird from Jewel and pinned it to her blouse. "And also a note. He scrawled a message that the peacock should go to you. Lucy Cook hid it. She says Nanine forgot all about the bird years ago."

"But if it belongs to Nanine—" exclaimed Jewel.

"Lucy Cook swears it doesn't. She says they came to some bargain about the jewel years ago and that Nanine gave it to him. Lucy even hinted at dirty goings-on—do you think Dinwiddie ever had other women?"

"There was someone once," said Jewel. "That first summer I came to live with them. You know, it's funny, Johnnie, but I haven't thought about that in years. And now I remember it—well, I wonder if he gave her up, that woman, because of me? He had been so happy but then suddenly he just sort of caved in and I guess it was over. It would have killed me to have him go, he was the only one," she continued, and her eyes filled. "Well, I will treasure it, I will wear the bird and think of him."

"Uncle Dinwiddie is pretty bad off, you know," he said. "She's got him trussed up like a hostage with Lucy Cook spoon-feeding him tapioca. I don't even know if he recognized me. Don't cry, Jewel, he doesn't need your tears—there's nothing we can do to make it better. He would like to know that you're happy. This jewel must have meant something beautiful to him—for him you are the jewel. There's nothing more relevant than that." After a moment he said, "But tell me, Jewel, are you happy?"

"Happier than I've ever been."

"I have never seen you so ravishing," he said. "But this Italian—Dal Bezo—who is he?"

"Far easier to say who he is not!" She laughed. "He does his best to disprove everything, all my deepest convictions, everything! These people are very cynical, you know, they are nothing like us—they don't believe in sincerity, not at all, and he has no reverence for anything sacred. And he is wildly suspicious of the most innocent, meaningless things I do and completely bland about things I consider positively sinister. He's got me all turned around—and I love it."

"Is that so exciting?"

"To be shaken up, disproved—it is exciting! I see the whole world in a different way. Somehow I don't feel so needy."

"And what do you do for him?" Johnnie asked.

"I'm not sure. It's odd but I'm not sure he loves me at

all. You'll see. You won't like him, I know you won't—
but when you know him a little I think you'll see that he
has something."

"Yes, but I came here to drag you away. It won't
matter how much I like the guy."

"We'll see!"

"Tell me," he said, "who is she?"

Jewel leaned over the balcony to look. "How funny!
It's his stepmother!" she cried.

"The Italian's?" he exclaimed. "His *stepmother*? But
how old is she?"

"Not very old at all. But Johnnie, darling, you've got
to stop calling him the Italian. His name is Lalo. And she
is his stepmother. The Contessa Dal Bezo—a wicked
woman if you must know."

"Can you introduce me?" he said.

"What—to the contessa? Certainly not! Lalo hates her.
Why do you want to know her?"

"Because I've never seen anyone like her," he said,
almost to himself.

"She is beautiful, isn't she?" said Jewel. "She's quite
famous here, everyone talks about her. Some people say
it's all Lalo's fault, not hers. I can't introduce you, I don't
even know her, and it's just as well—come away from
there, let's go inside. I have so much I want to ask you!
Did Buck Lamott ever marry that girl? And how is
Glenda Gumm?"

As Johnnie turned to go the contessa gazed up and
with a long glance met his eye. With a suggestion of a
smile she held him there for a long moment until at last
she looked away.

21

JEWEL LOOKED down from her little balcony at the Palace of the Lily and saw Lalo and another woman taking a late supper together outdoors, in the *campo* just opposite her window. The count had placed himself in among the rosy tables under the gay sweep of awning so that he might be seen: like a scarecrow, thought Jewel, planted among the startled birds. She spotted him instantly. Her first thought was that he wanted her to see him there. He faced her window but did not glance up. The woman— Jewel could not see who it was—wore a delightful purple hat with a curling feather.

This happened the same night her cousin arrived. She and Johnnie dined early and parted; Lalo had said he could not join them. She had been surprised at the time; it seemed he had no particular reason, only that it did not suit him to come, and he said he would meet Johnnie on the following day.

Now they were leaving. Together, like performers, they stepped out of the *ristorante* into the circle of light, bowed to one another at the lamp below, as if they meant

to part, but then Lalo detained her. Jewel saw then that
it was the contessa.

What did this mean? Lalo always made such a point of
saying he and his stepmother never spoke! He pointed
her out once, from a safe distance, hissing at the sight of
her. Jewel had said she could not see how such a marvelous creature could ruin someone's life. The remark was
innocent but Lalo seethed over it. "Do you doubt me?"
he roared at Jewel.

They were very handsome together, and sleek; it was
hard not to admire them, to think how perfect those two
were in this setting, with the church of Maria del Giglio
just behind, her façade of rippling maps and marble
galleons so dazzling and white, her pensive queen, high
up, triumphant against the night, and the soaring trum-
peting angel seeming almost to topple out from the gathering nimbus of rolling purple clouds. It was their
world, not hers—how could she ever hope to belong
here?

A party of shrill Venetians passed under Jewel's window and saluted the two beneath the light. Lalo and the
contessa joined them. Jewel shrank back. There was excited talk, a great laugh rose up. The others passed on but
those two remained, they stood facing one another and
spoke in low tones: what they said Jewel could not hear
for their heads were pressed close together. It was terrible to watch them—surely Lalo knew she was there!
What if the rumors were true—that he seduced her!
Jewel had decided she did not believe the rumors, that
Lalo did what he liked and never bothered to justify
anything and it seemed a relief to know someone who
refused to be burdened by the usual restrictions. But
now!? Hilarious groups passed back and forth in the
campo below and Jewel grew angry; she felt cruelly shut
away from the excited flow, the late-night caterwauling

of tourists and gondoliers, the whispers of those two below; she imagined they mocked her, shared secrets. Jewel suddenly understood that she had hoped for something more. He had not said he loved her and yet she believed it was so, she had taught herself to depend on him for her happiness.

She stuck her head over the balcony to hear what they said. She could barely restrain herself from shouting at him; she clenched her teeth and struggled for a deadly calm. Lalo stood just beneath her window. He took the handbag from his stepmother and moved with it into the light of the glass shop next door. He looked into the bag, found something—a match, and lit her cigarette. At that moment he glanced up and saw Jewel.

22

"MAY I introduce myself?" said the voice close to Jewel's ear. "I am Magda Priolia." Jewel looked up and saw the Contessa Dal Bezo. "May I sit down?"

"Oh!" Jewel cried. "Yes, please do!" It was early evening and Jewel sat in her usual spot on the Gritti terrace waiting for Johnnie to return from the Lido.

"You are surprised? Yes, a little shocked, and I think you do not like me very much—no?" began the contessa with a charming laugh. Jewel could not think what to say. "Yes, I see it in your eyes. How delightful—she does not pretend!" the contessa murmured, almost to herself, with an accent that sounded strange, guttural, yet pleasing, too; she pronounced the words with a lilt, emphasizing the wrong syllables. Jewel could not place the accent or anything about the woman from her looks. She had determined to dislike Magda yet this seemed impossible, for she was charming, her tone so pleasant, confiding! "He speaks of you," continued Magda. "Yes, often! He is mad about you—I have never seen him this way. No, please!" With one strong brown hand Magda reached to restrain Jewel. "Don't say anything yet, I beg you."

"I won't," Jewel said, mesmerized by that lovely hand. Magda searched in her bag, found a cigarette, smoked. Her hands were mannish and surprisingly sinewy, not those of a lady, Jewel noticed. Hands that worked. She remembered the other evening as the match flared and Lalo gazed into his stepmother's eyes—then looked up and scowled. The incident had mortified Jewel. She waited for him to refer to it but he had not. Then, a few days later, she spoke of it.

"You dined with the contessa night before last. I did not know you two were friends," she said coldly.

"Ah—friends!" And he smiled. "Yes, and I saw you, all Venice saw you on your balcony, my dear." This had been the end of it.

"It may seem strange, my interest in you," continued the woman, "but you see, I am pleased for Lalo. You cannot imagine how unhappy he has been." She gazed into Jewel's incredulous eyes with surprising softness. "I know, I know! You and I are meant to hate one another! He and I are enemies. I suppose he tells you he loathes me," said Magda, while her eyes strayed from Jewel's face to the diamond peacock pinned to Jewel's white cowboy shirt. "But I will confess something to you—I do not dislike my stepson at all, no, not at all!" As she lifted her eyes to Jewel's a curious thrill passed between them.

"But then why—" said Jewel.

"Why? It would take me days," said Magda. She was elated. She saw Jewel liked her. Something in Magda's face spoke out plainly, begged confidence. Jewel felt intrigued; she yearned to trust Magda because something in the other woman's eyes amazed her, a candid desperation. It almost seemed she courted Jewel. For the first time Jewel smiled.

"I come out so rarely," said the contessa. "You see, I am not very fond of people. Has he told you?" Jewel hated herself for a quick-darting thought: had Magda come to her for money? Had Lalo sent her? Was there a collusion—or did she imagine it?

"He did not send me, you know," continued Magda. "Perhaps you think I come to you for money? I could have come to you for that, it is true—I am capable of it! Yes. For we have nothing." There it was: *we.* A slow heat rose up Jewel's neck.

"I don't understand any of this," Jewel said.

"Ah, why would you!" Magda dipped in closer. Jewel felt lulled by the soft rolling words which sounded like some delightful foreign language, obscure, oddly lifting. Magda leaned in, pressed closer; she came away from the railing, the canal bubbling behind, green, thick as soup, it churned and rolled and Jewel let herself be lulled: golden sea monsters, she thought idly, with brassy tails, soft lights scudding through the waters; Magda dipped in closer, listing slightly, a sail listing to the sea then righting itself; darkly poised beneath a downward bleeding sky, beckoning like some lovely chimera. "May I be honest with you? I am afraid. So much is at stake. You are a stranger, yet I need your help desperately. Does this frighten you? I see it does. You know nothing of me except what people have told you."

"But I don't listen to that," said Jewel.

"I know."

"Anyway, I don't really know anybody here." This was not absolutely true. Several days ago Jewel had been asked to tea by a Baroness Uzo de Mar, someone Nanine insisted her niece call.

"I assure you I do not make an accusation," Magda said. This startled Jewel, for she frequently heard those exact words in Lalo's mouth.

The Baroness Uzo de Mar, a horse-faced lady with

yellow teeth, had got together a collection of moth-eaten English ladies and one giggling Englishman to meet Jewel. They did not pretend any interest in Jewel. Between sips of weak tea and the solemn crunching of biscuits there began an animated discussion of how splendidly the Buxtehude had gone off last Sunday. In a lull they finally asked Jewel if she had any acquaintance in Venice. When she mentioned Lalo's name the ladies all stared and the Englishman threw back his head and brayed like a mule from the sheer excitement of that name being said out loud.

"My dear, think of me as your friend!" said the baroness as soon as she got Jewel off alone to view the Tiepolo. "You are very far from home. Are you rich? I do hope you are! What? Not rich! Well, dear—beware! Tell me, has he forced his attentions on you yet?"

"I don't know what you mean," said Jewel.

"Yes, yes," said the baroness. "Well, then I suppose it's too late! My dear, the Count Dal Bezo is quite famous for it. Yes, quite the man, quite the bull." She gave Jewel a friendly poke. "But you see, dear Jewel, he runs after everything! You will have to be very rich to keep him— heehee!"

"And the contessa?" said Jewel.

"Yes, he's had her, too, I'm quite sure of it. They're like that!" said the baroness, who wagged two fingers at Jewel. "Stay away from them, this is my advice. Definitely stay away from the contessa—he at least is Venetian!"

"Jewel. May I call you Jewel?" said Magda. "And please—you must call me Magda. Jewel, may I ask you something? Do you love him?"

"Yes, I love him," Jewel said slowly. "I don't know what you want from me."

"I have offended you!" said Magda.

"No, not really. I guess I just have trouble understanding you Italians," said Jewel.

"But I am not Italian," said Magda.

"What are you then?" said Jewel.

"I will tell you everything I can, but later," cried Magda. "You see, Jewel, the world I have come from is nothing like your world." As Jewel gazed into that other woman's eyes she found herself being won over by an odd recognition. She felt as if she *knew* Magda. Magda smiled, reached out her hand, touched Jewel.

"You *do* understand!" she said almost tenderly. "Do you think it possible to care for someone without knowing anything—without knowing who they are or anything about their past?"

"Yes. I absolutely do," Jewel declared, and returned the slight pressure of Magda's hand. "How can I help you?" said Jewel.

"I place myself at your mercy by coming here. You see how nervous I am. I talk, I tell you things—I am trapped here, you see, I have nothing, nothing but the palazzo he says is his. Do you understand? Do you judge me?"

"No," said Jewel solemnly. "I want to hear it all."

"You see, I have what he wants—the deed to Palazzo Prioli—and he has what I want—my freedom!"

"Why don't you tell him these things? What have I to do with it?"

"I see," said Magda. For Jewel the silence was shaming.

"Whatever I can do I will do, but I'm not sure I understand."

Behind them at the Gritti dock they heard the motor launch arrive from the Lido; Jewel waved to Johnnie.

"You should meet my cousin," she said.

"Not now," Magda said quickly as she stood to go.

"But tell me, may I call you? Will you see me again?" As Johnnie came near, Magda touched Jewel on the shoulder, then turned quickly and slid away, disappeared into the Gritti and out the other side into the *campo* beyond.

"What was that all about?" asked Johnnie, not hiding his irritation. "Why did you let her walk away?"

"It's so strange, Johnnie, but she came to me for help. Isn't that odd?"

"And will you?" he asked.

"You're a curious man, Johnnie," said Jewel. "You don't ask why she came to me or what sort of help she wants."

But Johnnie said nothing; he only stared into the canal.

23

A DRAGON emerged from the basilica during Johnnie's second week in Venice, crossed Piazza San Marco, and sat down at Florian Caffé. Although he excited admiration from the tourists and was quite a splendid sight sipping coffee, legs crossed, his tail of silver scales trailing behind in the aisle, it seemed to Johnnie that in this surrounding the dragon really wasn't so remarkable. When he appeared the following evening in resplendent parrot green and in the next days in gold, peacock blue, a slithering cerise, his presence seemed so altogether natural Johnnie refrained from asking the waiter why he was there. In some way Johnnie felt sure the dragon was there for him. On the seventh evening the dragon did not appear. This, too, was a sign: Johnnie decided he must either leave Venice the next day—or tell the contessa he was in love with her.

Johnnie had not been alone with her yet, he had not even been introduced. Jewel and Magda were becoming fast friends but so far this did not include him. He had said no more than a few words to the woman—yet he felt sure he loved her!

Lalo gave Jewel his permission to befriend Magda; this delighted and amused him; Jewel seemed piqued. Was he playing with her? If so, almost to test him, she declared herself Magda's friend.

"In Venice, you see, we devour our friends. This may seem curious to you," said Lalo as he dined one evening with Jewel and Johnnie at Locanda Montin, "for I know Americans are squeamish. What does it mean—a *real* friend? There is no real friend. Are you sure you are my friend? Yes? If so, then give me everything, give Lalo all your money!" He cackled at them; he loved to tease her. "The honest man, he has no illusions about any of this. He is the only man worth having for a friend—and because he is honest, does not pretend, is not sentimental, he cannot be a friend, no, not as you would have it. His needs overcome everything. And why shouldn't they? We are put here to be used. The best do it first—no? I see you make a face—it is not pretty, life, it has a powerful stink, I agree. But what do you mean by friendship?"

"That we each give what we are able to give. And that we accept whatever the other gives, even if it isn't enough. This is the real generosity between friends, this acceptance," said Jewel.

"Bah! So friendship, for you, is a contract between merchants? For me this is not interesting," said Lalo.

"Would you have her give you her diseases?" demanded Johnnie, who loathed the man by now.

"Shall I tell you how it is?" asked Lalo. "They imagine they are friends, those two. See, there is already the fever of love a woman feels for her woman friend. They save it for each other, this fever. They don't trust us, you see. And why should they? I know all about it—and I am jealous! This one—" he laid his hand on top of Jewel's, "she will betray me like *that*—poof!" Lalo snapped his fingers at Johnnie. "But why suffer?" Lalo saw that in spite of everything they were amused; their fantastic American good humor appalled him, their innocence which he did not believe in for one second. No one stayed innocent who had lived three hours. He sneered, sending them into peals of laughter.

"You see, my dears, it will not last. Let the women bask all they like in this orgy of love, self-love in fact. Let them listen. Believe. Who else believes in their suffering? At last, she says—an accomplice!"

"It is true," said Jewel, calm enough, but Johnnie saw she was angry, "nothing is so passionate in the beginning as a new friendship among women, and do you know why? It's as if you have finally been given permission to be yourself."

"And a man? He does not give you permission?" demanded Lalo.

"Not at all! Most women feel they must perform to please some man, they don't value themselves unless they get his approval."

"What man?" said Lalo. "Am I this man? Or perhaps he is the handsome cousin here with the muscles. You see how frustrating it is for us." And he turned to Johnnie, smiling sleekly. "They hate us, I think, for wanting them, for not wanting them. It's a conspiracy, this pitiful need for us—I tell you, nothing binds people together so well as a conspiracy!"

Jewel looked disgusted. "You haven't understood anything. He never listens," she said to Johnnie. Lalo squinted at them like a sly child. He loved to provoke these little dialogues. Sometimes he so upset Jewel that she rushed from the restaurant in a fury.

"It was you who suggested we be friends!" she cried.

"Maybe he's afraid he won't be necessary anymore," Johnnie said.

"Afraid?" said Lalo, delicately, as if he were picking

up the word and holding it out before him on the end of pincers. "Afraid?"

"Yes, and why shouldn't he be afraid," said Johnnie softly. "He has everything to lose."

"What is it the handsome cousin thinks I have to lose?" Lalo asked. He still smiled.

"I think you know what I mean," said Johnnie.

"Say what you mean!" said Lalo. Jewel saw he was livid.

"He doesn't mean anything," she said quickly, scowling at Johnnie.

"Oh, but he does! This man—he says I have something to lose! You tell me! What! What is it? Go ahead, ask me! Isn't that why he is here? To interrogate me? What is it he wants to know? How much money I have? Ha! That waiter has more than I do! Tell him Lalo has nothing." Johnnie would only grin at him, eyes half shut, peaceful. Lalo thought, the man is an imbecile—why is he smiling? He is nothing like Jewel. Sometimes he felt sure she would produce a big knife, stab it into the table; he liked it, the hot words, her indignation, she believed in things, absurd things; her girlish truths meant nothing to him, he always won the argument because he didn't believe in anything. What should he do with this cousin? He turned it around suddenly: "Is this why you hate a man—because he has no money? Is this how you do it in America? Is it so contemptible to be poor?" Lalo turned to Jewel and cried, "If this is so—tell me now!"

"You know it's not true! I've never cared about that— you know it! You were very wrong to do this, Johnnie!" she cried. Johnnie sat quietly. He had never seen anything so contemptible as this aging Lothario with his spit-shined shoes. She had fallen for it. Johnnie yearned to slap that insolent face, smack him hard, but he understood that it was too late, he had lost. He lulled himself into thinking it no longer mattered who his cousin fell for. Again he must look on as she lavished herself on some fool, on the wrong man. He showed no contempt in his smile, only a disturbing quiet which she knew and dreaded. Across the table Lalo said, "I teach her to live. To enjoy. Yes, foolishness, I know—but what else are we here for? I see in your cousin's eyes, that word—money. He does not believe you can live without it. Money. And now, you must convince the rich cousin to pay the bill for Lalo has no money! It is one of the great luxuries of the poor, no? We don't pay the check."

Later, after Lalo had left them, Johnnie stood a moment at Jewel's door and said, "I used to think you chose these men to destroy yourself."

"And now?" she said coolly.

"Now I suspect you need them in order to resurrect."

"Resurrect myself?" she was stung. "Is it so terrible for you to see me happy—because of him?"

"Not at all," he said with that peculiar softness she did not trust.

"I won't listen if you're going to say anything hateful," she said.

"You remind me of those wild, strange, little hardy plants that seem so delicate and pure but will only grow in impossible places. Blooming, springing up miraculously out of swamps and dung heaps."

"You'd like to spoil it. You hate it that I found the way."

"Beautiful mushrooms," he went on, reaching for her but she pulled away, "and those translucent white poppies shimmering in the cow shit."

"It has nothing to do with you. Is that what you refuse to accept? That I can be so happy without the things you believe in? Well, guess what—he's shown me how. And you hate it. Maybe I am resurrected, brand new, what's

wrong with that? That's what kills you, isn't it—that I'm
free of your world, I don't even miss it, and you can't
survive without it. You would perish here—you have to
go back!" The words rang out with an unmistakable
triumph. Again he reached for her but she had the door
open and slipped inside quickly. "You would never survive here." she said and then disappeared.

Johnnie wandered toward San Marco with no particular destination in mind. His evening strolls sometimes
led him to the farthest corners of Venice. He had
searched out the most obscure passageways with an unhappy persistence, almost as if he knew something must
be hidden there and he had to go on till he found it. He
watched for Magda. He felt sure that one evening he
would encounter her; by now there was no other reason
to stay. Jewel seemed almost to have turned against him.
Why else would she refuse to arrange a meeting for him
with her new friend unless she felt he would interfere?
What a fool he had been to think he might have saved
Jewel—did anyone ever really want to be saved? But *this*
woman told Jewel *she* needed to be saved. His cousin, he
knew, felt thrilled at the prospect; between them those
two had arranged everything and he was in the way. At
the onset of this wonderful new friendship he had asked
Jewel, "Have you ever told these people you are penniless?" and she flew at him in a rage, insisting she had told
Lalo she was poor from the start but that he had only
laughed in her face. No, she would not suspect either her
lover or her friend of hidden motives. Johnnie she con-
demned for his meanness, for that appallingly conven-
tional American stance—suspicion of foreigners or
anyone at all odd or helpless or threatening. Why *should*
she introduce him to her friend and have him ruin everything?

He stayed in Venice though it made Jewel uneasy—

why linger? He admitted the place left him cold. Everything seemed too nice on the surface. This mirage; and the two of them, he and Jewel, were at odds. This was the longest he had ever gone without doing anything. He did not count seeing palaces and paintings and four-hour luncheons as doing anything at all. On the lookout for the contessa, Johnnie showed himself in all the right places: Harry's Bar before lunch, or the Cipriani for a swim, or in the Calle XXII Marzo for the late-afternoon promenade. Jewel said he left behind a ripple of disconsolate ladies in his wake but this meant nothing to Johnnie. He watched for Magda at every corner. He saw her only once, disappearing down an alleyway. He had even suited up one hellish hot evening and gone with Lalo and Jewel to the Fenice for the opening of *Parsifal,* an agonizing sacrifice, and still he did not find her.

He and Jewel fought over it more than once.

"I won't introduce you so don't keep asking me," Jewel had said. "I've told you—she doesn't want to meet you now."

"I've never heard of anything so goddamn strange. What has she got against me? How could she make up her mind based on one hello and—"

"You've got to stop this! Magda is in mourning, you know, and I don't think she wants to complicate things by meeting a man, no, not even my cousin—not till she clears up this mess with Lalo. She'll meet you after that, she's said so."

"She did? Well, then what did she say? It all seems silly to me—you spend hours with her, the two of you are thick as thieves all of a sudden, you see as much of her as you do of Lalo—more, I suspect—and you say she's become your close friend yet I'm not allowed to go near her. By God, Jewel, I won't stand for it!"

"You're jealous!" cried Jewel. "I've never seen you so

worked up over a woman. It's not at all becoming to you,
I can tell you that—and Magda doesn't like it. She hates
being stalked, so you might as well give it up."

"Magda! What does she know? She hasn't even seen
me—"

"Magda sees everything," Jewel said. "And I know she
doesn't like it."

Hardly a day went by that Magda did not leave some
little offering at Jewel's door. A bouquet or some exciting package tied with ribbons, and a note: "Will you
meet me for tea?" Or "Something sad and horrid has just
happened—how soon can you meet me?"

Without burdening her friend with what Magda
called the horrors of life she imparted to Jewel intoxicating snatches of her history: a mention of soldiers and
killings; as a child watching her mother being murdered.
Jewel suspected Magda was Hungarian and that she had
fled her country in 1956. Where she went from there
remained a mystery; Magda did not like to be ques-
tioned. She sometimes referred to a ruthless, fascinating
father and many servants. Her own father, Jewel said,
had been a good man, weak and lost, but tender. She
always began to cry when she thought of Horace and
could not bear to discuss him with her friend; she had
never told anybody about Horace's killing himself.
Magda always said the same thing when she realized
time and again how softhearted Jewel was: "My dear
Jewel, you really are a superb creature!"

If Jewel felt reluctant to discuss Horace and Mary
Lou, she spoke about Johnnie with great candor. As a
rule they mostly spoke of the present—that other world
out there beyond Venice had no real value for them.
Magda only recently learned that Jewel had been a
painter who fled from her career with disgust and disil-
lusionment. She never pressed Jewel about her work.

She was wonderfully discreet. Although Jewel really did not want her friend to meet Johnnie she often felt obliged to work the conversation back to him. One day Magda said to her, "I think you like him very much—I think you love him a lot, this cousin of yours, no?"

"Well, of course I love him!" exclaimed Jewel. "He's dearer to me than anyone else on earth!"

"Dearer than a certain Venetian count we know?" probed Magda with a curious little smile on her lips.

For a moment Jewel didn't answer, but then she laughed to cover her confusion. "It's different, you know. I'm in love with Lalo—but with Johnnie, what can I say? I am an only child, so is he, we grew up together."

"He was an ally, no? Your brother."

"Not that. In fact, sometimes I tell him he is anything but my friend. If he had his way he'd have me hog-tied and married to some cowpoke who never leaves the state! Me, of all people! Just to have me placed and secure. What he wants is to be sure of me, but of course that's impossible."

"Is it?" asked Magda.

"The way I see it, it doesn't pay to be too sure of anybody."

"Not even this wonderful cousin. But I thought—"

"You can love somebody without being sure of them! Why, I'd die for Johnnie and I know he'd do the same for me." Jewel's tone was fierce.

"But this is serious!" said her friend. Jewel stared at her.

"Don't you have anyone you feel that way about?" she asked Magda.

"No," said Magda. "I am alone. Tell me—what is so wonderful about this cousin who isn't a brother and is not an ally?"

"He's the only person I've ever known whose identity seems absolutely apart from other people's expectations."

"Then he has a revolutionary spirit?" asked Magda.

"He's what I'd call a maverick. Sometimes I think he needs no one," Jewel mused.

"Except his cousin." Magda smiled.

"He doesn't need me."

"Then perhaps he is cold. If he needs no one!"

"Cold? Not Johnnie. He's got a fire inside him all right, but it's not in the usual way. He's a quiet man. He doesn't spill out, he saves himself quietly and silently; he stores it up. But all the same, he's a romantic. Let me tell you a story about him. Well, out where he lives you often get the same telephone operator when you make a long-distance call. When he was about eighteen he fell for the long-distance operator. Her name was Rita and she had a voice like honey. Every time he placed a call they would talk, these two, and one day Johnnie asked where she lived and if he could take her to dinner. Rita said she lived in Willcox, a town about fifty miles away, and that she'd be delighted to have dinner with him. So Johnnie got all slicked up one night and drove to Willcox and found her door and rang the bell. There she was. Well, you can just about imagine! A huge fat woman, pretty old, too, a lot older than Johnnie, no beauty I can tell you, and there was Johnnie looking like a young god. Now any other man would've backed out of there fast and this Rita said, 'Son, I'm not going to hold you to it, hear?' But Johnnie wanted no part of that. He took Rita out to the nicest spot in town for a big steak dinner and they talked half the night and when he took her home Rita said, 'Son, I just want you to know—no one, and I mean *no one*, has ever treated me so nice.' "

Magda smiled at Jewel but didn't say anything.

"You see, all of the so-called gentlemen ranchers from our part of the world come up to Tucson and hang out at the M.O. Club," continued Jewel. "M.O.—you know what that means? Mountain oyster."

"Mountain oyster?" said Magda.

"Bulls' balls—they fry them and eat them," said Jewel, who laughed at Magda's revulsion. "They sit around all day long drinking whiskey and they talk cows, but Johnnie, he cut out on his own long ago. He keeps to himself. He likes to dream, to think. Or sometimes just for the hell of it he goes across the border to stay with one of the vaqueros and sleeps with the family on a mud floor or in a hammock in a house filled with snoring bodies. And in those little two-room mud-house villages they adore him. He speaks Spanish like a bandit, rides with the men, hunts mountain lion, goes off for days. You're seeing him here, of course, in his city clothes. But you'd be surprised if you could see him as he really is. In old Levi's, boots, chaps, spurs, a beat-up Stetson. He's quite a sight on a horse, just what a man ought to be. In *this* world, he doesn't seem nearly as beautiful as he is at home. I wish you could see Johnnie there, Magda."

Her friend's apathy on this subject disappointed her sometimes. Even when Jewel announced to Magda that Johnnie was taken with her, she did not seem sufficiently moved.

"Do you know, I really do think we talk more about Johnnie than anything else—and yet you know, my dear, I am intrigued that you don't want me to meet him!" Magda said.

Jewel stared at her. "But you said you wouldn't meet him!" she exclaimed.

"Did I?" Magda returned her friend's gaze with tender reproach. "Shall I tell you what I think, dear Jewel? You would hate it if I fell in love with this exciting cousin.

I know it. And if he loved me? No, my dear, I do not
think so. It is best we do not meet. And after all, perhaps
I am a little jealous, and want you all to myself. It is
enough that I must share you with Lalo, no?" She
stroked Jewel's hand and at last Jewel smiled but she felt
quite sure of one thing: Magda had insisted she did not
want to meet Johnnie. Why did she pretend Jewel had
forbidden their meeting?

AS JOHNNIE strolled toward San Marco he resolved to see
Magda, even if it meant going to her palazzo. He was
furious enough to do it and had just planned his attack
when at that moment he saw her coming out of one of
the little side streets emerging from Fenice and turning
into Calle XXII Marzo. She saw him and stopped. She
seemed momentarily at a loss but then quickly decided
to go on except that he caught her arm. The gesture
amazed them both, and he said to her, "Please wait. I
want to talk with you. Will you come with me over
there—for a drink or a coffee?" He nodded toward the
piazza.

Magda stood a moment, undecided. "I don't think I
should," she said at last, not unkindly but with a certain
abrupt intimacy in her tone that instantly gave him
hope. "It won't do any good, you know," she added with
a little smile. He led her toward Florian Caffé and found
them a table in one of the little coffee rooms. He ordered
for them and Magda waited for him to begin but he
seemed finally to feel no need to explain himself and only
watched her with what she took to be a satisfied, almost
humorous delight. After a moment of this she found
herself less sure. She hadn't meant for them to meet this
way. She would not have risked an encounter only he
had been so insistent; she felt intrigued in spite of her-

self. How much better it would have been if Jewel had
introduced them at last, perhaps when that other business was finished. She stared back at him coldly and said,
"There is no point to this." He grinned at her. Suddenly
she was angry.

"You stare at me. What do you want?" She seemed
disconcerted by his quiet, easy confidence. When he still
did not answer but only closed his eyes a moment, as if
to shut her out, and opened them, gazing at her with an
undiluted tenderness, she suddenly gave way. He saw
this and reached to take her hand but just as quickly she
pulled it away. Confused, she had never expected him to
be so sure of himself and of her. For a moment she
determined to go away but he fixed his gaze on her with
a steady brightness she could not resist; how delightful,
this admiration, it seemed he wanted to adore her. She
sank back with a little sigh, almost in assent, and said to
him in very different tones, "Don't you know how she
will hate me for this?"

"Leave Jewel to me," he said softly. "Are you afraid?"

"Yes," she said wearily.

"Of losing Jewel? Is your situation so—"

"Desperate? You know it is." She left her hand on the
little table near his own but not touching. "Jewel has
promised to help. You see, she loves me."

"I love you, too, you know," he said with that strange
fearless quiet and, soft as they were, the words leaped
inside her like a little fire.

She turned away, gathering up her handbag and
shawl, and murmured, "You say you love me, both of
you. But what does this mean? I am a fool to believe in
it." He half rose as if to prevent her from leaving—he
was so young, a great deal younger, Magda knew, than
she was, and he had shown her all his feelings in that first
instant, never suspecting that he had already excited her

interest, long before tonight. "A fool!" she said quietly. They were alone in the little room now, and before she could think what he would do he took her in his arms and kissed her deeply, fully on the mouth, a slow, long kiss, and Magda fell back against the banquette with a long sigh, arching her throat up toward him as he kissed her again.

24

LALO WAS at his wit's end. First, his tailor had absolutely turned him away. The humiliation! Then DiCicci, his lawyer, looked the other way as he passed him in the street: Scum! And yesterday the cousin took him aside to announce he would get nothing from Jewel—nothing! The blow was severe but he had carried it off with a bold flashing delighted glance, showing his teeth to the man in a derisive grin and then tapping his nostril twice, winking, nodding to show he knew something, that maybe he even knew something the cousin did not know, and he succeeded in annoying the man thoroughly. But the fact remained: Jewel had nothing! Had anyone ever been so unlucky?

He could hardly think how he must treat her now. She lay beside him in bed curled up in sleep, her fingers curled around two of his; she had cried to herself softly before falling asleep—he had seen—and the babyish blond curls stuck to her cheek damply. She was still slightly flushed, lovely; he saw this yet felt unmoved. Tomorrow was her birthday. She had made quite a thing of it—turning forty. The cousin had even offered to take her to Monte Carlo for her birthday but Jewel said she wanted to stay with him and he planned to take her to the island of Malamocco for the day. What should he do with her? He was a reasonable man, everyone said so, but if she really was poor, as poor as he was, why should he stay with her? Why hadn't she told him just how poor she was? Of course she had told him she had almost nothing, that money meant nothing to her, but women always said these things in the beginning, didn't they? Indeed, it began to feel as though he had been fooled. There really might be a conspiracy between those two. Magda must have known the girl was penniless—yes, she had known and she had a plan. This skulking lizard of a female had a plan to get the rich cousin for herself.

"I tell you they are lovers!" Lalo said to Jewel, earlier that evening.

"I don't believe a word of it," she said, yawning at him as she dropped her clothes on the floor and climbed into bed, knowing he hated this. "She wouldn't even meet him for lunch."

"I tell you I saw them with my own eyes! Play the fool, go ahead, what do I care . . . but you ask her, ask your precious friend if she fucks with your cousin—yes, and why shouldn't she? Why not?" he shouted. "He is big, he is American, he is rich—yes, you make an ugly face, you do not believe Lalo, I see it, but this friend of yours, she is interested in one thing, only one: to survive! Listen, carissima: what do you know about this gnawing rat hunger she feels? This woman, she survives with her teeth—don't you think I know?"

"I tell you, you're wrong!" said Jewel, and she believed it with all her heart. And the more he said to defame Magda the more Jewel began to doubt him. She loved him but he did not trust her as Magda did. He treated her like a wayward child. When she complained of this to her friend, Magda only smiled. "My dear, as long as you let them treat you like a child this is what you will be," Magda had said to her. "Do you really like a man to be your 'companion'? Isn't that what you call it in America? One has a dog for that. The whole point is that you find a worthy adversary. How else do we ever know who we are? It's the struggle that makes life so interesting, no? The others, these 'reasonable' men who understand, who accept everything as it is, they are your friends—but as lovers, dear Jewel, it never works. Poor things, they put one to sleep."

Magda never said a word against Lalo yet in so many ways she allowed Jewel to see his flaws as fascinations; outrages and absurdities were always suggested to Jewel in ways to make them seem intriguing. Jewel once had the impossible idea to make peace between those two, but even Magda admitted this was hopeless.

If, as Lalo always insisted, money is what Magda wanted, Jewel did not despise her friend for this. She offered to pawn the diamond peacock, much as she hated to part with a treasure given her by Dinwiddie, but Magda had been singularly reticent; it seemed she did not approve of her friend's selling the jewel to subsidize Lalo. Finally Magda asked where Jewel had gotten such a valuable thing and Jewel playfully told her it came from a secret admirer—guess who? "Actually, my uncle in New York gave it to me," Jewel said. "It's not at all like me, you can see that. I'm not much for fancy jewels, but there is something about this bird, I don't know what it is—do you see what I mean? I think of it as sort of a symbol of my new freedom. Turning forty; and this idea I have that now everything will be different somehow, that I've been set free." But Magda had turned the color of ash. She insisted Jewel must never again speak of pawning the pin. But how else could she help Magda?

She thought about it all the time and Lalo, merciless, tweaked her about it.

"And what is she planning to do for you, this wonderful friend?" he hooted at her constantly. "She can't give you my great-grandmother's seed pearl tiara, she's already sold that—maybe she will give you—"

"Oh, cut it out," snapped Jewel. "I'm tired to death of the horrid things you say about Magda. She doesn't say things about you!"

"And what should she say? That I've embezzled her out of her family's five-hundred-year-old palazzo? Or that I've arranged secret meetings late at night with the handsome cousin to weasel a little money out of that poor fool? I tell you she will do anything for the money!"

"Money?" Jewel laughed in his face. "Sometimes I don't even think we're talking about the same person! When I offered to sell my diamond peacock if it would help, she refused! It isn't money she wants—not at that price. She wants to go free. And no one thinks less of money than Johnnie does! He doesn't even give Christmas presents! For God's sake, look at his clothes—he had those boots at Yale, that jacket, too, they're almost twenty years old!"

Lalo shuddered. "So he is—how you say it?—a tightwad? You mean he will not help her even if she is desperate? What a charming fellow. I never heard of such meanness!"

"Look here, you'd better watch what you say about my cousin. I'm sick of you saying rotten things about both of them, I don't have to listen to this."

"Who keeps you here? Go!" he shouted. "Go!" And Lalo slumped forward with his head in his hands. Only this morning they had carted away the mouse-gray sofa; they sat in the salon on kitchen chairs; soon they would be coming for the chandelier.

"Lalo, darling." Jewel stood behind him and began to caress his head.

"Go!" he cried, but the word had a pitiful sound.

"Would you like me to stay here with you tonight?" she asked. She almost brought herself to suggest she move in with him. She still had a small sum of money set aside for the rent at the Palace of the Lily and if it might be better spent on his household— But she said nothing, remembering the look on Magda's face when she had suggested pawning the peacock; sometimes it was impossible to know how to help these people. Anyway, he was so disagreeable tonight, it had better wait.

"Do what you like," he said sulkily. "Lalo is too depressed to notice anything tonight." He appeared quite docile as he followed her into the bedroom but he was thinking: Trapped! Trapped! How will I ever get rid of her? He showed none of this, however, as he climbed into bed and Jewel petted him and made a great fuss over him and he pretended to be docile but his brain seethed with terrible thoughts. What should he do if Magda actually snared the fellow? Magda and that slab of American beef! Where would that leave him? They had an agreement, after all, didn't they? If they could arrange to have Jewel finance him and pay off their debts at Palazzo Prioli, he would give Magda everything else and she would leave the palazzo. Whenever Lalo thought of this "everything" he nearly moaned out loud, for this was the one treasure he had left besides the palazzo and despite his dire straits, and at the risk of losing his last belonging, he still managed to hang on to the Prioli emerald: a ring of surpassing beauty whose greatest fascination was that it had belonged to the gruesome Francesco III, the Mad Duke of the Archipelago, a maniac and murderer who was said to have stolen it somehow from Selim the Sot, a sultan in the Ottoman Empire some five hundred years ago. The ring had belonged to the Prioli doge; it had once been kissed by the young Ludovico Manin, who later became doge himself. Lalo's father, in a fit of uncontrollable bile, had once accused his son of selling the Prioli emerald—a dastardly accusation! Sell the Prioli emerald! The only thing worse would be to sell the palazzo and no Priolio had even whispered such an idea to himself, not even now, when everything might really be lost. And of course his stepmother knew of the ring, all Venice knew of the ring. He had said he would give her everything if she would help and she thought he had meant the emerald. Perhaps he had, in truth, offered it to her. She had sworn she would help him. Make sure of the girl's devotion so that both their interests would be served. But now, what if she snagged this rich cousin? Would they remove him from the palazzo, buy it out from under him? She could do that if he had no means to settle his debts. What if she remained here always to live in the palazzo with her American lover? Lalo would have nothing!

And what was he to do with Jewel? She had grown very fond of him. Lalo believed in the theory of geese: When the goose awakens he attaches himself to the first object he sees: a stick, a human, another goose, believing this to be his mother. So it was with Jewel. After a long sleep she awakened and saw Lalo. Indeed, it had been pleasant to seduce her but now that was over—what must he do? They had fattened her for the prospect of marriage. Magda had been sure Jewel would go for it. He groaned out loud, then remembered she was here in bed with him. But she was asleep. See how peaceful she seems now, she even smiles over some delicious dream. Drat the girl, she was beginning to infuriate him! She would stick to him, this he knew, for she was a passionate little creature; she would be loyal. Lalo groaned, rolling

in his bed, but it was Magda he hated. What a mess this
jezebel had gotten him into. Foul hussy. He felt sure she
was downstairs humping her rich American this very
moment. Fiend! And what if he had actually married the
girl thinking her to be rich! Endless years of domestic
bliss—he nearly swooned thinking of it—*married*! Then
he remembered: he had not yet married her! In a way
this cousin had done him a great favor. So it was he who
had all the money. He almost wished the rich cousin
would offer to buy him off. He was not too squeamish to
take their money. But then he remembered, his stepmother would now find some way to prevent the offer.
He moaned out loud and gnashed his teeth in the dark.
And what if she had known all along, this venomous
she-toad, that Jewel had nothing? Women are experts,
aren't they, at divining such things. What if all along it
had been Magda's purpose to ruin him, to revenge herself for that one night ten years ago when he had tried
to take her. What a perfect revenge, to ensnare him in
this vat of domestic goo with a penniless Florence Night-
ingale! Agggh! He almost felt like pushing Jewel out of
bed onto the floor. Tears of self-pity and outrage stung
at his eyeballs—Lucrezia Borgia had entrapped him. At
this very moment she was almost certainly in his own
house seducing that slab of beef, wallowing in the ancestral sheets, supping on dainties two floors below in the
piano nobile, lolling about on the baronial sofas, rolling in
all those heavenly piles of money while the last of the
tribe of Prioli shivered in his attic. Lalo had to put his
fist in his mouth to keep from screaming.

As the night crawled on, he took no comfort in the
body by his side except to rage at her occasionally for her
undisturbed slumber. Lalo gave himself up to imagining
various scenarios. What if ten days after he rid himself
of Jewel the cousin was killed in a cattle stampede and

left everything to her? Would Jewel take him back? He thought yes. What if he went to the cousin and threw himself down on those twenty-year-old boots and confessed everything—that Magda had dreamed up a plot to save them both, it had all been her idea, she had approached him with it—would Johnnie give him a reward? No. Not if the man was a tightwad. What if the other three left Venice with a pot of gold and he was left alone penniless? What a burden Jewel had become! Tomorrow she would be forty. She wasn't even young anymore.

25

"I WISH you had told me this before!" cried Magda, her voice filled with reproach. Jewel stared at her friend in amazement. "It seems extraordinary that I had to hear it from your cousin!" The two women sat together in Jewel's room in the Palace of the Lily. Magda had not visited her there before; usually they met somewhere else, as was the custom in Venice, but today was Jewel's birthday and in a few hours she would be leaving for Malamocco.

"But what are you talking about?" cried Jewel, alarmed.

Magda shook her head. For a long moment neither of them spoke. Jewel's thoughts began to race away crazily, then veer back from an unhappy suspicion, and all the while Magda gazed at her with utter disappointment—as if Jewel had done something unthinkable. The silence grew till it seemed unbearable. At last, in a low voice, Magda said, "I feel you tricked me."

"*Tricked* you!" The words flew out too sharply. Jewel felt on fire, the pulse in her neck quickened oddly. "Tricked you! What in hell are you saying?" Magda

would only shake her head sadly. She looked older suddenly; Jewel noticed lines at the neck, a certain coarsen-
ing there on the buttery sallow skin. Why, she must be
fifty! thought Jewel, and this made her even angrier. Her
friend had deceived people about her age and perhaps
everything else. "I won't have this, Magda—I won't be
accused! Did I ever say I am rich—did I? Of course I
didn't! Good God, what did you think—didn't I say I
would pawn the peacock for you?"

"I thought you were rich," Magda said at last.

"Magda, will you tell me something? Why did you
come to me that first day? There on the Gritti terrace—
what was it you wanted of me?"

"A friend," cried Magda. "An ally. I hoped . . ."

"What did you hope?"

"That you would rescue me! Rescue him! That if you
loved him—" The words rang out between them as an
accusation.

"But how? How was I supposed to rescue you?"

"How?" Magda stared. "Why, that you would marry
him, that you would buy him Palazzo Prioli, of course!"

"Buy Palazzo Prioli?" Jewel was flabbergasted. "But
how would that have freed *you*?" For a moment neither
of them said anything, then Jewel began to laugh. "And
you were to be rewarded somehow—is that it? But how?
He has nothing! What a disappointment I must have
been to you both—how could you bear it! And Lalo—"
Jewel's voice trailed away as she remembered Lalo, but
then again quickly she shied away from the suspicion
and said, "Buy Palazzo Prioli—my God! What did you
think? Did I ever do anything to mislead you? For God's
sake, Magda, how could you imagine that if I were rich
I would stand by and watch you two struggle for pen-
nies? Why, if I had anything you must know I would give
it to you! What do you think of me?"

"Look where you are living!" Magda answered her roughly. "You think I don't know what this place costs? And the jewel! The peacock—I know exactly what it is worth!" Jewel stared at Magda in horror. This was a voice she had never heard before. "I know exactly how it is. Those who have money, they like us to imagine they are poor. Do you think we are fooled?" Magda stopped, for the look on Jewel's face was very horrible.

Do you think we are fooled? Jewel stared at Magda as the other woman sank down onto the bed and buried her face in her hands. Magda saw that she had gone too far. What stupidity. She had lost everything, the weeks of careful work. Now she would have to stay here forever. The cousin—no, it was too painful to think of him. She had begun to care for him. But now that Jewel understood she would tell her cousin everything and he would believe her. They would go away. The truth of it was she had taught herself to care for Jewel; and she did love her, it was real enough; their friendship was the most tender and trusting she had ever known. But she had known it would not last. If only she could bring herself to some kind of confession, throw herself down, trust Jewel to be kind, it might not be too late. Magda's heart pounded at the thought, she snatched at it frantically. Was it too late? She would give it all up gladly, the emerald as well, the palazzo, and leave Venice a beggar if only they might not leave without her!

"Jewel, in all these weeks I have come to care for you! Please don't look away from me, I beg you!" The plea sounded genuine enough but Jewel had turned to ice. Magda dropped to the floor on her knees beside the bed. Jewel found the pose repulsive, she leaped up, but Magda clutched at her knees. Furious, Jewel tried to push Magda away. "Ask *him*!" Magda cried. Jewel knew im-

mediately that she meant Johnnie, and this angered her
more. "Ask him if I have been loyal to you!"

"What does my cousin have to do with this?" demanded Jewel.

"Nothing!" And Magda began to sob. "But he is the
one you will believe—ask him!" Now until this moment
Jewel really had believed that Magda would have nothing to do with Johnnie. She had believed her friend
rather than her lover. It pained her to do so but Jewel had
a dread of being unfair and it always seemed that Lalo,
who liked to make mischief with his accusations, was
testing her. Now, however, in the face of Magda's
strange behavior, what was she to think? She did not
believe Lalo ever had any business with his stepmother,
she could not believe this of him—and hadn't he tried to
warn her? All along he had sworn the woman was a
snake and Jewel refused to listen to him, even prided
herself on her magnanimity; it sickened her to think of
this now. No, it seemed far more likely that this
wretched woman would do anything to destroy Lalo's
character rather than bear the blame for this alone. And
now a far more terrible certainty bore in on her: Magda
and Johnnie were lovers.

"Have you been with him?" she asked, her face filled
with hate. "Look at me, Magda! Have you been with
Johnnie?"

"Only once."

"Where was I? When did you meet with him, Magda?"
She saw Magda hesitate. It seemed to Jewel that she
knew the worst and that to hear anything more would
be unbearable, yet she strained to hear what the woman
might say.

"It happened so quickly," Magda said at last. "It was
an accident. You see, we met in the street there by Fe-

nice. The night before last, I was returning from the
opera—"

"You said you didn't want to know him!" The cry
rang out, shocking them both. "Did you go with him to
his room?"

"No, I swear it, Jewel! We went to Florian's, we had
a drink, nothing more, it was late, I stayed a moment.
Just to talk—don't you believe me?"

But Jewel was turned to stone. Lalo had seen them, he
said he had come upon them kissing. And afterward he
followed them to the Gritti and watched Magda go inside. Later, the next day, he saw Johnnie emerging from
Palazzo Prioli. And Jewel had not believed him. She had
called her lover a liar. Magda choked over the words: he
had wanted her to go with him to the Gritti, this was
true, but she refused. "Because of *you* I refused!" Jewel's
friendship meant more to her!

"Tell me this one thing," Jewel said evenly. "Has
Johnnie been to Palazzo Prioli?" Magda gazed up at her
friend imploringly. Jewel's tone frightened her, yet she
drew herself together.

"Never, I swear it. On my life I swear to you he has
not been there."

"Never?" Jewel almost screamed. "Never? Lalo saw
him there!"

"Lalo—and so? Do you really believe what he says?"
Magda said with a sneer. And now Jewel saw how much
she hated the man. "You were the one who wanted your
cousin to be my friend. Didn't you want us to be
friends?" Jewel did not listen. She grew very pale, all the
anger left her suddenly. Something else remained, a
chilling fear. She could not think. Magda stood,
smoothed her clothes, and began to search in her bag for
a compact. She powdered her nose, her eyes, her lips,
tracing her features slowly with a puff of swansdown.

She lined her lips with red. "I can't think what friendship means to you if you won't trust me the first moment we quarrel. After all, Jewel, you were the one who insisted we be friends, Johnnie and I—and if you will remember, my dear, I refused! He will remind you—ask him!" Magda had made him swear he would not tell; she refused to let him leave her until he swore on his heart never to tell Jewel. They had made love the whole afternoon at Palazzo Prioli. Afterward she said, "Don't you know how Jewel feels? She is in love with you!" But he had laughed, he would not believe her. "No, it's you she's in love with!" he had said.

"You are such a fool," she told him, "she has always been in love with you."

After a moment's silence Jewel spoke. "You tried to get me to marry Lalo. You wanted me to marry him."

"But you love him, don't you?" said Magda. She snapped the compact shut. "What was I to think? You said you loved him!" She was beautiful once again, immaculate, and faced Jewel almost crisply, with the cool high-arched brows, the perfect lips framing a question in haughty tones; nothing was left of the wretched disheveled creature on the floor a moment ago and Jewel saw it all as for the first time—the dazzling length of bare brown leg in the sleek pumps, the dazzling rings, the clothes, the gold at her throat, the lustrous hair, all so expensive and fine—it nauseated her now, the whole terrible richness of the woman, her luxurious perfection which cost so much.

"You knew who I loved. You knew it even before I did!" cried Jewel. Her eyes filled with tears but she brushed them away.

"My dear Jewel, I am not a mind reader," said Magda. "I can only believe what you yourself tell me."

"But you knew."

"Shall I tell you what I know? You are terrified of love. You have loved him all your life—and what do you do? You send him away. What a child you are. A hopeless dreaming child, always wanting something more. Well, now look what you've done. Do you think you can play with people's lives and then dismiss them when it gets too hard? And now I am to be dismissed, too. Look at me, Jewel. You can't even look at me! Are you finished with me, am I to go? And Lalo? Are you finished with him, too?"

"I don't want to hear any more," said Jewel.

"No, of course you don't," said Magda. She stood a moment, undecided, then reached to pat Jewel's head, but Jewel pulled away. "I do love you, you know," she said in the most matter-of-fact way as she went to the bureau and straightened her hair, watching Jewel in the mirror all the while. "You are a curious girl. You really do believe in love, you believe in it more than the rest of us, yet you know nothing about it. Nothing. You are a ruthless child who smashes all her toys." Magda drew the comb through her hair slowly. "After a while when you are feeling better, darling Jewel, we will discuss all this calmly. Perhaps after—" Magda's voice trailed away. Three photographs crammed in a morocco frame drew her attention. She took the frame in her hand to examine it. A snapshot of Johnnie and a bleary photograph of Dinwiddie. And an old print of Jewel as a child: a little girl in chaps and boots sitting very tall on her horse. Next to the horse was a man. Magda froze. She turned to look at Jewel. Then, with a small terrified shriek, she threw the frame to the ground and ran from the room. Jewel did not move. At last she bent to pick up the frame and sat and studied the pictures. How odd, she thought, to be so like someone I scarcely knew. For the first time, she saw how much she resembled her father.

26

IT WAS one of those monumentally fine September days. A passing fog teased the morning with filaments of softly clinging moisture, a tender, billowing atmosphere, unearthly and caressing. All around their boat the Grand Canal trembled with splotches of freezing blue light, or now a glassy green. The Salute bore down on them from the opposite shore like a huge overdressed dowager bedecked in ropes of pearly light. In the basin just ahead, a CIGA boat cut through the water. Jewel squinted against the bright to follow its progress until far off, very small, it bobbed away like a thimble set to sea. She remembered something Johnnie said to her once: I rode into a rainbow, rode down into the very end of it, down into the bottom of some godforsaken canyon—but there was nothing, no pot of gold.

Now the sun burned a slow hole through the wet, light sprang out from sleep, the water breathed and fell away, now rising to a body of shivering diamonds, a beast rippling his shingled spine along the twisting canal, rolling, heaving up his diadem of gaudy morning light; or plunging down, the wanton shine, and glancing all around in lurid pools; metaled waters, copper eddies, a hard metallic light, acid green, a biting blue disappearing to oily black—a stinging shattered light raining down splinters of glassy air.

"Will it rain?" asked Jewel as a few jagged drops came down, but Lalo only pulled a face and whipped the boat faster still. Other boats passed them by, sudden boats, silvered apparitions, a sail, a cobalt scow, a streak of brilliant yellow, and vaporetti groaning under the happy burden of Sunday people. The beautiful young girls tossed and swished their manes like hot little ponies; a pack of young bucks, bored, furious, crowded in, sulked, sprawled, tossing insults around in the heat. She would refuse any sadness; the day was her own, a delirious new beginning.

"Tell me," she said, "are you happy? Because I am!" Lalo grunted. He thought it bad luck to admit to too much happiness. He looked wonderfully fresh this morning after his gruesome ruminations. He wore white linen trousers and a crisp white shirt with a faint blush of pink shine to the cloth and a bit of old blue silk with white dots knotted jauntily at his throat. And white espadrilles, the bare feet showing exquisite ankles.

"I've never seen you so handsome!" Lalo forced a smile.

The sun reached its full heat as they crossed the lagoon with its languid sloops dipping red sails to the sunlight. Out they flew on cut-glass wings of spume, faster now, beyond the stench of dying fish; Jewel felt her happiness bore them aloft. She would not think of Magda, not today; there would be time for that tomorrow. The world forgives everything. Jewel saw it all with tender eyes, bathed her wounds in the sparkling day. Old thoughts passed by sleekly; she was light, air; the earth had come unfettered.

She laughed. What a strange instrument for happiness this man was, and yet he had taught her to be alive. He aimed the boat at the tipsy little sloops and bore down on them gleefully.

"We are gods!" he cried to the dead lagoon. He slid his hand down to her bottom to find a handful of flesh, not caring who saw. With all her being Jewel fought him and he howled with delight. "Don't you see? We have invented all this—we have invented Him for our pleasure, so take it while you can!" How she hated him to talk this way. "What a delicious little hypocrite you are! You know there is nothing to believe in but this! Why drag behind you the great piled-up heap that is your past? Be free!"

"Free! To do what? Serve your god? You always end up serving somebody, you're never really free. We may as well choose our masters." And she laughed at him. "Or tyrants like you will choose them for us."

"You could do worse," he threw back at her. "You call yourself a free spirit but you are bogged down. Painters, you know, and poets—they are the ultimate materialists, too delighted by their own words, bound by the desperate need for immortality." He knew he had struck a blow; only this morning she had told him that she had decided to paint again, that she felt clean about it at last and joyous; he saw her fury, and it excited him.

"And you? Are you free? Dragging the dead carcass of all those centuries behind you! And your precious heredity? What does it amount to but all those disappearing tables and chairs?" She had not meant to go so far.

"It is true," he said evenly, "perhaps I am too fond of my tables and chairs. But who do I harm with this foolishness? My life is not a tragedy. You, my dear girl, punish yourself for being alive! You cling to this tiresome idea that you must pay some dreadful price just to be here taking up space. Do you really imagine the world cares? Are you so important? *This* is a tragedy." But he knew how to live. He had the very thing she wanted, this certitude that *now* is the moment. That a person could really exist separate from the incriminating evidence of his whole lifetime filled Jewel with wonder. The man's whole charm lay in this: for Lalo the moments of the day were little ecstatic feasts founded on the honesty of pure whim; her moments were the guilty response to that age-old grief of a civilization betraying itself in cupidity. Lalo saw that the final stupidity is not to enjoy.

He cut the engine and they bobbed up alongside the dock at Malamocco. A fisherman was slapping something flabby against the rocks.

"What is it?" asked Jewel.

"Our dinner," said Lalo. "Calamari."

They made their way into a little village ringed all around by fields of waving yellow marsh grass and a few bent trees. Jewel carried a small picnic basket with a Thermos of strong coffee, a few tangerines, and a cake. Lalo would not touch it. "I am not a mule," he said. He loathed sand in his food, and mosquitoes. He would take her to eat in a trattoria. Later they might feast her birthday on the rocks.

Malamocco had nearly been devoured centuries before by a monstrous wave roaring in from the sea, he told her. It was older than Venice. Its people fled into the lagoon—to what they now called Venice—and only returned much later to build the odd little corridors of chalk-green and red-rouged houses, the yellow church staring down at them from the end of the street. Early still, and hot, the only thing moving was a curtain flicking in and out of the dark hole of the church, like a lewd scarlet tongue. Jewel clung to Lalo's arm, bumping against him in a happy, sleepy languor, until at last it was

time to take their lunch. In the café the fishermen ar-
gued, smoked, drank wine. Lalo steered her to a corner
table. Wine was brought, red and also the local white,
sour as goat piss, and fish—platters of crab and squid,
langoustine, small staring silver-blue fishes floating in
green oil, and *pesce di oro,* fish of gold, with zucchini
blossoms deep-fried to a glorious saffron and gold. They
ate it all, drank the wine, and asked for more. Lalo,
purple with wine, could not tear his eyes from Jewel,
who devoured everything, crunching the last oily fishes
in her teeth. She was having a wonderful time. Lalo quite
forgot he had finished loving her. His heart was swollen
with plans to ravish her. Under the table he groped for
her thigh, and pressed her with his knee. At last, eating
ice creams, they stumbled out into the flat green afternoon.

Lizards darted along the rocks. Beyond the seawall a
meadow of stones stretched down to the sea. The place
appeared deserted except for two people at the edge of the
sea and beyond them, far out, tankers moored in the haze.
The woman dove into the sea, the man followed. Jewel
saw their heads bobbing in a fizz of jittery blue light rising
from the sea and remembered Magda and John. The two
merged, broke apart, disappeared into the sea.

"Come!" said Lalo in her ear. "It's still your birthday!
Let's go over there." He pointed to the grass. He took her
hand and led her to a place in the grass where the tall
fronds swayed and tangled themselves in a marshy nest
of gold. Lalo lay down and patted a place for Jewel.

"Take these things away," said Lalo, tugging at her
clothes.

"Not here," she said. "Someone will see. Tell me
something nice."

"Here," said Lalo, "here is something nice," and he
patted his groin. "We do it in the grass—my body will

tell you nice things." He began to undress her. "What more do you need? We have sun, see, he warms you a nest. And wind—look! See how he moves the grass. And shadows to cover us—all our friends are here. It's beautiful, no?"

How effortlessly she was aroused, how softly she came away. How strange it all seemed, and uncanny, this flesh spread upon the grass, breasts and bellies floating in the grass oddly. Who was he, this man? He tore open his pants, bent over her, and in the sighing grass she heard the snapping of mosquitoes and small avid flies. Farther off she heard the persistent whine of motorcycles coursing through the grass. And beyond that, the solemn, gentle slapping of the sea.

"Push me down!" she cried. "Push me down!" But the man seemed weightless, she scarcely felt him. She yearned to drown in him and be washed away but he didn't even feel as satisfying to her body as the feeble pulsing of tiny creatures crushed against her spine in the grass. Their bodies rocked; she grew amazed by how furiously he worked. The bite of air upon her flesh with teeth, a tongue, the stinging nest of marsh grass, the sea; and once before, there in a garden, she had stopped to dream: Who was it? Johnnie? Weeding in the garden. Shall I tell you what you look like? A huge red flower. A hibiscus, with the light coming through your ear, there at the back, your ear filled with sunlight, with red and gold fire.

"Tell Lalo you like it," he whispered in her ear hoarsely.

LALO FINISHED, he rolled off, panting. "It was good?" he said.

"Yes," she whispered. She heard the insistent drone of

motorcycles punctuating her thoughts, potent, unflagging; the violence reminded her of home. *Home.* The word brought tears burning to her eyes. Lalo began to drag on his pants. He tossed her her panties. Jewel stood and was just bending to put them on when suddenly four motorcycles roared down on them from the dunes and came crashing through the grass. Staring out blindly from behind huge goggles, four riders in rubber body suits and metallic helmets lunged at Lalo and Jewel, then veered off. Naked, Jewel began to shout. But they were gone, roared away. Lalo was outraged. He pushed Jewel away from him and screamed, "Hurry! They will come back!" Just then the cyclists came roaring back and Lalo, struggling into his shirt, hurried to the seawall, leaving Jewel behind. Jewel quickly got into her panties but was naked otherwise, dragging her clothes, walking slowly. She was steaming mad, too angry to be afraid. The cyclists circled her, whistled. They scissored back and forth in the path, whipping the machines as she got into her blouse, her trousers. They called to her, bucking the machines, hooting to one another, but she was not afraid. They roared off to catch Lalo. He streaked down the path far ahead as they exploded down onto him, calling to him with lewd noises. Their smirking insolence drove him mad, and he felt terrified. They had him surrounded and Jewel passed him in the path, still walking slowly. She did not stop as she passed, though he cried out to her. They surrounded him, nipping at his heels, spurting forward onto him with the machines, rubbing his legs, laughing. Lalo wound his way toward the seawall. His white linen trousers were soiled with streaks of engine oil and dirt.

Jewel climbed up onto the seawall. She was elated. How beautiful they were, these terrible young men twisting on their machines, eerily splendid in the rubber suits, vibrant grasshoppers poised for flight. Her drowsiness had gone, she felt light again, and young, completely unafraid. She laughed out loud, watched them herd Lalo in the path. How wonderful suddenly to hear every sound, see the colors separate, then fuse, the light sliding past, straying flinders of last light whirling past.

Lalo reached the seawall, hoisted himself up, and sat facing the sea. The bikers left their machines trembling on idle close by. They peeled off their helmets and mopped at deadly beautiful young faces. They smoked, stared at Jewel, grinned. They waited for her. One of them called to her, "Come with us, little beauty!" Then another said, "What you want with an old man?" They laughed and their ecstatic young voices shrieked onto the night with the shrill inconsequence of birds streaming out to sea. Moments in childhood, thought Jewel dreamily, and she smiled at them. Moments filled with exuberant terror. One moment, long ago, of unthinking happiness: with her ear pressed to grass she heard God's belly rumble far below. She slept in the grass, then awakened. A long moment of absent time, the silence perfectly still, bottomless: a first moment as it must have been at the beginning of all time, before there was any remembering. Into this each sound came separately and delicately; the first bird call she had ever really heard, the breathing grass, the earth sigh. She was astounded. She belonged to the earth absolutely, breathed life from it at its very root and heart, at one with all the scattered pieces. There was a great and simple belonging—it had always been there but she had forgotten. As a child she believed implicitly that the shimmer on the sea was her own ecstatic being. She remembered now. So there it was: she had not died or gone too far away. She was not lost. "Come!" cried the voices, "Come with us, little beauty!" She suddenly longed to run toward the bikers.

Lalo never looked around. His feet, Jewel noticed, had gone gray in their soiled espadrilles.

The young men revved their bikes. She waved goodbye.

"My mother brought me here as a child," said Lalo. "As a small boy. I wore shorts, a navy blouse with a sailor collar. My mother, she was so beautiful, I remember her skirt dragging along the rocks, catching up the little shells."

"Lalo," Jewel cried softly.

"And a hat. She always wore a hat. She liked so much to come here. She was very grand. Her mother was a duchessa. But she liked it—to picnic in the grass. We feasted on Baicoli and tangerines. Then afterward," Lalo sighed, "we came here to the sea wall."

It was nearly dark. At the mouth of the horizon a quixotic whorl of silver light trailed behind the vanquished day. The motorcycles roared off.

"Lalo, listen to me."

"You didn't go with them," he said.

"No, I didn't go."

PART THREE
1982

27

THE TOWN itself isn't much to look at these days. Anybody coming to Dragoon for the first time might not see what had got Old Lou so fired up years ago. There was a time when the land had been so rich it poured down from the mountaintops and out across the valleys like yellow lava, unabashed by its own virile heat.

On a white hot day in August 1982 when Lou lay dying, a tar-black Cadillac limousine with Tucson plates pulled up in front of Tiny's Bar and Grill. A chauffeur in uniform stepped out and walked toward Tiny's. A woman's voice called out of the back window.

"For God's sakes don't dawdle. I'm about to fry alive in this goddamn coffin. Where's the switch for the cooler anyway?"

"Air-conditioner don't work, lady. Not when the motor's shut off." With a *whap* of the screen door the chauffeur disappeared into Tiny's.

"This dumb crate's costing me eighty bucks an hour and I can't even use the lousy cooler."

"I told you I'd split the cost of this car."

Nanine stuck her red head out the window and took

a look around. They were parked on one of two dirt
roads that straggled together, then veered sharply apart
at unsociable angles farther along. There wasn't so much
as a mutt dog or a flower patch to ease the brutal landscape. Over to one side stood a small community of trail-
ers and some new wood houses with rows of planted
pinwheels and plastic swans in the yards, and here and
there a saguaro cactus done up in tinsel streamers. Behind the bar and grill there grew a single tree on which
were tied four mules. Even when the Southern Pacific
thundered through town a moment later no more than
ten yards behind them, pulling a hundred hissing rattling freight cars, not one of the mules looked up or even
flicked a tail.

"What a dump," said Nanine. The town's only visible
inhabitant, a fat lady in yellow stretch pants, sat opposite
Tiny's Bar and Grill on her porch drinking a root beer.

"Hey! Where is everybody? Yoohoo! Hello over
there!"

One small eye in a solid wall of blubber flicked around
to where the limousine was parked. The woman on the
porch took a look, deliberated, then decided it wasn't
worth the trouble.

"Drop dead," Nanine said, disgusted. "Can you believe we grew up in this place?" she asked Louise.

The fat lady, Sue Bob, surveyed them from her porch,
which rose up like a stage over a cascading bog of bat-
tered barbecues, old high chairs, tires, tin cans, a
smashed car, and hundreds of broken bottles, until at
last, and without seeming to budge her great progna-
thous jaw from where it hung suspended over an open
bag of Cheetos, she spoke.

"Everybody's down to church," she said. "Over yon-
der." With a roll of the eye she indicated a parked diesel

truck, on which was written, in gigantic red and gold letters, GOD IS YOUR FRIEND HE IS EVERYWHERE IF YOU DON'T FIND HIM HE'LL FIND YOU ROLLING DOWN THE HIGHWAY BRINGING YOU THE TRUTH.

"Who can think of God in heat like this?" sniffed Louise in the backseat. "My Lord, I'm simply dripping! I'll have to burn this dress."

The chauffeur emerged from Tiny's carrying a paper sack of refreshments, which he handed in through the back window. Tiny himself came out from the bar with a sidekick and approached the car.

"Well, Jesus H. Christ, will you get a load of this! If it ain't the McAllister girls!" cried Tiny, who stuck his head in at the window. "Hey, Bubber, git on over here! Well, Jeez! How do', Miz Nanine!? Get a load of you two! That you, Miz Lou-weez? Well, you two sure look mighty fine!" Tiny slapped his thigh and pushed Bubber on in to get a look but all he got was a limp hand fluttering out the window as the Cadillac, leaving plumes of bilious yellow dust, barreled out of town, heading for the Dragoon Cattle Company.

"The McAllister sisters! Well, now I've seen everything!" whooped Tiny, straining after the limousine. "Hell, Miz Nanine there, she's just plain exotic."

"Exotic? That old bag?" said Sue Bob. "Now my idea of exotic is that gal who passed through here day before yesterday. That foreign lady ridin' in the truck with Johnnie Truesdale. *She* was exotic."

"She had gold all over her," said Bubber. "And gaudy toes."

"She won't be wearin' no open-toe sandals if she means to stick around here," said Sue Bob, wadding up the bag of Cheetos and rolling it off the porch with her toe.

"Somethin' mighty powerful must be goin' on out there to the Dragoon Cattle Company if those two gals come back to town after all these years."

"Money, it's M-O-N-E-Y brings folks outta the woodwork," said Sue Bob.

"That other one looked like she was all made out of gold," said Bubber to be sociable.

MAGDA STOOD in the road by the ranch house out at the Dragoon Cattle Company and watched as far off down the long dirt road a whorl of yellow dust came slowly toward her. Johnnie was due home anytime now. Nothing else showed on the horizon, only a vast wasteland of low-lying yellow grass dotted through with sage, yucca, and an occasional clump of black mesquite. Beyond that, way off, a sweep of bald hills and low, fleshy pink mountains and, farther still, the little Dragoons, black humps rolling along a paste-white sky. After only two days she felt she'd seen it all a thousand times. Fighting back the tears, Magda thought how cruel this place was. Whatever she had done, surely she did not deserve this. She meant with all her heart to begin again. This man believed in her. Had anyone else ever really done so? Once, long ago. But how she loved this man! She would do anything to show him. It really did seem she was brand new—young enough, because of him, to do anything. Soon enough she would be fifty but of course no one knew. They took her for thirty-seven or -eight, nearer his age. She loved him. And this was it, her last chance. I have to love this place: I will learn to love it, she swore. What else was there? The memories, the horrors of a lifetime, disgusting defeats—so why couldn't she make this work? Magda began to think how she would grace his life with exquisite caresses, grace the clumsy land.

And he adored her. She believed he might have died if in the end she had not given way. She had never seen a man so besotted. Had any other man ever regarded her with so much devotion? Not for a very long time. All her life she had spent waiting. Then at last, just as it might have been too late, she had found someone worthy of her destiny. And she would be worthy of his. If embracing this hideous landscape would restore her destiny then she would do it. What did it matter that she had thrown herself away so many times before, had had other dreams? That other life, she would swallow it down. Today was the first day; she had someone to live for.

But he would have to be true to her. She would brook no betrayals. She had taught him, too, in these blissful months secreted away from intruders; taught him how to snuff out the specter of lingering disappointments. No one before had ever known how to please her.

What if she were to lose him? That bitch in New York, his aunt, Nanine Brown, was going to be trouble. She had looked Magda up and down. Magda knew her for an enemy and said as much to Johnnie, that she really did dislike the woman and hoped they would never see her again—and he laughed. He could not imagine that Magda would ever be afraid of anyone. But she was afraid; so much so that she made up her mind to separate him from his people as soon as possible. There were ways. And the others—they might *all* be dangerous if she didn't find a way to keep them in place. His mother, Louise, was coming and there was the other sister, that awful old Clara, and the dragon of a grandmother, upstairs sick in bed. Magda had been brought in only to say hello; she didn't expect much trouble from that quarter for it looked like the old lady was on her way out. No, it was Nanine she had to keep an eye on for there might be a possibility, however remote, for Dinwiddie to recover and talk. Imagine the horror of it—her encounter with him in New York! Johnnie's uncle! They had told her he was nearly dead, ailing and mute—that he had barely recognized Jewel and not spoken a word since the stroke. She had refused to go in but on this one thing Johnnie remained adamant: she must meet them all, he felt so proud of her. She could find no reason to stay away, so they had brought her in and presented her. A terrible sad ruin of a man sat collapsed in his chair—her former lover! He was clinging to life, dozing, then jerked awake when he saw her. His mouth opened and he tried to say her name, Madeleine, they had all heard the disgraceful scream: *"Muh muuh—Muuhhha—!"* Her heart leaped to her throat with terror. But he couldn't say it; none of them had understood! She ran from the room, could not stop trembling. Johnnie was contrite and said she need never go back. She had already resolved to stay away from New York until he died. How odd that the one person who really might harm her the most, Jewel, was the one she did not fear at all. She understood Jewel. Whatever she might think of Magda, she would never do anything to destroy Johnnie's happiness—of this Magda felt sure.

He had been thrilled to show her his place. A house and an enclave of outbuildings huddled together alongside a shaggy grove of eucalyptus trees, and for him it was all the world. It had been a terrific shock to her but she smiled up at him and curled in under his arm. "Home!" he said. "Oh, Magda, say you will be happy here, tell me that. We will be happy here, darling, I promise you!"

HE CAME at last, bouncing in over the cattle guard in the old beat-up pickup he liked to drive. She smiled when he waved. Most men that rich would have a Lamborghini parked out in the barn but it was just as Jewel had said—the man remained true to his code. It felt scary to know someone so true. She hadn't quite believed it at first, this simplicity. She waited for the hidden man to reveal himself as she might await some blow—but it didn't come, and it seemed unlikely now that it ever would.

"Did you miss me?" he said, taking her in his arms. "I've told them to treat you like royalty, you know. Anything you want you've only got to ask for. This is your home now, Magda. God, everytime I say that it gives me a thrill."

She smiled up into his eyes. "So happy," she cried softly, "I am so happy."

"This place may seem a bit rough at first but you'll get used to it. The people—well, they're rough, too, but they'll warm to you, honey, I know they will. You'll love them, I'm sure of it. You'll be safe here."

She couldn't imagine she'd ever feel safe—at least not until Dinwiddie died. If only she could have gone so far away no one would ever have heard of her—then she'd be safe. But there was nowhere else to go. There was nowhere else. Together, arms entwined, they stood in the road to greet the limousine from Tucson which carried his mother and the dreaded Aunt Nanine.

28

"SIR! SIR? Mr. Brown, sir, wake up! We want our lunch now, don't we, sir? There now, lookit here: minced lamb cut up nice and tiny and our favorite green jelly. And there's a pudding, sir, just the way we like it," said Nurse Flood into his ear.

Why do they shout? thought Dinwiddie. I can hear. Gad, why don't they leave me alone? I need time to dream. A man needs to dream. With his good arm Dinwiddie tried feebly to swat Miss Flood away.

On the other hand, thought Dinwiddie, what if she leaves me all alone? What if I die while their backs are turned? His hand began plucking at the air until it got ahold of Miss Flood.

"Now you let go, sir. You be a good boy! There's no call to go grabbing at me. I'm right here."

Nanine, thank God, had gone away for a few days. It shamed him to admit this but he felt scared of her sometimes. She and that gruesome Lucy Cook would stand there talking over his head like he was an imbecile.

"I don't see why he should be given that revolting jelly," Nanine barked. "It's nothing but sugar and some

vile chemical they stick in to make it bright green. Take
it away. He'll never notice the difference, poor thing.
Ghastly, isn't it? If I have a stroke, Lucy, I want cyanide
capsules immediately, you hear?"

"You ain't about to be having no stroke, for God's
sakes," said Lucy Cook. "Anyway, look out—I bet he can
hear."

"Come away, Lucy, it's too depressing," said Nanine.

Jewel wore the peacock when she came to see him the
day she returned from Italy. How it thrilled him to see
her! She leaned to whisper in his ear. "I know why you
sent it," she said. He heard her plain enough. "See? It has
given me wings and brought me safely home!"

Safely home—until Nanine had thrown her out! She
had spotted the bird there on his darling girl's dress and
shrieked and tried to snatch it away. She actually
claimed it was *hers*. Lied about it right in front of him.
Screamed like a fishwife. She told Jewel the bird had
been found in poor Horace's hand with its head snapped
off the afternoon they found him, that Horace had died
because of a woman who had stolen the bird and that
Dinwiddie found the woman and seduced her, a mere
child, but he had set her up at the Plaza Hotel and done
his whoring there for all New York to see. Dinwiddie
went rigid all over and strained against his chair, twisting, making a frightful noise, and they sent for the doctor. Nanine told Jewel she had better go away, the visit
had upset Dinwiddie too much. But Jewel still had the
bird.

In the days that followed, Nanine acted like a wild
woman. She tore through his things. Thank God he had
entrusted his will to Morley Barrett. He wished he could
see their faces—it was almost worth dying for. He could
still dream of his revenge. The old contest had ended, she
had won it long ago, scrapped him of every last dignity.

He had almost died when they brought Madeleine in. Madeleine—but she calls herself Magda now. "How do you do?" she said coolly, hanging back.

"He doesn't really hear us, you know," Nanine said. "In fact, we can't even be sure he recognizes us. But the whole point, you see, is to carry on." So Nanine never *did* know her. Madeleine stood rooted. *She* knew. She looked into his eyes and saw his soul swimming there. After all these years he loved her still. She saw that and looked away.

Madeleine was no longer young. They told him that she had married John. John? But this woman was old! See the old eyes, the terrible old eyes of a lynx. She had seen every horror—and John was so young! He ought to warn him.

"Yes, and he's been this way for ages," continued Nanine. "Wouldn't it be awful? If I believed in God I would be quite furious with him, wouldn't you?" She led them out of the room. "I'll tell you one thing—I'm not going to end up like that, no, I'm not, I'm going to live life right up to the hilt to the last day. Right up to the hilt!"

THEY HAD cabled from Sardinia, John and his bride, to say: ARRIVING JULY. Before that cables arrived from Tunisia, Cairo, and Venice. The one from Venice read: MARRIED (STOP) LETTER FOLLOWS, but the letter never came. This had been six months ago. Jewel came home without him last fall sometime. Jewel knew his wife, although she acted strange and would not say a word about her. It seemed incredible that John, of all people, would drop over the edge that way. A few spiteful people said that was what made Old Lou take sick. The news nearly killed her. John! Why, he didn't care two hoots about impressing people—if he had to go after the

woman, why marry her? And why hadn't he brought her
straight home to the ranch? The ranch meant everything
to John. Lou had seen it: the first time he came to the
ranch as a young boy. He soaked the earth in. She recognized the terrible longing, saw, too, he wasn't out to
disturb the earth but wanted only to become a part of it.

They had sent him out to visit her that first time when
he was ten; he had begged to come. After that he came
every year. Old Lou watched him and took his measure.
Not that she trusted him—Lou trusted nobody. But she
respected the boy, told herself he was a man who
couldn't be bought. His father left him a hefty trust fund
and John spent the money effortlessly, but she saw he
had a kind of elegant disdain for the process. The ranch
would be safe with a man who held himself above greed,
a man who knew what he had and valued it.

"What separates you from that cowhand over there?"
she asked him once, when he was fourteen.

"Only the thought that we are separate, I guess." This
answer pleased Lou.

They had always half expected Jewel to dazzle them
with some crazy-fool stunt—but John? Married to a foreigner? It just didn't make sense. What sort of a woman
had driven their John berserk? She said she was a countess, but out in Arizona they didn't believe much in
countesses, not in Dragoon anyway. He had told Jewel
he wouldn't be coming home till she would have him. So
he settled in at Venice, took Jewel's old room, and they
had not been able to lure him away from there, not for
roundup or the selling-off of the spring calves, not for
anything. He laughed when they called and told them
the Castillo brothers could handle things at the ranch till
he got home. Everyone knew Old Lou ran the ranch the
way she liked anyway; it was still hers.

Old Lou was fit to be tied as the months dragged on.

She turned ninety-seven while he stayed away and felt as mean as a rattler. She still had all her marbles, though.

"Cut him off!" she screamed. "Cut the damned fool lover boy off! Why should he have a ranch to bring his whore home to? Tell Rubirosa he can rot over there in Italy. We got plenty men here to run a ranch. What I want to know is why he had to go all the way to Italy to get him some poontang? What's wrong with the stuff we got right here?"

Not until she fell sick did they send a wire, and at last Johnnie called to say he was coming home.

"Never mind, it'll be too goddamn late," she roared into the receiver. "I'll be dead by then!"

So at last her boy had come home, bringing that foreign poontang as a wife. Old Lou was aching for a good fight. They all bored her now. Even Jewel bored her, especially now she'd crept home with her tail between her legs. Out of the whole lot it was only Johnnie who had the balls God gave a jackrabbit.

But then suddenly Lou took a turn for the worse. It was the hottest part of summer in a year when the rains never came and the desert lay bereft, its enchanted fruits rotting in their paradise of thorny arms, the long shimmering desert flats cooked raw under an obdurate sun. There was no feed for the cows, so they spent a small fortune bringing in hay. For the first time Lou hadn't the strength to carry on. Clara telephoned Nanine and the widow Louise, her husband Marshall Trimble, Johnnie's stepfather, being long gone. Neither of the McAllister girls had been to the Dragoon Cattle Company or seen their mother or Clara in more than twenty years. Lou would have wrung Clara's neck if she found out it was Clara who summoned the other two. She hated them; why should they pretend otherwise? They talked once a year on Christmas Day. That was enough.

But Old Lou had no intention of dying. The minute she heard the foreign woman was coming to her ranch and those other two she-buzzards were circling around her land she swore by all she believed in to rise up from her bed. The doctor said it wasn't possible but Old Lou lay there with a terrible bright fixity, muttering to herself that she'd be down there waiting for them in the dining room that very first morning—or lie down and die like a dog. No one would take her land, no one. Not until she decided to go.

She might be older than God but the land still meant everything to her. You had to be there year in and year out, as she was, to know what it meant; to scratch in the dirt, crawl over it inch by inch, taste it deep in your bones, howl over it. You had to live there even when it felt terrible, survive the many winters, whisper to some secret God for rain; see the burning summers, watch the earth curl and die, invoke the curse; and the sky turns away, the earth burns, cows die. I will die too, you say, I will sizzle and burn, but I will not go away. But then one day the gods weep down, the long wait is over, and now life, newly given, is grander, more vivid than before. Why should I die? Leave them my land? Leave the mountain behind? Never! They will have to tear me from this rock: on the last day of life I will lie down with the lizard in a cool place, and stay with the land!

It had all been written down, long ago, in the Escritura de Merced, the Mexican land grant made out to the first of the Ortiz in 1833, when Arizona was nothing more than a scraggle of untamed desert land. "From the core of the earth and the heavens above" this land belonged to her. The Tierra Grande, as it had been called then: the Big Earth. And when the big earthquake came and the Ortiz fled into southern Mexico, driving their cattle before them, Rufus McAllister, that scabrous old fire eater from Colorado who had come to Tombstone to mine silver, saw the land and took it. But he wanted that Escritura de Merced. He followed the Ortiz all through Mexico to get it and died on the way home. He had the paper, though, and bequeathed the land to his son and his son's son after him until at last it all belonged to her. From the core of the earth to the heavens above.

29

BREAKFAST AT the Dragoon Cattle Company was always served at eight sharp in the dining room. Lou positioned herself at the head of the table in a tall blackwood chair carved in curlicues, a Mexican grandee's throne. John took the other end. The long table had been hewn out of coarse Mexican walnut. Its only adornment was a clay bowl with some tangerines.

The place seemed just as he had left it eleven months before and yet Johnnie felt himself an intrusion, somehow, on the old order. He had a perfect sense of this: that *he* had changed, not the place. For the first time as he looked around he saw something of the stultifying complacency that had driven his cousin Jewel away. The same hot paucity of yellow light, the hush in the zaguan, Eulalia lost in dreams, moving slowly with a rag to wipe the waxy tables. Over there the prize Papago basket, the flints laid out, a stack of *National Geographics*, and the shards of a Gila monster. And there on the lime-washed wall soiled by the smoke of many piñon fires, the Navajo saddle blanket and the six famous arrow holes from an Apache raid. Over this there hung Rufus McAllister's

Winchester rifle. And the sounds—the loose flapping of
felt slippers as the Mexicans came and went in the courtyard, the insistent trickle of water in the horse fountain,
the saddle creak, the hooves backing in the dirt, the men.
And in the olive tree the desperate shriek of small birds,
the circling hawk, from the kitchen the high excited
jabber, the radio, a tremolo of careless Spanish palaver
crackling out: everything stayed the same.

John surveyed his grandmother at the other end as
though he had never really looked at her before. She had
shrunk somewhat; he guessed she weighed less than a
hundred pounds. But small as she was she ate like a man:
grits and refried beans for breakfast with a poached egg
riding on top and a sliver of fried ham. And sometimes
menudo, the famous old Mexican cure for whatever ails
you—tripe, the lining of a cow's stomach, in broth with
hominy. And always the Tabasco, hot as fire. Because she
liked an audience, they all had to sit put until Lou was
through.

This morning was the first time he remembered riding
out on his own with the men in thirty years. It had
always been Lou who led them out at the first light of
day; riding fence, hunting down some stray cow, watching over it all with the eye of a jealous lover, watching
always for some sign. He took no satisfaction in riding
at the head of the line, not even in the easy friendliness
of the men who were a little giddy without her and
horsed around like kids, slapping his back, grinning.
Magda had wanted to go with them but he hadn't let her.
He didn't think it right that she take Old Lou's place.
Johnnie hoped she wouldn't come on too strong, especially not at first. He liked that she was strong and proud,
not watered down, but the people out here wouldn't take
to a woman who insisted on doing things her way. They
had been home almost a week and Magda still didn't

seem inclined to do things the way anyone else did them,
or to bother with his grandmother except for a brief
haughty little hello now and then, sent down the table
almost as an afterthought. He spoke of it once but Magda
only stared back at him. He understood: she would not
be made to bow down—and although he almost wished
she would, just this once so they might all be peaceful,
he saw her point. The old lady hated his wife on sight.
"Well, Christamighty, John, what're we going to do with
a fancy piece like that?" To his wife she said, "Are you
plannin' to stick around?"

Magda flamed up but she answered the old lady cool
enough: "As long as John here wants me to stay, I will
stay," she said, staring Granma Lou in the eye.

"Well, if you do, see to it you abide by the rules. We
aren't runnin' some fancy dude outfit are we, John boy?
You tell her."

"I never could abide sloth," Lou said as Nanine sa-
shayed into the dining room trailing maribou feathers at
half past eight. "Now who you figurin' to git worked up
over you in that getup? If there's anything more embar-
rassin' on this earth than an old lady who don't know
when to quit I'd sure like to see what it is. I suppose over
there in New York everyone sits at the table in their
underclothes. Gad. And where, if I might be so bold as
to inquire, is the blushing bride? We got a ranch to run."
She fixed her eye on Johnnie.

"I told her to sleep in if she liked," Johnnie said.
"She'll get used to our ways, you'll see. She'll do fine."

Lou snorted. What remained of it, her coarse gray
hair, stuck out from her head like boar bristle. A gob of
something shiny and greasy rose on her chin and fell as
she chewed. He could not take his eyes from her. He had
come home fearing she might be dead.

"What you staring at, cowboy?" she demanded. She

called him cowboy and he liked it. It had been like earning his stripes to be called that.

"Well, my Lord, I never saw such a dull group at the breakfast table!" said Nanine brightly as she dropped down into a chair beside Clara. "Anyone would think we're a mighty peculiar lot with nothing to say after all these years. How you feeling, Mama?"

"You're late. And since when do McAllisters give a hoot what anyone thinks?" snapped her mother. "And you might as well forget about breakfast, miss, you hear? Take a look at the time! Nothing but coffee for those who can't get themselves down here on time. And there'll be nothing between now and lunch either. No snacking, you hear, Louise? She was late, too. I won't stand for it." Lou belched. "How long you two glamour girls fixin' to stay? I hope you don't expect entertaining. Can't figure why you two came to begin with. Not gettin' any money from me, you know."

Clara began to snigger, then held the napkin up over her face.

"If you're going to sit there braying like an ass, maybe you'd better finish your meal in the barn. I did my best with you girls, no one can say I didn't, but godalmighty, there isn't one outta the whole bunch got the brains God gave a chicken."

Buster Trotter, the head wrangler and Johnnie's good friend, poked his head in at the door. "Hey! Well, hello there, stranger, we heard you come home! Sorry I wasn't here when you and the missus arrived but we took some cows up to pasture in Colorado, you know." Buster and Johnnie shook hands, slapped shoulders, grinned, spoke of the drought. Through the door came Magda with her hair streaming way down her back, freshly brushed and with a thousand dancing little hairs catching at the light. Buster felt her go past, smooth, slim, and dark, like a

thrilling shadow. The others stayed silent, staring. Johnnie leaped up and placed her near him at the table, fixed
her coffee. Magda smiled into Johnnie's eyes as he put in
two, three spoonfuls of sugar, stirred, and slid the cup
toward her. Buster could not take his eyes away. Johnnie
introduced them; to see her smile up at John that way
made Buster feel as if he were spying.

"Maybe I'd better get back down to the corral. There's
work to do, I was gone all last week," he said. But he just
stayed there planted and watched.

"Jewel was out to the ranch last week, she said how she
wasn't coming back no more," said Clara with a furtive,
swift look down at Magda, who saw only John. "Yes, and
Jewel, she says how family or no family she's not coming
back to the Cattle Company as—"

"Buzz buzz buzz—sound like a buzz saw, don't it?"
interrupted Lou. "You two down there! How long's the
show going to last? You ought to sell tickets. Well, what
about it?" John looked up at Lou. Magda glanced her
way briefly and looked away. "Are we going to get in
some neighbors and have us a barbecue or does the
countess there plan to stay in-cog-neeto?"

"How about it, darling?" asked John.

"Barbeekew? And what is this?" said Magda with a
pretty little grimace.

She did not know what a barbecue was! They broke
out in an excited babble, arguing, wisecracking. Magda
looked over at Buster. He didn't laugh. "Come over here
and sit down," she said with that quiet voice. Now she
moved her smile to him, her eyes dilated strangely, almost in warning. "Tell me—what are they saying? Why
do they shout?" Buster grinned at her painfully. He
could not think what to say but he felt pleased to think
she had appealed to him.

"Go ahead, Buster," said Johnnie. "Tell her. Miss Lou

is always on the warpath about something. She likes to
stir things up. Beat the air. Buster knows—he's been
here almost as long as I have, darlin'. We grew up together." She looked at her husband with an amused tol-
erance, in no way unloving, yet in that moment Buster
wondered if maybe she didn't really love Johnnie; no,
she loved him all right—she must have loved him to
come all this way—but she didn't *hurt* over him.

"Old Spike Sanders from the Double Bar Six once
asked Miss Lou, 'How come you're not dead yet, Lou?' "
Johnnie continued. " 'Hell, Spike,' she said, 'I'm too
damn *mad* to die, that's what!' " Buster slapped his thigh
and shook his head appreciatively.

From way down at the other end of the table Lou
cackled her pleasure in the story. "Did he tell you about
the time I got up on Sinbad the Sailor over to the Tucson
rodeo and rode him to the finish?" she shouted down to
Magda. "Why, there wasn't a man that year could stay
on that bugger."

"Who is Sinbad the Sailor?" asked Magda.

"You mean to say you never heard nothing about the
meanest Brahma bull on the circuit? Well, Lord, he's
famous!"

"Well, as long as we're passing out the bouquets,"
said Nanine, "remember I rode that horrid Gold Rush,
didn't I?"

"And spent a year flat on your back, miss! That don't
count," said Lou. "Hell, there's no use braggin' on the
ones that threw you."

"I think I've won my spurs on this ranch," sulked
Nanine.

"Hell, I'm going on ninety-eight next May but it looks
like I'm still the only one got any gumption on this
ranch. Soon as I'm back on my feet, same as before, I'm

going out on that new animal I got out there—makes
Gold Rush look like a sissy. Finest piece of horseflesh in
Cochise County. Thoroughbred stallion. Big fellow,
eighteen hand high and with a neck on him that'll break
your heart. I call him Casanova. All he cares about is
doing you know what—but one of these days I mean to
ride him myself."

"You haven't ridden him?" inquired Magda. Was
there something in her voice that smacked of a challenge?

"Why should I ride him if I don't feel like it? But
maybe you'd like to go out on him," Lou added, eyes
narrowed. "What about it, countess?"

"I should like that," Magda answered her.

"Now, darlin'," said Johnnie, "let's take a look at him
first, shall we? How long have you had him, Lou?" he
asked.

"Two weeks. Ole Doc Skinner called me up. Said he
had a horse."

"I'd love to ride him," said Magda.

"Well, hold on now, have you ridden much?"

"I'm not afraid," she said, and smiled.

"All the same, I think it might be best to take things
easy at first."

"I'd stay away from that horse, miss, if I was you," said
Buster. "He's the meanest darn hunk of horseflesh I ever
saw. No right horse for a lady, Miss Lou excepted, of
course—and he hasn't been ridden clear onto a month,
either. None of the men like to go near him. Why, he
kicked Jesus in the—"

"Pooh! I never heard such sissy talk," said Lou. "And
that little lady there, the countess"—Lou took malicious
satisfaction in this title—"why, she don't look like she
ever been on a horse in her life. A big old Thoroughbred

like that'll scare the wig off a city gal right quick. If anyone here's going to mount Casanova it'll be me—you hear?"

Clara twisted her head around to stare down the table at Magda expectantly.

"No one's going near that horse till I've had a chance to take a look at him," Johnnie said.

"Say, boy! Who the hell's giving orders around here?" hollered Lou. "Isn't a man on this place knows horses like I do! I'll decide. I might just ride him today. Give the countess here something to write home about. You're a city girl, aren't you?" Magda kept silent but stared back at the old lady steadily.

"Let's wait a day or two, Lou," said John. "You've been laid up for a month—let's take it easy."

"I never felt better in my life," the old lady said grimly.

"You look fine, Lou, but maybe in another day or two—anyway, I got stuff I want to talk over with you. How about you and me taking the morning off to go over a few things? And the ladies here have been counting on a barbecue. They want to ask Jewel to drive out from town, have a real family get-together." This last was not true. Besides Clara, he was the only one who wanted to see Jewel. "It's been a long time, Lou. Be real nice to celebrate."

"What the hell're we celebrating?"

"C'mon, Lou," coaxed Johnnie.

"I'm going to ride that horse," she said.

"The doctor, he say no horse!" said Eulalia, standing in the old lady's path. Lou pushed her aside and made her way toward the door.

"Somebody'd better stop her!" said Nanine. Johnnie rushed toward the door and Buster turned to follow, but just then Magda drew out a cigarette and laid a hand on the cowboy's arm. The others all ran out of the room but Nanine stopped at the door and looked back. The cowboy reached in his pocket for a match, then leaned down over her. Magda smoked, and poured out a cup of coffee for Buster, smiling to herself.

30

"HEY! I been watchin' you!" Clara said with her sly smile. Her hair fizzled straight up and out in a grizzled halo of black with a stripe of white. No use giving Clara a hairdo, it wouldn't stay. Everything about her wriggled and strayed. Clara was sixty-eight, big and beefy, with swinging breasts and stovepipe thighs. She could outrun any cowboy and wrestle him to the ground quick as the wind, pin and tickle him till he howled for mercy. She acted like a regular menace on the ranch. Lou swore if she got any worse she'd sell Clara to the circus but she'd been saying this for years. Clara was no more crazy than anyone else. She fixed Magda with huge sooty eyes.

"You don't like us much, do you?" she said at last. Magda did not answer. Clara let her horse drop behind and began to sing. "Whooo hoo hoo, fancy lady ain't so glad, fancy lady sure feel bad, fancy lady hee heehee tuhtumteetum daddadee dahdah!" On and on she went, chattering and teeheeing behind Magda on the big buckskin. Clara rode a gray called Smoke. The two of them headed for Skeeter's Gulch down by the sycamore tree. Clara had packed sandwiches.

Clara began to wonder if there might be something dangerous in that other woman. She stayed so silent. And she was a foreigner. But how beautiful she looked— like a black snake! The others felt spooked by her. Clara didn't care a hoot for what they thought. Anyway, she ached for a best friend. So what if this foreign woman turned out to be dangerous? Maybe she had tricks she could teach Clara.

They rode on in silence. The horses dragged through a fiery wash of glittering pink sand that stretched out forever through a boiling white haze. Almost noon, the ferocious sun burned the sky white; they felt no moving thing, only the terrible fevered sizzling of dry things frying in the heat. Arid rock and small creatures dying there, curling up. Magda, so clean and cool-looking in her summer whites, never looked around. Clara, sweating like a vaquero, began to wish she hadn't come.

Then at last the dry wash twisted north into a gully and they picked their way some distance through rocks and low brush, glad to see some living thing. Up ahead stood a tree with spreading silver-white arms, an amazing tree splayed against a bleached sky.

"There it is!" Clara shouted. She tied her horse, pouncing down into a pool of brackish water that trickled weakly out from under a rock.

They settled under the tree and ate the sandwiches. Magda stretched herself on a slab of tilted granite, her back against the tree. Cool green drops of leaf splashed across the sky. Otherwise, all was burning hot.

"You brought me here to scare me," said Magda at last. "You thought I would hate it."

"No, I didn't," said Clara.

"Yes. It was a test."

"Well, so what if it was?" Clara sulked. Neither said

anything for a while. Behind them, the horses flicked, drowsed.

"Why are you all so afraid of me?" asked Magda.

"Maybe it's you who's afraid," said Clara. "Why wouldn't you stay and see Ma ride Casanova?"

"Why didn't you?"

"I wanted to be with you," said Clara.

"Even though it will get you into trouble with the others?"

"Well, I don't care! Phooey on the others!" muttered Clara. "They'll probably come looking for us. Johnnie'll be real sore. He don't like people taking the horses out this far in the heat. It's me he'll be mad at. But I don't care!"

"Clara—do you want me for a friend?" said Magda in her lilting, strange voice.

"Sure I do," said Clara.

"And what do you like to do, Clara?"

"Me? I look at things. I take a look around."

"You see things?" prodded Magda.

"You bet! Ole Clara sees everything. It's all I got to do," she said.

"I think that's wonderful," Magda said. "I need a friend, too."

"So why did you come here?" Clara challenged, eyeing the other woman with adoring eyes as Magda, easy as a cat, rolled onto her belly.

"Well, because of John." After a moment she said, "I'm starting over again."

"What was wrong with the old way?" Clara asked.

"It made me feel ugly, you see," Magda said.

"Oh!" said Clara, ruminating. "You mean you had to do ugly things?" But Magda did not answer.

"I have always needed to feel beautiful," said Magda at last.

"But you *are* beautiful!" cried Clara. "More than John-nie's other girl friends."

"No," said Magda with slow emphasis on the word, "not that. I want everything around me to be beautiful, you see."

"Well, you sure came to the right place!" Clara exclaimed.

"I would die if I had to be around ugliness."

"Oh," Clara murmured with a sinking heart.

"What about you, Clara, what do you want?"

"Oh, I guess I'm not too choosy."

"Clara, I think you're a lot more wonderful than you know."

"Hell, no—I'm not!" barked Clara.

"No, you are wrong there. I came out here with you, didn't I?"

"You wanted to show Ma you didn't care."

"Well, yes, that, too—but I came because I wanted to be with you." Magda began gathering the picnic things.

"You *will* be my friend, you promised, Magda."

"Here, Clara, take my hand, and let's make a vow: if you are good to me I will be your friend. And you?" Clara felt so pleased she almost sank down in a mortified heap. She reached out to touch that hand, then snatched hers back, quickly.

"Now I got two friends," she cried as she followed behind Magda. "You and Jewel! You'll see, I may not look like a movie star or anything, but I make a helluva friend once a person gives me a chance. You just be thinkin' what you need and ole Clara'll be there, hear? Yessiree, Clara knows how to be a real friend!"

The drone of Clara's love song came after Magda from behind. How can I live here? Magda wondered. Buried alive in this godforsaken desert with this imbecile for my only friend and the old one stoning me with every glance. What love could survive that? No, he cannot expect me to endure that old woman. But he sees nothing. This is his land, his earth; the uglier it is, the more he defends it. Yesterday they drove down one of those endless bone-hot highways that stretched on and on to nowhere—the closest market was fifty miles—and in a dead field of burned-out mesquite they saw a sign, a huge black cross framed in yellow on one of those tremendous billboards, and the sign said: JESUS SAID: WITHOUT ME YE CAN DO NOTHING—AND THAT'S THE WAY IT IS. It was the first time she had given vent to her disgust.

"How can they allow such a thing?" she said angrily. She nearly said, "And you ought to do something about it—why *don't* you?" He felt something of her scathing contempt but only laughed, shrugging it off with an easy grin.

"Hell, honey," he said—she hated this "honey"—"out here we go along with whatever it is a person's got to say. Some fellow has left his message there in the desert, that's all—it can't hurt anyone, not the way I look at it."

"It hurts *me,*" she said.

"You'll get used to it."

You'll get used to it. But she never would. And for some reason a swift vicious hatred of Jewel came coursing through her heart. She wanted to blame Jewel. Who else was responsible for Magda's coming here? Jewel had decided all their fates and walked away. Magda had done the only thing left to her, she had wound Johnnie in coils of irresistible light, wound him all around, tied him in ribbons of enchanted light, and he had stayed. But now she felt afraid. What if she lost him—her last chance? Soon she would be old. She had married him, abandoning the palazzo. He told her to leave everything to Lalo; let him have what furniture and rotted belongings were left. Her only satisfaction remained the sure knowledge

that the palazzo would choke him, cut off his air, bring
a slow death. But Johnnie didn't like to hear her talk this
way. He seemed curiously simple, without any idea of
revenge—an anathema to her and slightly revolting, this
goodness. She had not believed in it at first. How effortless it all appeared for people like Jewel and Johnnie.
Always so lucky, so privileged! That he never thought of
himself as anything special she found astonishing. He
even spoke of himself with an offhand disdain, saying he
ought to do more, ought to put some of it back. If anything he felt a certain contempt for his riches. Sometimes he joked about giving his money away. How
peculiar these people were, despising what they had,
feeling ashamed of their lucky fortune, hiding it. The
one luxury he allowed himself—in this he reminded her
of Jewel—were his ideals. These inflamed her; nothing
made her feel more impoverished than their grand
ideals. After all, when had these two been tested? As she
had been, again and again. How easy to be good if you
are rich. To be generous if you have too much. She once
found a note tucked in his wallet, something he copied
out from the Upanishads:

> *You are what your deep, driving desire is.*
> *As your deep, driving desire is, so is your will.*
> *As your will is, so is your deed.*
> *As your deed is, so is your destiny.*

Toys for the rich, these pretty ideals. How could she
resist taunting such dreams? He really did believe that
one day people must return to the wisdom of earth as
sacred or there would be no more earth. And that to
protect *her* was their greatest obligation. Magda, the sur-
vivor, knew better. If you've grappled with life you
know what matters: your own survival at any cost. Once

he had said he understood this but she began to see what he really cared for: that it was not enough just to survive. Animals survived. He never said so to her—but she knew. He was good—she had been contaminated. This is what she made of their difference. And if, in some corner of her heart, she hoped that to be near him might erase the taint, this prospect soon vanished. Nothing deepened her sense of having been sullied so much as his luminous acceptance, his sweetness. Always so unflaggingly compassionate: he soon made her bristle with savage little impulses when she ought to be grateful and soothed. Had he shown her his teeth she would idolize him. If only he could be as real as she was, absolutely real, brutally so, she might unmask herself at last. But how could she be honest in the face of so much goodness? At least with the old lady she had a genuine adversary and would know how to proceed. It might even be amusing now and then to put the old dragon in her place. But this—perhaps it would prove too much for her. This place will sizzle me up. Soon I will be old. Burnt by the sun, ugly. And I will die without finding my place. I will dry up in this desert, blow away, wizen and sour, grow stupid, coarse, unloved, rattle in the wind like that hollow gourd. . . . No, it was too much. The old lady would win.

31

JOHN STREAKED out toward them as they came in sight of
the barn. He waved and hollered, and Magda could not
make out his words. But Clara began to howl. She slid
from her horse and ran toward John, threw herself onto
the ground clutching at her sides, moaning like an animal. John grabbed Clara, held her, rocked her, and wept
into her neck.

How still the world, thought Magda, still as death. See
how it draws a circle all around. How far away they
seem, those two, enclosed and faraway. Old memories,
old lifetimes do not die; they wait, wrapped around by
stillness—no, she did not belong here with these people.

Johnnie shouted her name. Still in her dream, she got
down from her horse. The solitude was all around. Together they walked to the barn. John steered with his
hand under her arm. "You've had a great shock," he said
to her but she did not hear. She found a new distance.

"Lou was thrown from the stallion."

"Oh, John," she murmured.

"When I couldn't find you—Magda, I've been half
crazy!"

"I went with Clara. We should have left you a note."

"And he kicked her in the head," he said. "She fell facedown in the dirt, all broken—" He choked over the words. Tears streamed down Johnnie's face, yet she felt nothing. "Such a little thing, so old! I never realized. And Magda—" But he could not say it. He wanted to tell her that for *her* he had hated Lou. That for one terrible moment earlier that day he actually saw his grandmother with eyes of hatred. He looked in Magda's eyes—a little fire had sparked up in those careful eyes. He couldn't look at her.

"Is she dead?"

"Dead? No, thank God, she isn't!"

The old lady was alive? Magda could not suppress her fury.

"Buster and I scraped her out of the dirt. She was gray as a stone. We carried her up to the house. Nanine called over to town for the doctor but that was hours ago. Where the fuck were you, Magda?" She remained silent. He strained to look into her eyes but what he saw there seemed so hateful he jerked away.

"You go see to Clara," he said roughly. "We can't leave her there in the road. I'm going in there to take care of the horse." Magda saw the stallion pacing at the far side of the corral. He snorted wildly, knocking his hooves against the rails, then skittered away from the fence in terror.

"He's afraid!" Magda cried.

"The bastard knows what he's done and he knows I've got to kill him," said John. She noticed he wore a pistol. Magda could not take her eyes from the horse. The horse began to scream crazily. He was magnificent: sleek, huge, a fiery red, his tense haunches filled with light.

"I'm going to need you to be strong for me. I know you hate her. I know all that and, Magda, it isn't right, how they treated you. But Old Lou, well, that's her way, she didn't really mean anything by it, I swear. The thing is, she's my family. She's always been here for me, it was Lou who gave me everything."

She glittered at him strangely. "But don't you understand? We can be free."

"Free?"

"John, let me have the horse."

"The horse?" He could not think what she meant. Lou is going away, Lou is going, these words pounded in his head, the world without Lou. He had never thought she would die, not Lou. And the shame—he had nearly betrayed her. Lou gave him everything and in the end he had almost turned away from her.

"I never asked you for anything," she said.

"What is it you want?"

"The stallion."

"That horse is no damn good to anyone! He's better off dead. He's a killer, Magda, don't you hear me? You don't know anything about this."

"I want him." Her voice, rasping and foreign, struck him oddly. Almost as if he had never heard her before. He hated her arrogance. He saw her as the others must see her. For the first time he understood: he had brought her here and she would stay. Be here always. Lou would die and go away—and this one would stay. His head pounded so.

"Now you get on down and see to Clara," he said in a hard voice, hearing himself. "I want you out of the way." He tried to go near her but she jerked away.

"I'm warning you, John—shoot that horse and you shoot me! Do you hear?"

"For chrissakes, Magda, my grandmother is dying! That animal killed her—he has to go."

"You stay away!" She turned and ran toward the corral fence. "It's too much," she moaned. John went icy cold. He scarcely felt his own breath, so dead was his heart against her. "I cannot live here—you should have known, John! You should have known!" *I cannot live here.* The words shocked her as much as him. She had said too much, the words frightened her—yet she felt glad. He was so strange, she had never seen him so dead in the face, the eyes so cold.

At last he said, "No. He belongs to Lou. Everything on this place belongs to Lou until she dies." He turned away from her. Slowly he made his way toward the house. Everything had changed. She had changed for him. He felt it with a flat, almost uneventful finality and fell away from her, thinking he ought to be frightened by how easy this was, this coming away, but felt only a relief. How good to be separate again. He hadn't realized how she crowded him. John turned to look back: watched her cross to the gate, enter the corral. Better to let her go, an easy drifting-away; return to nothingness, to all the silences. He heard the animal's soft, furious nickering, and saw its hocks stiffen. She uncoiled the braid at her back and shook loose the soft mass of hair that came tumbling down in a dazzling play. The stallion waited, he tensed the fat slope of ruddy chest, stiffening the forelegs, hooves pointed sharply down. He began to blow softly, to snort, knead the earth. Magda was not afraid; she came toward him, locked her eye to his, and cawed to him in the throaty sounds of her own foreign tongue. The beast twisted up his neck, swelling out the long throat, arching back, muttering, the eye twisted sideways, staring down. And then he screamed, his head twisting, and curled his lip, stretching out his teeth toward her. She touched him with her nose, nuzzled his teeth, breathed in the shock of moist green horse breath. Now she rubbed against the velvet curling nostril and gently laid her cheek upon the foolish poking bristle along the velvet snout, the rumpled, wobbling chin, waiting. He sniffed her hair as she reached up to put her finger along the rubbery black lips and stroke him there and slide along the satin neck to smooth the straining flesh, the downward slope of belly. She untied the cinch and slid away the saddle, laid her cheek against the hurting places. She felt him through her skin, felt him shiver as she loosened his bridle and buried her face in the tangle of fiery hair. John turned away, back to the house. He heard the stallion shrill as Magda set him free.

32

MAGDA SAT at the head of the table in Old Lou's throne-backed chair. Johnnie remained in his usual spot at the far end. Buster Trotter stood between the two, slightly closer to Magda, receiving his orders.

"That should do it for the morning, Buster," said Magda by way of dismissal. "And then of course I'll be out a little later to have a look at that cow—but don't do anything about her till I come."

"No, ma'am, I won't," said Buster, holding his hat.

"I still think we'd better have Doc Waller over to take a look," said Johnnie. Buster listened but turned back to Magda for the final word.

"I'll be out after breakfast," she said curtly.

Lou died one year ago this August and Magda had claimed the ranch for her own. John did not interfere. Since that day at the corral when she fought him for the stallion, and won, the day Lou died, Johnnie had receded. Nothing she might try could bring him back. Never again would he look at her with anything resembling passion. He remained fair, of course; Johnnie was nothing if not fair. He would have deemed it unmanly

to abandon her here in this far place. But what did fairness mean in the face of his departed love? Magda cared
nothing about fairness. She hadn't come this far only to
be held in place by this unflinching correctness, casting
over their marriage a stately bogus grace that needled
and enraged her. What satisfaction could she feel in
wresting the ranch from him if nothing seemed to matter, if her worst ploy affected him as no more disagreeable than her best? She had taken away everything he held
dear—yet it seemed he scarcely noticed. It had the effect
of reducing her to nothing.

More and more frequently he stayed away. To let her
know she had forfeited his pleasure.

"Bastard! Damn you!" she hissed, riding out after
breakfast. Magda spat on the ground. The red Thoroughbred stallion, Lou's horse Casanova, whom Magda
now called Icarus, shivered suddenly and twitched sideways as if to dance across her shadow. They were riding
out to Skeeter's Gulch. Last night the rains had come and
Magda felt a desire to inspect the little pools in the desert. Clara wanted to come but Magda told her no. The
poor thing hung around Magda's neck so tightly since
Lou had died Magda could scarcely breathe.

Today the world was fresh and clean, softened. She
meant to revel in the day even if he did stay away. She
had seen the expression on his face as he drove off this
morning: not disgust, he was too reasonable for that, but
only a detached, slightly weary scorn. As if to say, My
dear, if winning these little domestic dilemmas day after
day is so important to you, why, by all means do so—you
see, I remove myself. Johnnie still decided the large is-
sues. But now that Old Lou was dead, Magda rode out
with the men every morning. They were used to her,
they called her a fancy lady behind her back, but there
wasn't a female in five counties who could stick a horse

as Magda did: smooth, silky smooth, the lady and the horse: she lay out flat on the stallion like a serpent. She had this uncanny way with the beast—he let her do anything. The men bragged about her.

And after her long battle with the place she had finally learned to love it. Magda turned Icarus off the trail, heading up the ravine, gloating a little over the thought that she had mastered this landscape.

Slowly the ferocity of the place forced her to see: if you taunt the desert, live there inanely, refusing its order, you condemn yourself to exile. The meanest parasite is more in harmony with the universe than you are, living off its back without any sense of what the place is. But to be at one with its spirit, caught up in its moods: better to give way and thrive here. She loved it now—the sizzling days, raw nights plunging down to a stinging cold; the mean June winds, tearing at your eyeballs, bedeviling thorny puffs of weed, funneling the hot sands in yellow twisters straight to the sky. Even the spiteful months when the toughest vaqueros fell down from their horses, wilting and ragged after the long day—she loved it all.

To the horse and the desert she bequeathed her spirit; the man remained her enemy. If only he would come to her clean, straight out as they did, and announce his needs. She would know then how to handle him. But he avoided her, skirted her like an adversary. She would notice sometimes, as he sprang down from his horse and headed for the house, he'd pause, as if remembering. He would stop and listen, the whole buoyant springing life leaking out from his being if he sensed her near. Then he stiffened. But with her, always that infuriating calm, the perfect correctness when his wife was around.

To the men he referred to her as Mrs. Truesdale or, worse, the missus. The missus! Like some old harridan.

Ma'am, of course, sounded very pleasant, but she did not like the men to call her Magda. She crowded in on him, knowing full well that his silence—what he termed his sanity—provided the mainstay of his life. That out of the silence there comes all possibilities. True understanding means relinquishing what you know. Every truth or conviction held is a bias which blinds. The things we are most certain of are the biggest traps, he explained to her once. Those things she knew about her own life, he said, were false assumptions. Conveniences really, pinning her down to old realities. But they weren't the truth. Conveniences! As if she weren't desperate to forget all that—but she would not pretend it hadn't been real. How could she bear to have lived such a life if it hadn't been—as she insisted—absolutely necessary? If her past meant nothing, then she herself was nothing. Never mind that she yearned to escape it—what right had he to take it from her? He told her nothing was true but the moment itself. In those first months this worked to her advantage: he showed no interest in her past or in the signposts by which she marked her progress. He refused any evidence. She had thought this was what she wanted yet the emptiness of it, the great silence surrounding everything, seemed to take on forms, presences filled with shadowy consequence. Silence is all very good if you love yourself. But in the absence of love, of his love, too, the ominous crept in; she began to imagine he could no longer see her, that she'd grown invisible to him; his very politeness had the effect of deleting her, removing her to some place far off—and in this landscape, more here than anywhere, in order to survive one needed to come in close.

Magda rode deep into the canyon, making her way toward the sycamore tree, spotting it at last, up ahead. She laid herself out on the rock, naked. Offered to the

sun, legs spread wide, arms, too, all the way out, spread-
eagled, a female offered to the sky. There were snakes,
she knew, and lizards, odd pulsing desert creatures
watching from the rocks, but Magda felt unafraid. An
Indian once told her no Indian was ever bitten by a
snake. Brother Snake, said the Indian, he lives here: this
is his path, his rock. "May I lie here, Brother Snake?" she
said out loud. Magda felt at peace with all creatures.
They knew that she honored them. Her love for the little
beings filled her soul with rapture, lying there, offered
to the rock. Icarus bent to sniff her hair and wobble his
big lips at her as they heard a small summer wind moan
along the canyon wall.

"I hate that sound," she said to the horse. "It's the
sound of pure loneliness, you only hear it when there's
nothing else to hear."

The rock pool was deep enough after last night's rains
to sit in and Magda plunged down into the icy water,
sinking the hot flesh of her back and shoulders down and
down with shivers of delicious cold, singing little words
of love to the horse but thinking to herself, all the while,
of John. If only she could find some way to fix his attention on herself. The other men in her life all remained
fixed on her till the very end—it had been she who discarded them. Idly, she wondered if he had a mistress. No,
these Americans have their strange morality, Magda said
to herself. He would prefer to suffer rather than betray
her; live in his dream of how things ought to be rather
than stray into the real world, seeking pleasures there
which would only tear down his silence, make him feel
rotten. At heart she remained convinced he was a puri-
tan. He judged no one but himself, perhaps, but this only
made the condemnation worse. And she despised him for
this. Better to have him fucking his heart out and come
home to her with fire in his eyes than to endure more of

this restraint. What good was virtue if it dulled one to the point of imbecility?

Why then haven't I taken a lover? Magda asked herself, rising from the pool to stretch out onto the rock. But what man here is so exciting as this stinging wind? she said to Icarus. Or the sun boring down, the flood of new rains? Her mind returned to the vision of Buster Trotter, who had come upon her here one day as she sunbathed, given to the rock. The fear in his face on seeing her, then the quick fire, the shame—she hadn't even covered herself. Buster stiff upon his horse, the thighs full and round, packed like meat, straining to the animal—but no, if those thighs came wrapping round her she would heave him off with disgust. It might amuse her to go with a man who never read a book, but only once—and what then? Better the beast for that matter. These men were less than beasts to her. Buster squinting at her sideways, roaming her with his eyes, pawing, licking his chops. But what pleasure was there in being taken like a cow by some man? No, there had to be the fury. You had to howl and run leaping onto their backs, biting with your teeth, straining over them with your brain, or it was better to be alone.

But she could communicate none of this to John. They still made love sometimes but only with the weary fury of two disappointed adversaries. But the man had finished with her. And she was not finished with him. If she had loved him before, filled with dreams, she loved him now with a keener edge. The dream had gone but the reality, his dislike, stimulated her in a deeper place. She saw it as a contest: he for his solitude, his sanity—she for her survival. She saw the signs of his agony: how her nearness and the feelings she aroused in him compromised his soul. He did still desire her, then despised himself for it. He groaned over it in the dark, that none

of his ideals could save him from her. Her presence only
reminded him of his failure. He brought her here with
an expectation of how it should be, only to cave in at the
first blow. Where were his ideals now, his compassion?

If only she could smash away this silence, feel the
desire, engage with him once again. He shrank from her
as she expanded, filling herself on the land. His retreat
had the effect of whipping her on. She almost yearned
for him to hate her—anything would be better than his
horrified compassion. He pitied her. And she felt no
mercy for the struggle tearing at his soul. If only he
would dash at her, crush her down, love her. But he
shivered away from her in his soul. He wanted nothing
to do with her. Relentless, Magda resolved that no matter what, he would never be free until she made him love
her again.

33

THAT AUGUST Jewel called out to the ranch to tell them Dinwiddie had died. He had been ill so long, no one knew how he lingered on. Nanine insisted he did it to spite her. She could be having a whole new life by now if he'd had the decency to go.

"May I come out and see you two? There's something about his will," Jewel said to Magda, who answered coolly, Yes, come. In the year Magda lived in Arizona she had seen Jewel twice: the day Lou McAllister fell from the horse, and three days later at the funeral. Johnnie made some early attempts at peace between them but soon gave up. He stayed away from his cousin—not because it angered him that she snubbed his wife—but he knew it wouldn't be possible to hide his feelings from Jewel. And nothing she could do would help. The trouble between him and Magda had no resolution, he believed this; the only thing left to do was bury his disappointment deep in his own heart and somehow get through the rest of his life. He'd made a mistake but he saw no point in whining about it to anyone. He yearned to have done with Magda—but she would never leave.

Jewel arrived at the ranch on a Sunday afternoon.
Clara was overjoyed. Magda stood to one side as Johnnie
lifted Jewel off the ground and held her in his arms. The
greeting between the two women was unsentimental.
They all took their places in the front room, seldom used
in Lou's time: Jewel and Clara in the two big wing
chairs, Magda slightly apart from the others in a straight
chair. John found a place near Jewel. Jewel's natural ease
in this surrounding, her intimacy with the servants who
rushed out to squeeze and exclaim over her, put Magda
at a loss in her own house. The servants merely tolerated
her, no more. Clara bubbled over with excited stories,
and Johnnie, always so remote, suddenly leaned forward
in his chair to hear Jewel's response. It was bitter for
Magda to watch.

"What about Nanine? What did she get?" said Clara.

"Well, he left her almost nothing," said Jewel. "We
were all amazed, let me tell you. Of course the house in
Southampton is hers for life—but she can't sell it. She
can stay at Ninetieth Street, but he left that to the Audubon Society in his mother's name. You should've heard
Nanine: 'The *Audubon* Society! That musty old bunch of
warthogs! They already have a house!' I tell you, she was
beside herself."

"Heehee!" screamed Clara as Magda glared at them
from the other side of the room. Magda hardened against
them—this was *their* place, yes, but she would outlast
them all. How she hated Jewel, so blooming and rosy
with her new millions, and Johnnie looking on fondly,
the two of them seemed so much younger. Magda felt
desiccated, burnt, ravaged by the wind, the stinging
heat; her once-lustrous mane was spoiled by coarse wriggling gray hairs. How Clara cackled over this unlovely
transformation— Now you look like me! said Clara,
heehee! Magda felt her age to be all the more disgraceful

since she could not acknowledge it. Jewel looked lovely, fresh, brimming over with happiness.

"But everything else?" asked Johnnie.

"He gave it away years ago, mostly to charities. She knew nothing about it. Imagine her fury! What it boils down to is that she can live on in that house but not much else. He's left her on a budget, so to speak—a budget! You know Nanine!"

"And the millions he left you? What are you planning to do with those? Do you remember, Jewel, how once you said that if you ever got any money you'd give it away. Well?" he teased, as if they were alone in the room, the old cocky half smile showing itself for the first time since Lou McAllister died.

"You know me too well," said Jewel with a sigh. "It all rests upon this—if I give the money away I can be the person I always wanted to be. And if I can't—" she continued with a slight flush, "if I can't, I guess I'll have to be the person I am."

"Don't be too hard on yourself," he said softly. "Maybe the timing's all wrong. Sometimes the best thing is to wait a thing out. To accept that you're not a hero—"

"I'm no hero—give it to me!" screamed Clara. Everyone but Magda laughed.

"But that's a cop-out, too, you know," said Jewel, gazing across at Johnnie with real tenderness. "I mean if we all just wait—well, don't you see, action is the only thing that really matters."

"Action," he said. "But it has to be the right action."

"Almost any action is better than none at all," she said.

Magda could not restrain herself. "Not to act—not to act is death itself!" Magda said harshly. They all turned to her in surprise. "It kills everything around it, it stifles everything—the air, people, everything." For a moment no one spoke. Johnnie vanished into himself at the first word from his wife, a pained look showing on his face. Jewel stared at him in surprise.

"Some actions," said Jewel, who addressed this to John with a particular insistence, "are never felt till much later—and the best actions are those no one ever gets credit for. You know—the kind that make you want to go out and change your entire life." She chuckled. Johnnie shot her a look, grateful but something more, almost a look of pure love. It confused Jewel more than the other, this obvious hatred between John and his wife. Magda saw this; all at once she knew Johnnie loved his cousin as he would never love her. Jewel didn't know— Magda scrutinized the other woman closely—but *she* knew. And Magda remembered something she had said to Jewel in Venice several years ago: It's *him* you love, not Dal Bezo—you've *always* loved him, only you refuse to act upon it.

He never gazed at her with those eyes. Always the aloof face. Or sometimes, thinking to make it up to her for the absence of his love, he might say how handsome she was, or clever. Handsome! What woman who has been a great and dazzling beauty wants to be told she's handsome? She caught him staring at her with bewilderment—or was it horror? Then quickly his eyes glazed over. He could not bear to see her. No matter that she graced this clumsy ranch of his, mastering the men, the horses, insinuating all the rare beauty of her being into the very plaster of these old adobe walls. Burnished the stones, lent them her fire. Why, the place looked spectacular now, a regular showpiece of early American restraint—subtle, a perfect Mayan bowl placed just so, the severity was admirable—even he said so—any other woman would have spoiled the place, the harsh little windswept desert garden with potfuls of petunias. He told her so—yet he could not bear her.

She saw it all perfectly: how delighted he felt near that happy laughing creature with her plump hips and flushed face looking newborn always, like a brand-new child, and all this nauseating talk of giving the money away. What had these two ever had to suffer over? She yearned to crash down on them: slap her hard, sting him with a bullwhip, rip his eyes, tear away that chilly smile, snap him awake, out of the reverie—it was all so smug and superior, this hiding place of his, this dreaming silence. She yearned for an encounter. The other two laughed like excited children. Magda had said to Johnnie once, Funny, isn't it—how love can spoil things. And he had said to her, No, it isn't funny.

She watched them through hooded eyes. They were not lovers, no, and Magda's lip curled, thinking how Jewel might have had him for herself only she'd spoiled it all with her false virtue, lost him in the end.

"Look!" said Jewel in a whisper, "Clara in her chair, dreaming. Like an old dog dreaming of liverwurst."

And just then Clara twitched and gave a great yelp in her sleep and cried, "I'm not asleep, I'm not asleep!" Magda pretended to be as amused as they were.

"I'm amazingly fond of that old thing, you know," Magda said.

"Magda has been good to her," Johnnie said. "After Lou died, Clara was in pretty bad shape. Mother and Nanine wanted us to put her in a home somewhere—can you imagine Clara in a home? One time Magda and I drove back from Bisbee and Clara had stretched herself out across the drive stark naked." Johnnie threw back his head and laughed. "Stark naked! Damdest thing you ever saw. Like a great beached whale, huge in the headlights, dead white, stretched across the road. Said she was waiting for us—"

"I was lonesome," Clara muttered in her sleep.

"My God—listen to this," Jewel cried. "I haven't told you the best part. Well, they read the will and of course Nanine went into a furious sulk when she heard he'd left me three million but then the lawyer kept reading and all the rest—*all* the rest he left to this unknown person: Madeleine Boldiszar was the name."

Magda's face turned to ash. She stared at the others stupidly. Madeleine Boldiszar! But she hadn't understood—had he really left her his money?

". . . More than me," Jewel was saying, "and *that* was a surprise!"

"How much did he leave her?" asked Johnnie.

"Five million dollars."

Magda froze in her chair. A clammy sweat broke out on her forehead and neck. She felt absolutely sure Jewel knew who this Boldiszar woman was. And that at any minute she would stand and scream out an accusation. Then all would be over, finished at last.

". . . And that my father died because of this woman. It all came out that time I went to see Dinwiddie after he sent me the diamond peacock. When Nanine saw it on me she shrieked at me something about how my father died for that bird and how Dinwiddie had a whore shacked up in the Plaza—and of course I felt dead sure she was lying—but then I went to Uncle Dinsie's lawyer, old Morley Barrett, who was still alive at the time, and I asked him. And it was true."

Magda could scarcely breathe. And now she glanced at Jewel, who stared at her strangely.

"Yes, and I know that this Madeleine Boldiszar person must have been one of those cunning, deadly, intriguing creatures who prey on men—there are women like that, you know, eating off the flesh of their lovers. And there was something about the peacock," continued Jewel, never taking her eyes from the woman. "It was hers. My

father had it in his hand when he died. I suppose we'll
never know why—and this is a curious thing, too, because Dinwiddie had it in his hand, too, that evening
years ago when he had the stroke. Almost as a warning.
Lucy Cook found him. Perhaps he was trying to tell us
something. And Father, too. I think she killed them.
She's a killer," Jewel said flatly, two red spots coming to
her cheeks as she stared at Magda, who looked quite ill.

This was unbearable for Magda. She grew faint, could
not trust herself to speak. That she must sit here pinned
before them all, endure that hateful gaze—she nearly
cried out. But she was afraid. They despised her for
surviving by her wits. And he pitied her—it was too
much! She longed to fly at them, scream out, I am Madeleine Boldiszar! The money is mine! Do you know how
I earned it? And your father—your pig father raped me!
Filthy pig! But she kept still in an agony of silence.

"But this is a terrible story!" said her husband at last.
If he saw her face he gave no indication. "To think that
Uncle Dinwiddie suffered all those years and none of us
knew! But who is this woman—and why leave his money
to her?"

"In revenge, I think," said Jewel. "More to punish this
Boldiszar woman, perhaps, than Nanine. And as a way
of telling us all straight out: this is who he was. That he
was forced to buy his happiness. He bought his love. And
it cost everything, it destroyed his peace of mind. But
this is who he was—and I think he wanted us to know.
This always keeping up a perfect front must have
crushed him in the end. I can't imagine that anyone on
earth loathed himself more than Dinwiddie: for deceiv-
ing Nanine, yes, but for the shame of it, of contaminat-
ing himself with a creature who never loved him."

"Then why reward her with money?" said Johnnie.
His wife glared at him with burning eyes.

"Reward? Do you think it is? Dinwiddie had no illusions about money. He always said he didn't think he would do me any favors by leaving it to me. He said to me once, 'You know, dear Jewel, money was given me to teach me who I am. And I discovered that, oh, dear, yes, in the most awful way for I failed all the tests. It's a terrible thing to be rich, you know. A poor man can dream. He can imagine he's a good person. He can get away with it. But those who have the money, they can buy off remorse and self-deception, but sooner or later they know who they are. You see, there is no reason on earth that justifies the money. In the end—no reason good enough. I cringe yet I cannot part with it. And knowing this only makes it worse. Nothing keeps a man feeling so clean, so innocent as refusing to know things, refusing to see. Whatever we know, don't you see, creates an obligation.' That's what he said," continued Jewel, and her eyes filled with tears. "And that each piece of information crowding his head took the place of an unborn possibility. A moment of real creativity. 'Oh, it's all too crowded in here,' he used to say. No—" continued Jewel, staring at Magda, "I know why he left her the money: to force her out into the open, to force her to see—there is nothing so painful as that, in the end. Having to see who you really are."

"Yes, but he seemed to think—*he* seemed to think she had earned it!" The words broke out of Magda in a harsh little scream. She trembled violently. Johnnie stared at her in surprise.

"Are you feeling all right?" he asked. They all stared. Johnnie, struck by her drained face, thought with a shudder how ill she looked and wizened, how old. Magda stood suddenly as if to escape them and moved quickly toward the door.

"I do feel—I do feel unwell," she brought out haltingly. "I'm sorry not to hear the end to your story." She turned to Jewel, oddly formal, almost pleading, "But you see—no, never mind." Then, as she turned, Magda said, "Will they find her? This woman he left all the money to?"

"If she doesn't claim it," said Jewel softly, "I guess the money will come to me."

"You will be very rich," said Magda.

"Yes," said Jewel.

"Sure wish someone'd leave *me* all their money!" shrilled Clara. "I'd do a lot dirtier than what that woman did to get it." The laugh came, the high cawing shriek of a sea gull. "I ain't too particular—not when it comes to money."

Magda suddenly gave out a little cry and fled from the room.

"What did I say?" asked Clara. "Did I say something wrong?"

34

ONE MORNING a few days after Jewel visited them Jesus
the cowboy came through the door of the dining room
to hand the mail to Johnnie. This irritated Magda. Why
should it always be Johnnie who saw the mail first? He
glanced up now and said, "Here's a package for you,
Magda—it has a Tucson postmark." She waited to see if
he would have Jesus bring it to her. Then she stood,
walked to his end of the room, took the mail, all of it.

The two men discussed ranch business. This annoyed
her even more; she had told him again and again she
didn't like the men standing around in her dining room
in their dusty clothes hemming and hawing and slapping
their hats, hoping for a cup of coffee. Buster Trotter was
one thing, he was the foreman. But the men adored Johnnie. All he had to do was look at them and they leaped
to his side.

"Who is the package from?" he asked as Jesus left the
room.

Magda did not answer. She had no friend in Tucson,
she felt reluctant to open the box. He buried himself in
his paper, seeing she would not open the package. When

he looked again he saw Magda staring at it with horror.

"What is it?" he said. She threw the thing away from her violently, staring at him, aghast.

"Magda!" He stood and moved toward her as she scrambled to grab the box—but he had seen. She stared at him with crazy eyes as he took the thing in his hand— he knew it well—the diamond peacock. The bird was missing its head. He saw it had been severed, hacked off crudely, perhaps twisted from the neck—and the head was nowhere to be found. He examined the box for a note but found nothing, only now he recognized Jewel's handwriting on the label. Still he did not understand. Magda stared at him with a ghastly trembling face, half rising in her chair, then sank back down, throwing her hands over her face. And at last he understood.

"Is this yours?" he said finally. "Are you—?" But he could not say the words: Madeleine Boldiszar. Then suddenly he tore her hands away and shoved his face up against hers, and shouted: *"Madeleine? Is this yours?"* His hands gripped both of hers roughly. "Say it!" he shouted. "Are you the one who destroyed that old man's life? Say it!" Her fear vanished. She opened her eyes. He hung over her, ugly, his face all distorted, and she smiled. He hated her and she was glad! He fell back in horror from those excited triumphant eyes, and almost staggered, but she rose up toward him and suddenly he raised his arm and brought it smashing down hard, the hand opened out flat against her face, and struck her a great blow. It sent her reeling sideways but she recovered instantly. She was still smiling.

35

"HELLO THERE, stranger, it's been a long time," said Jewel. "It's late."

"Late for what?" asked John.

"*La Bomba Atómica*—showing at the drive-in. I thought you might like to go."

"Drat."

She stood in the doorway waiting. From the back of the truck he took a six-pack of beer and a sack of groceries.

"Just like old times." He grinned.

"You still bring me food," she laughed, peeking into the sack. "Tamales! Good. And you remembered the salsa." He slid his arm around her.

"I've missed you," she said. For answer he squeezed her. She looked him over carefully and felt shocked. He knew without her saying a word how changed he was.

"Do you think it'll rain?" Jewel said lightly as he followed her in through the studio and out the other side to her little garden.

"There's lightning over the Empiritas tonight—times

like this you ought to be out somewhere in the country, Jewel. The city's no place to wait for rain."

"Would it surprise you to hear my idea of heaven on a hot night is to head on over to the Tucson Five Drive-in? Haven't you been? There are five screens, John—five! You can see all five at once. What you do is lie up against the hood of your car out there under the stars, your back pressed against the windshield. Or if you've got a truck you back it in and lie on a mattress with your sweetie hugging in the moonlight, drinking beer—some people take lawn chairs and spread out. And all around you in the night the cars throb with lovers doing it. One night," Jewel laughed, cracking open a beer, "I saw two lovers glued like frogs humping away on the hood of a Chevy Impala—and suddenly they rolled down with a big crash onto the dirt, still doing it. No," said Jewel, "you can't say you know the desert till you've experienced a sunset at the Tucson Five. Just there beyond the screens the highway stretches out and all the rigs fly by, the trains . . . it kills me to hear the Southern Pacific howl by just as the sun sinks down—and what a sun! You wait, almost with dread, then here it comes. Slow, easy, firing up the sky, rolling down like some terrible ball of fiery calamitous doom sliding down from heaven. An outraged eye that sees," cried Jewel as she sank down beside him on the shabby garden sofa. "Sees everything," she went on, breathing near him in the dark garden, "but wait! Suddenly it flattens, this boiling red eyeball, and all the world is soothed. Cool now, sinking slowly down, a gong of some miraculous copper effortlessly hung, soundless in the sky. Oh, Johnnie! Gone the day, the endless day. And then you almost long for something wild. A disaster maybe—to shatter the false serenity. How smooth this gong, this disk of molten copper suddenly gone cold, sinking down behind the five screens into the Tucson mountains. I always feel tragic and absurd in that last light, a little dissatisfied. Do you know what I mean?"

He knew. The words tickled up old half-forgotten feelings.

"And are you dissatisfied?" he said at last. She laughed awkwardly.

"No—should I be? Do you find me very changed?" The question irritated him. She *was* changed, she bloomed out at him with a new heady exuberance that only made his own gloom more oppressive.

"You know you've changed," he brought out sullenly. She recoiled from him slightly.

"Don't resent my happiness," she said.

"I don't resent anything. Or maybe I resent everything," he said.

"I *am* happy," she said in a softer tone. "Be glad for me." How smooth she seemed, self-confident. She wanted him to know it. She smiled but not with a happiness that included him. The smile slid over him, silly, adoring, then passed on. Until this moment he had not known how wretched he felt.

Not that he expected her to remain the same—and certain little gestures had not changed. The way she stretched her chin to stroke her throat, catlike, the same yet somehow rearranged; as if she had been broken and the pieces put back oddly. He had heard stories about her. That she lived like a squaw with the Hopi Indians shucking corn for a number of months; or that she had traveled to India, and come back a Hindu—or was it a Buddhist? Someone told him she had not given all the money away, but that she drifted away from old friends and hung around with poor people. It had been six months since that day she came to the ranch to tell them about Dinwiddie and the will.

"Why didn't you come to me sooner?" she said abruptly. He said nothing, the pain of her nearness after so long nearly overwhelmed him. Yet she never seemed further away.

They sat under the lemon tree without speaking. Over the wall and out across the city the sky filled with rain. At last it came weeping down in plumes of soundless gray, curling down the sky along the ragged mountain. Streamers of saffron cloud held aloft in puffs of silver air, then a crimson spill of sudden liquid air seeping through the heat, they held their breath, this quickly disappeared and the rains came down in darkness. But over there, far off over the mountain, not near them here in the city.

"You need an ally for all the grand moments," she said at last. "Thank God you're here." How dark now under the lemon tree. He could barely see her face, only the flight of her hand darting from lap to throat.

"How long has it been," said John, "since you had a man?" Near him in the dark she quickly rose and passed behind, disappearing into the house. She returned with a hurricane lamp. As she lit the candle it was Magda he saw. A swift vision of Magda poised against the dark there on the Gritti terrace so long ago. A fear came wriggling across his soul.

Jewel, pale and strangely delicate in a long gauzy caftan of some ghostly trailing white, attenuated in this light, agitated, shadowy and improbable, flitted before the candle, then darted away like some large smoke-white moth. He remembered now: how he had spurned her in this garden that time long ago. He had not been here for several years. Since his marriage he hadn't seen many of his old friends. Magda called them uneducated, said she could not possibly take them seriously. *Specimens,* this is what she called them: that one over there a perfect

specimen of drooling incomprehension. She had them all
terrified.

"Why did you come to see me?" said Jewel a moment
later. *See?* The word scratched at him oddly. I didn't
come to *see* anything, he said to himself, I came to find
you. But he did not answer. Perhaps it really wasn't a
friend he wanted, or a woman; lately he noticed more
and more how people got in the way. If only he might
be left alone with the silence. But Magda had seen to it
the silence had fled. After she received the peacock he
feared her. Sometimes when she drove him in the car he
felt she might crash them. Murderously, against some
boulder. If he had a beer Magda drove. She stayed deadly
sober always. Not that he drank much—but lately he
found himself wanting more. Better to give way to her
in these things. The discussions, the words drove him
further from himself. Let her think she had won. And
she had won. She confessed to loving the power of driving him. She set her jaw and took the curves like a man:
tense, alert, glaring at the road as she mastered it, whipping through the turns with icy disdain, glorying in the
near misses. He bought her a Ferrari; driving around in
the truck, she said, did not amuse her.

After that day nothing could ever be the same again.
She had written to Morley Barrett to claim the five million dollars. At last she was rich. John said he wanted a
divorce but she only laughed at him and swore she would
never leave.

"Leave this ranch!" she cried. "Never! You'll never get
me to leave! I've earned my place here if anyone has. You
leave!"

And again, at other times, she wept and pleaded with
him. "What have I ever done to you? Who has loved you
as I have? Jewel? Did she love you? Well then, why did
she throw herself away on that fool Dal Bezo if she loved

you? Do you really imagine she loves you? She will run like a frightened rabbit the first time you show her your belly. But I have stayed! See? Oh, John—what has happened to us? Can't you love me again? You do still love me, I know it! I know it! Don't turn away from me—it will kill me!"

How should he rid himself of her? She claimed this was her land and in the eyes of the law it was half hers. If he divorced her she would take half of his ranch and then the Dragoon Cattle Company would be spoiled, lost forever; she even threatened to subdivide her half so that once, where there had been the awesome hush of flatlands, scrub, and sacred mountains, he would now look out over a sea of vile prefab houses. It was hers: no choking weed had ever insinuated itself more adroitly, curling itself around with softly spreading tendrils to squeeze away the life—it all belonged to her. Yet how could he go away? His only hope of protecting the land was to stay.

"Johnnie—for God's sake, say something!" Jewel said. "Is it so terrible for you? Is *she* so terrible? You frighten me!"

"You've heard of the spider wasp," he said after a moment. "Do you know what keeps them alive? They wait for their prey, these dazzling silky-black wasps, then swoop down on the tarantula, sting and paralyze it. They drag it off to their lair. A hidden hole somewhere. While the spider is paralyzed they lay their eggs in its fur. The eggs hatch, the babies feed on the comatose spider. Feed slowly, devouring the vital organs last. The mother, meanwhile, feeds on milkweed. Milkweed! Have you ever seen it? The whole complete head of an entire milkweed cluster is no bigger than the end of my thumb. There's this perfect ordered universe collected around the ritual of survival, dozens upon dozens of extraordinary flowers, beautiful beyond imagining. This perfect little cosmos is so wonderfully constructed, so concentrated upon its survival, any interference from without must absolutely destroy it. Each flower is perfect. At the heart of each cluster there is a sex organ. It is here the wasp plunges down her quivering proboscis, searching, sucking out the life."

"And Magda—"

"I'm saying that this is what the desert is. And no one understands it better than Magda. In order to survive you have to feed on something else."

"But this is terrible!" she cried.

"No. This is how it is. It's not terrible at all," he said.

"But—if she's destroying you—"

"I'm not sure anyone can really destroy anyone else," he brought out slowly. "Not as you mean it."

"Then you've chosen her to do the job," she said almost angrily. "But why be destroyed? My God, Johnnie—you can stop her, it's not too late!"

"It is too late. From the first moment I saw her it was too late." He said it flatly, the words uneventful, final.

"I won't listen to this—you're just punishing yourself because your life was perfect." She became very angry. "If there's one thing that makes my blood boil it's sacrifices that don't count! What is this? Some kind of misplaced chivalry? Do you think you'll get a medal for sticking to a woman who's out to destroy you?"

"You know it's not that," he said.

"But then why?" He had never heard her more ferocious. "Is it the land? Is that why you stay—for the land? Would you really sell out your life for that burnt-out scraggle of land?"

"Lou was right," he said bitterly. "You never did get the point, did you? Do you really think the whole point of life is to get what we want? Do you? And is that

enough? Is happiness enough? Is it even the point? Isn't
there something larger out there?"

"And you think it's the land?" she asked, incredulous.

"I do! If people like me don't protect it, who will? If
I give the place over to her she'd subdivide it in a week—
just to spite me. You've got to live for something, Jewel,
beyond yourself."

"So you'll stay there till she destroys you?"

"I'll stay there because no one likes to lose what he
puts himself into. It isn't Magda I'm afraid of losing, it's
that piece of myself. Or maybe I stick to her because in
some way I feel she's what I deserve. It was too good, it
was all too goddamn easy. And now, suddenly, everything is hard and the hidden things, deep inside, they're
coming to life. I can't kid myself anymore, Jewel. I know
who I am. She's given me that. You never know who you
are until you have to do something you never thought
you could do. Until you force yourself out of hiding and
everything you were absolutely sure was good and right
and honorable, everything you lived for, gets broken
down and you have to do the things you never thought
someone like you would do. She taught me that, to survive."

"You still love her."

"Maybe I do. I hate her more than I've ever hated
anything in my life—but maybe I do love her."

"What about me?" she asked.

"You know how I feel about you."

She waited a long moment. "Then what is it you're
clinging to?" she asked.

"I'm not clinging."

"But you are. What else keeps you there? Is it that you
love to suffer?" He heard the soft bite in her voice. "Is
this what you live for—the suffering? Is it enough?"

"And what about you?" he said angrily. "What holds

you here? Is there anyone—you used to love men, you were the one woman I could count on to love men and not get complicated about it."

"Complicated!" Her laugh was loud, potent, widening the distance between them. "Don't you know how awful it was for me? Do you really think a man makes me happy? What man? My whole life all I ever thought about was finding myself in some man. Well, that's over—you hear?"

"And you can live without a relationship?"

"Is there anything so boring as a relationship?"

"What happens between a man and a woman—even if it's terrible—is everything," he said.

"I want something larger!"

"God?" She heard the sneer in his voice.

"Of course I mean God—I mean life itself!" she threw back at him passionately. He groaned.

"Is it so big and so simple? Can you really reduce all life down to this?"

"Show me something better," she almost screamed at him. "I want something more! I want to go beyond where I am, I want to be carried off—" She leaped up.

He felt a sudden fury. What was it to him, this God of hers, pungent, erotic? She would go free, ardent little being, while he stayed behind with the lacerating truths. He felt her lift off, rush past—and his life seemed cruelly inert, sterile. He smelled her perfume.

She threw herself down again, near him on the collapsing sofa. She said his name. "I wanted you once," she said at last.

"I waited for you all those years," he said. "Then I gave up." He said this with a certain hateful finality, his voice going flat. "You always wanted something more. But there isn't anything more. Everything you ever wanted was here all along—but you never saw it."

"I did want you," she said softly, almost pleading.

"Hell, one of these days maybe you will find a man. The right man." His laugh grated on her. "You know of course who the right man is—"

"No," she said sullenly. "You?"

"Buck Lamott," he said. "He always was the right guy for you—only you never saw it. I'm married, remember?"

"I don't want Buck Lamott," she said angrily. "It was you I wanted."

"Magda said it was so—but I never believed her."

"She always knew," said Jewel. "I wish to hell you'd figured it out."

"There's no point in starting anything now," he said bitterly.

"I didn't say there was!" Just then a hilarious little burst of rain air shivered up the lemon tree, rattling the leaves, and the flame leaped, John saw her strain toward him, undecided, the moon of her pale face ringed all around by a fluff of ghostly baby wool hair, preposterously soft hair, how it had intrigued him as a child.

"If I thought . . ." But he let it lie.

"You've changed so much," she said. He heard the disappointment in her voice. "Do you think it is finished," she said, "this thing between us?"

"Nothing's ever finished," he said, "but I feel dead."

"But I tell you, you're not dead!" she cried softly, reaching for his hand. A jagged hissing light lit the little garden suddenly and he saw her face, the question hanging there, and also the happiness. "Look!" she cried. "Lightning!" Silver tongues of sizzling light, ominous, quick-darting, flickered high up in the churning sky, then disappeared into a creeping cloud. Black beast rolling up the sky, a buffalo cloud grumbling in his bowel: he roars, thunders out, cracks apart the sky, roars again, hacks down on earth a dry misery—but still no rain.

"Don't go back to her," cried Jewel. "I have a terrible feeling about it—Johnnie, stay with me!" He sprang up suddenly to get away from her.

"God, I never knew what you wanted," he said angrily, pacing back and forth in the little garden.

"I don't think I ever loved anyone else," she said.

"I don't believe you!" He smelled her perfume, the sweet flesh coming near in fragrant gusts. The rain, too, pungent cool of new air; and now the lemon tree, sharp, dark-pointed succulent leaves mingled in a liquid air, joined, and the coming of the rain. "I wish to Christ I could believe you, but I don't."

"But I believe it," she said. The rain came close. Somewhere nearby the first sweet rush of rain air came slicing through the heat tickling up a green perfume from out the dusty jalousie where a forgotten fig vine curled. Jewel sank back against the lemon tree.

"You almost yearn for some shattering roar to tear apart the sky," she said. In the dark she saw the pearl snaps glittering on his white shirt. "So that it will finally be over."

"I waited for you," he said roughly, "all those years—and you never gave a sign. I wanted you so goddamn much. I never wanted anybody like I wanted you!" She came rushing up at him and clasped him in her arms, dragging him down, sinking down, and she pressed her mouth to his throat, coming softly down, the old ache melting her down, and he came away too, the old wild feeling came back to him, sliding down, clasping her in his arms, and he called to her—remember, Jewel? Your ear is filled with sunlight, with red and gold fire. Like a hibiscus, and she wept against him, buried in his breast: it was always you, she cried, always you, and she carried him down with her, down onto the ground, it was always you.

36

"TONIGHT, MY darling boy, you'll have me all to your-self," said Magda, who lay forward on the stallion's neck to place her mouth near his ear. "We'll be happy," she whispered, as she slid from his back to open the gate. "That sonofabitch bastard has gone to his whore." Icarus came alongside and waited while Magda straddled him from the rail fence. On these hot days she rode him bareback, loving the touch of his flesh. The meaty fleshy belly pressed to her leg and the bristle, the hard-ridge spine so damp, smelling of beast, the mane harsh, sting-ing her cheek. "Yes, and I will bathe my darling tonight, rub him—then smooth him down, my darling darling," she crooned as they headed for the barn. "Just the two of us."

"He says he's going away—but he's not! He'll never leave this place. I told him so straight out. If he tries it he'll have a surprise—won't he, darling? Yes, and by God I'll do it too—kill myself if he goes!" The beast nickered low in his breast and stepped along fast to the barn. "Yes, but it's only you who would mind."

When they reached the barn, Magda slid down and

went for the hose. Icarus came from behind and nudged
the back of her neck with his nose, whinnying with that
strange ominous high trill. He loved the water. He
pushed her gently, knocking the bucket and brushes
with his nose, then fell back, stiffened all over when she
turned the hose on him, trembling in his body as she
squirted him.

She brightened, remembering how she'd sent the peacock to Nanine. *She* earned it after all, she was the one
who stole it, Magda thought. If only she could have seen
Nanine's face when she opened the box. She's such a
greedy goddamn bitch she'd probably wear the disgusting mangled thing—but so what? I've got her money, she
mused. Icarus pushed against her again.

"Yes yes, my darling, come, here's the soap. There—
see how good it feels?" Magda worked his sides, lathering
him, crooning a little song, then fell upon the haunches
scrubbing vigorously. Icarus, tense, alert, let her scrub
him down with the scraper.

"Shall I rub you with a blanket?" she asked. "No—
come, I'll walk you. See how still the air is tonight. Do
you feel it? Listen, the cicada!" The two stopped a moment, waiting. "The sound fills up the world."

The horse strained against her, his skin was alive with
some hot crazy current of life; he was edgy tonight,
knocking against her angrily, muttering under his
breath, then stopping suddenly as if to listen. It was
nearly impossible to walk him and Magda began to scold.

"What am I to do with you? You're a big baby. A
hopeless darling baby. What's that—why do you keep
stopping? You make me afraid," she chided as Icarus
yanked back violently, almost pushing her away. Magda
turned and saw John standing there, watching them
from the corral gate.

"What are you doing there?" she said. "You know he hates you."

"You taught him how," he said smiling at her. She could tell he had been drinking, but he was not drunk.

"Well?"

"I'm going, Magda."

"Going?"

"Yes, tonight," he said gently. "I wanted to say good-bye."

"How decent of you."

"Magda, don't," he said, coming toward her. Then he stopped.

"Are you afraid?" she sneered.

He had had a few drinks but at the same moment he was also deadly sober. He hated the stallion but he was not afraid.

"Well, are you?"

"No more games, Magda," he said wearily as he came toward her. "We can do this nicely, can't we? I'm leaving you everything—"

"Everything!" She spat the word out. Icarus, behind her, went rigid. "Everything but what I want! Do you think this ranch means anything? If you leave—" she challenged him, "I will sell this land to the first one that comes along, I swear I will!"

"It's yours," he said. "Do what you've got to do." He was peaceful, standing there with that soft smile. This enraged Magda.

"Are you going to her?"

"Yes."

"She won't make you happy," she said bitterly. "She doesn't know what she wants, she never knew—"

"Magda!" He said it so quietly. And suddenly she knew he really was going and that she would be alone.

She felt a cold terror grip her in the gut, a cold desperate fury, and began to tremble violently, falling back against the stallion. She sank onto his chest, letting go the reins.

"Listen!" he cried. "The cicada! Is there anything more beautiful? The sound of night. I will miss it."

"You'll kill me."

"Magda." He took a step toward her. "Let this bring you new life. You've got the money and now the ranch, you could—" But this only drew her fury.

"Killer!" she screamed, then again, violently, "*killer*— you are killing me!" A shocking scream, savage, ungodly. It terrified the horse, which reared up, knocking Magda to the ground, but she quickly scrambled away. John stayed, he stared at the horse with a surprised silly little smile, almost tender, as if waiting. The horse came crashing down onto John and sank his teeth into him. He took hold of the man's neck and John made no sound. The stallion snapped his neck from behind, then dropped John to the ground. Icarus danced toward Magda, whinnying, pawing the ground. She had not moved. She said nothing. Then suddenly she threw herself down on the lifeless body and began to scream, calling to him. She shook the body, then clasped it to her—but he was dead. She screamed at him to speak to her; clutching at him, she began to moan that she couldn't bear to be left alone—but all was silent. The horse fell back, hearing her wailing. She laid Johnnie down in the dirt and stretched out next to him, pressing herself onto him, moaning. She pressed her lips to his. There was some warmth still, perhaps he only slept. Hear the night! The cicada—was anything more beautiful? I shall miss it, he said. Yes, they would stay together in the night; and she would lie beside him, watching over his dream, she would not disturb him, only lie here awhile, as he did, listening.

37

MARCH. COLD though it was, and early, Jewel took her breakfast in the garden. This year she had planted a garden. Gardens in the desert swallowing all the water—how Johnnie would have hated it!

Strange though how free I am now he's gone. Jewel settled herself in the hammock, feeling instantly ashamed of the thought. In a way it terrified her, this new freedom. Who was there to live for, now that he had gone? Dinwiddie and Johnnie, these two had been the only ones who believed in her and now they were gone. And the ranch, that was gone, too, it belonged to Magda. She lived all alone out there in the middle of nowhere with no one but Clara and a few cowboys who stayed on. All the old crew quit. It was Johnnie they loved.

Soon Jewel would turn forty-three. Still quite young, and she had a sense of the years stretching out forever. She had lived it wholeheartedly yet she didn't feel she had begun. So many possibilities remained, so much she had yet to face about herself.

She had kept the money. The flurry of spending delighted her at first but then she wished she had her old

car back. She did give some of it away but not enough
to make her feel transformed. She still thought sometimes of moving to Calcutta. But where would she go
now? Perhaps every place really was the same. Why
deny it—the money had made her sad. These months
since Johnnie died had been discouraging. A great and
terrible drowning, a descent to nothingness without
Johnnie. Jewel couldn't get it out of her head that Magda
had murdered him. They blamed it on the horse but
Jewel knew. Black and cruelly hateful thoughts thrived
in her head after his death. She would try to remember
if she had ever been happy. Even those last days with
Johnnie—well, they were tinged with an awful sadness.
Almost as if he had known he would die. He had said that
she saved him and there had been a terrible beauty to
those days—but then he died.

But lately new feelings were coming to her. The garden, for example—how sweet it was! One day not so long
ago as she lay in the hammock under the olive tree she
stopped wishing she had died instead of Johnnie. She
gazed up into the sky, at the blue light piercing the dusty
green leaves, the purple fruit, ragged holes of freezing
blue light torn from the fabric of a winter sky, dotted
over with prim clouds, and it suddenly seemed she *had*
died. A vision of herself lying curled in a heap at the foot
of a tremendous tall tree somewhere deep within the
forest. She lay in a shallow hole. A nest of leaves: she
sniffed them, they smelled of death, rank, fermenting,
and she knew she had come here to die but did not cry
out or struggle to live; and just then as she sank down
and down into that soft hole something happened. Some
billowing miraculous thing filled with light fluttered up
out of her body like a diaphanous airy white handkerchief and disappeared into the tree. It came whisking up

out of her body, spirited high up—her soul; she knew
this to be true, and it disappeared high up where the
leaves and the frothy heavenly light joined and were
oblivious—and she was free. Then she remembered
what he said to her that last day: everything is perfect as
it is. This was the last thing Johnnie said to her and she
felt it to be so.

She thought of this now, lying in the hammock. What
a glorious day! Just this month she had begun to paint
again. Gone the old constraints, the cloying self-consciousness. She wouldn't paint for the world ever again.
Strong voluptuous new canvases amazingly bold and
free. It felt glorious to paint and that would be enough.
To feel the day. Nothing existed beyond the day.
Splashes of slicing green light: separate leaves growing
from their stems in silhouettes of acid light blotting
against the pink wash of winter sky: now the dark, pur-
ple-black olives, falling: the gentle plop. Yes!

The phone had been ringing. Jewel deliberated
whether or not she should answer it. Here was the new
joy, the new possibility—that it did not matter who
might call or if she answered the phone ever again. She
smiled thinking about the last time Johnnie had called:
Come away with me!

Dusty leaves, a soiled green, the olive leaves; rows of
stiff young plants, thriving, hopeful; and strange lilacs,
a hybrid desert breed; and bright false young reds, salvia
and hollyhocks, California poppies: chaos in the garden.

Again the phone began to ring. As if in a slow dream
Jewel wandered toward the house. The ringing stopped
just as she got there and she smiled, but then it began to
ring again. Come away with me, Jewel!

"Hello?" she said.

"Hi! Guess who?"

"Who is it?"

"Well, it's Buck Lamott. How are you, Jewel? What are you doing?"

"You mean right now?"

"Sure! Can I come over and see you?"

There was a silence.

"Jewel?" He said it again. "Would you like that?"

In the garden, dizzy bees, voluptuous bees returning to life. Big juicy black bees wallowed drunkenly in saucers of light: scarlet, gaudy first poppies of winter opening out flat to soak in the light, the hairy stems wobbling up from the earth in a decadent disregard for the cold. Jewel listened, she stood transfixed.

"Jewel?" said Buck with a wonderful chuckle. "Shall I come see you?" Odd poking bouquets of hyacinth and heliotrope staggered along the path in exuberant rows—she felt it stirring, the new day.

"Yes!" she said at last. "Come see me."

ABOUT THE AUTHOR

INDIANA NELSON is a painter from Tucson, Arizona.